APPLES
and
CINNAMON

STACY JOHNSON

ISBN 978-1-0980-9015-9 (paperback)
ISBN 978-1-0980-9016-6 (digital)

Christian Faith Publishing, Inc.
832 Park Avenue
Meadville, PA 16335
www.christianfaithpublishing.com

Printed in the United States of America

CHAPTER

*J*ULY 1960—MEMORIES OF THAT TIME COME back periodically like pieces of a jigsaw puzzle. One thousand pieces scattered throughout my prepubescent mind. Sometimes I feel like if I could just reach up and hold tight to whatever memory decides to float through my mind, maybe I would remember my mother's voice—how she wore her hair or her favorite perfume. But I can't. Sometimes when I'm asleep, it feels as though she is near. I hear her calling my name. But I wake up with tears streaming down my face only to discover that it was all a dream. Memories of my mother were truncated by my father in a jealous rage. I was two years old when my mother died. She took me to the roof with her to hang clothes. As always, she gave me strict instruction to remain where she could see me and to stay away from the pigeon coop. But the White King pigeons fascinated me, and I ventured toward the coop anyway. I was talking to the pigeons when I heard my father's voice.

Immediately I hid behind the coop and watched my parents through the mesh wire. My father sounded so angry. Why was he yelling at my mother? I could tell that my mother was afraid of him. Her hands were out in front of her. But he kept advancing toward her yelling something unintelligible. I could see my mother shaking her head from left to right as she backed away from him. Then the unthinkable happened, in a fit of rage, my father threw my mother off the roof of the building where we lived. I was aware that my mouth was open wide, but I do not remember hearing a scream or cry escaping from it. I could hear someone yelling to call the police.

When they finally arrived, they found me still hiding behind the pigeon coop sitting in my own urine. A police officer picked me up and carried me off the roof of Building 20, away from the White Kings, and away from the memory of my mother's death. Maybe the smell of urine did not bother him because he held me like I was one of his children. A crowd had gathered, and yellow police tape cordoned off the scene of the crime. I could hear "poor baby havin' to grow up with no momma." Some even speculated that my father probably was suffering from some sort of mental breakdown. Echoes of "What a shame," "That baby is only two years old," or "I hope he has people to take him in," followed by "You don't want no strangers raising him" rang throughout the growing crowd. Pity was evident on the faces of the residents of The Gardens Housing Development.

The police looked for my father for three weeks before finding him hiding in the boiler room of the apartment building where we once lived. The police were baffled that he was able to elude them for three weeks and insisted that the boiler room had been checked. According to granny, he was crying when they led him out of the basement of the apartment building in handcuffs. She said he kept yelling about how much he loved my mother. Had it not been for ole Ms. Carmichael, my father probably would have still been hiding in the boiler room. She called the police when she saw a suspicious person sneaking into the basement of Building 20. That's where I lived with my parents before that fateful day. After my mother died and my father incarcerated, I went to live permanently with my grandparents on Madison Avenue. You would find a lot of working-class families living on Madison. It seemed like worlds apart from The Gardens and the broken swings and missing nets on the basketball hoops. For as long as I could remember, my grandparents lived on Madison Avenue. My mother was raised in that house.

Granny would tell me childhood stories of my mother; the only memories I have of Mom are the ones granny shared. My mother was a beautiful woman; Granny kept pictures of her all over the house. My grandfather worked long hours at the construction site, which gave me plenty of time with my grandmother. When he wasn't working, however, he would take me fishing, play catch in the backyard, or take me to a baseball game. One day, the police showed up at the house on Madison Avenue and informed granny there had been an accident at the construction site where my grandfather worked. I overheard the police telling her that granddad was electrocuted when the crane he was operating became entangled with live powerlines. The scream escaping from my grandmother caused people to emerge from their homes up and down Madison Avenue. Death seemed to follow me around; *1966*... I was eight years old.

Twenty years later...

I walked the three blocks to Garcia's Grocery store on the corner of W. 125th and Lenox Avenue. Around 9:00 p.m. every Friday, the produce truck arrived at Garcia's with bushels of apples. If I didn't time my arrival, the ladies in the neighborhood would wipe Mr. Garcia out and leave me without my weekly apple fix. When I arrived, Mr. Garcia smiled and told me in broken English that I was his first customer. I took my time, inspecting each apple for bruising, firmness, and coloring. When I was satisfied with my choice, I walked to the front, paid Mr. Garcia $3.60 and started my journey back home with pride.

I enjoyed an apple on my walk back home; the crunch of this succulent fruit took me back to simpler times on Madison Avenue— *reminiscing*. The tree in my granny's backyard yielded bushels of red delicious apples every summer; Leroy and I would go door to door selling apples to people in the neighborhood. We charged 10 cents an apple. Some thought paying 10 cents was highway robbery. Some even vocalized it. Mr. Jones raising his cane high in the air, making like he was going to hit us over the head. We probably lost a half-dozen apples jumping off Mr. Jones's porch. When Leroy and I were a safe distance from Mr. Jones, we turned around and saw him collecting the apples we dropped. From that day forward, we decided to stay far away from Mr. Jones. No more free apples for him.

"Come on over here, Leroy…Myles," we heard Mrs. Jackson yell.

She was one of our best customers. Me and Leroy picked up the basket and raced across the street to her house.

"How you two doing today? You sell many apples?" she asked from behind the screen door.

"Well, it's early yet," Leroy replied. "I'm quite sure we will sell all these apples before the end of the day."

Mrs. Jackson studied us for what seemed like an eternity before exiting the house and going through our basket of apples. She would slowly turn each apple in her hand; gently smelling the aroma of each one before placing them in her apron.

"Yes, these apples are just right for baking pies," she said to no one in particular.

I counted each apple that she placed in her apron. "That will be $1.20, Mrs. Jackson."

She smiled. "You boys wait here, and I'll be right back with the money."

Twice a week, Leroy and I would go door to door selling apples. Mrs. Jackson would always buy apples from us. How could one woman bake so many pies? She was a widow and didn't have any kids, according to granny. What was she doing with the pies? The opening of the screen door and the soft shuffle of Mrs. Jackson's house shoes snapped me out of my daydream.

"Here you go, boys, $1.20. Don't spend it all in one place," she called over her shoulder as she disappeared back into the house.

It was October 17, 1980; two weeks before Mrs. Jackson died. I remember it like it was yesterday. She invited me over for dinner. For dessert, we had apple pie. I wonder where she bought her apples. Mr. Garcia's store was long gone. She served up slices of apple pie on her good china in the dining room that she only shared with her late husband Harold. I asked about all the apples she bought from me and Leroy when we were kids.

She smiled warmly and considered her words for a minute.

"Myles, I always felt sorry for you and Leroy. I would watch you go door to door trying to sell those apples to people who were not nice to you boys. I didn't mind paying you the $1.20 a week for the apples because seeing you two working so hard gave me joy. A lot of kids your age was getting into trouble and just being miserable. I saw something special in you and Leroy and I felt it was my duty to help nurture whatever it was God had placed in you. Your grandmother, Leona, and I were in school together and were best friends growing up. You didn't see one without the other. Kind of like you and Leroy. My husband and I didn't have any children, but had we been blessed with children, I would have wanted them to be as kind, hardworking, and respectful as you and Leroy."

Now it was my turn to smile.

"Mrs. Jackson," I said tentatively. "Why did you bake two pies a week? That's eight pies a month."

Mrs. Jackson slapped the top of my right hand playfully and laughed generously.

"Mind your manners, young man, I baked those pies and took them over to St. Mark's. What better way to give back than to provide some form of comfort food for those that are a little down on their luck. What did you think I was doing, baking pies and eating them myself? Lord, I'd be big as a house if I did that." She roared with laughter at the thought.

Was she reading my mind all that time? I quickly answered, "No, ma'am."

Now that I think back on it, Mrs. Jackson and my grandmother are the main reason I decided to become an accountant. I can still hear my granny's voice saying, "Myles, you sure are good with numbers. You're like a human adding machine." After the deaths of my mother and grandfather, granny was all I had to hold on to. We were so tight, it's a wonder she wasn't out there selling apples with me and Leroy. I mentally scolded myself for allowing most of the week to go by without seeing my grandmother. There are people her age at Chesterfield Assisted Living, but it is not like having your own flesh and blood visit with you.

By the time I arrived at the front stoop of my six-floor walk-up, I had finished my jaunt down memory lane as well as the apple. Mothers up and down W. 128th Street were hanging out their windows calling their children in for the night. I sat on the stoop for a while, taking in the sounds of summer in Harlem.

One of my co-workers told me about a dance tonight over at the Glitz on W. Thirty-fourth Street. That place was always jumping with live music and pretty women. Yep, the Glitz was the place to be. I called Marion, but she informed me that she had other plans. I silently wondered if those plans included another guy, but I decided to play it cool.

"My girlfriends and I made plans to go out about a week ago," she offered.

"Cool." I hung up and called Cinnamon.

Cynthia Marie Harrelson got the nickname Cinnamon back in high school. She was the type of girl that could thwart a man's concentration in a heartbeat. She had her mother's looks but her father's complexion. Those two knew what they were doing when they decided to get married and have children. Good genes.

I was almost ready to hang up when Cinnamon's sultry voice floated through the speaker causing me to hold the phone a little tighter.

"Hello."

"Hey, beautiful… I was about to give up."

"Give up?"

"Well, let's just say I'm glad you answered."

"Why is that?"

"You've been on my mind a lot lately. Right now, I feel like the luckiest man on the face of the planet just being able to talk to you."

Her soft laugh made me forget all about Marion. At least for the moment.

"You got plans for tonight?"

"What if I do?"

"I would be heartbroken if you did."

"Shut up, man! You would not be heartbroken."

"I'm going to meet up with friends at the Glitz tonight. You down?"

"What time you trying to be there?"

"Coupla' hours maybe."

"Pick me up at ten-thirty."

I hung up with Cinnamon and called Leroy and told him I would come through the spot around eleven o'clock. I had a strange feeling about tonight, but I quickly dismissed it. What could possibly go wrong? I arrived at Cinnamon's promptly at ten-thirty, but I could tell from the expression on her face that she didn't expect me to be so prompt. She invited me in and continued to get dressed. "Never keep a lady waiting," granny instilled in me.

"You wanna fix yourself a drink?" she called out from the bedroom.

"Naw. I'm good."

I slouched a little on the couch and closed my eyes, resting my head on the back cushion.

"I see you. If you go to sleep, I might have to wake you up."

I smiled at the thought of Cinnamon waking me up.

"Come on…wake me up," I pleaded playfully.

Cinnamon laughed as she entered the room. I couldn't take my eyes off her. The red dress with the plunging neckline fit her in all the right places. Her soft, black curls draped her face cascading down her neck brushing the top of her shoulders. My eyes lingered a little too long.

"Wow."

Cinnamon smiled as she turned around very slowly. She knew that she turned heads. How could she not know? A woman possessing that much sexual prowess had to know that she would stop traffic on Mars. I'm a blessed man to be seen with this woman.

Cinnamon broke into my train of thought when she asked, "Is that all you have to say?"

"You look gorgeous." I wasn't just paying her lip service.

She moved in closer to me, pressed her body against mine, and gave me the softest Cinnamon kiss.

Yep, tonight is going to be a good night.

We hopped in the ride and I'm trying not to smile like a young boy out on his first date. I need to play this one cool. Cinnamon and I have been out before so why is this night so different? We pulled up to the Glitz, and I tossed my keys to the valet. The place is packed, and Cinnamon started to dance before we can get in the place good. All eyes are on her.

Leroy and his lady are posted up in a booth across from the bar. I took Cinnamon's hand and guided her through the throng of people. A waitress appears like magic to take our drink orders as soon as we sit down. Cinnamon ordered a lemon drop; me, a Hennessy neat.

I caught a glimpse of Leroy's lady friend when Cinnamon gave the waitress her order. Nice-looking but something seems a little strange about her. My spider senses are kicking in again.

We are sitting there doing what people do when out on the town, when suddenly Shakira questioned Cinnamon's choice of drink. Couldn't she wait until we had been properly introduced? The only person that knew her was Leroy and he was taking his time making introductions. Shakira was sitting there grittin' on Cinnamon for whatever reason. Things were getting a little strained, so I decided to break the ice by extending my hand to Shakira. She ignored it.

"What the hell kinda' drink is a lemon drop?" Shakira blurted.

"Aww, hell," mumbled Leroy. "Shakira, cool out."

"Don't tell me to cool out!" slurred Shakira.

Shakira turned her attention back to Cinnamon. "Why can't you order a real drink? What's wrong? You not woman enough to handle a real drink?"

Cinnamon ignored Shakira.

"Myles," Cinnamon cooed. "We came here to have a good time. Let's dance."

Her timing could not have been better. Maybe Shakira will sober up by the time we get back. From the looks of her, we might be on the dance floor all night. Here I was thinking that tonight was going to be high-quality hanging with Leroy and his lady friend. Something was going on with her and I needed to talk to Leroy before things went south.

Cinnamon and I returned to our seats; our drinks were waiting for us. Leroy told us to catch up as he was on his third drink; Shakira clearly had outpaced everyone in the club, and he was down to his last ten dollars. Not only was she wasted, but she was singing louder than the band on the stage. I couldn't help but notice people pointing and laughing. Leroy and I needed to have a long talk. He's my boy… I can't let him go out like this.

The band was on fire, and Cinnamon and I had graced the dance floor several times since Shakira's misstep, but it was time to sit down as the band had just announced a fifteen-minute intermission. Cinnamon seized the opportunity to head to the ladies' room. As I was making my way back to my seat, Shakira stumbled past me toward the ladies' room. I took the opportunity to rap with my boy about his lady.

"Leroy, what's going on with Shakira?"

"I don't know. I'm trying to figure this craziness out myself. She started buggin' after you guys showed up."

"So, we're the problem now?"

"No. That's not what I meant."

"We've been friends for a long time, but I can't allow her to disrespect Cinnamon like that."

"What? Is Cinnamon your lady now?" Leroy said with a sly grin.

"Come on, man. Cinnamon is my home girl. We've been chillin' since high school. I kid you not, nobody better disrespect none of my friends. That includes you too, negro."

"Yeah, you right. I'll say something when she gets back."

No sooner had I ordered another lemon drop and Hennessy for me and Cinnamon when two shots rang out. People began screaming and running toward the door. We couldn't tell where the gunshots were coming from. Leroy and I pushed through the crowd toward the ladies' room in search of Shakira and Cinnamon. Pushing the door to the ladies' room open slightly, I called out to Cinnamon. Shakira was standing there holding a gun pointing it toward me. I jumped back and informed Leroy that Shakira was in there with a gun, but

I couldn't see Cinnamon. I prayed that she wasn't. Leroy crouched near the entrance to the ladies' room and called out to Shakira.

"Shakira, baby, I'm coming in. But I need you to put the gun done."

Leroy pushed the door open enough to get a glimpse of where Shakira was standing.

"Shakira, please put the gun down."

Shakira lowered the gun. Leroy slowly entered the ladies' room with me following closely behind. That's when we saw Cinnamon laying on the floor in a pool of blood. I removed my jacket and placed it over the spot where I thought she was bleeding from. I kept pressure on the area, but I wasn't confident that it was helping. There was so much blood.

"Shakira, what happened? Why did you shoot her?" Leroy asked repeatedly.

My head was spinning trying to make sense of all of this. In the distance I could hear the sirens.

Leroy was looking at Shakira in disbelief. She kept mumbling that Cinnamon had taken what rightfully belonged to her and she couldn't let her get away with it. Shakira walked around in circles, mumbling the same thing repeatedly.

"What did she do, Shakira?" I bellowed while trying to stop the bleeding. "What did she do?" By this time, I felt helpless.

Shakira retreated to the far end of the bathroom and slid down the wall. Seated with outstretched legs, she let the gun slip from her right hand. Two officers entered the ladies' room with guns drawn.

"Let me see your hands!" the male officer shouted. A female officer rushed past him with her revolver trained on Shakira, kicking the gun far away from her. Both Leroy and I were handcuffed and escorted out of the ladies' room. Tears of anger and frustration filled my eyes and ran down my face.

Shakira's countenance was crestfallen as the female officer led her out of the ladies' room in handcuffs. The paramedics rushed in to check on Cinnamon. I heard them radio in that she had a faint pulse and time was of the essence if she were to survive. In a matter of minutes, she was loaded into the ambulance and rushed toward the nearest hospital as Leroy and I remained in handcuffs.

Thirty minutes after the ambulance left, the handcuffs were removed from me and Leroy.

"You good?" Leroy inquired.

"I don't know. Hey, look, I gotta bounce. Catch you later."

"Yeah, I'll catch up with you at the hospital. I need to stop by the precinct first. Man, this has been one crazy night."

We turned and proceeded in opposite directions. I turned back in time to see Leroy turning the corner. I couldn't help but think about all the times Leroy and I have been together. You never saw one without the other. But tonight, we both had a different road to walk.

I tracked my car down and headed to Mercy General Hospital. During the drive to the hospital, memories of losing my mother flooded back. Granny always said to pay attention to those feelings. Why didn't I pay attention? I knew something didn't feel right before leaving home, but I never would have guessed it would come this way and to someone I care so deeply for.

Hold up! Did the voice in my head say that I care deeply for Cinnamon? When did this happen? For years, I kept my emotions in check. I never allowed myself to get too close to anyone. There have been plenty of women in my life; however, when they started talking about "catching feelings" for me, I pulled a disappearing act out of the rabbit's hat. Yes, that's my MO. I would go ghost in a heartbeat. I thought I was safe with Cinnamon because we're just friends. How did I allow myself to fall asleep and "catch feelings" for Cinnamon? What makes matters worse, I realized all of this on the night she was shot. I said a silent prayer before emerging from my vehicle.

I entered the hospital and walked up to the information desk and inquired about Cinnamon. The young lady at the desk informed me that she was in surgery and to take the elevator to the fourth floor. The elevator doors opened down the hall from the nurse's station. I informed them that my friend, Cynthia Harrelson, was brought there and was currently in surgery. The nurse instructed me to have a seat in the reception area directly across from the nurse's station. She assured me that the surgeon on duty would find me after the surgery.

With my eyes closed and head resting in the palm of my hand, I thought of running far away where no one could find me. In the past several hours, I went from reminiscing about simpler times as a kid on Madison Avenue to admiring the most beautiful woman in my world to seeing her covered in blood. None of this made any sense.

Not long after I arrived, Detective Donaldson showed up. An hour later and my head continued to spin as he questioned me about events leading up to the shooting.

"Did you see what happened?"

"No."

"How do you know the victim?"

"She was my date for the night. I've known her since high school."

"Do you know the shooter?"

"I just met her tonight. You will have to ask Leroy about her."

"Who is Leroy?"

"Leroy Jones is my friend. She was his date."

"Was there an argument prior to the shooting?"

"Not really."

"What do you mean by not really?"

"Shakira made an offhanded comment when Cinnamon ordered a lemon drop."

"Is Shakira the shooter?"

"Yes."

"Who is Cinnamon?"

"*The gunshot victim.*" I was slightly annoyed with the detective by this time, but I kept my cool.

"Her given name is Cynthia…Marie…Harrelson."

Detective Donaldson stopped writing in his black notepad long enough to fix his eyes on me. I got the message.

"Is that spelled with one *L* or two?"

"One."

"Well, okay, Mr. Beyers, I think I have everything I need. Oh, one more thing. Where can I reach you if I need you?"

I handed him my business card.

"I'm not going to take up any more of your time. Of course, you are aware that Ms. Harrelson is in surgery. The doctors are working diligently to determine the damage and where the bleeding is coming from. They know that you are here and as soon as the doctor knows something, you will be informed. Please know that your friend will be in my prayers. I have been on the force for twenty years and I have seen utter destruction during those twenty years. It is not pretty working these streets. Does Ms. Harrelson have any family that I can call?"

"Her father and brother live on Palmyra Street. I'm sorry but I don't have their number."

"That's okay. What's the address and last name?"

"Eighty-eight zero nine Palmyra." I must have stared at the police officer for ten minutes before answering the question about the last name. I don't know why it bothered me so much. Cinnamon had never been married. Maybe it was a valid question, but it bothered me, nonetheless.

"Mr. Beyers?" the police officer looked at me with questioning eyes.

"Ah, yeah, last name Harrelson."

"Got it." With that Detective Donaldson closed his black notepad, turned, and walked down the corridor toward the bank of elevators. I watched as he waited patiently for the elevator doors to open. Before the doors closed, he turned facing outward and for a brief second, I thought I recognized a glimmer of sadness in his eyes. He was staring into space. His lips were in a downturned position with a slight pull to the lips. At that moment, it appeared as though he carried all twenty years of working these streets on his shoulders.

The elevator doors closed, and Myles was left alone with his thoughts. Cinnamon had been in surgery for about three hours when her father and brother arrived. I looked up to see them rushing down the corridor toward me. I got up from my seat; it seemed like the proper thing to do. Mr. Harrelson looked like he wanted to pummel anyone and anything that got in his way, fight through the pain. Sitting wasn't an option for him that night; he paced back and forth for what seemed like hours before asking the question I had been wrestling with all night.

"Myles, what happened?"

I pondered his question for a minute before responding.

"Mr. Harrelson, everything happened so fast. Leroy, Cinnamon, Shakira, and I were all there having a good time listening to the band play, or so I thought. Cinnamon and I were on the dance floor, but during intermission Cinnamon ducked into the ladies' room. I was walking back to my seat when Shakira stumbled past me headed in the same direction. I didn't think anything of it as she had had a lot to drink. Leroy and I were talking when we heard two gunshots. It was total pandemonium. People were running in every direction, pushing, and screaming. Leroy and I pressed through the crowd toward the ladies' room in search of Cinnamon and Shakira. When Leroy and I got there, I pushed the door open slightly and called out to Cinnamon. From my vantage point, I could only see Shakira. I pushed the door open a little more but jumped back when I noticed Shakira pointing the gun toward me. I told Leroy that Shakira had a gun and I wasn't sure if Cinnamon was still in the ladies' room. I noticed Leroy had crouched low to the ground and opened the door only enough to see Shakira. He called out to her and told her that he was coming in, but she needed to put the gun down. I followed Leroy in and that's when I saw Cinnamon laying on the floor in a pool of blood. Shakira was standing there with a gun in her hand mumbling. I couldn't make out what she was saying. She sounded so crazy. Mr. Harrelson, I tried to stop the bleeding with my jacket, but it was just too much blood."

"Shakira? Are you talking about Shakira Fleming?" This was the first time Kyle had uttered a word since arriving at the hospital.

"Yes."

I caught the exchange between Kyle and his father. All the blood seemed to have drained from Kyle's face. What did they know about Shakira that the rest of the world wasn't privy to? It appeared they were watchful of her but failed to share their wariness with those that mattered, especially Cinnamon. So I stepped out on that limb.

"Mr. Harrelson, I couldn't help but notice the exchange between you and Kyle. What is it about Shakira that I should know? Better yet, what should Cinnamon have been warned about?"

"This ain't your fight. Stay out of it," cautioned Mr. Harrelson.

Mr. Harrelson's voice trailed off as he retreated deeper into his thoughts. Thoughts that had been neatly filed away in the deep recesses of his mind had just made a house call.

The three of us retreated to neutral corners of the waiting room, silently anticipating news…any news about Cinnamon. Suddenly a sound came from the depths of Mr. Harrelson's soul. The cries erupted with such force that it sent shock waves through everyone in the hospital. Nurses scrambled from every direction in search of the wounded animal sitting in front of them. One brave soul sat and held his hand; another brought him water while the others quietly made their way back to their stations.

The chaplain appeared to relieve that one brave soul and proceeded to minister to Mr. Harrelson. He got him to discuss Cinnamon's childhood—his experience as a single parent, how he felt when his wife died, and his faith. Listening to the chaplain talk to Mr. Harrelson in such a fatherly way made me smile. I smiled because now I know why Cinnamon was such a special person. She grew up with a father that loved and cared for her. Mr. Harrelson poured his values into his daughter and that's something no one could take away from her.

I glanced at the large clock on the wall in the nurse's station. It was now four hours into the surgery, and we still had not heard anything from the surgeon. Cinnamon's brother, Kyle, and I were afraid to leave the waiting room for fear of not being in place when the surgeon emerged from the operating room. However, the chaplain stayed with us the entire time which gave all of us, I would like to believe, much needed comfort.

Leroy arrived. The look on his face as he walked down the corridor was one of pure defeat and confusion.

"Mr. Harrelson…Kyle…I am so sorry this happened to Cinnamon. I really don't know why Shakira shot her. I just left the precinct. She's been booked for attempted murder and will go before the Magistrate on Monday."

Before anyone could stop him, Mr. Harrelson shot out of his seat and grabbed Leroy by his shirt, ripping part of the shirt and popping several buttons in the process.

"Don't nobody care about Shakira! You hear me! Don't nobody care about Shakira! She shot my baby in cold blood. So help me God, if Cynthia dies tonight, nobody will keep me from showing up at the magistrate's office on Monday. She gonna know what it feels like to get shot. I will shoot her dead right where she stands." Kyle and Myles had interlocked arms with Mr. Harrelson's attempting to pull him off Leroy. Kyle really had to talk to his father to get him to loosen his grip on Leroy.

The chaplain hung back in disbelief. An armed security guard had joined the skirmish.

"Sir, let him go," the security guard commanded. "I don't think anyone wants to go to jail tonight. We can do this the hard way or the easy way. Now, how do you want this to go down?"

Mr. Harrelson waited a beat before releasing Leroy's shirt. The armed security guard remained on the fourth floor for the rest of the time we were there. I could only imagine what was going through his mind.

Leroy tried to straighten his clothes out, but the altercation with Mr. Harrelson left his appearance a little shambolic.

"You're right to be upset, Mr. Harrelson," Leroy surmised. "If I was in your shoes, I would be upset too."

"Ain't nobody ask you to be upset for me. Did I ask you to be upset? No. I didn't. So spare me your pity."

The security guard made his way back to the reception area and gave us a silent warning with his eyes. I prayed that no one would say another word.

At that point, Leroy decided to give it a rest. Nothing he said would make a bit of difference to Mr. Harrelson anyway.

I felt sorry for Leroy. He didn't put the gun in Shakira's hand or tell her to shoot Cinnamon. She came up with that craziness all on her own. Leroy took the seat next to me. Without saying anything, he knew that I had his back and he had mine…friends for life.

We all looked in the direction of the woman in green scrubs walking toward the reception area. She stopped by the nurses' station. One of the nurses pointed our way. The woman in green scrubs walked toward us.

"Harrelson family?"

"Yes. I'm John Harrelson…Cynthia's father." The doctor searched the strained faces of Cinnamon's loved ones. Dr. Monge knew that all too often having to talk to family members could be stressful for families as well as dangerous for the doctor. But today she was privileged to provide the family with good news. Let's all have a seat, shall we?"

"No. I'm not sitting down. Just tell me…is she alive or not."

"Yes, Mr. Harrelson. She's alive. However, I must tell you that it was a little touch and go during the surgery, but your daughter is a fighter. Once we established where the bleeding was coming from, we were able to stop it. There was an entrance wound but no exit wound."

"What do you mean by no exit wound? Is the bullet still in her somewhere?" Mr. Harrelson inquired.

"The bullet lodged itself in the spleen. Therefore, it was necessary to remove the organ. The severity of damage was just too great. A blood transfusion was essential as she lost a lot of blood in route to the hospital. She is lucky that there was no damage done to any other abdominal organs."

"I'm tired of all this talking. I need to see my daughter now. Can I see her?"

"Not yet. She will be in recovery for about an hour, after which time she will be transported to intensive care. As soon as we get her settled, you will be allowed to visit with her."

Mr. Harrelson was visibly upset. We all eyed him cautiously as he looked like a person ready to explode at any moment. He was trying desperately to process everything the doctor was saying. All of us were for that matter. I didn't want to overstep my boundaries, but I needed to know what was facing Cinnamon on her road to recovery.

"Dr. Monge," I heard myself say. "What is the recovery time for this type of surgery? Also, her spleen was removed. What function does the spleen play in the body? Can a person survive without a spleen?"

"These are all very thoughtful questions...thanks for asking. Well, for one, the spleen filters blood and helps the body fight off infections. However, people can and do live without a spleen. With respect to her recovery time, that depends on the absence of infection in the body. Typically, recovery time from a splenectomy is four to six weeks. However, the gunshot wound will add a few more weeks to her recovery time. I would estimate somewhere around eight to ten weeks. Again, it depends on whether infection sets in."

I uttered, "Thank you." That thank-you was just as much for the doctor as it was for God.

"I know this must be hard for you. Please know that she is in good hands here at Mercy General. I will oversee her care personally. Should you need anything, please let me know."

"Doctor, I was very rude to you earlier. My emotions were and still are all over the place. I apologize."

"Apology accepted, Mr. Harrelson. When a loved one has been injured, in Cynthia's case by gunshot, it's human for our emotions to be raw. You are sitting there praying for a favorable outcome. Sometimes it's not that way. As a doctor, I have had my fair share of delivering the news of a loved one's demise to several families. It's not a pretty sight. As a matter of fact, it's heart-wrenching. I'm quite sure you noticed the armed security guards. They are in place for a reason. I've seen chairs thrown, fights break out and doctor's threatened with bodily harm because the family believes the surgeon didn't do all they could to save the life of their loved one. Tonight, is a good night, Mr. Harrelson. A really good night."

With that, Dr. Monge went back to work.

We were so relieved that Cinnamon was still with us, we forgot that the chaplain was sitting there until we heard him say, "Let us pray."

We all joined hands and bowed our heads as the chaplain led us in prayer. I listened as he thanked God for giving Cinnamon another chance at life. I, too, was thankful for her life. I tried to focus on the rest of the prayer; however, my mind kept taking me back to the exchange between Kyle and his father. What did they know about Shakira that had them spooked? They were holding this information a little too close to the vest in my opinion. John Harrelson had a story to tell, and I needed to hear it.

I had been at Cinnamon's side since the night it all happened, but I needed to make time to go visit with my grandmother. It was not like me to miss my weekly visits with her and I was certain that she would let me know in certain terms that she was feeling neglected. The thought of her feigning neglect brought a slight smile to my lips. The two women that meant the world to me were on opposite sides of town.

It was the agency's busiest time of year—forced to put in long hours at the office. There were days when the numbers on the pages were a blur; but I, and the coffee machine down the hall, became fast friends. I realized I was not getting enough rest but felt I owed it to Cinnamon to show her how much I cared. It hurt me to see her lying in that hospital bed knowing that I could have lost her for good that night. Again, I thanked God for sparing Cinnamon. This opportunity was not lost on me. Going forward, I was determined to make every second count. At that moment, I decided to knock off work at five o'clock. I got up from my desk, took the elevator to the twelfth floor and walked through the double doors leading to the executive suite. Mr. Brimmer's executive secretary, Veronica, looked up from her typewriter and met me with a generous smile.

"Good morning, Veronica," I said quietly.

"Good morning."

"Is the big guy in his office?"

"Actually, he just arrived."

It was 10:30 a.m. according to the clock on the wall. I guess that's a luxury afforded to the president and chief executive officer of Brimmer Financial Services. John Brimmer started offering financial services to friends and family right out of college. When he discovered how good he was at it, he branched out of the basement of his family home to a one-room office. Thirty-five years later and look at him now. He is the founder of one of the most successful financial services agencies in Manhattan.

Earlier that day, Myles arrived at the office at 6:00 a.m. and got the most important projects out of the way. The financial statement for Young & Bourne was complete and ready for their eleven o'clock meeting. The conference room on the tenth floor was scheduled and prepped with coffee, water and soft drinks thanks to his very efficient secretary, Gloria. He was even ahead of the game with the financial reports needed for next week's meeting with Mr. Brimmer. The company is in great shape—nothing for the "big guy" to be concerned about. When I grow up, I want to be just like him. For now, I am there to inform him that I need to leave work at five o'clock and not a second later.

I snapped back to reality when I heard Veronica's sultry voice usher me into his office. The door was slightly ajar, but I knocked out of respect.

"Come in."

One would think that John Brimmer was a big man upon hearing that rich baritone voice of his; however, he was of average height and kept himself in good shape by working out every morning.

He looked up from the stack of papers on his desk and motioned for me to have a seat in front of the massive mahogany desk that threatened to swallow him whole. I eased down into one of the leather chairs in front of his desk, mindful to sit fully erect in the chair.

"Myles…how is everything going? I do not have occasion to see you on this floor very often. What can I do for you?" I noticed that he placed his pen on the desk and settled back in his chair. I decided to mirror his body language and settle into a more relaxed position in my chair.

"Mr. Brimmer," I began.

"None of that Mr. Brimmer stuff," he countered. "Call me John."

"So, Myles, what brings you to my office?"

"Mr. Brimmer, uh, John, I need to leave at five o'clock today. I know that this is an extremely busy time for the agency. However, I arrived at six o'clock this morning and completed the most important projects. The financial statement for Young & Bourne is complete and ready for the eleven o'clock meeting. My secretary, Gloria, has scheduled the tenth floor conference room and stocked it with coffee, water, and soft drinks. She is currently making copies of the financial reports for the meeting. In addition, John, we are ahead of the game with the financial reports for next week's meeting.

"Impressive," he replied. He studied me for a while before leaning forward, resting his arms on the desk. "You remind me of myself as a young man." There was a far-off look in his eyes and memories of times long gone.

I did not know what to say, so I smiled instead.

"I really like your dedication, but I don't want you working so hard that you forget about family." Puzzled at the mention of family, but I shrugged it off. He had this fatherly tone in his voice, so I took note of his advice. We talked a little while longer. When he picked up his pen, I rose from my seated position, thanked him for his time, and exited his office as quietly as I had entered.

Promptly at five o'clock, Gloria and I were getting on the elevator. She was all smiles and excited about getting home while still early enough to enjoy time with her family. She confided that getting home after her children were in bed was hard for her. I was shocked when she told me her husband was let go from his job about six months ago and she had become responsible for all things financial. I made a mental note to make sure she got her just due when raises rolled around.

"Thanks, Gloria, for all your hard work today."

"No problem. Thanks for letting me go early. My kids are going to be so excited to see me."

"Yeah, John said something about family today that resonated with me."

"Oh, so you two are on a first name basis now?" she said jokingly.

I laughed a little and shrugged my shoulders as if I were the man. "Well, he asked me to call him John, so who am I to disobey his orders."

We laughed, said our good-byes, and went our separate ways.

I caught the cross-town bus to Chesterfield, a senior's living facility on the west side. As I walked up the walkway and climbed the marble steps leading to the lobby, I noticed seniors were out soaking up the sunshine and fresh air. Some lined the walkway on benches while others played checkers, card games, or were deeply engaged in conversation. My grandmother was sitting on the veranda facing the lake. A nice breeze wafted through the honeysuckle trees making it extremely pleasant on this side of the facility. I stood there and watched her for a few minutes with two dozen long-stemmed roses, twelve red, twelve deep pink. My grandmother was my rock after Mom died and Dad incarcerated. These roses let her know how much I loved and appreciated all she had done for me. I could have easily been swallowed up by the streets, but my grandparents were determined that I would not end up dead or in jail. They were a constant fixture in my life, and for that, I would be eternally grateful.

I walked up behind her, leaned down, and kissed her on the top of her head. She knew instantly that it was I as I was the only one that had ever kissed her on the top of her head. That was reserved for me only. Everyone else kissed her cheek.

"Thanks for coming," her words smiled at me.

I handed the red roses to her. As she reached for them, I walked around and kneeled before her. When I handed the deep pink roses to her, tears welled up in her eyes. She knew without me saying a word what these roses meant.

She looked me in the eyes and whispered, "And I would do it again."

During dinner, Grandma and I had an opportunity to talk about what happened to Cinnamon. She listened thoughtfully to my recount of that fateful night. The only movement she made was a slow shake of the head from time to time. It was during the mention of Shakira Fleming that I noticed something different about her.

"What is it?" I queried.

"I-I-I," she stammered.

"Are you okay? Should I call someone?" I looked around for an orderly, but she grabbed my hand. I turned toward her. Tears were streaming down her face. What is it about Shakira that had everyone spooked? Whatever it was, I was determined not to leave there without the answers I desperately needed.

"Grandma, let's go inside. I think you will feel better if you lay down for a while," Myles quickly surmised.

She shook her head in agreement.

When we got inside, she laid down on the sofa. I put on the teakettle. She closed her eyes, but I could discern she was not asleep. Her breathing was too shallow for sleep. Things were getting more interesting by the day.

I could hear the teakettle just beginning to whistle in the distance.

"Grandma, where do you keep the tea bags?" I asked.

"First cabinet to the right of the stove; first shelf," she shot back.

As I got up from the chair, I smiled to myself at how well I knew my grandmother. Yes, tonight was going to be interesting.

She emerged from a reclining position as I reentered the living room with two steaming cups of tea. My grandmother never used sugar in her tea, only honey and lemon. I took my tea the same as hers.

I waited a couple of minutes before asking why she reacted the way she did during dinner.

"Oh, it was nothing. Sometimes I get a little faint," she offered.

"Grandma, I couldn't help but notice that all of this came on the heels of me mentioning the name of Shakira…Shakira Fleming."

"Mr. Harrelson and his son Kyle reacted the same way the night Cinnamon was shot."

She patted the space next to her on the sofa. I moved from the chair next to her. Grandma grabbed my hand and squeezed it tight. The only time she did that is when she really does not want to discuss something but feels there is no way around it. Therefore, I prepared myself mentally for a rollercoaster ride I believe I was about to embark upon.

"Baby, the young lady you call Cinnamon and that other one with the funny name are sisters."

I could not believe what I was hearing. "What do you mean they are sisters? Grandma, maybe you are getting them mixed up with someone else. They cannot possibly be sisters. That night was the first time they met each other," I explained.

"Baby, listen to me. I know I am getting up in age but there is nothing wrong with my memory. Cinnamon's birth name is Cynthia, right?"

"Yes," I eyed her cautiously.

"Her father's name is John Harrelson, right?"

"Yes," I responded by dragging the word out slightly longer than necessary.

She stared deeply into her teacup like one of those women around the neighborhood who offer to tell your fortune by reading tealeaves.

Finally, she found her voice, "Myles, something terrible happened to Cinnamon's mother. I remember now. It's a shame how the sins of the father come back on the children," she said thoughtfully.

"What happened to her?"

"Talk to John Harrelson about that," she responded. "He alone holds the key to why Cinnamon was shot. It might be hard for him to acknowledge his part in this, but for him to have peace he has to take ownership in his part."

The sun was just beginning to set when Myles boarded the cross-town bus back to the east side. He sat silently mulling over the revelation his grandmother disclosed. Cinnamon and Shakira sisters…this was too crazy to be true. On the other hand, was it?

Myles bypassed his building and continued to Palmyra. He knocked on the door and Mr. Harrelson answered.

"Myles, what brings you to my house this time of night?"

Mr. Harrleson eyed Myles warily. He was not sure what to think about Myles showing up on his doorstep this time of night. It was uncharacteristic of him. One thing he knew for sure is when a man shows up on your doorstep, he has something on his mind, and he will not rest until he has gotten whatever it is plaguing him off his chest.

Myles looked him in the eyes and said, "I know."

There it is Mr. Harrelson thought to himself. Now I know what brought Myles to this side of town so late at night. Mr. Harrelson stepped back from the door allowing Myles access to a story he thought he buried with his wife.

He escorted Myles into the living room. The two men sat in chairs opposite one another. He knew that one day what happened all those years ago would come back to haunt him, but why tonight. Why the past could not remain in the past was beyond him.

Myles sat across from John Harrelson, trying to understand what he must be going through. He searched John Harrelson's face and saw a man that carried a heavy burden. Life certainly was not easy, and people prone to mistakes. However, those mistakes do not come without consequence. As Myles sat there in the presence of a broken man, he searched himself. He thought about the mistakes he made along the way. His grandmother's voice drifted into his thoughts. "Myles, we have all sinned and come short of the glory of God." The anger and self-righteousness he felt when he entered Mr. Harrelson's home, began to dissipate. Everyone has a story to tell, and Myles believed John Harrelson was ready to tell his.

John Harrelson cleared his throat. Glancing around the room, he leaned back in his chair and rested both elbows on the arms of the chair. Interlaced fingers became the focal point as he struggled with how to tell Myles the deadly secret carried all these years.

Myles did not move or look at Mr. Harrelson until he heard a deep sigh coming from the other side of the room. From the look on Mr. Harrelson's face, Myles believed he had made peace with the situation and was ready to unburden himself.

"Myles when I opened the door, you said that you know. What is it that you think you know?"

Now it was Myles's turn to lean forward.

"Mr. Harrelson, I learned this evening that Shakira and Cynthia are sisters. Is this true?"

"Yes."

"How could this happen, and Cynthia not know anything about it? Why would Shakira shoot her own sister? None of this is making any sense."

"Myles, it is a long story. A story I hoped I would never have to tell...again."

"What do you mean by again?"

"Well, it was twenty-seven years ago when I first told this story. There are times when I cannot believe that I caused another human being so much pain. The day I told her about Shakira and Melba, Shakira's mother, I thought I would lose her for sure that day. When I was a young man, I was arrogant and self-centered. I worked at night and it was easy for me to do things under the radar. My wife, Janice, was so trusting. When I think back on our relationship, I fully understand that I caused every problem in the marriage. I take ownership for that. Janice managed this house, the bills, and the kids. She had control over everything but me. I was determined to be my own man and do what I wanted to do. Truthfully, Myles, I do not know how she put up with me."

"Mr. Harrelson, how did your wife die?"

John Harrelson shook his head from side-to-side like a tormented soul. His body shook with silent sobs. Finally, he regained his composure long enough to tell Myles what happened to his wife on that fateful night twenty-seven years ago.

"I was living a double life, Myles. In all my arrogance, I thought that I could get away with it. During the day, I lived by all appearances the perfect life with my wife and son. Kyle was the only child at that time. I worked at night but on my off days, I stayed on the other side of town with Melba. It was just the two of us. No kids… no worries. This double life went on for about two years. Then one day, Melba told me she was pregnant. I panicked and walked out. I avoided Melba. She would call me at work, and I would refuse to take her calls. Then, one day, everything stopped. She stopped calling me. She stopped showing up at my job. I thought, finally, I could live the rest of my life in peace. We had an agreement that she would never come to my house or tell Janice anything about our living arrangement. If she did, I would make her life miserable."

"Let me guess. She showed up on your doorstep."

John Harrelson got up and poured himself a drink to calm his nerves.

"Can I get you a drink?" he asked.

"Nope."

28

He returned to his seat and watched as the ice cubes gently swirled in the glass.

"That night," he continued. "Janice walked the three blocks to God's Grace and Holy Tabernacle for Bible study. She was six months pregnant with Cynthia and it was a beautiful summer evening. I was sitting on the front porch and I watched as she talked to our neighbors along the way. It was about nine-thirty that evening when my neighbor, Joseph Carmichael, knocked on the door. I will never forget that knock. It was one of urgency. When I opened the door, he told me that someone shot Janice. He said it happened as she was exiting the church and I needed to get to the hospital immediately. I ran to get Kyle, but he told me to go; that he would look after Kyle. My mind was racing. Who would want to shoot Janice? She never did anything to harm anyone. She was in surgery when I arrived. I never got a chance to say goodbye. Not long after I arrived, the doctor took me into a conference room and told me that they did all they could do but Janice succumbed to her injuries. They were, however, able to save the baby. The doctor asked if I wanted to see my baby girl. I was in shock… I did not know what to do. I asked the doctor if I could see Janice first. When I saw her lifeless body, I cried and kissed her goodbye. I walked to the nursery and held my daughter. I told her that her mother had picked Cynthia Marie as her name. She was born prematurely and had to remain in the hospital for about three months."

Myles reached up and wiped the tears from his eyes. His thoughts turned back to the day his father killed his mother. His mind was racing.

"Mr. Harrelson, was Melba responsible for your wife's death?"

For the second time, Myles witnessed a soul-stirring cry erupting from the bowels of John Harrelson. He sat quietly, lost in his thoughts, until he was ready to finish telling him about that night.

"The police were milling around the hospital when I arrived, but I was too distraught to talk to them that night. A detective handed me his card and told me he would stop by my house the next day. The detective told me the following day that there were several witnesses to the shooting and that the woman who shot Janice appeared to be pregnant. I didn't want to believe it was Melba. I didn't want to believe that she could be capable of shooting someone. Nevertheless, I told the detective about my affair with Melba and the pregnancy. I provided him with her address. The detective called me later that day and informed me that she confessed to the shooting."

Myles was speechless.

"Myles, my life has been a living hell since that night. I replay it over and over again in my head."

"That night at the hospital when I mentioned Shakira you and Kyle looked at each other. Does Kyle know about the circumstances surrounding his mother's death and that Shakira is his sister?"

"Kyle was six when his mother died. When the detective arrived that morning, it was early. The detective and I were sitting in the living room and neither noticed that Kyle had entered the room. He heard me tell the detective about Melba. I wasn't sure how much he understood at his young age, but as the days went on, he began asking questions."

"What kind of questions?" quizzed Myles.

"He wanted to know who Melba was. One day he asked why Melba didn't like his mommy. Kyle was seventeen the first time he encountered Shakira. One day after school, Kyle told me that some girl was following him. She wouldn't say anything, just stare at him. Kyle played basketball at Joiner High and was used to girls vying for his attention. However, this girl kinda spooked him a little. I played it off and told him it was nothing more than a school-girl crush."

"Kyle doesn't appear to be the type that would let something like that go," Myles countered.

"You're right. He didn't let it go. One day he had enough of Shakira following him around and confronted her. She told him that she was his sister and that her mother was in prison because of me with no chance of parole."

Hollywood couldn't write a script this good Myles thought.

"By this time, Cynthia was about eleven. I was in the kitchen packing my lunch when I heard the front door slam. Kyle was shouting wanting to know where I was. When I walked toward the living room, he was pacing back and forth like a caged animal. He lunged when he saw me. Now, see I'm no slouch, but I had a hard time with Kyle that day. During our scuffle, we broke everything in this living room. I had to work overtime every day and picked up a Saturday shift here and there for two months to afford new furniture."

Myles laughed at the thought of Mr. Harrelson and Kyle fighting. But he could understand why. His mother taken away from him and the one responsible for all the craziness is standing in front of him. Yep. Myles could understand the frustration and pain Kyle felt.

"Who told Shakira about you?"

"Well, when Melba was convicted and sentenced to life in prison, she was six months pregnant, so was Janice."

"Oh, man, this just keeps getting better and better. Mr. Harrelson, I think I will take that drink now."

John Harrelson got up to fix a drink for himself and Myles. When he handed the drink to Myles, he gulped it down and got up to fix himself another.

Myles returned with a strong drink in hand.

"You okay, Myles?" asked John Harrelson.

"I'll be fine. Please continue."

"Melba gave birth to Shakira behind bars and Melba's sister, Connie, raised Shakira. My name is on her birth certificate. Connie wanted me to be a part of Shakira's life, but I couldn't. I told her that I would provide child support for Shakira, but it was best that she be raised on the other side of town. Well, I don't know for certain, but I can only imagine what Connie and Melba told Shakira."

"It's ironic, isn't it?" stated Myles.

"What's that?" asked Mr. Harrelson.

"That she and her mother followed the same path. I could be wrong, but both Melba and Shakira wanted your attention. They achieved it by removing what they viewed as obstacles. Those obstacles: Janice and Cynthia."

Mr. Harrelson considered Myles's theory.

"Well, Mr. Harrelson, It's getting late, and I have an early day tomorrow. One more thing, Mr. Harrelson, you gotta make this right. You have one daughter sitting in jail as we speak and another one in the hospital. I am not one to judge, because we all make mistakes. My father killed my mother in a fit of rage and jealousy. He is still in prison and I go to see him from time to time. Had it not been for my grandmother, I would not have been able to forgive him for taking my mother away from me. I was mentally prepared to forgive him when he asked for forgiveness and I haven't looked back since that time. I understand your pain, however, you gotta make it right. I can't tell you which one to start with, that's between you and God."

It had been several weeks since the shooting at the club. Cynthia was now out of the hospital and recuperating at home. Myles stopped by every day after work to ensure she was following the doctor's orders. They would talk and laugh for hours about everything and nothing. He was falling deeper in love with her by the day. One Saturday afternoon, Myles stopped by to check on her. When she answered the door, he knew something had upset her.

"Cinnamon, what's going on?"

"I don't want to talk about it."

Myles took her hand and led her to the sofa. He wasn't sure if he should press her to let him in or let it go.

"Cinnamon, obviously something has upset you. As someone who cares very deeply for you, I don't like seeing you like this. The night you were shot, I thought I had lost you forever."

Cinnamon rested her head on his shoulder.

"Myles, I don't know how to feel about this."

"Feel about what?"

"My father stopped by this morning and told me about the night my mother died."

Myles put his arm around Cinnamon and pulled her closer. He knew that she had a long road ahead of her, making peace with how her mother died.

"Myles, I experienced a rush of emotions when he told me what happened. I was angry and hurt all at the same time. I never got a chance to know my mother. All this time, I thought my mother died giving birth to me."

Myles remained quiet.

"For years, I could only imagine what you were feeling seeing your mother fall to her death. Now, the truth is right in front of me, and I am having a hard time accepting it. I never thought of my father as a selfish person, but now I see that I never really knew him."

"Cinnamon…"

"Please do not try to defend his actions, Myles. He was wrong and indirectly responsible for my mother's death."

Myles thought back to the night he confronted Mr. Harrelson with his knowledge of Shakira. He had struggled many nights after that with disclosing what he knew about Shakira and her mother's death. Eventually, he realized it wasn't his place to tell her about a conversation had between him and her father. Now, the elephant was in the room and he wasn't sure how to handle it. He decided now was not the time to bring it up. Cinnamon had been through too much already and he did not want to add to it.

Several weeks after Cinnamon's discharge from the hospital, Myles awoke to an early morning call. He rolled over—the clock on the nightstand blinked 6:00 a.m.

Myles brought both pillows up along the sides of his face to cover his ears. When that did not block out the incessant ringing of the phone, he decided to answer it with an attitude.

"Hello," barked Myles.

"Myles? Why are you answering the phone like that? Were you asleep?" his father asked.

Myles could not believe what he was hearing right now.

"Well, it is six o'clock on a Saturday morning. I am typically asleep at this hour on a Saturday morning," Myles shot back.

"Oh, I'm sorry. I guess all those years of incarceration has me trained. You know in the joint you gotta get up when they tell you, go to sleep when they tell you, eat when they tell you. A man can't even form a thought in his head unless they approve it first," his father chuckled at his ill-fated attempt at prison humor.

"Dad," Myles started. "I don't mind talking to you but going forward can you try not calling so early? I would suggest not calling before noon."

"Yeah, son, I can do that," he said obediently. "I guess I should invest in a watch or a clock for my room."

Myles's eyes opened fully at his father's last statement.

"Room? Since when are prisoners allowed to wear watches or keep clocks in their prison cells?" Myles asked.

Myles listened to his father's soft chuckle. He slowly threw back the covers and sat on the side of the bed. Myles was unaware of how hard he was holding the receiver or that he pressed the receiver so close to his ear that he could hear his own heartbeat.

"Dad?" Myles said into the receiver. "When did you get out?"

"This morning. Man, I tell you…it really feels good. I have been walking around the city taking in the sights and sounds. I sat on a park bench and watched the sun come up. I listened to the birds singing and watched as the squirrels scampered up and down the trees in the park."

Tears streamed down Myles's face as he listened to his father recount the first few hours of freedom on the outside. The joy coming through the receiver was contagious. There was no way Myles could go back to sleep after this. Myles listened for the next hour as he saw the city through his father's eyes.

Now that his father was no longer incarcerated, they both experienced shades of freedom. Myles embraced the understanding that they could visit with each other whenever time allowed and get to know the man he had become. His father now had the freedom to come and go as he pleased. Their visits were not always pleasant, but Myles got a chance to understand his father better and see his mother through his father's eyes. What Myles came to understand about his father is that he loved his wife, but the drugs and alcohol distorted his ability to see clearly. He was insanely jealous, which did not make matters better.

During his incarceration, finally he was able to take ownership for his actions. He told Myles during one of their visits that it is never right to take the life of another. He asked Myles for forgiveness. Had it not been for Myles's relationship with God, he never would have been able to show his father the benefits of unconditional love. For years, Myles was angry with his father for turning his life upside down. No child should have to go through what he went through. He blamed his father for everything that did not go right in his life. Being able to forgive his father and to love him was hard but necessary for him to go on with his life. He wanted Cinnamon to be able to do the same. He knew she was capable of it.

It had been several weeks since Myles and Cinnamon had seen each other. Myles picked up the phone and dialed her number.

"Hello?"

"Hey, Cinnamon…do you have plans for tomorrow?"

"I don't have anything planned. What's going on?"

"I have someone I want you to meet."

Myles's father lived at a halfway house in the old neighborhood. He felt that if Cinnamon could witness firsthand the freedom that comes with redemptive love, she might see her father differently.

"Oh yeah, who might that be?"

"My father. He was released from prison a few weeks ago and is living in a halfway house on the other side of town."

"Hello…Cinnamon?"

"Yeah, I'm still here."

"Okay, so I told him all about you and he is excited to meet the woman in my life."

"What time should I be ready?"

"I will stop by your house around eleven o'clock. We can go out to eat and get to know one another. How does that sound?"

"Okay. I will see you at eleven tomorrow."

The line went dead. Myles stood holding the receiver for a beat before returning it to the cradle. Something seemed a little off with Cinnamon. Maybe he was making too much out of nothing. He got dressed and went out to meet up with childhood friend, Leroy.

When Myles arrived the next morning, Cinnamon was dressed but reluctant to go. She was not sure she wanted to visit with a man that had murdered his wife. What purpose would it serve? All she could think about was how she was feeling about this revelation dumped on her by her father. She was not in the mood to meet Myles's father. After all, he had murdered his wife in front of his own son. She did not trust herself to be civil when her emotions were so raw.

"Are you ready?" asked Myles.

"I'm not going," responded Cinnamon.

Myles stood there staring at the woman that held his heart captive. He wanted so desperately for her to see forgiveness up close and personal. To experience how freeing forgiveness is. But he also knew that she had to be a willing participant. She wasn't ready.

"Look, Cinnamon, I'm not going to stand here and act like I'm not disappointed because I would be lying. And I'm not going to preach to you because I understand your anger and your pain. I went through the same thing with my father. However, with God's help, I was able to move on and do something that is extremely hard for all of us to do. I forgave him. It was necessary for me to break the chains that had me bound for years. Once I did that, it felt like the weight lifted off me. At that moment, I knew what it felt like to be free. But hey, we can do this at another time."

Myles took her in his arms and hugged her tightly before opening the door and closing it gently behind him.

As Cinnamon stood staring at the space once occupied by the man she cared so deeply for, she realized that she needed space. Space from Myles, her father; she needed time to sort out her feelings.

CHAPTER

IT HAD BEEN SIX MONTHS SINCE Cinnamon last spoke to her father and Myles. Six months of therapy brought her to the place where she was now strong enough to talk to her father about the night her mother died. She called him and asked if she could stop by. When she parked in front of the house on Palmyra, her father was sitting on the front porch.

Cinnamon rested her head on the steering wheel, "Mom, I am doing this for you," she whispered.

Cinnamon exited the car and climbed the cement stairs leading to the front porch. Her father got up and stood there awkwardly not knowing what to do. Cinnamon walked up to her father and extended her hand to him.

Her father looked at her hand, "Fair enough," he said. He took her hand in his and they entered the house. For the next several hours, Cinnamon listened as her father gave an accounting of that night. He blamed himself for what happened, not being man enough to take ownership of lives wrecked. She confided in him about her hurt, her anger, and having sought professional help. She put space between the two men she loved more than life itself: her father and Myles. Now it was time to rectify all the wrongs.

Later that day, Cinnamon called Myles and invited him over for dinner.

Myles was surprised to hear from Cinnamon, as it had been six months. He thought he might not ever hear from her again. He knew she was struggling with the knowledge of her father's double life and all the consequences surrounding his indiscretion, but when she shut him out, he went on with his life. Debbie was now a huge part of his life and had been for the past three months.

"Myles, it would mean a lot to me if you would join me for dinner," Cinnamon said.

"Let me call you back in about an hour," replied Myles.

"Okay, I will wait on your call," she said. "Myles," she continued, "I really need to see you tonight."

Cinnamon hung up and wondered if she and Myles would be okay. She knew it wasn't fair to push him out of her life for six months, but if he of all people didn't understand why, then who would.

Myles and Debbie had planned to spend a quiet evening together. For the past three months, they had spent every available moment going to concerts in the park, long drives in the country, boat rides, and a weekend getaway to the Bahamas. Debbie was cool and he loved spending time with her, but Cinnamon had his heart.

Debbie answered the phone on the second ring. "Hello."

"Hey, you," Myles said.

"I was hoping you would call," cooed Debbie. "Do you need me to stop and bring dinner?"

"About tonight," Myles started. "Can I get a raincheck? I have something I need to do. Tomorrow is Friday…we can spend the entire weekend together."

"Uh, sure," yielded Debbie.

"Cool. I will call you tomorrow." Myles hung up giving her no time to ask questions. His next phone call was to Cinnamon.

Cinnamon was busy in the kitchen when the phone rang. "Hello."

"What time is dinner?" queried Myles.

"Six o'clock," she responded.

"Cool, see you at six."

Myles leaned back in his office chair and closed his eyes. After six months of silence, why was Cinnamon reaching out to him now. He could not get this question out of his head. Maybe he was over-thinking the situation, but he did not know how to handle this. Six months of not seeing Cinnamon, holding her, or talking to her made him question everything about himself.

"Enough of this," he said to himself. "All I have to do is ask."

The clock on his desk illuminated four o'clock. Myles made a mental note to himself to be out of the office in precisely one hour.

Myles could not believe his good fortune. Traffic was very coop-erative. He parked his car a block away from Cinnamon's apartment.

When he arrived at her apartment door, he stood in the hall listening to the soft jazz coming from her apartment. He allowed the smell of good cooking to envelope him before lightly knocking on the door.

Cinnamon opened the door allowing the aroma of chicken and dumplings to fill the space. She remembered Myles's favorite dish was chicken and dumplings with apple pie for dessert. Myles appre-ciated Cinnamon with his eyes and for the moment, Debbie was a distant memory. He constantly reminded himself that he was just there for dinner and to find out why Cinnamon cut him out of her life six months ago. Myles wondered if she thought they would pick up where they left off all those months ago, or that she thought he would sit around and wait on her. If so, she was delusional. He was a man and men don't sit around waiting on a woman to make up their minds. He couldn't wait any longer for her, and if provided the opportunity, he would say as much.

Myles entered the apartment. Cinnamon took his jacket and hung it in the hall closet.

"Myles, thanks for accepting my invitation to dinner. Honestly, I did not think you would come. I've been so nervous about seeing you today. But you are here now, and I cannot tell you how pleased I am to see you.

Cinnamon sat down beside him on the sofa and reached for his hand.

"Myles, I know…"

Myles cut her off before she could finish.

"Cinnamon," started Myles. "It's been six months. Why now?"

Cinnamon let out a sigh. "Myles, I was in a dark place. I needed time to process what I learned about my mother's death, my father's infidelity. Consequently, I pushed everyone out of my life that I cared for and that cared for me. I'm sorry if I hurt you in doing so but I needed time to myself. During that time, I sought professional help. My therapist helped me process what I learned about the circumstances surrounding my mother's death."

"Why didn't you say something? The last time I saw or heard from you was when I asked you to meet my father. I tried calling you but no answer. I called you at work but no answer. So I did what I had to do, I moved on."

Cinnamon stood and walked over to the window. So many thoughts raced through her head. She turned and looked in the direction of Myles. Cinnamon understood what he meant by moving on.

"Is she nice?"

"She's not up for discussion."

"Believe it or not, I'm happy for you. Thanks for being honest. Most men would have seized the opportunity."

"You should know that's not me."

"Yeah, I know."

Myles retrieved his jacket from the hall closet and walked toward the door, "Thanks for the invite, but under the circumstances, I think I should leave."

"Wait!" exclaimed Cinnamon. "I understand where you are in your life, but our friendship shouldn't change. I would love it if you would stay and have dinner with me. That's all. Just dinner. Anyway, you cannot leave without dessert. I made apple pie."

I am so in trouble, Myles thought. She is serving my favorite meal of chicken and dumplings with apple pie for dessert. What is she trying to do to me?

Myles closed the door and leaned against it. He laid his jacket across the back of the sofa and joined Cinnamon at the dining room table. After dinner, Cinnamon grabbed his hand and led him to the

APPLES AND CINNAMON

sofa where she spoon-fed him apple pie. Myles struggled to keep his thoughts on Debbie, but the seductress sitting in front of him was making it difficult to do so. Cinnamon leaned in a little closer to Myles as she brought the next spoonful of apple pie to his mouth.

Myles put up his hands in surrender. "Cinnamon, I know what you are trying to do, and it is not going to work."

"What isn't going to work?" asked Cinnamon.

"Don't play with me, Cinnamon. You knew exactly what you were doing when you cooked my favorite meal and dessert. You are trying to seduce me. I already told you this game you are playing is not going to work."

Cinnamon pulled back gently placing the dessert plate on the coffee table.

"What happened to us?" Cinnamon asked quietly.

"Cinnamon," Myles said while turning to face her. "You happened to us. I was prepared six months ago to take our friendship to the next level, but you shut me out. What was I to think? What did you expect me to do?"

"Myles, I was hurting," Cinnamon cried. "I know now that I was wrong, but I didn't know what else to do. Please don't hold my poor judgment against me."

Myles leaned forward, interlocking his fingers attempting to process everything. He slowly rose from his seat and grabbed his jacket.

Cinnamon stared at Myles as he opened the door to leave.

"Take care, Cinnamon," Myles said over his shoulder before closing the door softly behind him.

A solitary tear fell from Cinnamon's eyes as Myles walked out of her life.

Myles needed to clear his head. He didn't understand why this was happening to him now. Cinnamon held a special place in his heart, she always had; but none of this was making any sense to him. He needed time to process what just happened. He hopped in his car and drove around the city. The loss and abandonment Myles felt was overwhelming. The closest person to him was his grandmother. She became both mother and father to him. A freak accident took his

41

grandfather and the penal system stood between him and his father most of his life. Three months wasn't enough time to fill the void. However, Debbie filled the empty space created by Cinnamon.

As Myles drove around the city, he reflected on that Sunday when Cinnamon reneged on going with him to visit his father. He was so excited to introduce Cinnamon to him. He wanted her to see how love conquers all. Of all the people who should be angry, it's me Myles thought. I grew up without my mother and father.

Myles slammed an open palm down hard on the steering wheel. "God, how many times did I ask you why did my mother have to die? Why didn't you save her from my father? Why did I have to continue in this life without them? I was just a little kid."

Choking back the cry that threatened to escape, Myles eventually yelled out of frustration. Right now, he felt like his life was crumbling down all around him. Soon he found himself parked outside of Leroy's eight-story walkup. He could not believe his good fortune. He found a parking space right in front of the building. Any other time, he would have to circle the block several times only to end up parking three or four blocks away and walking back.

"It's a good thing I go to the gym," Myles said to himself as he took the steps two at a time. When he reached Leroy's apartment, he knocked three times twice. He and Leroy developed customized knocks years ago.

Minutes later, Myles heard the unlocking of several locks. That's the cost of living in the inner city. Myles smiled at the thought.

Leroy opened the door wide allowing his childhood friend to come in.

"Hey, man. What brings you to this side of town?" Leroy inquired.

Myles plopped down in one of the many chairs Leroy had strategically placed around the apartment. Leaning forward, he folded his arms across his knees allowing his head to rest until he felt the cool of a bottle of beer on the back of his neck.

Myles reached for the bottle and leaned back in the chair, taking a long swig from the bottle. Leroy watched his friend cautiously.

"What's going on, man?" Leroy asked again. "I can tell you have something that's weighing pretty heavy on your mind."

Leroy got up to get another beer. He brought another bottle back for Myles.

"I think this is going to be a two-beer night," he said, returning to his chair.

Myles looked at him, silently turning the bottle up draining the amber liquid.

Leroy pulled his chair a little closer to Myles, choosing his words carefully. "Man, we been friends for a long time. We been through some things together. You know I always got your back. But honestly, Myles, why are you here? I know this ain't no social visit. This is what I do know. You showed up at my apartment looking like the world is ending, and you sat down and drank two beers without coming up for air. By the way, you need to replace those two beers you drank."

Myles smiled at the comment. He knew Leroy was joking about replacing the beer. That was his attempt at bringing him out of the funk that had settled on him after leaving Cinnamon's place. After their third beer, Myles shared what he knew about Cinnamon, Shakira, and their father.

"What kind of craziness is this?" Leroy asked. "You are seriously telling me that Cinnamon didn't know that Shakira is her sister and that her daddy kept this a secret from her all this time."

"Yep," Myles replied while nodding his head up and down. "Not only did he keep it a secret, he allowed Cinnamon to believe that her mother died while giving birth to her."

"Myles, you want another beer?" This stuff has my head spinning and I think I need another beer or something stronger tonight." Leroy rummages through the kitchen cabinets in search of the bottle of liquor he keeps for special occasions.

He found the bottle and retrieved a shot glass from the cabinet. "You want one?"

"No."

Leroy put the shot glass back in the cabinet and turned the bottle up to his mouth twice before putting the top back on the bottle.

"What are you going to do?" he asked upon returning to his seat.

"I don't know. I would have been okay had she not laid this on me. After all, she was the one that cut communication with me. I tried calling her. I even stopped by her apartment several times and there was no answer. There was one time I knocked, and I could have sworn she was looking through the peephole. What does she want from me?"

"She wants you," Leroy responded. "That's not hard to understand."

"I understand that she wants to be in a relationship, but what I don't understand is how she could expect me to feel the same way about her after six months of nothing. It's as if she pushed the pause button on our friendship and said sit until I am ready to see where this might go."

"Hold up…weren't you the one who told me you two were just friends?" asked Leroy.

"Yep."

"Well, I don't see the problem," slurred Leroy. "Or did I miss something?"

"Leroy, I was ready to go there with her six months ago. Now Debbie is a part of my life and Cinnamon is trying to pick up where we almost left off. Man, I'm confused."

"Not half as much as I am," laughed Leroy. "Well, I wish I could help you solve this mystery, but I need to get some sleep. You are welcome to stay here."

"Where would I sleep?" questioned Myles. "Man, have you taken a good look around your apartment?"

"What's wrong with it?"

"Leroy, all you have is chairs in your living space. Can't nobody get a good night's sleep in a chair!"

"Well, don't say I didn't offer," Leroy shouted at a closing door.

Myles exited the building and eased into the driver's seat. He sat there for a moment thinking about his conversation with Leroy. Maybe he was right about there not being a problem. Although he felt something special for Cinnamon, they never got a chance to be in a true relationship. He and Debbie, on the other hand, had spent a romantic weekend in the Bahamas. Cinnamon had been through enough. He did not want to add to it.

Myles turned the key in the ignition and pulled slowly away from the curb. Tomorrow is another day and he promised Debbie the entire weekend. When the timing was right, he would have a conversation with Cinnamon. Until then, it's business as usual.

The next day, Debbie arrived at Myles's apartment carrying dinner in a brown paper bag. It smelled delicious, whatever it was. She kicked off her heels as she entered the apartment and immediately started to complain about the horrible day she had at work. Myles thought she must work for the worst boss in the world. He watched as she busied herself in the kitchen scooping out helpings of the mystery meal onto dinner plates for him and her. He scolded himself for drawing a stark contrast between how Cinnamon went all out with cooking his favorite meal and dessert. She even served him. Myles knew that was all part of the seduction, and she almost had him. Debbie, on the other hand, came in with dinner in a bag and has not stopped talking yet to ask about his day.

Snap out of it, Myles, he thought. Debbie has a high-profile job in the mayor's office and does not have time to cook. More and more women are taking their rightful place in this world even if it meant that positions traditionally held by men would soon see a woman at the helm. He got up from his seat on the sofa, walked up behind Debbie, and wrapped his arms around her waist.

"It sounds like you had an extremely hard day. Why don't we put dinner off for a while? I will run a hot bath for you so you can relax. How does that sound?"

Turning to face him, she looked in his eyes and said, "Heavenly."

Myles leaned in and kissed her gently. He sought her mouth again, each kiss hungrier than before until they found themselves fully engulfed in the essence of lovemaking. He made good on his offer to run her bath, both gently easing down into the bathtub. Debbie closed her eyes and leaned back into Myles. Her soft hum of Myles's favorite song caused him to check off two things on his list: the bedroom and her beautiful singing voice. Her gentle hum brought back memories of his mother humming as she would go about cleaning the apartment.

Later that evening, Myles complemented Debbie on her choice of meal as they ate by candlelight.

"By the way, Everfest Jazz Festival starts tomorrow. You wanna check it out?"

"Sure," replied Debbie.

Myles mentally checked off another item on his list: jazz lover.

Myles took her again. Debbie slept softly in his arms.

After breakfast the next morning, Myles and Debbie headed out to Everfest. Performances held at specified locations throughout the city, Myles and Debbie tried to see as many of their favorite artists as they could that Saturday. Sunday lent itself to other artists at venues closer to his neighborhood.

They returned to Myles's apartment late in the evening, he invited Debbie to stay the night. Debbie liked preparing for life's little expectancies so she packed an additional outfit on the off chance that she would stay with Myles through Sunday. The two were growing closer and getting more comfortable with each other. Debbie silently pondered what it would be like waking up next to Myles every day or accepting his last name as hers. Myles's entrance into the bedroom caught her off guard.

"What are you thinking so intensely about?" inquired Myles.

"Oh, I was thinking about how much I enjoyed hanging out with you this weekend," she replied with a smile.

Myles crossed the room and sat down next to Debbie on the bed. A few errant hairs went astray and lay in wait across Debbie's left eye. Myles reached up and gently moved them out of the way before taking her mouth in his.

"I enjoyed hanging out with you too," Myles said. "But we both have to get up early tomorrow. Let's get some sleep."

Debbie turned off the light and folded herself into Myles's arms. He lay there listening to her soft snores, mentally revisiting his "must-haves" in a mate. That night he decided the list was no longer necessary.

Several months into his relationship with Debbie and they were still seeing each other; splitting their time between his apartment and hers on the Upper East Side. Myles continued to put in the hours at work and received a promotion that landed him a corner office on the twelfth floor. His new position brought with it more work and longer hours. There were times when he would go into the office on Saturday fully expecting to put in a couple of hours but end up spending the entire day trying to catch up on his workload. He hated to call in his secretary on a Saturday, but there were times when it was unavoidable. According to his grandmother, he had to find a way to manage work-life balance. Maybe this is what "the big guy" was referring to when he said not to forget about family. It didn't take long for things to shift in his and Debbie's relationship. Things were beginning to cool off between them. If Debbie were going to be a part of his life, he could not forget about her. He had to find a way to make it work.

One fall Sunday afternoon, he and Debbie took a walk in Central Park. It was beautiful there. So many colorful trees as the leaves were just beginning to turn. He would come here with his grandparents after his mother died. He remembered his grandmother saying, "Myles, God didn't forget a thing and his canvass is magnificent. Look at the leaves and their vibrant colors."

He would choose leaves of different shapes, sizes, and colors stuffing them in his pockets for further examination. Now that he was older and sharing this childhood experience with Debbie, he believed his grandmother wanted him to experience all that was right with the world, not focus so much on the negative events that sometimes paints our canvass.

"Myles, there is a lot of bad in this world but there is also a lot of good. Remember, the good," his grandmother would say.

This was his Sunday to visit with his grandmother. He informed her earlier in the week that he would be bringing Debbie with him to dinner. His grandmother assured him that she was eager to meet the woman that was filling up so much of his space. He trusted his grandmother's intuition. He reminisced about the time he had a huge crush on Carlotta. He was a senior in high school, and they shared a table in biology class. He really liked her so when prom rolled around, he asked Carlotta to be his date. When he told his grandmother about her, she did not say anything—not one comment.

Before he could get out of the door for school the next morning, he heard his grandmother call out from the kitchen. "Myles, I want to meet Carlotta. You hear me Myles." He really liked Carlotta and looked forward to her being his date for prom, but he also knew that his grandmother had not been wrong in the past. He silently hoped she would be wrong this time.

Myles arranged for Carlotta to stop by his house the next day. She was prompt, beautifully adorned, oozing with sweetness. Grandmother was pleasant and Myles thought the visit went well. After the visit, Myles walked Carlotta home. When he returned, his grandmother told him that Carlotta was "full of it" and that he should reconsider taking her to the prom. He argued that it was too late to get another date and that he was taking Carlotta. Period.

Myles remembered his grandmother's surprised look, as he had never questioned her judgment. She left him standing in the living room. The slamming of her bedroom door let him know that he had messed up big time.

The following weekend was prom and Myles dressed in a black tuxedo with a white carnation corsage in hand for Carlotta. He knocked on Apartment 8A. Carlotta's father answered the door and asked if I had the right apartment.

He stood frozen in place. Sweat accumulated in his armpits; sweat rolled down both sides of his face. The entire incident began to play out in his head.

"Is Carlotta here?"

"No. Carlotta went to school prom," answered her father.

"But I'm her date for prom. I told her that I would pick her up."

By this time, Carlotta's mom was at the door and she and her husband conversed back and forth in Spanish. He remembered thinking that he should have paid closer attention in Spanish class but could make out that she left with Diego about an hour ago.

"Sorry," her father continued. "She at school prom." I stood there staring at a closed door and no date for prom. Granny was right, Carlotta was full of whatever it is, and I fell for it hook, line, and sinker.

Myles and Debbie arrived at Chesterfield early. Debbie didn't want to go in right away, so they sat in the car and talked about the upcoming mayoral election. She felt that her boss was a shoo-in for reelection as there was not much competition in her opinion. Myles felt that the mayor had not done much for the taxpayers in New York. Lately, people have been coming out of the woodwork accusing him of kickbacks received from awarding contracts to certain businesses. If that man is reelected to a second term as mayor, Myles swore he would pack up and leave New York.

Myles looked at his watch. It was four-thirty in the afternoon and his grandmother was a stickler for eating on time. When she said dinner was at five o'clock, she meant that everything was on the table and we were eating promptly at five o'clock, and not a second later. He got out of the car and walked around to the passenger side. He opened the door and held his hand out for Debbie. They walked arm-in-arm up the sidewalk leading to the entrance of Chesterfield.

Leona watched her grandson and Debbie from the balcony of her one-bedroom apartment. She stayed on the balcony until she heard the doorbell chime. She entered the apartment from the French doors connecting the balcony to her bedroom. She scurried down the short hallway opening the door wide. She was excited to finally meet Debbie.

"Why, hello," she said cheerfully. "Won't you come in?"

Myles leaned in and kissed his grandmother on the top of her head; something he had been doing from the time he realized that he towered over her. Debbie extended her hand to Leona.

"Well," Leona continued. "It is so nice to finally meet you. Would you like to freshen up before dinner? I just have a few more things to do in the kitchen and then we can all sit down to eat. The bathroom is down the hall, first door on the left."

"Yes, that would be nice," Debbie said casually. She smiled at Myles touching his arm ever so lightly as she left the room.

"Well, while she is freshening up, why don't you help me in the kitchen?"

Oh no, Myles thought. *Granny is starting early.*

"She is pretty," Leona said.

A broad smile crossed Myles's face. "Yes. She is very pretty. Smart too," he threw in for good measure.

Leona busied herself in the kitchen; directing Myles as to where to place each dish on the table. When Debbie rejoined them, the table was adorned with the finest china and silverware and each dish steaming with the aroma of roasted chicken, asparagus tips with garlic herbed butter, wild rice with glazed baby carrots. They feasted like kings and queens.

"What would you like to drink? I have fresh squeezed lemonade, sweet tea, water. Oh yeah, I also have a nice bottle of Chardonnay chilling in the refrigerator," Leona offered.

"Let's see," Debbie said touching her index finger to her check playfully. "I believe I will have a glass of Chardonnay."

"I will join you," said Myles.

"Well, I guess it's Chardonnay all around," exclaimed Leona.

Myles secretly wondered if his grandmother had not already had a glass before they arrived. He chuckled at the thought of her kicked back in her one-bedroom mansion with a glass of Chardonnay in her hand. Why not...she did not have anything else to do. She earned the right to a glass of wine whenever the mood struck.

For the next hour, Debbie and Leona made small talk about the upcoming mayoral election, her job as the procurement officer for the mayor, and Debbie's thoughts on all the candidates who recently have thrown their "hats in the ring" for the mayor's job.

Myles sat back and observed how the two women interacted. He was impressed with his grandmother's knowledge of the political climate in New York, senior citizen's issues, as well as the City's budgetary constraints. That one bottle of Chardonnay did not stand a chance between Debbie and his grandmother. Next time, he would bring a bottle with him.

"Whew," Debbie said while glancing at her watch. "It has been a real pleasure visiting with you, but it is getting late and I have an eight o'clock briefing with the mayor in the morning."

"It was a pleasure visiting with you as well," said Leona. "I hope that we are able to do this again some time."

Leona walked Myles and Debbie to the door.

Myles leaned in and hugged his grandmother tightly. "I love you so much, Granny," Myles whispered in her ear.

Leona squeezed his arms before pulling back.

"Good night, you two. Drive safely. Call me in the morning, Myles," she said before closing the door.

There was a slight chill in the air. Debbie and Myles quickened their steps to the car.

"I really like your grandmother. She is so sweet and enlightened about the issues plaguing our senior citizens," Debbie articulated.

"That she is," pronounced Myles.

Debbie settled into the passenger seat and drifted off to sleep as Myles maneuvered the car out of visitor's parking at Chesterfield onto the expressway. He glanced over at Debbie as she slept.

"What am I going to do with you?" he uttered under his breath.

Thirty-five minutes later, he pulled up in front of Debbie's building. Like clockwork, Debbie popped up looking around.

"Wow, I must really be tired," she conjectured.

"Yeah. You looked like a drunk with your head rolling around. At one time, your head leaned so far toward the dash I thought it was going to bypass the dash," Myles joked.

Debbie joined him in laughter.

"Come on, I'll walk you to your door." Myles exited the car and walked around to the passenger side and opened the door for Debbie. She took his hand and stepped out of the car. When they arrived at her door, Myles hugged her tightly.

"Why don't you stay the night?" Debbie suggested.

"Uhm, I don't think that would be a good idea. Maybe some other time. You have to be at work early tomorrow and so do I," replied Myles.

"Are you sure?" she said playfully.

Myles smiled but was determined not to give in. If he stayed, she would not get any sleep and the meeting with the mayor would be null and void. He kissed her lightly on the lips before turning and walking toward the elevator. He looked back only to see she was still standing in place.

"Go inside," he urged.

"Make me," she said laughingly.

"Girl, if you don't go inside…" his thought trailed off.

"You know I always get what I want," she continued.

"Oh yeah, and what is that?" he asked while walking back toward her.

Debbie gave him a knowing smile and Myles knew both were in trouble tonight.

Debbie lay soundly asleep as Myles slipped out of bed and retrieved his clothes from the floor. He quietly exited her bedroom and quickly dressed in the living room. He was tired of all the interrupted nights shuffling between his place and hers. They have been dating for almost a year now and Myles had considered proposing a couple of times. Every time he came close to proposing, something stopped him. He did not know if he feared marriage—of not being a good husband and father, or that they needed to get to know each other better before making such an important decision. Maybe they were moving too fast.

Debbie was still on his mind when he awoke several hours later. When he arrived at the office, he instructed his secretary to send flowers to Debbie with a card simply stating, "Thanks for a lovely evening."

Debbie arrived at work ten minutes before the start of the briefing. She quickly grabbed her files. She did not have time to wait on the elevator; therefore, opting to run down the hall and up two flights of stairs. She entered the conference room seconds before the start of the meeting.

Mayor Stevens looked over at Debbie and smiled. "Safe," imitating a New York Umpire at home plate.

Everyone around the conference table chuckled. Debbie joined in.

"Now, let's get down to business. We have a busy day with the elections coming up and, as all of you are aware, I am seeking reelection. However, there are a few looming issues that might present a problem if not handled with care," said Mayor Stevens. "In the coming weeks, people will go to the polls to vote for who they perceive the right person to fill this office. Today, we need to take a serious look at the issues and put a plan in place going forward that will ensure my reelection. I do not, and I repeat, do not want to be caught off guard on the campaign trail."

"You sound as though you are anticipating strong competition this time around," said Glen, his campaign manager.

"I am not taking anything for granted. I have worked too hard putting things in place to allow someone to come in and take it all away. Okay, everyone back to work. Glen, Debbie, I need to talk to you."

Mayor Stevens waited for everyone to leave the room before continuing his conversation with Debbie and Glen.

"Debbie, I need you and Glen to get together and craft negative campaign ads. Dig up whatever you can find on Michele Dobbs, Darren Jenkins, and Julius Carbozza. As always, I need you to leak this information to your friends in the press. If we play our cards right, all of us will have jobs for the next four years."

"Glen, I need you to set up a meeting with Davis Construction. See if ole Danny boy can meet with me later this afternoon. If not, let him know that it is in his best interest to meet with me first thing tomorrow morning. Next, I need you to talk with Jim Donaldson at Premier Architects. I did not get a good read on him the last time we talked. Finally, I need an exhaustive list of new prospects. The old ones are still on board with our pay-to-play scheme. However, I smell new blood. This city is ripe for the picking," he laughed enthusiastically.

Debbie left the conference room and thought about all the money directed into offshore bank accounts monthly. She was living the life that existed only in the minds of most people. She remembered people from the old neighborhood who spent a portion of their rent money in hopes of winning the lottery. However, the mayor and Glen had found a way to hit the lottery with every contract. She reflected on their international travel, offshore accounts, and investments. If all went according to plan, she thought, a house in Turks and Caicos would be in her immediate future. Soon, she would leave her job and New York far behind.

Debbie stepped off the elevator and noticed a delivery person holding the loveliest bouquet of white roses.

"Oh, here she comes now," she heard the receptionist say.

The delivery person turned toward Debbie. "These are for you, ma'am," he said with a smile. "Can I get you to sign here?"

Debbie signed for the flowers and marveled at how the petals of each rose were perfect. She picked up the vase and walked into her office. Placing them in the center of the table near the window ensured plenty of sunlight for such beautiful flowers. She removed the card attached to the flowers and smiled with fond recollection of the magical time spent with Myles the previous evening. She was still smiling when Glen walked into her office.

"Well, somebody has been a very good girl," he conjectured.

What a pig, Debbie thought to herself.

"I did not know you had a social life," continued Glen. "Who is the lucky guy?"

"My private life is not open for discussion," Debbie countered.

"Well, I'm thinking the whole white roses thing. You do know the meaning of white roses, right. You really left a lasting impression on this guy, whoever he might be," Glen chuckled slightly. Okay, I am through teasing you. Let's get down to work."

Debbie's thoughts turned toward Glen's last statement of leaving a lasting impression with Myles. Was he truly in love?

"Earth to Debbie," she heard Glen say.

"Yes."

"You looked as if you were a million miles away."

"Uh, no, I was thinking about the best way to attack the competition."

"Okay, that's the Debbie I know. So what do you have so far that we can use? I would like to get a jump on our negative ad campaign." Debbie pulled out files on each candidate.

Glen's eyes grew wide with the knowledge learned on each candidate. This was going to be an all-out brawl.

Glen walked into the offices of Premier Architects the next morning. Jim Donaldson was at his desk going over drawings for the new gymnasium in one of the poorest burrows in New York City. He looked up when he heard Glen walk in.

"Hey, Jim, how's business?" Glen smirked.

Jim rolled up the plans and placed them on the right side of the desk.

"Are those the plans for the gymnasium?" Glen inquired.

"Yes, but they are not finalized yet," Jim responded nervously.

"Can I take a look?"

"Sure."

Jim unrolled the blueprints, allowing Glen to view what promised to be a state-of-the-art gymnasium at The Winchester School. Glen thought about the stark difference in living conditions of the families only a short distance from the luxury he and his family enjoyed. He justified what he was doing by telling himself that everyone was benefitting from this. Jim Donaldson's architectural firm was growing by leaps and bounds. Just this past year, he hired eight new architects. The kids were benefitting from new gymnasiums and equipment. Then, there were the other businesses that were profiting. Roofing companies, electricians, landscapers, asphalt companies: all that were willing to play the game benefitted. Of course, that meant that the same companies received the contracts, but that is how one plays the game.

"My reason for stopping by so early," Glen started, "is to go over our little arrangement. You have a thriving business with a complete staff. Your kids attend private school and your wife spends her time at the country club. You have a summer cottage in the Hamptons and your family has gone on luxurious vacations. When the mayor approached you a few years ago about this arrangement, you were more than willing to play along as your firm was flailing. The mayor threw you a lifeline. You grabbed on tight and did not look back. However, the mayor thinks you might be having second thoughts about this little setup. Are you having second thoughts, Jim? If you are, then we need to reach a new agreement."

Jim looked Glen in the eyes and knew instantly that this new agreement would not work in his favor. He wiped the sweat from his brow.

"No. I am not having second thoughts. I appreciate everything the mayor has done for me. Look around, Glen. Do you really think this firm would have grown so quickly without the mayor?" Jim laughed nervously.

Glen stared intensely at Jim. "I know for a fact it would not have. It probably would have been a pile of ashes by now."

A slow smile crossed Glen's face.

"Well," Glen said while slapping his knee. "Now, that we have reached an agreement. I will let you get back to work. Have a great day." Glen got up from his seat and left the office of Premier Architects as quietly as he had arrived.

While Glen was reaffirming the agreement with Jim Donaldson, the mayor was meeting with Danny of Davis Construction.

"Danny, come in. It's good to see you," the mayor declared.

"It is good to see you again, Mr. Mayor," Danny said while extending his hand.

"Well, let us get down to brass tacks. I just wanted to check in with you to see how everything is going with your construction business. Are you enjoying the little arrangement we have?"

"Uh, yes, sir, Mr. Mayor. Everything is going great. I really appreciate what you have done. Also, working on the contracts with Premier Architects has been a true delight."

"Good, good. I am glad to hear that. As you are probably aware, I am running for reelection. If I win, the contracts will keep coming. What that means for you and the others is money. As long as contracts keep coming your company will continue to roll in the dough."

Danny shook his head in agreement.

"What do you need me to do, Mr. Mayor?"

"I need your vote and your loyalty," the mayor articulated.

"You got it," Danny said emphatically.

The two men shook hands and Danny exited the mayor's office with a sense of relief. When Danny received the telephone call from the mayor requesting his presence, he did not know quite what to expect. He was extremely nervous on the drive to the mayor's office, but no sooner had he navigated his car into an empty space, all anxiety ceased. He was ready to face the day with a new perspective. He whistled an up-tempo beat as he stepped onto the elevator pressing the button for the lobby.

As Glen predicted, it was a brawl. The attacks delivered on the candidates were brutal and unrelenting.

Throughout the campaign, more city contracts were awarded to Davis Construction and Premier Architects, as well as a few new companies. Employee bribery, kickbacks, and payoffs were widespread, but no one seemed to care. Money was flowing into bank accounts and the city and its taxpayers bilked for millions. With no true oversight, it was like taking candy from a baby.

Myles was hard at work when he heard his intercom buzz.

"Myles," said Victoria, "Mr. Brimmer would like to see you in his office."

"Let him know I will be right there," Myles verbalized.

Myles walked down the hall to Mr. Brimmer's office.

"You can go right in," Veronica directed.

When Myles appeared at the door, Mr. Brimmer waved him in and quietly closed the door to the office.

"Veronica uses discretion, but I am not taking any chances with what I am about to reveal to you," John Brimmer said.

Myles sat up a little straighter in his seat and leaned forward.

"Myles I am revealing this information to you in the strictest of confidence. Last week I met with a federal government employee from the Department of Justice who told me that the mayor and some of his employees have been under investigation for the past year. Apparently, one of the vendors complained about the same companies winning City contracts year after year. The Justice Department set up a bogus company so they could witness the crime firsthand. What they discovered is that the mayor and some of his staff have set up an elaborate "pay-to-play" scheme. The Justice Department believes that the bribery, kickbacks, and payoffs go deep."

Myles sat back in his chair trying to process what he had just learned.

"Who, besides the mayor, is involved?" Myles asked.

"They did not tell me. What I do know is that they would like this firm to become involved in the investigation. There are four people associated with this firm authorized to work with agents from the Department of Justice: You, me, Veronica, and Gloria. Starting tomorrow morning, two agents will set up office next to yours. Inform Gloria of what is underway. Veronica already knows. Please make sure that Gloria understands the magnitude of the investigation and that she is not to disclose any of this to anyone in the office or outside of the office. We do not want to jeopardize the investigation in any way."

"I understand completely."

"You're a good man, Myles."

Myles got up from his seat and walked back to his office down the hall. He asked Gloria to come into his office and close the door behind her. She took a seat in one of the two chairs positioned on the opposite side of his desk.

"Gloria, I just learned that our firm is assisting the Justice Department in an ongoing investigation of possible corruption in the mayor's office. Tomorrow, two federal agents from the Justice Department will set up office next to mine. The only people that know what is going on are John, Veronica, you, and me. It needs to stay that way. I must warn you to not disclose this knowledge to anyone. Do not, and I repeat, do not talk to anyone within the firm or outside of the firm, to include your little pillow talk with your husband, about the work of these agents or the Justice Department. I am not sure how all of this is going to play out, but we do not want to be in a position where any of us is responsible for jeopardizing the investigation. So please keep this under your hat.

"You don't have to worry about me. This information is in the vault."

Myles gave Gloria a look that said otherwise.

"What? Why are you looking at me like that? Have you ever known me to talk about sensitive matters?

"Okay, are we going to play this game right now? What about the time Chester was under investigation for embezzling the firm's money and you tipped him off that he was being watched?"

"I really liked Chester and I did not want him to get fired. I felt like if I told him he was being watched that he could put the money back before Mr. Brimmer lowered the boom on him."

"You do know how ridiculous that sounds, right?"

"No."

"That's exactly my point. It's okay to like the person, Gloria, but you don't climb into bed with them when you know they are doing dirt. Chester was siphoning money from this firm by padding his timesheet. The misappropriation of funds over a three-year period was staggering. Mr. Brimmer built this firm from the ground up and employs close to one hundred people. Remember, thou shalt not steal."

"I know it was wrong and that I could have lost my job behind my lack of judgment."

"Yes, you could have. However, I did not want to see you go down in the flames with your boy, Chester, so I asked Mr. Brimmer to give you another chance. However, both of us needed to know that your loyalty was with the firm before moving forward with keeping you on staff."

"Thanks for that walk down memory lane. Please know that I learned my lesson from that one incident, and it will never happen again. Discretion is my middle name."

"Okay…discretion. Let's get to work."

Myles looked up and met Gloria's gaze. "What's on your mind?"

"Doesn't Debbie work for the mayor?

"Yes, she does." Myles leaned back in his chair and secretly wondered if Debbie was under investigation too.

The unspoken passed between the two for what seemed like an eternity before Gloria arose from her seat and returned to her desk.

Myles arose from his chair and stood staring out the window at the hustle and bustle of the people in Town Center. From his vantage point, he had a clear view of the mayor's office building. He never gave it much thought until now. His office faced the front of the building where the Mayor's Executive Office is located. Why had he never paid attention to this before?

When Myles and Gloria arrived the next morning, the agents were in deep conversation with Mr. Brimmer.

Their conversation stopped abruptly when they saw Myles and Gloria. Mr. Brimmer gently closed the door.

Special Agent Karl Simmons turned his attention back to John Brimmer. "Like I was saying, the mayor's office and several of his cabinet members have been under investigation for a year. During the investigation, we have uncovered an elaborate pay-to-play scheme spearheaded by the mayor."

John Brimmer adjusted himself in his chair. "I find this hard to believe. I've known the mayor for a few years. He has done great things for some of the most underserved parts of this city. The people love him."

Special Agent Julia McBride sat down across from John Brimmer assessing his body language. "How long have you known the mayor?"

"Well, let's see. After his election to office, I received an invitation to one of his gala events. If I am remembering correctly, the gala was at one of the museums downtown. I was impressed that he called me by name when we shook hands. I remember commenting to my late wife that out of all the hundreds of people at that event, he called me by name. Strange, isn't it?"

Agents Simmons and McBride exchanged knowing glances.

"Well, you are a well-known figure in this town," offered Agent Simmons. "Your philanthropic work puts you up there with some of the greats like Warren Buffet and Michael Bloomberg."

Mr. Brimmer chuckled at the thought of placement in the same category as Warren Buffet or Michael Bloomberg.

"Thank you for that but these gentlemen surpassed me in their giving." Mr. Brimmer got up from his seat and walked toward the door. With his right hand on the knob, he turned toward Agents Simmons and McBride and quietly said, "If you need anything, Gloria and Myles have been instructed to assist."

John Brimmer exited his office and stuck his head into Myles's office. "Good morning, Myles. I've just had a brief meeting with Agents Simmons and McBride."

Wait one moment. Mr. Brimmer turned toward Gloria. "Gloria, can you join me and Myles for a moment?"

When Gloria entered the office, she closed the door and sat down next to Mr. Brimmer.

"Gloria, did Myles explain to you why agents from the Department of Justice are here?"

"Yes."

"And do you understand that their work here should be treated with the highest level of discretion?"

"Yes, sir."

"Okay, with that said, I would like to bring you two up to speed on my meeting with Agents Simmons and McBride."

Both Myles and Gloria leaned in a little closer to Mr. Brimmer.

"Will you two relax?"

Myles looked at Gloria. "I believe he is talking to you."

Gloria looked back and forth between both men before all three broke into laughter.

"So this is all I know thus far. The mayor's office has been under investigation for a year. Apparently, the mayor is spearheading an elaborate pay-to-play scheme. I don't know how deep this goes. However, they will be using the office next to you for an unspecified time while gathering more information. What makes this more interesting is that the mayor is up for reelection. Additionally, several senior level officials in the mayor's cabinet are under investigation as well."

For the second time in as many days, Myles's attention turned toward Debbie. He silently prayed that she was not involved in the corruption impregnating the mayor's office. Myles wished that he could talk to his grandmother. He desperately needed to talk to her and get her perspective; however, he could not.

Of course, he could not talk to Debbie to see what she knew about this scheme. The same warning issued Gloria, he had to abide by. At this moment, he felt stuck like Chuck.

His attention returned to the others in the room in time to hear Mr. Brimmer conclude with "It's business as usual as far as everyone is concerned."

"Why are they setting up office here?" asked Myles.

"From what I understand, our office is the perfect vantage point to record the comings and goings of those suspected of doing business with the mayor. Listen, this investigation is within the purview of the Justice Department—they know what they are doing. We can accommodate them so that they can rid this city of corruption."

Myles made a mental note to have Gloria fill him in on what he missed.

Across town, Debbie's mom sat in the kitchen of the small apartment of Baruch Houses, a public housing development on Manhattan's lower east side. In stark contrast to the condo that Debbie had grown accustomed, Lois, had a perfect view of the Browery and the East River from her bedroom window.

When Debbie left the old neighborhood, she never returned. Lois reflected on the long hours she spent working for Housing Authority. She picked up a second job cleaning office buildings to help finance Debbie's education. On what she made working for Housing and her second job, she still needed to apply for loans. After Debbie graduated from college and secured full-time employment in the mayor's office, Debbie would send money so that she could quit her second job.

As Lois polished off a bowl of cereal for dinner, she thought about all the times Debbie would call for money so that she could buy food. Debbie never wanted any of her classmates, or her coworkers to know her background. Even as a child, Debbie was different. She never played with any of the other children in Baruch. She was determined even from a child that her life would be different. Debbie never knew her father and Lois didn't offer any information on him.

Lois appreciated the monthly checks from Debbie, but what she desired more than money was a relationship with Debbie. She never received an invitation to any of the events that Debbie attended as part of her job with the mayor or been invited to her condo or taken out to a fancy restaurant. Lois thought it would have been nice to receive a telephone call from her only child telling how much she appreciated the sacrifices made so that she would have.

The ring of the telephone startled Lois out of deep reflection. She answered the call on its fourth ring.

"Hello, Mom?"

A huge smile spread across Lois's face when she heard her daughter's voice. Tears began to spill out from the fringes of her eyes as she mouthed a "thank you, Jesus" into the silence of her apartment.

"Hi, baby, I was just thinking about you. It is so good to hear your voice."

"Mom, I know that I haven't kept in touch and I do not want to fall back on the excuse of being so busy that I don't have the time to call anyone. The truth of the matter is that you are my mother and I should never have neglected you the way that I have. I want to make it up to you."

"Debbie, I know you might not want to hear this, but I have been praying for you. Every day I ask God for a closer relationship with you. I have been waiting a long time for him to answer my prayers."

"You said prayers. That would indicate there are more than one. Are all of these prayers pertaining to me?"

Lois chuckled lightly. "One might say that."

"Also, I am thinking of leaving New York."

"What? Wait a minute. What do you mean by leaving New York? Where are you going? Is it job related?"

Now it was Debbie's turn to chuckle.

"Calm down, Mom. I will tell you all about it tomorrow over dinner. I will send a car to pick you up at six o'clock sharp. Have a good evening. I love you."

"I love you too, baby. Goodbye."

Lois hung up the phone and tried to process this new information. What was Debbie up to?

The next day, a nervous energy consumed Lois. Her mind raced with anticipation of having dinner with her daughter and learning of her plans to leave New York. Why is she leaving? Did she accept a position in Washington, DC? That might be it. She probably wants to tell me that she has accepted a position in a senator's office in Washington thought Lois.

The next day, Lois sat patiently waiting. It was four o'clock and she was already dressed for dinner. While waiting for the car she picked up the Bible that sat on the side table by the window facing the mom-and-pop businesses on Canal Street.

She carefully opened her Bible and turned to a well-known passage: The Lord's prayer. As her eyes fell on the words, she reclined and let her head come to rest against the back of the chair as she recited:

"Our Father which art in heaven, Hallowed be thy name. Thy kingdom come, thy will be done in earth, as it is in heaven. Give us this day our daily bread. And forgive us our debts, as we forgive our debtors. And lead us not into temptation but deliver us from evil: For thine is the kingdom, and the power, and the glory, forever. Amen."

Just as she was finishing the story about the prodigal son, she heard a knock at the door. The clock on the wall illuminated five o'clock.

"Who is it?" she inquired.

"I am your driver, ma'am. Ms. Debbie asked that I pick you up and take you to her residence."

Lois left the chain on the door and opened it slightly. The driver looked around nervously.

"My name is Orlando James. If you have any reservations about my validity, please call your daughter."

"No, that's okay. I don't need to call her. However, I wasn't expecting you until six o'clock."

"She asked that I pick you up an hour earlier so that we could avoid some of the rush-hour traffic."

"Okay, let me get my purse and I'll be right with you."

"I appreciate that, ma'am."

"No worries. I will protect you. Everybody knows me around here. I won't let anything happen to you."

The driver tipped his hat slightly in appreciation.

Lois could not wait to talk to Debbie about the skittish driver that came to pick her up. He was totally out of his element.

Orlando James opened the door for Lois and waited for her to situate herself in the backseat of this massive car before closing the door. A glass partition separated the driver from her. Lois was not sure how to feel about it. It had been many years since she had been east of the river. That part of her life was a distant memory. But right now, she felt like the old Lois Adderly. The daughter whose father was a judge and mother a socialite. Her thoughts quickly turned to her attire when the driver pulled up in front of the building where Debbie lived. For some reason, her navy-blue dress with matching navy-blue two-inch heel pumps did not seem fitting for such a place as this. The gold stud earrings and modest gold watch adorning her right wrist were unassuming against the women exiting the property. Suddenly she felt like she did not belong.

That's why Debbie never returned to the old neighborhood, Lois thought. She did not belong there. Lois suddenly felt what her daughter felt all those years ago growing up in Baruch Houses. It was Lois's turn to feel out of place.

As she exited the car and walked toward the front of the building, the Doorman tipped his hat as he opened the door. Not in the time before leaving her father's house has anyone opened the door for her.

The concierge greeted Lois as she entered the building.

"Hello. May I have your name and the name of the person you are visiting?"

"I'm Lois Adderly. I am visiting my daughter, Debbie Adderly."

"Thank you."

"Ms. Adderly. Lois Adderly has arrived. Would you like me to send her up?"

The concierge hung up, escorted Lois to the elevator, and pushed the button for the sixteenth floor.

"Ms. Adderly will meet you at the elevator. Have a wonderful visit."

Lois watched as the concierge walked back to his post.

"If this is what money does to people, I don't want no part of it."

When the elevator doors opened on the sixteenth floor, Debbie was there to greet her mother with a big hug and a kiss. Lois was so happy to see her daughter that she forgot all about her surroundings and allowed the tears to flow.

Lois made a mental note that Debbie was in Unit 16B, exactly five units to the left of the elevator.

Debbie had dinner catered from Eleven Madison Park. Tonight, she wanted nothing but the best for her mother. Upon entering the condo, Lois did not know what to look at first. The décor and views were simply breathtaking. The Manhattan skyline was simply stunning from the sixteenth floor.

"After dinner, I will give you the 10-cent tour," Debbie smiled as she escorted her mother to the table on the balcony. The outdoor fireplace was the perfect backdrop for dinner and taking in the sounds of summer in Manhattan. At this moment, both Debbie and her mother were living in the moment. As Debbie sipped from her glass of wine, she allowed her mind to contemplate her exit from New York. Soon Turks and Caicos would be their future and New York a distant memory. Debbie's thoughts of Turks and Caicos were interrupted when Lois inquired of Debbie's plans to leave New York.

"So tell me. Why are you leaving New York? Did you get another job offer?"

"No. I have always planned to retire early enough to enjoy life. Now I am in a position to do so."

"Really? When do you plan to retire?"

"Next year. By then I will have enough money saved to leave New York forever. Mom, I want you to come with me."

"Where are we going?"

"Turks and Caicos."

"Turks and Caicos? Why?"

"Mom, you will love it there. I have always wanted to live in the Caribbean. It's only a couple hours flying time from Miami and only about a few hours more from New York. Mom, I have been in New York all my life and worked hard to get to where I am. Now, it is time to do something different and I want you with me."

Lois covered her daughter's hands with hers. "Baby, it sounds nice. Truth be told, I am just as tired of New York, especially Baruch Houses. But I want you to be very sure about the decision to leave New York and retire early to the Caribbean."

It was getting late and Debbie needed to arise early for work. She offered her mother the guest bedroom for the night. Debbie was asleep before her head hit the pillow. Lois lay in bed staring at the ceiling for hours before drifting off to sleep.

The next morning, Debbie opened the door to the guest room to check on her mother before leaving for work. Her mother's soft snores brought a smile to her face. Debbie's thoughts drifted back to when she was a little girl growing up in Baruch Houses. She allowed her eyes to roam around the room where her mom lay sleeping peacefully. Debbie's eyes rest on the luxurious bedroom set creating an oasis that would draw applause from the most privileged person. The floor to ceiling custom-designed drapes was her proudest moment. The Italian drapes dressing the floor to ceiling windows allowed for a beautiful soft glow of sunlight to enter the room without being too intrusive. The adjoining spacious en suite with oversized soaking tub and huge windows was simply breathtaking. The white marble tile flown in from Carrara, Italy was Debbie's biggest achievement. Debbie stood there for several minutes, mentally patting herself on the back, before quietly pulling the door shut and exiting the condominium for work.

When Debbie arrived at work and entered the executive office of the mayor, there was a different feel in the atmosphere. She was used to people in and out of the mayor's office, but this morning it felt more like the quiet before the storm. She quickly brushed the feeling away.

"You are being paranoid for no reason," she quietly said to herself.

As she approached her office, she could hear her phone ringing. She quickly unlocked the door and ran to answer the phone before the caller had a chance to hang up.

"Hello, Debbie Adderly speaking."

"Good morning, lovely lady," Myles said.

"Good morning to you as well, kind sir," responded Debbie while gently easing into her chair.

"How was your evening with your mother?"

"It went better than I expected."

"You can tell me all about it over dinner tonight. That is if you are available."

"Well, let me check my calendar," she said playfully. "It appears that you are in luck."

"How is that?"

"There is an available slot on my calendar for six-thirty this evening."

"An evening with Debbie Adderly…yes, I would put that in the category of luck. Sometimes I have to pinch myself to see if I am dreaming."

Debbie laughed at Myles's attempt at humor.

"What did I ever do to deserve such a sweet, gentle, considerate, loving, passionate, and compassionate man as you?"

"It is easy to be all those things you think I am when a man is in love with a sweet, gentle, considerate, loving, passionate, compassionate, and beautiful woman like yourself."

"Oh my, I might have to leave work early just to be ready for you."

"Woman, please! You know you are not leaving work early. Get to work and I'll do the same."

"Yes, sir!"

"Oh, so you are really putting on the brakes right now?"

"Yes, sir!"

Myles chuckled at the thought of Debbie putting on the brakes. That is so not like her.

"How does Carmine's sound for dinner?"

"Mom and I had Italian last night. What about Sylvia's in Harlem?"

"I haven't been there in years. I will call later and reserve a table, and with any luck, there will be live music. Have a good day and I'll see you outside of your office at six o'clock."

"Okay, baby. See you then."

Debbie returned the receiver to its cradle and leaned back in her chair in anticipation of dinner with Myles. Abruptly her thoughts interrupted by the buzz of the intercom on her phone.

"Debbie, the mayor has called an emergency meeting in his office stat," announced the mayor's secretary.

"On my way," shot Debbie.

When Debbie arrived, Glen and the mayor were in hushed conversation. They both looked her way when she entered the room.

Debbie looked from one face to the other as if to read them. She secretly wondered if the conversation they were engaged in when she entered the room pertained to her. She would soon find out.

The mayor waved her over. "Debbie, come join us."

She pulled up a chair and placed it so that she could see their faces as they talked. Whatever they discussed before she walked in, she was determined to find out.

"Debbie, I need to bring you up to speed on the situation with our clients. Glen paid a visit to Jim Donaldson of Premier Architects. Glen informed them of upcoming contracts around the city. He is so hungry for money that he sees the benefit of the 'play' aspect of the pay-to-play scheme."

They all laughed in concert.

The mayor turned toward Debbie, "The negative campaign ads are doing what they are designed to do, but we need more. What have you been able to dig up on these three?"

"Well, people were not as forthcoming with information as during the last campaign. However, I was able to find one person who was willing to assist us unearth information. Of course, he doesn't come cheap. This is what I was able to find out."

The look on Glen's and the mayor's faces were of someone waiting with great anticipation of a long-awaited Marvel movie.

"Well, let's hear it," urged the mayor.

Debbie pulled out her file on Julius Carbozza.

"It appears as though Mr. Carbozza has an illegitimate set of twins. Prior to his marriage, he committed a crime against a young girl. The girl was sixteen years old; he was twenty-six. She became pregnant by him and gave birth to twin girls. Mr. Carbozza comes from a wealthy family and his father smoothed everything over with the girl's family."

"Are we talking hush money?" inquired the mayor.

"Definitely we are talking hush money to the tune of ten million dollars."

"We can definitely use the hush money angle, but we need to tie it together with something more damning," interjected Glen. "How old are the twins and where are they now?"

"Well, I was able to track down the mother of the twins who now lives in Colorado. Initially, she did not want to discuss Carbozza's past indiscretion, but I offered her $100,000 for anything she could tell me about the unfortunate incident."

"Okay, what else do you have on him that we can use to discredit him?" asked the mayor.

"From what she told me her mother worked for the Carbozza family as a housekeeper. On holidays and summer break, her mother would take her to work with her. She would help her mother clean the house, do laundry, load the dishwasher, etc. When she was done with her work, sometimes her mother would allow her to relax by the pool or swim. All of this was with the permission of Mr. and Mrs. Carbozza, of course."

"Don't tell me that Julius was watching her?"

"That's exactly what he was doing. She told me that one day her mother went grocery shopping and she asked her mother if it would be okay for her to stay behind and swim. Her mother gave her permission to do so and told her to stay by the pool and not go into the house for anything until she returned. However, she disobeyed her mother's directives and entered the kitchen through the side door. She opened the refrigerator door to retrieve a soda. As she was closing the door, Julius was standing there. He took the soda out of her hand and forced her into a back room where he raped her. He held his hand over her mouth to muffle her cries. When he was done, he forced her to her feet and walked her to the pool where he proceeded to push her in."

"So his father paid ten million in hush money and I am thinking he used his influence to keep this story out of the press. I need you to do a deep dive. In other words, follow the money. Who received pay off to keep this story out of the press? We really need to work this to our advantage," instructed the mayor.

"When did this happen?" asked Glen.

"Ten years ago."

"Ten years ago? Wait a minute! Didn't Julius Carbozza and his wife Sydney just celebrate their ten-year wedding anniversary?"

Glen got up to retrieve the newspaper from the mayor's desk. He quickly scanned the celebrity news section of the paper.

"Yes. Here it is," handing the paper to the mayor.

The mayor read out loud, "Celebrating ten years of blissful marriage, mayoral opponent Julius Carbozza and his wife Sydney are still happily in love and supportive on one another. When asked how they keep the romance in their marriage after ten years, they simply respond with, 'Respect one another and boundaries, listen to what one is saying, never allow anger to dominate a discussion, and laugh often. In addition, be truthful.' Sydney Carbozza said that spending time together, allowing integrity to take its rightful place in our marriage is the recipe for longevity in our marriage."

"Debbie, see what else you can find out about Julius Carbozza, who his father paid off to keep this story quiet and what happened to the ten million dollars paid to—what's her name?"

"Who?"

"The mother of the twins!" exclaimed the mayor. "We have exactly six months before elections. Let's get all of our ducks in a row so that the campaign will go as planned."

"What do you have on Michele Dobbs and Darren Jenkins?"

"I should have information on Darren Jenkins later today. However, I am running into brick walls with Michele Dobbs. She might be a modern-day Mother Theresa?" she said jokingly.

"Not an option. Everybody has skeletons in their closets. Old boyfriends, time at college, or any mental illness or drug use in her background. I do not care what it is—just get me something I can use. Need I remind you that our jobs are on the line? No pressure."

Walking back to her office, Debbie thought of the endless possibilities another four years of working for the mayor would afford. It was time to plan a vacation with her mom to Turks and Caicos. Her mother had already confided that she was tired of New York. Island life was calling her name.

Although the mayor said no pressure, Debbie knew she was under pressure to perform. She hurried back to her office where she immediately put in a call to her contact.

"Hey, it's me. What do you have on Darren Jenkins?"

"I'm still working on it, but I think you will be pleased with what I provide," said the mysterious voice on the other end of the call. "Come through the spot around ten o'clock tomorrow night."

"I'll be there."

"Don't forget payment for services rendered."

"If it is all you say it is, I might add to it."

"Oh, it is all I say it is and more."

"Later."

The call went dead.

CHAPTER

MYLES LOOKED AT HIS WATCH. HE had been hard at work since he talked to Debbie that morning. It was now five-thirty and he needed to finish work on the file for Premier Architects before leaving for the day. For a new company, they seemed to be doing very well. Of the ten contracts submitted by the city over the past year, the city awarded all of them to Premier Architects and Davis Construction. How could this be? He had to meet Debbie in thirty minutes and did not have time to consider why or how right now. He quickly scribbled a note to himself to research both files the following morning.

It was six o'clock and Debbie was just exiting the front of the building as Myles pulled up. She entered the car and leaned over and gave Myles the sweetest kiss. He matched hers.

"Was your day as stressful as mine?" inquired Myles.

"My day consisted of a lot of planning for the upcoming mayoral campaign," replied Debbie. "There are three opponents, of which you are probably aware. They are strong candidates."

"Yeah, I am trying to familiarize myself with them so that I will be prepared when time to vote."

"So, what do you know so far about these three," quizzed Debbie.

"Well, I know that Julius and his wife Sydney are celebrating their ten-year wedding anniversary and they are expecting their first child in nine months."

"Oh, really! Where did you hear or read this?" asked Debbie.

"I saw an earlier interview of the wedded duo today as they were leaving the doctor's office. I ducked out of the office and slid into the Irish Pub across the street from where I work to grab lunch at the bar. I typically do that when I'm eating alone."

Debbie was lost in her thoughts and did not hear anything else Myles was talking about. Given this news, would she be able to move forward with the smear campaign on Julius Carbozza? Would she be able to live with herself knowing that she was a willing participant in ruining another person's life?

"Debbie, where did you go?" asked Myles. "Am I boring you?"

"No. Not at all. I was thinking about the campaign and if making all those appearances would be too much for Sydney Carbozza."

How could she tell Myles the truth? Hired less than four years ago as the mayor's procurement officer, she was successful in accomplishing whatever task given her. She wanted to be a major player in the mayor's office, and she had become just that. If the mayor instructed her to make sure Premier Architects got all the contracts for a year, she made it happen. If he instructed her to make sure to award Davis Construction with all contracts for a year, then she made sure of it. Her goal was to retire early and leave New York for good. She wanted a house in Turks and Caicos more than she cared about sparing Sydney Carbozza's feelings. At that moment, she decided to take the gloves off.

Myles and Debbie rode the rest of the way to Sylvia's in silence. Each one lost in their own thoughts. The live music at Sylvia's Soul Food restaurant allowed both Myles and Debbie to kick back and not be worried with making conversation.

The set finished at ten o'clock. Myles gently reached for Debbie's hand as they walked the block to reserved parking.

As Myles pulled off the lot, he asked Debbie, "Your place or mine?"

"Can I get a rain check?" I need to go into the office tomorrow.

"Tomorrow is Saturday. When did you start working weekends?"

"As the mayor's chief procurement officer our office has been flooded with contracts. We are about six months out from the election, and I need to stay on top of things."

"I understand. I was just hoping that we might get to spend a little time together this weekend. Don't get me wrong, tonight was lovely, but you can't fault me for wanting to spend a little more time with my lady."

"Baby, I want to spend time with you as well. I promise that as soon as I can, I will make it happen for us."

"So as the chief procurement officer for the mayor, what are your responsibilities?"

"Well, my office supports all the procurement activities of city agencies throughout New York. My office oversees the public access system that provides online entry to public contract information. Additionally, my office fosters relationships with the vendor community and holds public hearings for contracts."

"So if I understand this correctly, your office also awards contracts. Is this correct?"

"Yes."

Myles found a parking space in front of Debbie's condo. They both got out of the car and walked toward the building in silence.

When they arrived at the elevator, Debbie reached up and gave Myles a kiss good night.

"Don't you want me to see you to your door?" asked Myles.

"I'll be okay," replied Debbie playfully. "If I allow you to see me to my door, I'm afraid I might allow you to come in. Like I said earlier, I have an early day tomorrow and I need to get some sleep. I hope that is okay with you baby."

She gave him another kiss before disappearing into the elevator.

Myles was not sure what to make of Debbie's behavior. This is the first time she has stopped him at the elevator. Myles thought the sudden shift in Debbie's actions was strange but accepted her excuse—at least for now.

Myles exited the building and walked back to his car. He navigated the car away from the curb into the honking horns and never-ending traffic of the Upper East Side and pointed it toward the other side of town. Thoughts of the investigation, Premier Architect and Debbie filled his head as he maneuvered traffic. He made a mental note to perform a computer search on Monday of all contracts awarded to vendors in the past year to determine if they are clients of Brimmer Financial Services. If so, then that would answer why agents from the Department of Justice chose to set up office at the firm. He always felt a little uneasy about them being there and quietly hoped Debbie was not under investigation. There was a pulling at his gut that told him otherwise. Myles was so preoccupied with his thoughts that he never noticed the black sedan following him.

Richard Stephenson, retired police officer turned private detective and investigator, has been following Debbie and Myles since they left Sylvia's in Harlem. If anyone were to ask him what he liked best about his job, he would tell them being in the field. He enjoys conducting interviews and surveilling people. With the irregular hours he worked as a police officer turned detective, he got used to working irregular hours. Retiring from the police force, this new profession of private detective and investigator helps him live a more comfortable lifestyle than from collecting 50 percent of his pension.

His wife divorced him two years ago and since remarried. The one child they had together chose to study abroad in Australia. He receives the occasional father day cards and sporadic birthday wishes from Bryce; however, he has not returned to New York once for Christmas. Maybe he will take some time off after this case and fly to Australia to visit with his son.

Richard entered the police force after dropping out of City College after two semesters. His father suggested he try applying for the police force. He took the test and was accepted and placed at Midtown Precinct South for two years. From there, he went to the 19th Precinct for five years. He got into a little trouble there and transferred to the 28th Precinct. The 28th Precinct was home for retired police detective Stephenson until retirement after twenty-five years on the police force. How many people do you know retire at the age of forty-two? He had to. There are only so many dead bodies one can tolerate or hostage situations. It takes a toll on a person's psyche after a while. Yes, surveilling people is slightly safer than responding to situations more volatile in his estimation.

The soft chime of the elevator indicating arrival on the sixteenth floor brought Debbie out of deep thought. She wanted Myles to stay but she was not ready to introduce her mother to the man in her life. There would be too many questions. Questions she was not ready or willing to face. Debbie allowed her mother to stay with her a few extra days after the initial invitation to dinner but after tomorrow, it was imperative she return to the old neighborhood.

Debbie opened the door to her condo and saw her mother sitting on the balcony. The soft glow from the outdoor fireplace danced across the right side of her face. Her mother looked at home—like she was born into this lifestyle. Debbie did not know how accurate her perception was.

As Lois sat on the balcony overlooking the New York skyline, her thoughts drifted back to a life she once knew. Tears ran down her face as memories of a former life flooded every crevice of her mind. Lois Adderly, daughter of famous socialite Josephine Adderly and chief judge Dennis Adderly do hereby divorce their daughter for bringing shame upon the Adderly name. How dare you get pregnant out of wedlock? Lois remembered those words spoken from the mouth of her father as if it were yesterday. She searched her mother's face. She was desperate for her mother to intervene on her behalf. But she stood there silently beside her husband with downcast eyes.

Lois Adderly is not to attempt communication with Josephine or Dennis Adderly for the remainder of her life. She is not to tell her illegitimate child about its lineage. You and your illegitimate child are hereby cut off from the family trust and will. You will live by the sweat of your brow from this day forward.

Judge Adderly instructed the servants to place her suitcase outside of the front door and escort her off the property. When she got to the front gate, a cab was waiting for her.

London, Josephine Adderly's private secretary, told her there was an envelope in the suitcase from her mother. London gave the cab driver the address of a private home for unwed mothers. Lois would be safe and comfortable there as Josephine and the founder were best friends. Discretion was paramount to Josephine and Dennis Adderly.

Debbie crossed the living room floor and opened the sliding door to the balcony. As she sat down across from her mother, she noticed tears running down her mother's face.

"Mom, what's wrong? Are you okay? Are you in pain?" Debbie asked while drawing closer to her mother.

How could Lois tell her only daughter about her former life? A life filled with luxury and privilege. Sworn to secrecy the day her father dismissed her and her unborn child as being part of the great Adderly name, Lois felt she had done Debbie a great disservice. Her parents were up in age now and her father retired from judgeship several years ago. What difference would it make to any of us to divulge the truth?

Lois quickly wiped the tears from her cheeks. "I'm fine, dear. I was just sitting here thinking about how proud I am of all your accomplishments. I am so glad to have you as my daughter."

A smile quickly crossed Debbie's lips as she embraced her mother for the first time in years.

Debbie pulled back and looked at her mother. For the first time she allowed herself to truly look at her mother. The beauty and love harnessed by her mother had gone unnoticed for decades by Debbie. Why had she not seen it before? Was she so closed off and self-involved to take note of the wonderful qualities her mother possessed?

Before she could stop herself, words began to tumble out of her mouth at a rapid clip. "Mom, I could not have asked for a better mother. I realize I have not been much of a loving daughter to you. I am selfish, self-centered, egotistical, and downright rude at times. Please know that I love you. I always have."

Debbie looked down at her hands and continued, "I have not been nice to you. The sacrifices you made for me while I was in college were not lost on me. I don't know what is wrong with me. Sometimes all I can think about is what I want."

Lois gingerly took Debbie in her arms and held her tight. Her earlier thoughts of abandonment replaced with thoughts of a beautiful baby girl wrapped tightly in a blanket sleeping quietly beside her.

Thoughts of a little girl growing up in Baruch House who never felt at home there, who wore dresses and ruffled ankle socks and read books instead of playing with dolls, or hopscotch with the neighborhood girls. The little girl she gave birth to was now a grown woman who navigated her way all the way to the mayor's office. Her grandparents would be so proud of her. If only they knew her.

Debbie pulled back from her mother and rested her head against the cushion of the love seat she and her mother shared. With interlaced fingers, they sat in silence staring out into the night sky as they took in the sights and sounds of the Upper East Side before quietly retiring to their respective bedrooms.

While at breakfast the next morning, Debbie and her mother discussed her plans for leaving New York for good.

"Debbie, let's talk about your plans to leave New York. I have given it great thought and I have decided a change in scenery would do both of us some good. You mentioned traveling to Turks and Caicos was in your immediate future."

Debbie chuckled. "No, Mom. It is not just in my immediate future but yours as well. I have my eye on a plot of land that I believe will be right for the both of us. Currently, a shell of a house sits on the land, but it can be torn down and a beautiful house to replace it."

"Should I make flight arrangements or no?"

"No worries. I will arrange the flight, as I need to clear some things off my calendar first. As you know, we are six months out from election. I need to ensure that everything is in order before we go."

"I understand. I have to admit that I am looking forward to this trip and spending more time with you."

"I have a great idea," exclaimed Debbie. "Why don't you and I go shopping? Although I did stop by the old neighborhood after work the other day and picked up a change of clothing for you, I think it is time I spent some of this hard-earned money on my mother. What say you?"

"Sweetie, you do not have to buy me anything. Two tickets to Turks and Caicos is going to be expensive."

"Mom, I have already budgeted for the trip. Anyway, you want to travel to Turks and Caicos in style, don't you?"

As their attention turned back to their breakfast, thoughts of Josephine Adderly filled Lois's head. Her mother would prepare for weeks prior to their trips. She would go through Lois's closet inspecting every article of clothing in preparation for their trips.

She could hear her mother's voice, "Lois, one must look stylish while traveling."

Had Debbie inherited this trait from her grandmother? The mere thought pleased Lois. All Lois had were memories of times long gone. Memories of her childhood she desperately wanted to share with her daughter but could not. These memories she kept safely tucked away until the right time.

Debbie and her mother returned to the condo after a full day of shopping, giggling like little girls.

"Debbie, I don't remember the last time I have had so much fun."

"It was fun, wasn't it?"

"If you want, you can leave the clothes we bought in the closet. Of course, that's just a suggestion. You are more than welcome to take the purchases with you. I just thought you might want to leave them here as it would be easier when we leave for Turks and Caicos."

"Uhm…I think that is a brilliant idea. The people in my neighborhood are so nosey. I do not want them seeing me walking in with a ton of bags. They might get the idea that I'm rich."

They giggled like two schoolgirls.

Bedford Hills Correctional Facility

John Harrelson arrived early at Bedford Hills Correctional Facility to visit with Shakira. He was nervous. He sat in a large room with others waiting to visit with their loved ones. Two months ago, he requested placement on the visitor's list and every Saturday he would make the drive to Bedford Hills in Westchester County only for the guards to inform him that his name was not on the list. I guess he could not blame Shakira for not wanting to see him. For years, he denied her very existence. However, he desperately needed to see her, to make things right, to ask for her forgiveness. One day, he conjectured, she would see him. Until then, he would continue to make the trip to Bedford Hills every Saturday.

Two hours after John Harrelson left Bedford Hills, a prison guard appeared at Shakira's cell.

"Shakira Fleming, you have a visitor."

Cinnamon was the only person Shakira had agreed to see. She needed her sister to know how sorry she was for what she'd done to her. Jealousy had consumed her. The thought of what she had done that night tormented her in her waking hours as well as in her dreams. That night played over and over in her mind like a bad movie. Her sister lying on the floor in a pool of blood from a gunshot wound she administered. Jealousy saturated her every thought. That is what landed her in prison. It wasn't Cinnamon's fault or her father's fault, it was hers.

Shakira followed the guard. She sat down behind the glass and looked at her sister for several seconds before slowly lifting the receiver from its cradle.

Cinnamon mimicked her movements.

"Hey, sis," Cinnamon whispered. "Where do we start?"

Shakira placed her hand over her mouth so that none of the other inmates would hear her cries.

Cinnamon placed her hand on the glass.

"Shakira, look at me. Come on, sis, open your eyes."

Shakira opened her eyes and into the smiling face of Cinnamon.

"Shakira, I forgive you. None of this is your fault. What I need you to do for me is forgive yourself. Can you do that for me? Can you forgive yourself?"

"I don't know if I can. Cinnamon I hurt you. How can I live with that hanging over my head?"

"It doesn't have to hang over your head. Pull it down and stomp on it."

"Shakira, you are my sister. We cannot deny the blood. We have different mothers, but the same father and his DNA runs through both of us."

Shakira noticed that all the time Cinnamon was talking she never removed her hand from the glass that separated them. She reached up and placed her hand on the glass to mirror her sister.

Tears ran down Shakira's cheeks when she heard Cinnamon praying, "Our Father, which art in heaven, hallowed be thy name. Thy kingdom come, thy will be done in earth, as it is in heaven. Give us this day our daily bread. And forgive us our debts, as we forgive our debtors. And lead us not into temptation but deliver us from evil. For thine is the kingdom, and the power, and the glory, forever. Amen."

When Cinnamon finished praying, both were shedding tears.

"Shakira, we are going to get through this as a family. I know you don't want to see anyone other than me right now, but I need you to know that Dad has been coming here every Saturday since your incarceration. He sits patiently in the intake room waiting to hear his name. I did not come here to force you. All I ask is that you take your time, consider his request, and go from there. He believes that you will have a change of heart and have his named placed on the visitor's log."

"Cinnamon, I'm not ready yet. First, I need to get my head wrapped around the fact that I am doing five years in prison for shooting my sister. In the State of New York, that is a Class B felony. It does not matter that I am a first offender. The only thing that matters is that I was in possession of a firearm and I used it in the commission of a crime. That crime being attempted murder."

"I'm sorry. You are right. Sitting down with him has to be in your time and on your terms," Cinnamon said while looking at her watch. "Oh my…we have been at this now for an hour and a half. I need to leave but I will be back next weekend. Take care, sis, and know that I love you regardless."

Both placed the receivers back in their cradles. Cinnamon watched as the guard escorted Shakira through the heavy metal doors back to her cell. On the return trip to Manhattan, Cinnamon meditated on God's word "do not despise these small beginnings."

*****

Debbie could not remember a Saturday morning when she allowed herself to lounge in bed past seven o'clock. However, this Saturday was different. Scheduled to meet with her contact later that evening, her mind raced with what information she might find in her possession.

"Jenkins is the least of my problems," Debbie said as she turned to watch the sunrise slowly illuminating the New York skyline.

Down the hall, Lois began to stir from a very restful sleep. She never awoke before nine o'clock, but today, it's as if her body wanted her to take in all that life had to offer. She kept her eyes closed and imagined the city awaking along with her as cars emerged from underground garages, lighted from parking spaces along the streets and New York and circular driveways. She imagined cars filing onto the bridges and freeways connecting one borough to the next and shop owners slowly lifting the gates protecting the windows of their stores from attempted burglaries. Lois smiled as she saw herself sitting in the chair by the window of her tiny apartment as she sipped coffee and listened to the voices of the children playing in the courtyard.

Soon all of this will be a distant memory, she thought to herself. Although Lois could see the New York skyline with the drapes closed, she wanted to feel the New York sunshine on her skin. She reached for the switch operating the drapes and pushed the button. The soft whir of the drapes as they opened allowed all the beauty New York had to offer into the room. She quietly got out of bed, walked across the room, and stood in front of the massive window spanning the entirety of the wall. From her vantage point, Lois's eyes rested on the tops of trees and thick foliage common to this part of New York. It would be a lie if she told herself that she did not miss this lifestyle, or, that it was not a daily struggle raising her daughter on little to no money.

However, all of that is a moot point as these past couple of days with her daughter were both enjoyable and satisfying. Debbie has done very well for herself and a daughter any mother would be proud of, Lois thought.

She returned to the king-sized bed with overstuffed pillows and allowed the warmth of the morning sun to rest on her face.

Debbie decided that soaking in a nice hot bath was just what the doctor ordered for a Saturday out of the office. She would lounge most of the day until it was time to meet up with her contact later that evening. Her mind was racing with endless scenarios of what dirt her contact was able to dig up on Darren Jenkins.

Debbie slid down further into the water and rested her head on the back of the tub. She closed her eyes and allowed Michele Dobbs to fill her thoughts.

There must be something she has done in her lifetime that we can dig up thought Debbie. She made a mental note to herself to review Michele's resume once more before meeting her contact. She needed to push this fact-finding mission along a lot faster as time was running out and the mayor's campaign manager needed all ammunition to put together negative ads that will sway the voters toward reelecting the mayor.

A day of relaxation and small talk was something both Debbie and Lois needed. They spent most of the day sitting on the balcony with the fireplace pushing out the right amount of heat. They decided to eat breakfast and lunch outside on the balcony but ate dinner by the fire inside as the night chill settled in.

Later that evening, Debbie drove her mother home and saw her safely to her apartment. She gave her mother a big hug and kiss before wishing her a pleasant evening.

"Mom, I will call you tomorrow," said Debbie.

"I look forward to it," responded her mother.

Debbie waited outside the door listening for the click of the locks before skipping down the six flights of stairs. The building had an elevator, but Debbie always took the stairs. This was her way of keeping fit. Debbie returned to her car and glanced at her watch.

"Nine-fifteen," Debbie said with a sigh. She sat there with her head resting on the steering wheel for several minutes before starting the car and pulling away from the curb.

When Debbie arrived at the agreed upon meeting location, her contact was already there. She got out of her car and slid into the passenger side of his. He handed her an envelope upon which she quickly opened. She could not believe her good fortune. There were photographs of Darren Jenkins with other women. There was evidence of offshore bank accounts with dates, times and amounts of wire transfers to banks in Switzerland and the Cayman Islands.

"How were you able to get his bank statements?" Debbie inquired while turning toward her contact.

"I have my ways."

Debbie returned her attention back to the bank statements. She noticed several large deposits within days of each other. Her contact provided her with bank statements dating back five years. Presenting the mayor with this information might prove futile. Every candidate must file a campaign financial statement thirty days after the election declaring contributions and expenditures. However, that only covers contributions and expenditures from ten days before the election through the election period.

Debbie returned everything to the envelope.

"Thank you. This is just what we need to secure the next four years." Debbie reached into her purse and pulled out a thick envelope containing the money she promised with a little extra.

"I have another job for you," Debbie said.

"Whatever you need, boss lady," her contact said jokingly.

"I need whatever you can dig up on Michele Dobbs. I am having trouble turning up anything on her. I have never met anyone as squeaky clean as her. See what you can do, and I will double what is in that envelope."

Debbie thought she noticed something different about her contact when she mentioned Michele Dobbs. Maybe it was her imagination, but she thought she saw his eye twitch ever so slightly at the mention of her name.

"What was that?" she questioned.

"What was what?" he countered.

"I don't know…but when I mentioned Michele Dobbs, I thought I saw your eye twitch."

"If my eye did or did not twitch, what does that have to do with Michele Dobbs?" asked with the street attitude all New York had to offer.

"Well, I got the impression that you might know her personally. That's all."

"So you are going to double what's in this envelope with anything I can find useful on Michele Dobbs, huh?"

"Yes."

"All right, consider it done. I will be in touch when I have something."

"Thank you."

Debbie exited the car and walked briskly to hers.

Her contact waited until after she left before driving away and finding the nearest payphone.

"Hello," said the voice on the other end.

"We need to talk."

"I have a fundraising event tomorrow evening and will be staying in the city for a couple of days. Meet me around two o'clock at the Four Seasons—Room 1015."

"See you then."

From his hiding place, Richard Stephenson watched as the black Dodge Charger snaked its way from behind buildings long past their prime before disappearing into the night.

He pulled out his black notebook and quickly scribbled down the New York license plate number. It is time to find out who he is and what business he has with Debbie Adderly.

On his way home, he stopped by his old precinct.

He ran into his former partner, Jim O'Connor as he entered the precinct.

"Richard, what brings you back to the twenty-eighth?

Richard smiled and shook Jim's hand. "Jim, just the man I was looking for."

"Here I was thinking that you missed us and wanted your old job back."

They both laughed.

"Retiring from the police force was the best thing for me," replied the private investigator. "However, sometimes I wonder if I chose the lesser of the two evils."

"Walk with me," Jim said pensively. "How can I be of service?"

Under normal circumstances, Richard Stephenson was extremely tight-lipped as they come when it comes to his clients and his investigative work; however, this case kept him up at night. People just kept crawling out of their respective holes and, quite honestly, it left him wondering how all of this was going to play out.

"Jim, I need you to do something for me."

"Sure, what is it?

"I need you to run a license plate for me."

"I don't know, Rich. We can only run plates as long as we have probable cause."

Richard Stephenson wasn't sure he should divulge that he was hired by the Justice Department to help them with their investigation of the current mayor, several of his staff, as well as the accounting firm and at least one employee of that accounting firm. This case was getting deeper by the minute and he had just hit his first legal roadblock.

As a former cop, Richard Stephenson knew all too well the repercussions associated with attempting to circumvent procedure. There was something afoot and Stephenson could smell it.

He leaned toward Jim O'Connor to prevent any chance of being overheard by others working around them.

"Jim, I would not ask you to do anything that would get you in trouble. Heck, I worked here in the twenty-eighth for many years, and I am well versed on the procedure, but this case goes deep. Deeper than any could ever imagine—for investigative purposes, I need to know who the car is registered to. I believe money is being exchanged on the highest level and whoever is tied to this license plate is a vital piece of the puzzle."

Jim looked at his former partner for several minutes before picking up the phone and calling in the license plate. He leaned back in his chair and waited.

Several minutes later, his phone rang, and he copied down the information and handed it to his long-time friend and former partner, Richard Stephenson.

The two men shook hands and vowed to keep in touch.

Richard Stephenson looked at the slip of paper when he returned to his car. Jim O'Connor wrote Lonnie Smith, 815 Amsterdam Avenue in East Harlem.

"Well, this is truly good news," said Stephenson. "This just keeps getting better and better."

The next day, Debbie sat in her living room poring over the information she received from her contact, Lonnie Smith. The amounts of money Darren Jenkins had received over the past five years far exceeded the kickbacks she received in the mayor's office. What was he doing to receive such large payments? Debbie gathered up all the information and drove to her office.

Her first stop was to the copier room where she proceeded to make copies of everything given to her. Placing the photocopies in her briefcase, she then locked the envelope in the top drawer of her desk.

"Game on," Debbie said as she exited her office.

Lonnie Smith arrived at the Four Seasons early. His mind raced and he needed a serious attitude adjustment. In all the years of living in New York, he had never crossed the threshold of the Four Seasons. There was no reason to. He sat in the lobby, watching people check in and out of the hotel. He noticed the way people were dressed and suddenly felt out of place. He got up and asked the first friendly face he saw where he could get a drink. He was quickly directed toward the restaurant. He noticed not many people were in the restaurant and he had his choice of seats. The seat at the bar directly in front of the television was perfect.

"What can I get you, sir?" the bartender asked.

"Uh…let me get a Heineken."

The bartender retrieved a bottle of Heineken and proceeded to pore the golden liquid into a tall glass.

"Is there anything else you would like?" asked the boyish-looking bartender.

Lonnie was clearly out of his element and the bartender knew it.

"Are you strictly a Heineken man?" the bartender asked.

All Lonnie wanted was to be left alone with his beer, but he decided to play along.

"For the most part I am a Heineken man. However, I have been known to indulge."

Now it was the bartender's time to be amused.

"Might I suggest Samuel Adam's Utopias? You look like a man with a little time on his hands so I'm going to set you up with some samples of beers. You let me know which one you can't live without."

"Okay. That will work."

With that, the bartender proceeded to place four small glasses in front of Lonnie. She opened one bottle at a time and poured sample amounts in each glass and waited for his response to each.

Lonnie was so relaxed sitting at the bar that he almost forgot why he was at the Four Seasons. He discretely checked his watch.

"Man," Lonnie whispered under his breath. He had been wheeling and dealing on the streets for years. Certain people were familiar with his skill set and were not afraid to hire him to get information on people. That was supposed to keep their hands clean, but what they didn't know is that their hands were just as dirty as his. The truth always comes out in the wash.

Lonnie paid handsomely for the beers he consumed and left the bartender a very generous tip before heading for the elevator. Promptly at two o'clock, he was standing in front of Room 1015. He knocked lightly on the door and waited for what seemed like hours before he heard the door unlock. The door was left ajar for him to enter. Lonnie's street sense kicked in. Before entering the room, he gave a cursory glance to his left. He did not notice anything out of the ordinary, so he looked to his right. He heard the ding of the elevator. A middle-aged woman with a tiny dog exited the elevator and walked in the opposite direction.

"Get it together," half-whispering to himself. "That beer has you trippin'."

While at the bar, Lonnie had consumed three Heinekens; however, he had been doing this long enough to know that he had to feed the alcohol. He ordered lunch, took in a little television, and engaged in sports talk as well as the upcoming mayoral election with the boyish-looking bartender.

He checked the small of his back and removed the gun he always carried before entering the room. Slowly pushing the door open, he quietly stepped into the suite. From his vantage point, he could see the soft glow of the television and the clink of ice being added to a glass.

"Lonnie," a woman's voice called out. "Would you like me to fix you a drink?"

"No," he responded. "I've already had enough. This is not a social call."

"Well, we can be social while discussing business," she countered.

Lonnie fully entered the room taking in every inch of it before facing her. He noticed the door to the bedroom was not fully open. This made him nervous.

"Are we the only ones here?" he asked.

She slowly sipped on her drink before replying. Now it was her turn to be nervous. Lonnie had never acted like this before. What had him spooked?

"Yes, we are the only ones here. Can you put that gun away? You are making me nervous."

"Not so fast," Lonnie said while waving her toward him with the gun.

"I have to admit that I am a little taken aback by your actions. I've never known you to be so paranoid," she said while slowly walking toward him.

"In my line of business, it pays to be cautious. If I let my guard down, that might be the day life as I know it ends."

He used her as a human shield as they went from room to room checking every area that someone might have been able to hide. He wasn't satisfied until he pulled back the drapes and checked the lock on the sliding glass door leading to the terrace. The door was unlocked.

"You should be more careful," he suggested as he secured the lock. "There are a lot of crazy people in this world."

"I feel safer already," she said while lifting her glass to him.

"Shall we?" she said while extending her hand to the living room. They both sat down opposite one another.

"Are you sure I cannot get you a drink? It might calm your nerves."

"I'll pass on the drink. I need my wits about me tonight."

"Okay. Well let's get down to business. You said last night that we needed to talk. Have there been any new developments that I need to be aware of?"

"I met with Debbie last night. I handed off all dirt on Jenkins and Carbozza."

"That's great!"

"Not so fast. Let me finish before you break out the champagne and confetti."

"Okay, proceed."

"Debbie asked me for information on you. Of course, this should not come as a shock to you as you have been spoon-feeding me information on the other two for months. Now, the way I see it, this can go one of two ways. I can go back to Debbie with no information on you which would put you in the category of Mother Theresa. That would work in your favor and guarantee your spot as the new mayor of New York City. Or I could feed her your whole life story, which might carry a jail term and prevent you from ever seeking public office again."

She sat there quietly mulling over her options. With glass in hand, she absent-mindedly swirled the ice with her index finger.

"How much would it cost for your silence?" she queried.

"Five mil," he replied.

"Dollars? Are you seriously asking me for five million dollars? Where do you think I can get that amount of money?"

"Not my problem. You came to me for help. I did what you asked me to do but the stakes have just gotten a little higher. Let's be clear on this one thing… I am not taking the fall for you. I am giving you one week to come up with all five mil, or I write a tell-all book with New York's finest. You had a fundraising event today. How much did that bring in?"

"That's none of your business."

"Well, since it's none of my business," he continued "I suggest you have a few more fundraising events and add to that what you took in today and have all that I asked for in one week's time."

"I cannot possibly raise that amount of money in one week's time. You are being unreasonable. Even with the best of fundraisers I do not know how I can raise this amount of money on such short notice," she reasoned.

Lonnie rose from his seat and headed for the door.

"One week," he said again before opening the door and exiting the suite.

Michelle sat in silence.

*****

With coffee in hand, Debbie arrived at her office an hour earlier than normal and patiently waited for the arrival of the mayor. When she noticed him entering his office, she removed the envelope from the top drawer of her desk and quickly walked to his office.

"Good morning, Mr. Mayor," Debbie said rather excitedly.

The mayor looked up at her with slight amusement. "Giddy is not an emotion I would typically associate with your demeanor," said the mayor. "It must be something good."

"Mr. Mayor we need to talk," she said while closing his door.

"I met with my contact over the weekend and this envelope contains very damaging information on Darren Jenkins. There are photographs of him with other women as recently as two weeks ago. In addition, there is evidence of offshore accounts in Switzerland and the Cayman Islands. What is even more interesting than that is his bank accounts right here in New York. You will notice bank statements dating back five years with many large deposits within days of each other. We can use this information to get him to drop out of the race. In my opinion, all of those large amounts deposited into his account are suspect and smell like kickbacks."

The mayor leaned back in his chair and considered his words carefully.

"Debbie, you and your contact did a great job of uncovering damaging information on Jenkins. However, I will have to consider this information very carefully before calling a meeting with you and Glen. I will get back with you before the end of the day."

Debbie turned and left the mayor's office with a strange feeling. She thought he would be overjoyed with the information she uncovered; however, it was the complete opposite. She returned to her office and tried to concentrate on her work.

It was six o'clock when Debbie finally left the office. As she exited her office, Glen raced up beside her.

"Great work, Debbie! The mayor shared your findings with me, and I must say that you did an outstanding job. The mayor wants to meet with us later in the week to formulate a plan of action. Again, good job at potentially securing him another four years in office."

Debbie watched as Glen breezed down the hall exiting the building to the right.

A smile eventually spread across her face.

"Game on!"

Across the street from City Hall, Myles decided to stay late at the office. It would be easier to research files after work while the office was quiet. The Department of Justice agents had asked for a file on Premier Architects earlier that day. He made a mental note to pull the file. He wasn't sure if he would be able to ascertain what they were looking for, but he would give it the old college try.

Mr. Brimmer stuck his head in Myles's office before leaving for the evening.

"You are burning the midnight oil, I see," said his boss. "Remember what I told you about family." With that, he chuckled and headed for the elevator.

"Have a good evening, Myles," Gloria called out as she placed her sweater on the back of the chair.

"Enjoy the rest of your day," Myles replied.

Myles got up from his desk and walked down the hall to the restroom. On his way back to his office, he decided to stop by the kitchen for a cup of coffee. He heard voices. He recognized the voices as Agents McBride and Simmons. Were his ears playing tricks on him or did he hear Debbie's name. He quietly walked toward the entrance to the kitchen and stood quietly trying to hear the rest of their conversation. Just then, he heard the chime of the elevator arriving and their voices fading away as the elevator doors closed.

Time seemed to escape Myles as he was unsure of how much time passed since he overhead the federal agent's conversation. His biggest fear had come to life… Debbie was under investigation. So many questions crowded his mind. He needed answers but how would he get them answered? Who could he talk to about this? He couldn't go to Debbie. All of them had received an official gag order. They were not to talk about the investigation to anyone. Suddenly Myles felt like he couldn't breathe. He loosened his tie as he walked back to his office. *What kind of craziness is this?* he thought to himself.

"This has to be a mistake," he muttered. "Debbie could not be mixed up in a pay-to-play scheme. She's too smart to allow herself to get caught up in something like this," he rationalized.

Myles got up from his desk and headed toward the file room. He pulled the file on Premier Architects and headed back to his office.

"Okay. What would Agents Simmons and McBride be looking for? What's in this file that would implicate Debbie?"

It had been several hours since Myles overhead Simmons and McBride discussing Debbie and a potential pay-to-play scheme. He looked at the clock and decided he had enough excitement for one day. He closed the file and placed it in his desk. This was too much information to process right now. Suddenly he placed both palms flat on his desk and pushed back.

"I can't let Debbie go down like this," he said to himself. "She needs to know what's coming her way."

Myles grabbed his suit jacket and pressed the elevator button taking him to the garage. He ran to his car and turned the key in the ignition. The garage was empty allowing him to speed out of the parking structure with relative ease. When he arrived at street level, he took the right lane with no regard for oncoming traffic. All he could think about at this moment was Debbie and how to warn her without drawing suspicion to himself.

Myles drove around the city for what appeared to be hours until he found himself parked in front of Debbie's condo. Gripping the steering wheel, he felt he had reached an impasse. He considered Mr. Brimmer and how hard he worked to build the most lucrative accounting firm in New York City. He thought about all the times his competition had insinuated that Mr. Brimmer had to have done something illegal to reach such status in a short period of time. As he sat there contemplating the situation with Debbie and Mr. Brimmer, he turned the key in the ignition and pulled slowly away from the curb.

He looked at his watch and decided it was another night of cereal for dinner.

"Man, what a day," exclaimed Myles.

Myles unlocked the door to his apartment and plopped down in the chair nearest the living room window. He stared out into the night, oblivious to the sights and sounds of the New York City night. His mind was still trying to process the possibility that Debbie had done something illegal. Something that could get her years of jail time.

Myles awoke hours later to a knock at his door. He sat up straight in the chair with his chin coming to rest in both palms. He remained in that position until he heard a second knock at the door. Reluctantly, he got up from the chair to answer the door. Through the peephole he saw Debbie standing in the hall.

Debbie heard the familiar sound of locks being turned. She smiled in anticipation of Myles's response to her impromptu visit.

"Debbie, what are you doing here?" Myles asked in a concerned tone.

"What's wrong? Can't I pop up to see my man?" she said while playfully peering around him.

"Of course, you can," he said while opening the door wide for her to enter.

Debbie chuckled bumping Myles as she passed him.

"You are the last person I expected at my door at this hour," Myles continued.

Debbie crossed the living room and made herself comfortable on the sofa. She patted the space beside her. Myles locked the door and followed her nonverbal request.

"Can I get you something to drink?" Myles asked. "You have your choice of water or juice. I'm afraid I have not been to the grocery store in weeks."

"How about a hot cup of tea?" she asked. "I'm in the mood for tea."

Myles smiled as he always kept tea if nothing else. That is something he and his grandmother had in common. They are both ardent tea drinkers.

"Have you had anything to eat?" Myles queried. His stomach was on empty. The nap he took when he got home helped to refresh him; however, did nothing for the fumes he was operating on right now.

"We can go out and get something to eat, if you like," he offered.

"Uhm…I really don't feel like going out, but I am a little hungry," Debbie said. "When I was little, my mom used to fix pancakes for dinner. She called it upside down day. This is when you have breakfast food for dinner."

Debbie smiled at the thought.

Myles searched the cabinet for pancake mix. He looked in the refrigerator for eggs and sausage. As fate would have it, he had all the ingredients needed for a nice meal shared with someone he was growing fonder of by the day.

Myles and Debbie shared the kitchen, laughing and telling jokes while they prepared their meal.

"Wow…so this is upside-down day?" asked Myles.

"Yep! So do you think this is something you could get used to?" asked Debbie.

"Well…let me say this. I think your mother is on to something."

Debbie pierced the last piece of sausage on her plate and fed it to Myles.

As Myles began to clear the table, Debbie took the dishes from him, "Why don't you sit down while I clean up the kitchen," suggested Debbie.

"No, you sit, and I'll clean up the kitchen," countered Myles.

Truth be told, Myles needed time to think about this situation with the Department of Justice, the firm, Debbie's involvement in a potential pay-to-play scheme. This was all too much.

"Would you like another cup of hot tea?" asked Myles.

"No, one is enough. After the meal we just had, I feel like I need to walk around the block to burn off calories," said Debbie.

"Well, it would be nice but not at this hour," said Myles. "Too many crazies on the street at night."

"Yeah, I agree."

Myles finished cleaning the kitchen being careful to place the dishtowel up so that it could dry. He exited the kitchen to find Debbie sleeping peacefully on the sofa. He sat down in the chair by the window wondering how someone so beautiful and brilliant could do something so imprudent. He knew more than he cared to know about the situation and yet he held out hope that somehow implicating Debbie was a huge mistake.

She began to stir from her sleep about an hour after she lay down. She stretched her body in catlike fashion before coming to rest in a fetal position. Myles was amused by her ritual. He looked at the time and determined it was too late for Debbie to drive home. He got up and walked down the hall to the linen closet where he kept an extra blanket. He returned to where Debbie was sleeping and gently covered her with the blanket.

The light on the hall table gave off a soft glow as Myles headed toward his bedroom and lay across his bed. His mind swirled with thoughts of "what if" scenarios about Debbie, the mayor, kickbacks, and jail time. Things appeared to be spiraling out of control and the more he thought about it, the more he feared Debbie might be in the thick of it.

Myles closed his eyes only to awaken to the alarm clock. He quietly got up and walked down the hall.

"Sleepyhead," he called out while walking down the hall.

There was no answer.

"I know you heard the alarm go off. Unless you plan on calling off from work, you better get a move on," continued Myles.

Myles reached the sofa and discovered a neatly folded blanket and no Debbie. Sometime during the night, she had awakened and quietly slipped out.

A half smile crossed Myles's face as he turned and headed back down the hall. He quickly jumped in the shower, dressed, and headed out for work. It was Friday and he was ready for a little R&R. Work at the firm picked up with the induction of several new clients. Also, having agents from the Department of Justice in the next office to his only added to the discomfort felt.

No sooner than Myles sat down at his desk, his phone rang. Normally his assistant would answer his direct line and transfer the caller. However, it appeared as though she was running late so Myles had no choice but to answer the call. He is glad he did as the call coming in was from Debbie.

"Hey, you," Myles said while reclining in his office chair.

"Hey, sweetie," returned Debbie.

Myles loved it when Debbie used terms of endearment such as *sweetie, babe,* and *lover* when addressing him. His whole day became magical after hearing those words radiate from her.

"Babe, do you have plans for lunch?" she queried.

"Not until now," Myles teased. "What do have in mind?"

"Do you think you can get away for a couple of hours?" Debbie asked.

"Uhm, we just took on a few new clients," Myles countered. "Let me get back with you after my boss arrives and I've had a chance to discuss the needs of the clients with him."

"Sounds good," Debbie said. "Give me a call when you can."

They both hung up.

Myles looked up when he heard the chime of the elevator. The doors opened and his assistant and both special agents exited the elevator.

His assistant busied herself rearranging the items on her desk. Myles noticed that she always rearranged her desk when she had something on her mind. Whatever it was, she would not rest until she spilled the tea.

The agents walked past Myles's office speaking in a hushed tone. Myles thought he saw Agent Simmons glance his way but, his look left Myles with an uneasy feeling. Myles secretly wondered if any of this had to do with information gleaned from their files.

Then it occurred to Myles. He got up from his desk and walked toward the window. As he stared down at the people scurrying about and the never-ending barrage of yellow cabs on the streets of New York, he suddenly realized that they must know that he and Debbie are a couple. A wave of anxiety rushed over him as he began to connect the dots. He finally realized that if Debbie was under investigation, then everyone connected to her was under investigation.

He grimaced at the thought.

Myles heard Mr. Brimmer's baritone voice as he exited the elevator, speaking to staff on the way to his office. At this moment, Myles wanted to march into his boss's office and ask him if the reason for the FBI agent's larger than life presence in the office went deeper than they were led to believe. He wanted answers and he would not rest until he got them.

What is the worst that can happen, he thought to himself? Mr. Brimmer is a reasonable man. A real straight shooter, not one to pull the wool over a person's eyes. He has always been transparent and upfront. The more Myles thought about marching into his boss's office, the more his paranoia dissipated. Nonetheless, Myles knew beyond a shadow of a doubt that Debbie was under investigation. He overhead the agents discussing this very fact while waiting on the elevator several days ago. What was he supposed to do with this information? The only thing he could do. Myles dialed Debbie's office number.

"Hey, babe. I was just thinking about you," cooed Debbie.

"Really? You will never get any work done if you keep thinking about me," joked Myles.

Debbie found his attempt at humor amusing.

"So…can you get away for a couple of hours?" Debbie probed.

"I'm sorry, sweetheart. I am swamped. Also, my boss called a meeting to discuss our new clients."

Myles felt bad lying to Debbie, but he needed to discuss his concerns with Mr. Brimmer. Maybe he had seen too many James Bond movies, but he suddenly felt like he was under the microscope. He needed to get his boss out of the office to discuss his suspicions. Myles exited his office and walked down the hall.

"Veronica, is Mr. Brimmer in his office?" asked Myles.

"Whoa, are you okay?" inquired Veronica.

"Yes, why do you ask?" countered Myles.

"Well, it could be the serious look on your face, the tone in your voice, and your body language."

Myles was not in the mood to entertain Veronica, so he posed the question again.

Veronica buzzed Mr. Brimmer.

Myles heard Mr. Brimmer's response. He did not wait for Veronica's formalities; he turned the doorknob and entered his boss's office closing the door behind him.

"John, thank you for taking time out of your busy schedule to see me."

"Myles, my door is always open to you. I cannot say that about some of the other people on staff. But you have unlimited access to my time."

"Thank you. I really appreciate that."

"So what brings you to my office?"

"I need to discuss some things with you but, I would prefer not to do this in the office. How about lunch? My treat."

"Well, it's not very often that I get asked out to lunch. Where are we going?" asked John Brimmer while putting on his suit jacket.

"I know the perfect spot."

John Brimmer grabbed his suit jacket and followed Myles out of the office. He stopped by his executive assistant's desk on the way out. "Veronica, I'm going to lunch now. I should be back in the office in a couple of hours."

"Yes, sir. Also, I should have those documents you requested when you return."

"Thank you." With that, both men turned and headed for the garage.

Agent Simmons answered the phone when it rang.

"Agent Simmons speaking…what do you have?"

"Our subject and Mr. Brimmer are on their way to lunch."

"Why are you calling me with this? Everyone has to eat, right?"

"The subject said he had some concerns he wanted to discuss with his boss. However, he did not want to do it in the office."

"When did they leave?"

"About two minutes ago. They haven't exited the building or garage yet."

"Follow them," said Agent Simmons. "You know what to do."

The elevator chimed and the doors opened to the upper third level of the parking structure. John Brimmer's reserved parking space was two spaces to the left of the elevator. What better space could one ask for?

Myles thought about all the times he had driven from level to level looking for the perfect parking space. It was for that exact reason he had decided to change his hours. Of course, he was not on the executive level, but at least he had his choice of spaces nearest the elevator.

"Myles, we can take my car. It's the least I can do since you are springing for lunch," John Brimmer chuckled as he tossed the car keys to Myles.

Myles climbed in behind the wheel and gently navigated the car out of the garage. He cautiously pulled out onto the main street maneuvering noonday traffic with ease. Both men rode in silence until they reached Jessie's. Myles exited the car first and handed the keys to the valet. John Brimmer got out of the car and followed Myles's lead.

The maître d' greeted Myles by name and escorted him and his boss to a reserved table. After they made themselves comfortable, John Brimmer looked around the restaurant before making small conversation with Myles.

"You know, I've lived and worked in this city most of my life and I never knew this restaurant existed."

"Yeah, I believe it is one of New York's best kept secrets. I stumbled across it one night after work."

"Well, I must admit that I am impressed," John Brimmer said with a slight nod of the head.

"Thank you," replied Myles.

Within minutes of sitting down, the waiter was at the table. "Hello, gentlemen. My name is James and I will be taking your orders. Have you decided on your selection or do you need a little more time?" he said with perfection.

Mr. Brimmer chimed in with, "Hello, James. This is my first time at this fine establishment and I'm not sure what to order. Can you assist me with something light?"

James did not move from his position as he rattled off a few suggestions for Mr. Brimmer.

"My first choice would be the Thai Broiled Salmon with a homemade chili sauce," offered James. That is my go-to selection at Jessie's. There are two other items on the menu that are not too heavy. They are the chicken tostadas and the caprese chicken and zucchini," said James.

"Thank you, James, for the recommendations. I believe I will have the Thai broiled salmon."

"Perfect! You are going to love this dish."

James took John Brimmer's menu and turned toward Myles. "And for you, sir."

"I will have the Thai broiled salmon as well."

"Very good, sir."

James took the menu from Myles and disappeared into the kitchen.

John Brimmer picked up the glass in front of him and took a long gulp of water.

Richard Stephenson entered the restaurant and approached the maître d' and asked for a table in proximity to Mr. Brimmer and Myles. Before the maître d' could protest, he flashed his badge along with a $100 bill.

The retired detective hoped that the high-tech listening device attached to the lapel of his suit jacket would be adequate in capturing the hushed conversation between Myles and his boss. He had not been a detective for many years, still he had not lost his knack for surveilling persons of interest.

He was careful not to draw attention to himself as he and the maître d' approached the table next to Myles and his boss. With the aid of the listening device, he was able to determine that Myles was informing his boss of his suspicions of the FBI agents at the firm as well as Debbie. This was about to get ugly real fast.

John Brimmer did not know what to make of this revelation shared by Myles. As far as he knew, agents from the Department of Justice were in place as there was an ongoing investigation into the activities of the mayor and certain mayoral staff. Of course, he knew that Debbie was under investigation; however, he had been sworn to secrecy. Now to learn of Myles's suspicions that he might be under investigation resulting from his relationship with Debbie, this might be bigger than any of them could ever imagine.

As they sat in silence, the waiter arrived with their lunch. An eerie reticence enveloped them as they picked at the food on their plates. Halfway through lunch, John Brimmer removed the napkin from his lap, wiped his mouth, and placed the napkin on the table indicating to Myles that it was time to go. Myles followed suit and notified the waiter to provide him with the check.

Richard Stephenson did the same.

As they rode back to the office in silence, John Brimmer's thoughts turned toward the firm. Myles had mentioned going through the files. "Myles, when we get back to the office, I want you to bring the files that Agents Simmons and McBride requested. Between you and I, the firm cannot afford to be blindsided. If possible, we need to connect the dots."

Within minutes after returning to the office, Myles knocked on his boss's office door with files in hand.

Mr. Brimmer opened the door gesturing for Myles to enter.

Turning to his secretary, "Veronica, can you reschedule my appointments for the remainder of the day and hold all calls, please? Thank you."

"Yes, sir. Will there be anything else?"

"Yes, I do not want to be disturbed under any circumstance."

Mr. Brimmer walked back to his office and closed the door.

"Myles, I hope you do not have any plans for this evening. We need to go through these files with all diligence to make a connection."

Myles took off his suit jacket and rolled up his sleeves. He reached for the file on Premier Architects while his boss reached for Davis Construction. They needed to make sure they had not overlooked anything that would bring disgrace to Brimmer Financial.

"Well, let's get to work," exclaimed Mr. Brimmer with tone of admiration.

In the distance, Veronica could hear the ringing of a phone and the muffled voices of Agents Simmons and McBride.

"Hello, Detective Stephenson. This is Agent Simmons. Since you are calling me, I would assume you have something to report back."

"Yes, I do. Myles is on to you."

"Why do you say that?" asked Agent Simmons.

"I overheard him revealing as much to his boss during lunch. It appears as though he was in the office kitchen not long ago and overhead a conversation between you and Agent McBride discussing the case."

"Is there a recording?"

"Yes."

"Okay, you know where to meet me. Be there in twenty minutes."

"What's going on?" asked Agent McBride.

"Apparently, Myles overheard our conversation about Debbie being under investigation."

"Do you think he tipped her off?"

"I don't think he would be that stupid. He might have thought about it, but he doesn't strike me as the type that will go down with the ship."

Agent McBride chuckled slightly before making light of the situation. "Even if he did think about telling her, how do you think it would have happened? Would it have been before or after their time of intimacy?"

Agent Simmons shook his head. "You are one sick puppy. You know this, right?"

"In our line of work, we have to keep our sense of humor."

Special Agents Simmons and McBride arrived at City Hall Park and quickly located Richard Stephenson.

"Walk with me," instructed Agent Simmons.

Richard Stephenson and Agent McBride followed him to the plaza area. When they reached an area where it was less populated, Agent Simmons asked for the recording. He took the recording from Richard Stephenson and played it where all of them could hear the conversation between John Brimmer and Myles. The recording confirmed what Stephenson revealed in an earlier conversation with Agent Simmons. Myles knew that Debbie was under investigation. The recording further revealed that Myles wondered if he might also be under investigation.

"Good work, Stephenson. Do you mind if I hold on to this for a while?" asked Agent Simmons.

"Not at all. Hold it as long as you need to," responded Stephenson. What Special Agents Simmons and McBride did not know is that he made a duplicate copy of the recording before informing them of Myles's suspicions. He had been in this business long enough to know that sometimes evidence goes missing.

After listening to the recording, Special Agent McBride wondered about the best way to proceed. She was anxious to discuss this with her partner. However, she would have to wait until this new revelation with Myles played out. She needed to know what his next step would be.

"Thanks, Stephenson, for recording their conversation. This helps us move forward with the investigation," announced Simmons.

"If you need anything else let me know," Stephenson said as he shook hands with the agents.

Simmons took his hand in a firm grip and exclaimed, "I am glad you offered. I need you to continue to keep an eye on Myles and Debbie. I have a feeling that Myles might try to tip Debbie off about the investigation. Who knows...he might be in cahoots with her? If they make any sudden moves or something does not look right to you, contact us immediately."

"I will be in touch when I have something to report," Stephenson said as he turned and disappeared into the crowd.

Agents McBride and Simmons arrived back at the office an hour before close of business. They entered their temporary office and closed the door to discuss what they had just learned.

"Now that Myles knows that we have his girlfriend in our sight, we have to move quickly," offered McBride.

Simmons folded his hands over his stomach and leaned back in his chair.

"I agree."

"Do we have enough to move in with federal law enforcement? This man is an elected official that betrayed the public's trust," continued McBride.

"Let's go over what we have. I do not want anything to go wrong by moving too fast," countered Simmons.

"Okay. You want to stay late and go over what we have or call it a night?"

"Let's call it a night. It will not take us long to go over this tomorrow morning. We've already gone through the files and determined that this firm does the accounting for all the companies that are consistently awarded city contracts. We have already determined that Ms. Debbie Adderly awards all city contracts. Go home and get a good night's sleep. Tomorrow is another day and we need to have all of our ducks in order before we move in."

"Sounds good," McBride said softly.

Agents Simmons and McBride gathered their belongings and headed out. As they passed by John Brimmer's office, they saw a light spilling out from under the closed door. Suddenly, the door opened, and they came face-to-face with John Brimmer.

"Leaving for the evening?"

"Yes. It has been a long day," said Agent Simmons.

From McBride's vantage point, she could see files spread across the large conference table in Brimmer's office. Myles got up from his chair and closed the door.

"Have a good evening, sir," Agent McBride said leisurely.

As Agents McBride and Simmons headed toward the elevator, they were careful not to say anything until after the doors of the elevator closed.

"Did you get the impression that something is going on?" asked McBride. "I couldn't help but notice Myles get up and close the door while we were talking to his boss. Normally, he would inquire about the status of the investigation. With him being such a creature of habit, I wonder why he didn't ask this time."

"You're right but there is no reason for concern. We have more information than they have and the files you saw on the conference table may or may not be the same files we asked for," said Simmons.

"If not the same files, why did Myles get up and close the door. That was very suspicious as we were not even remotely close enough to see the files in question," countered McBride. "Think about it. Myles overheard our conversation. If they are trying to connect the dots, they will have to start with the files we requested. Is it a coincidence that the companies that are consistently awarded city contracts are also clients of this accounting firm? Is it a coincidence that the person on the mayor's staff responsible for awarding these contracts is the girlfriend of one of the top people on staff here at this firm?"

Simmons could see the wheels turning in McBride's head. He had to admit, she was the best partner he's had since arriving at the Department of Justice ten years ago. McBride graduated at the top of her class and could hold court with the best Bureau profilers. Sometimes he thought that maybe she had chosen the wrong government agency. The more he worked with her, the more he felt like she should transfer to the investigative arm of the Department. The Federal Bureau of Investigations would be a great fit for her. He did not want to see her go but that's a conversation for another day.

CHAPTER

I T HAD BEEN ALMOST TWO YEARS since Shakira was sentenced to five years at Bedford Hills Correctional Facility for attempted murder. The only visitors she agreed to see were her mother's sister, Connie, and Cinnamon. Two years in this place, and she still could not get used to the sights and sounds of this place. I guess that is by design. No one should get comfortable with being told when to get up, go to bed, or when to eat. A total loss of freedom—being held captive. This could not have been God's plan for his creation.

Just then a guard appeared at her cell. "Shakira Fleming, you have visitors. You know the drill." Shakira walked over to the door and turned so that her back would face the door. She placed her hands through the small opening in the door so that she could be handcuffed and escorted to the area where she could visit via telephone.

She was more nervous than usual today as John Harrelson was one of her visitors. When Cinnamon asked her to put their father on the visitor's list, she was resistant. She held so much animosity in her heart toward him she did not trust herself to be civil. But she watched Cinnamon very closely during their visits. Every Saturday she would make the drive to visit with her. During those bonding moments, Cinnamon talked to her about the love of God. She told her how God sent his only son to die on the cross for all of us. She explained the concept of unconditional love. She thought about the transformation taking place in the six short months that Cinnamon has come to visit causing tears to well up in her eyes.

When she entered the visiting area, the guard removed the handcuffs. Cinnamon picked up the phone and placed her hand on the glass. Shakira did the same.

"Hey, sis. How are you holding up in here?" asked Cinnamon.

"Well, you know me. I am getting a lot of reading done. And because of you, I am attending church services," replied Shakira.

A big smile appeared on Cinnamon's face. "God is good!"

Cinnamon removed the phone from her ear and placed it on the small counter. John Harrelson took her place. With tears streaming down his face, he sat down and picked up the phone. He placed his hand on the glass. Shakira did the same.

For years, Shakira longed for her father's attention. She longed to hear his voice, to be held by him. She looked at the glass preventing them from embracing each other and she cried. The inability to have what she so desperately wanted caused deep convulsive cries to escape. Cries so violent that she frantically banged on the glass hoping it would break so that her father could hold her.

Before her father could apologize for all the pain caused, two guards appeared escorting her away in handcuffs.

Cinnamon placed her hand on her father's right shoulder. "C'mon, Dad. Let's go."

John Harrelson arose slowly from the chair, placing it neatly under the counter. He stared briefly at the glass petition that separated him from Shakira. He couldn't blame her for any of this. He placed the blame squarely on his shoulders. Selfishness walked into his life years ago causing torment, hatred, bitterness, and jealousy.

"Dad...are you okay?" Cinnamon asked quietly as she pulled out of the parking space.

"I'm so sorry, Cinnamon," he said through intermittent sobs. "I didn't do right by any of you."

Tears formed in Cinnamon's eyes and raced down each cheek with reckless abandon.

They rode back to the city in silence.

"Dad, I'll call you later to check up on you," Cinnamon said as she pulled up in front of her father's house.

With his hand on the door handle, her father shook his head in agreement before exiting the car. Cinnamon watched as her father climbed the cement steps leading to the front porch where she had spent so much time as a young girl. She continued to watch her father as he retreated into the house closing the door behind him.

As she pulled away from the curb, she began to pray. "Thank you for small beginnings. Shakira and our father have both made steps toward forgiveness and reconciliation. They don't yet see it... but it's there. Circumcise all hurt from their hearts and open their eyes to the benefit of wholeness. Fill them up with your love. In the name of Jesus. Amen."

Arriving back at home, Cinnamon unlocked the door to her apartment, kicked off her shoes and stretched out on the sofa. She stared at the ceiling for what appeared to be hours before picking up the phone and calling her brother.

Kyle answered on the third ring. "To what do I owe a call from my beautiful sister?" he teased.

A smile crossed her lips.

"I just need to talk to my big brother," Cinnamon shot back. "Do you have any plans for this evening?" she asked.

"Nothing that I cannot get out of," replied Kyle.

"Great! Pick me up at seven o'clock. Dinner is on me."

"Bet. See you at seven."

Kyle arrived promptly at seven o'clock. He knocked on the door and to his surprise Cinnamon was ready.

"I'm shocked. I cannot believe you are dressed and ready to leave. This has never happened in all the time I've known you," Kyle teased.

"Man...shut up! I know how to be on time."

"When?"

They both laughed.

"So where are we going?

"Remember Patsy's?" queried Cinnamon.

"Of course, I remember Patsy's! I haven't been there in years," replied Kyle.

"Well, we are going to East Harlem tonight for pizza," announced Cinnamon.

When they arrived, they were told the wait time was between fifteen to twenty minutes but were seated in ten.

"Hi, my name is Connie and I'll be your waitress this evening. Can I start you off with something to drink?" she asked.

"Sure. I'll have a ginger ale," responded Cinnamon.

"And for you, sir?" asked the waitress.

"I'll have a Heineken."

"Do you know what you'd like to order, or do you need a little more time?"

"I think we need a little more time," replied Cinnamon.

"Okay. I'll be right back with your drinks."

"I can't decide on what to get. Everything looks so good," whined Cinnamon.

"Now I remember why Dad stopped bringing us to Patsy's. It was all your fault. You could never make up your mind on what to order."

"Not true."

"I'm not lying. So that we won't be here all night, I'm placing the order when the waitress returns."

"We aren't going to talk about this?"

"Nope. You are exhibiting shades of indecisiveness," explained Kyle.

"Shades of indecisiveness? Man, you have fallen and bumped your head hard. I don't have an indecisive bone in my body."

"Okay. Here comes the waitress with our drinks. Go ahead and place our order," said Kyle.

"Here are your drinks. Are we ready to order?" asked the waitress.

"Uhm…yes. However, I am having a hard time deciding between the margherita and the macellaio," replied Cinnamon.

"I feel your pain," offered the waitress. "You can't go wrong with either one. When I am in the mood for a lot of meat, I go with the macellaio. The juice from the pepperoni, sausage, and meatballs give this pizza a unique taste. However, I can eat the margherita every day. The fresh basil, paired with the tomatoes and mozzarella will make you want to dig up five thousand of your dead ancestors, smack them, and place them neatly back in their caskets."

"Well, that settles it. We will go with the margherita," said Cinnamon.

"Hold up," said Kyle. "I'm a big guy and I like for my pizza to have a lot of meat."

Cinnamon fastened her eyes on Kyle and chuckled, "I thought you were allowing me to place the order."

"Yeah, but that's before you went all healthy on me."

Cinnamon turned to the waitress and placed an order for one of each.

"See how decisive I can be?" Cinnamon asked.

Kyle couldn't hold back his laughter.

They were halfway through their respective pizzas when Kyle asked Cinnamon what was on her mind.

"I took Dad with me today to see Shakira," confessed Cinnamon.

Kyle took a napkin and wiped his hands before looking up at Cinnamon. "I didn't think she wanted to see Dad. What made her change her mind?" queried Kyle.

"Shakira has been locked up for two years, and Dad has been driving to the prison every Saturday for two years hoping that she would consent to see him."

"Again, what made her change her mind about seeing him?"

"After I was shot, I was really messed up. I sought out a therapist who helped me get in touch with my emotions. She walked me through that night; how I felt when Dad told me that Shakira was my sister, the betrayal. But I had to remember that I was not the only victim. There are plenty of victims to go around. Shakira is a victim too."

Kyle sat motionless as Cinnamon walked him through the various stages of her therapy.

"Kyle, I was in therapy for months. I pushed Dad away, you, and my best friend Myles. I didn't want to see any of you. I needed time to myself. I felt like the walls were closing in around me."

Kyle reached across the table and took his sister's hands in his.

"Cinnamon…how did it go today between Dad and Shakira?"

Cinnamon's hands slid from her brother's as she leaned back in her seat.

"Not good. Shakira had a meltdown. I thought everything was going to be okay when she saw Dad but then she started crying and banging on the glass partition. She was crying so hard that the guards escorted her back to her cell. Dad never got a chance to talk to her."

"Man. That's rough. What about Dad? Is he okay?"

"He was very emotional. I told him I would call and check on him later tonight."

Kyle made eye contact with the waitress. She appeared like magic carrying two boxes with her and the check. "Here's your check. I'll take that whenever you're ready."

Cinnamon quickly whipped out her credit card and handed it to the waitress.

"I'll be right back," the waitress said as she scampered through the crowded restaurant.

Kyle and Cinnamon busied themselves with packing up the leftover pizza.

"Cinnamon, I think you and I need to stop by dad's house tonight. This situation deserves an in-person visit, not a phone call."

"I agree," Cinnamon responded.

The waitress returned with Cinnamon's credit card. She placed the card back in her wallet and left Connie, the bubbly waitress, a generous tip.

John Harrelson was sitting on the front porch staring off into space when Kyle and Cinnamon arrived. They sat in the car for several minutes before exiting the car.

"Dad," started Kyle. "You okay?"

John Harrelson was at a loss for words. He looked down at his hands and allowed the tears to flow.

Kyle moved closer to his father and placed his hand on his shoulder. "Come on, Dad, let's go inside."

Cinnamon moved toward the front door and held it as her brother and father entered the house. She carried the boxes of pizza to the kitchen and placed them in the refrigerator before joining her brother and father in the living room.

"Dad, do you want to talk about what happened today?" Kyle asked cautiously.

Their father removed the handkerchief from his back pocket and wiped his tear-stained face before indicating with a shake of the head that he was more than ready to talk about what had happened on his visit with Shakira.

Both Cinnamon and Kyle made themselves comfortable on the sofa directly across from their father. It had become second nature to them, as kids that is where they were expected to sit whenever their father wanted to talk to them.

"So what happened? From what Cinnamon told me, Shakira was ready to visit with you," inquired Kyle.

John Harrelson held the gaze of his children before responding, "I did too. But when she started banging on the glass, it broke my heart. All I could think about was that I was responsible for her pain. Had I not been so selfish, none of this would have happened. How do I undo all the pain and suffering I caused?"

Cinnamon got up from her seat and walked over and kneeled beside him. She took his hand and looked up into his teary eyes. "Dad, we are a family and we will get through this as a family. Please stop beating yourself up about something you can no longer control. What happened in the past is in the past. Do I wish my mother were still alive? Yes, I do. I'm quite sure Shakira feels the same way. You are still here. We will get through this."

Kyle sat silently trying to process what he had just heard. Memories of the fight he had with his father when he found out that Shakira was his sister floated to the forefront of his mind. He remembered how angry he was. He understood Shakira's anger, but he also understood that to move on, all hatred, malice, and unforgiveness had to go so that love and forgiveness could enter in.

Kyle got up and walked toward his father. He took his father's hand and pulled him to a standing position. He embraced his father tightly. He held his father closely as he cried and asked God to forgive him of his transgressions. That night healing came to the Harrelson household.

The sound of heavy iron doors closing was a sound that Shakira was all too familiar with. "Lights out!" cried the guard.

Shakira reached for the Bible and positioned herself at the foot of her bunk where she was able to get a little light streaming from the hall. She reflected on the events that happened during her father's visit. It was all a blur now. Why had she reacted the way she did?

"Father, God, I thought I was ready to see him," she prayed. "Please place it on his heart to return. I promise I won't make a scene. I'll be good. I'll be good. I promise. Just give me one more chance to see him." Shakira held the Bible close as she thumbed through the pages until her eyes fell on a scripture that read, "Let all bitterness and wrath and anger and clamor and slander be put away from you, along with all malice. Be kind to one another, tenderhearted, forgiving one another, as God in Christ forgave you."

She read that same scripture several times before closing the book. She climbed under the covers and slept peacefully for the first time in two years.

Kyle, Cinnamon, and their father stood in a circle holding hands as they prayed. They took turns adding to the prayer until they were satisfied every issue plaguing their family was covered. While praying for Shakira, they asked God to assist them in an early release for her. This family needed to be made whole.

Cinnamon kissed her father goodbye while Kyle headed to the kitchen for the pizza. Cinnamon and her father could not help but laugh when Kyle turned the corner with a huge slice of pizza in his mouth.

"All that praying made me hungry," said Kyle.

"You're always hungry," replied Cinnamon.

"In all seriousness, the next time you go visit Shakira, I'm tagging along. If we are going to get through this as a family, then family needs to show up so that she will know we are serious about this thing. Cinnamon, how often do you two talk?"

"At least twice a week."

"Dang, twice a week! How much do those calls set you back?"

STACY JOHNSON

"Shut up, man!" Cinnamon said playfully.

"I'm only joking. Okay, dad, I need to get your other bigheaded daughter home, so she won't oversleep for church tomorrow."

"Nope, that would be you."

John Harrelson stood back and watched as his adult children continued to tease each other as they disappeared from the house and walked into the night. He did not close the door until he saw the car pull away from the curb and a short honk of the car horn, indicating good night from Kyle.

"Well, that went well don't you think?" asked Cinnamon.

"Yeah, I think we are well on the road to recovery."

"Who are you and what have you done with my brother?" teased Cinnamon.

"Hey, I'm just taking a page out of your playbook!" exclaimed Kyle. "Also, I'm serious about visiting with Shakira. Ask her to put my name on the visitor's log."

Cinnamon settled back in the passenger seat while her big brother navigated New York's city streets.

"So when is the last time you saw Myles?" asked Kyle.

Cinnamon was a little taken aback by the question as she had not seen Myles in months.

"I haven't seen him in quite some time. Anyway, he has someone in his life, and I don't want to be a distraction."

"A distraction? Aren't you two just friends? How would you be a distraction?"

"Geez! Your questions are coming like rapid fire."

"So who is the new person in his life?" continued Kyle.

"All right, settle down. He is dating but I don't know anything about her. The last time I saw him he specifically said she is not up for discussion. But that's okay. I saw Leroy not long ago and he told me everything about her. Her name is Debbie Adderly and she works for the mayor."

"Okay. A woman with a good job. You can't beat that with a stick. You know at one time I thought you and Myles were going to get married. Well, maybe it wasn't meant to be," Kyle surmised.

Cinnamon considered her brother's comment before asking, "What made you think Myles and I would marry?"

"I don't know. Maybe it was the way he took you in with his eyes. Not in a lustful way. It was more like respect and admiration."

Cinnamon turned her face toward the window and allowed her thoughts to consume her. If only Myles knew how much she loved him. She feared he would never know now that there was someone else in his life. She had taken their friendship for granted. He wanted more from her, but she pushed him away. What made her think he would wait for her? Cinnamon discretely wiped a lone tear from her cheek.

Kyle parked the car and walked Cinnamon to her apartment. They hugged and Cinnamon unlocked the door and gently closed it behind her. Kyle did not leave until he heard the click of the lock. A change in Cinnamon's demeanor did not go unnoticed by Kyle. It wasn't until he mentioned Myles that she got quiet. He secretly hoped that she would be okay. She mentally shut everyone out after she was shot. He did not want her to go back into a black hole.

After placing the pizza in the refrigerator, Cinnamon walked down the hall to her bedroom. Kyle was right. She noticed it too. Myles made her feel so special whenever he was around. She felt safe with him. He was so attentive after her surgery. Self-pity consumed every fiber of her being preventing the love and admiration he held in his heart for her to enter in. She hurt him and she did not know how to make it all better. The clock on the nightstand screamed ten-thirty. It was late but after what happened earlier this evening, Cinnamon decided not to let another hour go by without apologizing to Myles and asking for forgiveness. She reached for the phone and dialed his number. He answered on the third ring.

"Hello?"

"Hey, Myles," Cinnamon said quietly.

"Cinnamon?" asked Myles.

"The one and only," gushed Cinnamon.

"Wow... I didn't think I would ever hear from you again," confessed Myles.

Cinnamon allowed the tears to flow.

"Cinnamon? Are you still there?"

"Yes," she sobbed.

"Cinnamon, are you okay? What's going on?" he asked.

"I don't know where to start. So much has happened since we last saw each other."

Myles was expecting the worst. He reached for the remote and turned the volume down on the television.

"Hey, c'mon. It can't be that bad, right?" suggested Myles.

Myles sat silently listening to Cinnamon's soft sobs. At that moment, he realized that no matter how hard he tried to bury his feelings for her, it would never happen. All he wanted at that moment was to take her in his arms and tell her that everything would be okay. Together, they could weather the storm. But those days were long gone. All he could do at that moment was to try to be there for her from a distance.

"Cinnamon, sweetie, you okay?" Myles asked.

"Yeah," Cinnamon answered slowly. "I'm sorry that I fell apart like that. I have been holding so much inside…man, this is harder than I thought it would be," confessed Cinnamon.

"Just say it," urged Myles.

"When I heard your voice, I couldn't hold back the tears."

"Hey, that's okay. What are friends for if they can't be there for each other, right?" quizzed Myles.

"Yeah, you're right," agreed Cinnamon.

"So I'm curious. What's been going on with you? It's been like a year or more since we last saw each other," asked Myles.

"Uhm…it's been a little longer than that but who's counting," Cinnamon gently corrected.

"Cinnamon, I know you. You didn't call me at this hour just to shoot the breeze. What's really going on?" inquired Myles.

"You know me too well, Myles Beyers. I could never get away with anything with you. Never have, never will."

"There she is ladies and gentlemen," teased Myles. "Will the real Cinnamon Harrelson please stand up!" exclaimed Myles.

They both laughed.

"I really missed having you around," announced Cinnamon.

Myles was caught off guard.

"Myles? Myles, are you still there?"

Myles brought the phone back to his ear. Clearing his throat, "Yeah, yeah, I'm still here."

"You scared me for a minute," continued Cinnamon.

"Well, while we are playing True Confessions, I missed you too. More than you know."

A delicate smile crept across Cinnamon's face.

"Myles, my reason for calling you tonight was to apologize. Like a true friend, you were with me, helping me out and caring for me after I was shot. Don't think that went unnoticed."

"Cinnamon, hey, you don't have to—" started Myles.

"No, let me finish," commanded Cinnamon.

"Yes, ma'am," teased Myles.

"After I found out that Shakira was really my half-sister, I didn't know what to make of it. I pushed everyone out of my life. I needed space to breathe…to make sense of it all. I pushed my dad away. I pushed you away. Emotionally, I was a train wreck waiting to happen. Once I realized that I needed help…that I couldn't do this on my own… I sought therapy. Twice a week for six months. That was the best decision I've ever made. Prior to that, I thought I was going to lose my mind! When my father disclosed how my mother died, I couldn't process the information. For years, he allowed us to live his lie."

Cinnamon continued to bare her soul to Myles, catching him up on her reconciliation with her father, the weekly visits with Shakira as well as giving him the blow by blow that unfolded during she and her father's last visit with Shakira. As she talked, Myles thought about the power of forgiveness. Only God could pick up the pieces of a fragmented family and make that family whole. He settled back on the sofa and silently thanked God that his friend had thought to call him at the exact moment he was at his lowest. By the time they were finished catching up, the hour had grown late.

"Wow, can you believe we've been on the phone talking for hours?" asked Cinnamon.

Myles looked at his watch. It was officially Sunday morning.

"It has been awhile since you've talked me into another day," laughed Myles.

"Haha…you're so funny," Cinnamon shot back.

"Well, try to get some sleep," instructed Myles. "I don't want you falling asleep in church."

"Later," Cinnamon said sleepily.

"Later," responded Myles as he gently hung up the phone. There was so much he wanted to tell Cinnamon, but tonight wasn't the time. Tonight was her time.

Myles awoke to an early morning call from Debbie. He looked at the clock. It was extremely early. He placed a pillow over his head to ignore the ringing. Finally, he reached for the phone.

"This better be good, he said to the person on the receiving end."

"Hey, lover," Debbie cooed.

Myles removed the pillow from his head and rolled over onto his back.

"Do you know what time it is? Why are you calling so early? You know that's rude, right?" he scolded.

"Wow…good morning to you too. I've called you before at this hour and you've responded differently. What's wrong?" she inquired.

"I'm just tired," he replied.

"Okay, how about I call you back later this afternoon. Maybe we can grab something to eat or take a walk in the park," suggested Debbie.

"I have a couple of things to do today so I'll call you when I'm done," replied Myles.

As she listened to the dial tone, Debbie wondered at the sudden shift in attitude toward her. She made a mental note to speak to Myles about it.

Myles set the alarm for nine o'clock and fell back asleep.

Less than two hours later, the alarm clock sounded. For a moment, Myles contemplated staying in bed all day. Ten minutes later, he threw back the covers and headed for the shower.

Bethel AME was in the old neighborhood. Myles couldn't remember the last time he attended services. He found a seat in the back of the church and quickly scoured the congregation for his grandmother. He located her. She was wearing the purple hat he gave her for her birthday. He smiled inside knowing how excited his grandmother would be to see him at service. She never failed to mention it whenever they were together. Today, he needed to spend time with her...talk to her...seek her advice. From the time he went to live with her, she had been the one constant in his life. She kept him grounded.

Myles was startled out of his thoughts when he heard the pastor say, "Hast thou considered my servant Job, that there is none like him in the earth, a perfect and an upright man, one that feareth God, and shuns evil?"

After service, Myles stood in the back of the church watching as his grandmother made her way through the crowd, stopping to talk to people along the way. When she saw Myles standing there, she greeted him with the biggest smile and hug.

"Lord, thank you for answering my prayers!" she cried out.

Myles hugged his grandmother tightly as he shared in her excitement.

"It's so good to see you, Myles. You haven't come by to see me in a while. That young lady you are seeing must be keeping you busy. Tell her that she can't be monopolizing all your time because there is another woman in your life. Your granny needs to see you some time."

"Oh, do I detect a little jealousy?" Myles teased.

"Yes, you do and I'm not ashamed. One might say I am unapologetic," she shot back.

"Wait a minute now. Didn't we just leave church?" Myles continued to tease his grandmother.

"God understands my pain," said his grandmother.

With that, they both broke out in hearty laughter.

"Okay. I have an idea. That is if your dance card isn't already filled. How would you like your favorite grandson to take you to lunch?"

"Well, let me check my schedule. I just might be able to squeeze you in."

"Okay, go ahead and check your schedule. I'll wait."

His grandmother made a big production of pulling a pocket calendar from her purse. She opened it up and exclaimed, "Well, will you look at that? I've had a cancellation and I am free for the rest of the day."

Myles smiled as he extended his arm toward his grandmother. "Shall we?"

She gracefully folded her arm into his as they exited the church. After lunch, Myles drove his grandmother back to Chesterfield Assisted Living.

"Make yourself comfortable while I get out of these clothes," his grandmother instructed.

Myles removed his suit jacket and loosened his tie. He stepped out on the balcony to take in the fresh air, allowing the sun to warm him up. *Why is life so complicated?* he mused.

Soon his grandmother appeared by his side. "I spend a lot of time out here. It is so peaceful and beautiful. I wouldn't trade this for anything in the world. As we age, we yearn for simpler times. Living here is as close to those times as I'm going to get on this side."

Myles knew to which his grandmother referred. The cycle of life is not something he wanted to think about today. Today, he just wanted to spend as much time with her as humanly possible. He wanted to talk to her about some things that have been bothering him. He needed to glean from her today…if she would allow him.

His grandmother eyed him cautiously. "Myles, I raised you. I know when something is weighing heavily on your heart. Let's go inside. I'm going to fix us both a cup of tea and you, young man, are going to tell me everything that's bothering you about that young lady you are seeing."

"How did you know it was about her?" asked Myles.

With a twinkle in her eye, she turned and faced Myles. "I didn't get to be the age that I am by being a fool. I can read people like a good book. Also, you showed up for Sunday service today. People always run to church when they are searching for answers. And young man you are searching for answers. It's written all over you. C'mon.

Sit down and I'll be right back with the tea. Then you can tell your granny all about it."

As he drank his tea, his thoughts turned toward his boss, Debbie, the agents from the Department of Justice, and the conversation he overheard. He wanted to unburden but he had been sworn to secrecy. The only person he talked to about his suspicions was John Brimmer. Today, he could only talk to his grandmother about the call from Cinnamon.

With a clink of the teacup his grandmother looked him straight in the eyes. "Tell me. What's going on?"

"Do you want the good news or the bad news first?" he asked.

"Why don't we start with what you perceive to be the good news first?" countered his grandmother.

"I received a telephone call from Cinnamon last night," started Myles. "Grandma, I must admit that I was taken aback by her call. Let's face it. We haven't seen or spoken to each other in over a year. I always wondered how I would react if I ran into her on the street. I played it repeatedly in my mind. You know how guys are. We try to act like nothing phases us because we are so macho. But it's a façade. Let me be clear on that. It depends on the woman. If we have deep feelings for the woman, and that woman rejects us, then we hurt. We are so deeply hurt that we think we will never recover. Sometimes, we find it difficult to love another the way we loved that woman and vow never to let that happen again. We don't want that woman that cut us so deeply to know how broken we are inside. I was prepared to be that way with Cinnamon. At first, I was. Especially when everything was new and fresh with Debbie. Yep, Cinnamon called me up and invited me to her place for dinner. I knew what she was trying to do, but I shut her down. I felt vindicated in doing so, too. I wanted her to feel the same rejection I felt."

"So when she called you last night, how did you feel?" his grandmother asked cautiously.

"Every reaction I thought I would have didn't materialize. Like I said earlier, I was taken aback by her call. She was so apologetic and real. In my head I thanked God that my friend was back. She revealed how she sought therapy after learning Shakira is her half-sister and about her journey to forgiveness. She was able to forgive her father, and as a result they have a much stronger relationship. Her biggest accomplishment is traveling every Saturday to visit with Shakira."

Myles's grandmother sat silently sipping on her tea as he continued to unburden himself.

"She told me that Shakira had a meltdown the last time she was there. When she saw their father, she started screaming and crying and banging on the glass."

"My Lord" was all his grandmother could utter.

"I found out that all three of the Harrelson's are going to see Shakira together as a family. All I can say is God is working it out for them."

"Amen to that! Now, tell me about you, Cinnamon and Debbie. I sense a triangle forming and you will want to avoid that at all costs," cautioned his grandmother. "Believe me when I tell you, Myles, nothing good is going to come of this if you don't nip it in the bud right now."

Myles placed his head in his hands, massaging his temples with his thumbs. He knew he needed to distance himself from Debbie. The investigation had him spooked. He didn't know how deep she was in this, but when news breaks, he doesn't want his name associated with hers. What a tangled web we weave he thought to himself.

"Myles, where did you go?" asked his grandmother. "You look like you are a million miles away."

"Granny, I am going to confide something in you. Just know that I am breaking all the rules in telling you this as I have been sworn to secrecy."

"Myles, what kind of trouble are you in?"

"Granny, what I am about to tell you cannot be shared with anyone," cautioned Myles.

Myles brought his hands together and closed his eyes as if he were in prayer.

His grandmother sat patiently waiting for him to share.

Finally, Myles opened his eyes and began to confide in his grandmother.

"Granny, I have always been honest with you. We have never kept any secrets from each other and keeping this from you is no longer an option."

"Myles, you are scaring me."

"Granny, I don't want you to be scared, upset, or worried about me. But for the last several months, agents from the Department of Justice have been investigating the mayor's office. Two of these agents have moved into an office next to mine to better surveille foot traffic at City Hall."

"Okay, what does this have to do with you?" asked his grandmother.

"Well, I don't know how deep the corruption goes in the mayor's office, but Debbie is one of the people under investigation."

His grandmother got up to make herself another cup of tea. "You know, if I were a drinking woman, I would be tempted to add something to this cup of tea."

"It's a good thing that you aren't because you are on your third cup of tea right now."

Myles waited for his grandmother to return to the kitchen table before he continued. "Not long ago, I was working late at the office. I went to the kitchen to make myself a cup of coffee when I overheard the Department of Justice agents discussing the investigation. I heard Debbie's name mentioned along with the mayor and his campaign manager."

"Myles, if I were you, I would put some distance between me and that woman," suggested his grandmother.

"Before they got on the elevator, I heard them mention my name. Granny, I am also under investigation."

"What? How can that be when you don't even work for the mayor?"

"Granny, I think they believe I might know something. The agents asked that I provide them with specific files. I didn't think anything of it until I overheard their conversation. The files they asked for are those companies that are consistently awarded contracts by the city. Guess who awards those contracts?"

"No, don't tell me it's Debbie!" exclaimed his grandmother.

"I invited my boss to lunch last week and told him about the conversation I overheard and about the files the agents requested for review. When we returned to the office, he asked me to pull those files. We went into his office and poured over the files to determine what they were looking for. The only thing we could determine was the amount of money awarded for the contract and the amount of money claimed on taxes did not add up."

"What disturbs me about this whole situation is the fact that you are under suspicion. Debbie is getting her palms greased just like the mayor and his campaign manager," his grandmother said matter-of-factly. "If she says any different, she is lying."

"You are probably right. The elections are coming up. I suspect they are going to move on the mayor and the others very soon."

"Have you seen the campaign ads?" asked his grandmother.

"Yes, I have. Each ad gets more vicious by the day. I wonder where they get their information."

Myles looked at his watch. It was going on four o'clock. As much as he dreaded seeing Debbie today, he knew he had to face her. The drive to her place would give him the time needed to get his thoughts together.

"Granny, I have to leave. I promised Debbie I would stop by."

She eyed him warily. "Myles, please be careful. I have lost so many people that I loved already. I refuse to lose you too."

Myles walked over to his grandmother and kissed her on the top of her head.

"Granny, I promise you that nothing will happen to me."

He kissed her again before calling Debbie to inform her that he was on the way.

When Myles reached the door, he turned to see his grandmother staring at him like she would never see him again. He caught the imaginary kiss she blew in his direction and placed his hand on his heart.

Traffic was congested, but Myles didn't seem to mind. He needed time to himself to consider the situation with Debbie. It was getting messy and felt it was about to get even messier.

Myles arrived and parked his car in front of the building where Debbie lived at approximately five-thirty Sunday afternoon. He entered the lobby and walked toward the elevator. Several minutes later he was standing in front of the door to Debbie's condo. He rapped lightly.

Debbie answered the door and pulled him into her arms. She reached up and planted a kiss on his mouth. Something was wrong. She noticed that he wasn't as receptive to her advances as in previous times. She desperately searched his face for a clue, any clue that would tell her why the sudden shift in demeanor.

Myles moved away from Debbie and walked toward the living room. He intentionally avoided sitting on the sofa and sat in a chair allowing him to focus on the New York skyline. The more he thought about Debbie and the investigation, the more he realized that he had to put some distance between them, and he had to do it quickly.

Debbie moved slowly toward the sofa. She knew Myles had something to say but she wasn't sure she was strong enough to hear it. She had allowed herself to fall deeply in love with Myles and had dreams of them spending the rest of their lives together away from New York. Debbie sat on the sofa crossed-legged waiting on Myles to reveal what was weighing so heavily on him.

Myles noticed that Debbie positioned herself to obstruct his view. Forced to look upon her beauty, he fought within himself to remain strong. He knew undeniably she would do some time for crimes committed. What a pity. What a waste. He felt anger rising in him.

Debbie cleared her throat.

"Okay, Myles, say what you came to say," demanded Debbie.

Myles folded his hands together with both index fingers resting against his mouth in a steeple stance. He rested against the back of the chair and stared at Debbie for several minutes before speaking.

"Debbie, I came here today to break it off with you. This is the last time you will see me. This is the last day that we will call each other. We're done!" Myles got up from his chair and headed for the door.

Debbie sat in stunned silence.

"Myles," Debbie called after him. She jumped up from the sofa and ran toward the door. She positioned herself between him and the door. "Myles, you cannot do this. Why are you doing this to us?"

Myles remained resolute.

Debbie softened her tone as she was determined not to allow him to leave without giving her answers she so desperately desired.

"Myles, why the change of heart? I'm standing here going over things in my head and I haven't been able to identify one thing in our relationship that wasn't good. We always had fun together. You cannot deny that, can you Myles?"

Myles knew she was right. The relationship was perfect except thievery was now part of her resume. That was a serious game changer. Not that he was a "Goody Two-shoes" but he could honestly say that he has never taken anything that did not belong to him.

"Debbie, move away from the door," Myles said quietly.

"No. No, I will not move until you have given me answers. You owe me that!" she exclaimed.

"Why can't you accept that we are done?" asked Myles.

"Because I have been with you long enough to know that there is something behind your decision. It is too abrupt. Something or someone has pushed you to make this decision, Myles. It is as simple as that," explained Debbie.

"Debbie, some things are better left unsaid," retorted Myles.

"I cannot accept that from you. I thought we were good together. I honestly thought that you were the one I would spend the rest of my life with. But today you waltz in here and tell me that we are over. Did you expect me to open the door and allow you to leave without so much as a fight? No. I cannot allow this."

"It doesn't matter what you will or will not allow, Debbie. You don't call the shots as far as my life is concerned. Now, I'm going to need you to step away from the door."

The tone in his voice let Debbie know that he meant business, so she sidestepped the door allowing him free access to walk out of her life. Or so he thought.

"Did you get all of that?" asked the FBI agent.

"Yeah, this guy knows something," replied the other agent. "Maybe he should have stayed a little longer. You know…gotten her to talk."

"Yeah, that would have been nice. Put in a call to Agent Simmons. Let him know that the boyfriend is now the ex-boyfriend."

"Hello, this is Agent Simmons."

"Agent Simmons, I thought you would like to know that Myles Beyers is no longer the boyfriend of Debbie Adderly. He just broke up with her, sir."

"Thank you for the call."

"Sir. Do you still want to keep surveillance on her?"

"Yes. I want to know her whereabouts and the people she is in contact with."

"Yes, sir."

Agent Simmons hung up the phone and immediately called his partner.

"Simmons, it's Sunday. Don't you ever stop to take a break?" asked McBride.

"McBride, we've got a problem. I just learned that Myles and Debbie are no longer an item."

"Wow… I wonder what brought that on?"

"I am going to need you to meet me at the office earlier than usual tomorrow morning. We need to strategize. I have a suspicion about Myles."

"Care to share?" inquired McBride.

"I'm not certain of my suspicions yet. However, I will get your thoughts on it tomorrow. Enjoy the rest of your day and I'll see you bright and early tomorrow."

McBride hung up the phone, reclined with a glass of her favorite wine and turned Coltrane up to an appreciable level.

Monday arrived way too soon. When the alarm clock sounded at six o'clock, Myles hit the snooze button and pulled the covers over his head. He thought about calling out sick but that was out of the question. He needed to assist his boss in preparing for a kickoff meeting with a new client. The alarm sounded again. This time Myles turned the alarm off and headed for the bathroom. An hour later, Myles was in his car headed downtown.

He was making good time until traffic came to a standstill. Rush hour traffic in the city was always horrific, but today was different. Every turn he made, landed him in the middle of a traffic jam and honking horns. Why the city would decide to work on the roads during rush hour was beyond his comprehension. He checked his watch. It was now 7:45 a.m. and he knew from experience that if traffic didn't let up soon, he would not make the scheduled nine o'clock meeting with John Brimmer.

He checked his watch again. It was too early to call the office. His secretary did not arrive until eight-thirty so he decided to stay the course praying traffic would subside. Several blocks later, traffic began to flow, and he was able to make up time by cutting through alleyways and other side streets. He mused, knowing the layout of the city can work to one's benefit in times like this.

Myles pulled into a parking space with ten minutes to spare. He hopped out of his car, quickening his pace to make the scheduled meeting with John. When he arrived, he immediately gathered the files he needed for the meeting and started out for his boss's office.

Before he could get there, he noticed that agents McBride and Simmons were in deep conversation. He mentioned it to his secretary, Gloria, who told him that both agents were already in the office when she arrived. Myles considered this information and made a mental note to bring it up with the boss. Something was afoot. He could feel it.

Three hours later and Myles felt like he had worked a full day. Gloria looked up when he appeared in front of her desk.

"Myles, Agents McBride and Simmons would like to see you."

Myles stopped and turned to face Gloria. "Can a brother get a break? I have been in an extremely difficult meeting with our new clients and…"

Gloria signaled for him to stop talking as the agents were exiting their office and heading in their direction.

"Myles," said Agent McBride. "Can we have a word with you, please?"

"Actually, I just got out of an extremely long meeting. Can we do this after lunch?"

"Lunch sounds wonderful," offered Agent Simmons. "McBride and I were just heading out to lunch ourselves. Why don't you join us? Our treat."

"Gloria, can you put these files on my desk? Also, let John know that I will be out of the office for about an hour or so with Agents McBride and Simmons."

"Certainly." Gloria took the files and watched as the three walked toward the bank of elevators. She secretly wondered what they could possibly want to talk to Myles about. She would just have to wait patiently until Myles returned.

Myles was prepared to walk across the street to Carl's Burgers for the Monday special, however, when they got on the elevator, Agent Simmons pushed the button for the garage. Agent Simmons noticed the look on Myles's face. "I thought we might go somewhere else other than Carl's Burgers."

Myles had never mentioned Carl's to them; therefore, he was feeling a little nervous. He quickly surmised that they had been watching him all the time. What else did they know about him? C'mon, Myles. You are being paranoid, he told himself. He felt sweaty all over. He mentally scolded himself, *Get yourself together. Don't let them see you sweat.*

When they arrived at the car, Agent McBride climbed into the driver's seat, Simmons in the passenger seat. Myles was more than comfortable in the back seat. They rode in silence. Myles could not help but notice that they took him to the same restaurant he introduced to his boss, John Brimmer. Was this by accident or intentional? Myles was determined to find out.

Richard Stephenson was already at the restaurant when they arrived. He had received a call earlier that day from Agent McBride instructing him to go to the restaurant and be prepared to record their conversation with Myles. Stephenson was more than happy to oblige. He knew that once the FBI and local law enforcement were brought in, his assistance would be scaled back. McBride informed him that there was a sudden twist in the investigation and that they needed his assistance once more.

Agents McBride and Simmons exited the car and waited for Myles to get out. They all walked into the restaurant together.

"Nice restaurant," exclaimed Myles. "You come here often?" he queried.

"First time," answered Agent Simmons. "Actually, it comes highly recommended."

"What about you?" asked Agent McBride. "Is this your first time?"

Myles thought about lying; however, there were too many coincidences. So he decided to tell them what they already knew. "I've frequented this restaurant once or twice."

Both Agents McBride and Simmons exchanged knowing glances.

The restaurant was busy. They stood and watched the hustle and bustle of busboys and wait staff for several minutes before the maître d' approached apologizing for the wait.

Agent McBride informed the maître d' that she had a reservation for three. They were seated promptly at a table near the back of the restaurant. Myles noticed that they were seated in an area of the restaurant that did not see much traffic. If he did not know any better, he would have thought all of this had been set up by Agents McBride and Simmons and the maître d' was a part of the set up.

A waiter appeared with three menus and three glasses of water. "I am Anthony, and I will be your waiter for today. The specials for today are…"

"That's okay, Anthony," said Agent McBride. "We are a little short on time, so why don't you bring us three specials."

"Sure." Anthony collected the menus and disappeared through the crowded restaurant.

"Why don't we cut through the chase?" said Agent McBride. "We know that you and Ms. Adderly are no longer an item. What we would like to know is why you decided to break it off with her?"

"My personal life is none of your business," replied Myles.

"Let us make something perfectly clear Mr. Beyers," offered Agent Simmons. "Did you actually think that when we told you about our investigation into possible corruption in the mayor's office that we would not find out about your relationship with Ms. Adderly? Did you honestly believe that your name would not come up as we delved deeper into our investigation? We are good at our jobs. Please don't insult our intelligence."

"Okay, since we are putting everything on the table, why am I under investigation?" asked Myles.

Once again, Agents McBride and Simmons exchanged glances. None of which went unnoticed by Myles.

"Is this why you broke it off with Ms. Adderly?" asked Simmons.

"Yes, that's why I broke it off. I don't know what she has done or not done. However, when I overheard your conversation a few weeks ago I decided that it was time to put some distance between Debbie and I," explained Myles.

"Well, Myles. To be totally honest, we moved into the office next to you to keep an eye on you as well as track the finances of certain companies that have complaints registered against them. Not only do we think it strange that both companies use the same accounting firm, but one of the persons under investigation is your love interest. And the cherry on top of the cake is your firm is located directly across the street from City Hall. Brimmer Financial is not the only accounting firm in New York, but it happens to be the only firm that these companies sought out to do business with. Doesn't that strike you as more than a coincidence, Myles?" asked McBride.

Like clockwork, Anthony appeared with three specials. "Here you go, three specials for the table. Enjoy."

Agents McBride and Simmons broke into laughter. "The look on your face is priceless," McBride said through her laughter.

"Burger and fries? Really?" voiced Myles. "A slow smile creeped across his face."

Midway through their meal, Agent McBride looked at Myles and said, "Myles, we need you to apologize to Ms. Adderly for breaking it off with her. Tell her that you gave it some thought and that you made a huge mistake."

"What!? No, I can't do that," protested Myles.

McBride stopped eating and stared directly at Myles. "Look, Myles. This investigation is complex. The mayor has been under investigation for over a year and we are close to the end of our investigation. I really don't have to reveal anything to you, but for you to understand our position, I have decided to break the rules.

Agent Simmons eyed his partner. He knew that his partner was breaking protocol but trusted her technique.

McBride continued her conversation with Myles, "We now know that you are not a part of whatever Ms. Adderly has gotten herself into. All we need is for you to get her to talk about the major players. We suspect there is a pay-to-play scheme within her office. She works for the mayor. If you can get her to talk about it, then we will know how far up the 'food chain' this thing goes."

"When we get back to the office, call her up and invite her to your place. She might be a little salty with you because of yesterday. However, I am willing to bet she is willing to give you another chance. I listened to the tape," confessed McBride.

Myles looked back and forth between the two of them. "What do you mean you listened to the tape?" Myles asked.

Both Agents Simmons and McBride took a big bite out of their burgers.

"Did you hear..." Myles's thought trailed off as both agents shook their heads yes in unison.

Myles placed his napkin over his plate and waited patiently for Agents Simmons and McBride to finish their lunch.

They drove back to the office in silence. Myles silently scolded himself for not realizing that Debbie's condo might be bugged and made a mental note to check his apartment for bugging devices.

Gloria eyed them as they returned from lunch. She could not wait to get the 411 from Myles.

Agent Simmons continued to the office he shared with his partner.

Myles walked into his office. He heard his office door close and turned to see McBride standing there. "Whatever you must do to get back in her good graces, do it," she instructed. She exited Myles's office as quietly as she had entered.

Agent Simmons was standing with his back to the door looking toward City Hall when McBride entered the office. He asked, "Do you think he is going to follow through with this?"

"I bet you $1 that he places a call in the next ten minutes inviting her to his place tonight," McBride said with confidence.

He looked at her with a sly grin.

"What? You don't want to take the bet?" queried McBride.

"I don't like losing," replied Simmons. "If I lose the bet, you will not like being in this office with me."

"So it's like that?"

"You know it."

"Well, I still believe that before the night is over, the man next door is going to put a call in to Ms. Adderly."

"You're probably right," Simmons said thoughtfully.

Myles sat at his desk and pondered the events of the day. It was only 2:30 p.m. and it felt like he had been through the ringer. He leaned back in his desk chair and closed his eyes; meditating on what Agents Simmons and McBride revealed. He could not get his brain wrapped around the fact that the only reason they moved into the office next to him was to keep an eye on him. Not only were they keeping an eye on him, he was under investigation purely by association. This sounded so crazy to him that he was considering calling Debbie and bringing her back into his life just so this craziness would be behind him.

He picked up the phone to dial Debbie's office but quickly returned the receiver to its cradle. He wasn't ready to talk to her yet.

There was a knock at the door. "Come in," Myles said.

Gloria entered the office and closed the door behind her. "Myles, I'm worried about you." She walked further into his office taking a seat in a chair on the other side of the desk. "What did Agents Simmons and McBride want to talk to you about?"

"Gloria, let me ask you something," Myles said cautiously. "Are you truly worried about me or are you just nosy?"

"Honestly?" Gloria stated as a question.

"That would be a good place to start," Myles responded half-heartedly.

"Well, to be honest, both," she confessed.

Myles looked at Gloria and chuckled. What could be worse than the day he has had so far. He thought back to when the alarm clock sounded at 6:00 a.m. and he contemplated calling in sick. Why didn't he just stay in bed?

"Gloria, can we talk about this tomorrow? Right now, I am mentally drained. Agents McBride and Simmons are..." Myles started.

"They are what?" Gloria asked.

"Never mind. I promise that I will tell you everything tomorrow. But today, I need to focus on..." his thoughts trailed as he looked around the office for the files given to Gloria earlier. "Where are the files?" he continued.

"They are on your desk," she said. Gloria rose from her seat and walked around to the other side of the desk and pointed out the files to Myles.

"Thank you," Myles said. "I really need to get some work done. Can you close the door behind you, please?"

"Sure," she started. "However, I am concerned about you and as your secretary and best friend, I don't want to see anything happen to you. Don't think I won't tell the agents in the other room to stand down," she said as she closed the door.

Myles buzzed Gloria within minutes of her returning to her desk.

"Yes, sir. How can I assist you?"

"So when did we become best friends?" Myles asked.

"Right after your return from lunch," she said. "I looked at your face and knew that something happened while you were with them. Tomorrow we will sit down and discuss this as promised."

Myles chuckled at Gloria's motherly instinct. "Okay, I promise we will discuss this tomorrow."

Myles was so engrossed in his work that he did not notice people were leaving for the day. There was a soft knock at the door. He looked up just when McBride poked her head in the office.

"Myles, are you okay?" she asked.

"Yeah, yeah, I'm okay."

"Well, I just wanted to let you know that we appreciate your willingness to assist with this investigation. The mayor's office wreaks of corruption and the people of this city deserve better. Because you have a close relationship with Ms. Adderly, chances are you can get her to reveal her part in this. It's a long shot, I know. But it's worth a try."

Myles fixed his eyes on McBride for several minutes before releasing a sigh. "You're right. Give me a couple of days to get my head wrapped around this. I will get back with you and Agent Simmons soon."

"That'll work. Have a good evening."

"You too."

Myles looked at the folder in front of him and decided it could wait until tomorrow. He grabbed his suit jacket and soon joined forces with rush hour traffic. "Yep, tomorrow has to be better than today," he told himself. He turned up the radio allowing Earth, Wind & Fire's classic "Keep Your Head to the Sky" to fill the car. This song brought back memories of the old neighborhood and hanging out with Leroy and Cinnamon. They would sit on his granny's front porch playing this song repeatedly. Soon, Myles was singing along with the song.

Keep my head to the sky
for the clouds to tell me why
As I grew with strength
Master kept me as I repent.

The matchless voices of brothers Maurice and Verdine White along with Phillip Bailey filled the air on those summer nights in the old neighborhood. There were times when Myles wished he could go back to those times. Simplistic and carefree.

Myles stopped and got something to eat before heading in for the night. As luck would have it, there were no parking spaces close to his apartment building. He circled the block several times before he gave up and drove to the next block. He found a spot a block and a half away from his building. It didn't matter…he was tired. He grabbed the bag of food and headed home.

Why couldn't he live in a building with an elevator he thought to himself. Today he did not feel like climbing six flights of stairs. Complaining is not something he engaged in at all, but today he felt justified. Some might say he was wallowing in self-pity. Maybe he was but he was so tired of the craziness surrounding his life. Between Debbie and the DOJ agents, he didn't know who was worse. As he walked the six flights to his apartment, he had time to think about his lunch with Agents McBride and Simmons. He weighed his options. If he did not call Debbie, what is the worse than can happen? If he did what Agent McBride suggested, would he be able to get her to talk about her work and those companies she awarded contracts without making her suspicious? After all, he had never shown much interest in her work.

In the distance, he could hear the ring of a telephone. As he drew nearer, he realized the ringing was coming from his apartment. He fumbled with his keys attempting to get to the telephone before it stopped ringing. He opened the door and rushed toward the kitchen and snatched the phone from the cradle.

"Hello?" Myles said before he heard the click of the answering machine. Myles hit the play button and stopped in mid-stride as Debbie's voice floated out from the machine.

> Myles, I am glad I got your answering machine. I know you said that we were done, but I cannot let this go. I'm not one of those women who beg, nor do I like loose ends. That's exactly what yesterday felt like…loose ends. I cannot get the thought out of my head that there is something you are not telling me. We need to talk. Call me. I don't care what time. Myles, if you ever cared for me, please do me the favor of returning my call.

"Dang!" he said as he spooned his food onto a plate. Why did he think walking away from Debbie was going to be a walk in the park? He was too hungry to think about this. All he wanted was to enjoy his dinner and a good basketball game. He picked up his plate and headed for the living room.

Cinnamon was at home relaxing with a new book by her favorite author when the telephone rang.

"Hello?" she said softly.

She heard the familiar automated message, "This is a collect call from Bedford Hills Correctional Facility. Will you accept the charges from Shakira Fleming?"

"Yes."

"Hey, sis," Shakira said.

"Hey, girl," responded Cinnamon. "How are you doing?"

"Much better than the last time I saw you. I'm sorry our visit did not go the way I envisioned it," confessed Shakira.

"Hey, don't beat yourself up. You can make it up to us this Saturday," teased Cinnamon.

"Dad wants to see me again?" Shakira asked in disbelief.

"Girl, did you think you were going to scare him off with all that crying and beating on the glass?"

They both laughed.

"I guess I was a sight, huh?"

"A little bit."

"Hey, can you put Kyle's name on the visitor's list? He wants to be included in on the visits with you. Shakira, it doesn't matter how we came to be family, it's a moot point. We are family and dad, Kyle, and I have decided that we are going to get through this as a family. Okay?"

"Okay. Cinnamon, I have been reading my Bible and I prayed last Saturday for God to give me another chance with Dad. I guess he answered my prayer."

Cinnamon held the phone tightly as tears welled up in her eyes. "Yes. He is a God that hears and answers prayers," consoled Cinnamon.

"Love you, sis," said Shakira.

"Love you more, sis," replied Cinnamon.

She hung up and immediately called her father and Kyle informing them of her conversation with Shakira. It finally looked like things were turning the corner for this family. Cinnamon hung up and got on her knees and thanked God for turning an unconventional situation around.

This coming weekend, she envisioned the four of them having a nice conversation. The glass between them kept their healing at bay. Once an ardent reader of Aristotle, Cinnamon remembered reading that human beings are social animals and therefore naturally seek the companionship of others as part of their well-being. Before getting in bed for the evening, Cinnamon prayed for God to direct her family to the right person to help petition the court for an early release for her sister. Incarceration was wearing on Shakira. Last Saturday was a prime example of this.

CHAPTER

MYLES AWOKE THE NEXT DAY WITHOUT the assistance of an alarm clock. Instead of lazing in bed, he decided it would be better to get up and prepare for work. He was warming to the idea of getting to work early. The previous day certainly wasn't the best commute into work. On his way out, he grabbed an apple and banana from the kitchen. He didn't know what it was but today he felt like he could conquer the world.

He walked the block and a half to where he left his car last evening. Before pulling away from the curb, he checked the time. It was 6:45 a.m.

"Young man," he voiced to himself, "you are doing good this morning. Look at you, leaving home early! Something tells me that you are prepared for anything that comes your way. Look out ladies and gentlemen, Myles Beyers is coming through."

He let out a hearty laugh.

He turned on the radio and invited Marvin Gaye to ride along with him. He joined the musical artist as he sang:

Mother, mother
There's too many of you crying
Brother, brother, brother

There's far too many of you dying
You know we've got to find a way
To bring some lovin' here today

Yeah, he was in a good mood this morning. The message Debbie left last night was in the recesses of his mind; however, he was in too good of a mood to let it bring him down. He was in the driver's seat and wasn't about to let anything or anyone call the shots where his life and happiness was concerned. He turned the music up to drown out his thoughts about Debbie as well as Agents McBride and Simmons.

The commute was much better this morning than the previous day. Leaving home earlier made a difference. He didn't have to take any alleys or side streets this morning. It was a straight shot downtown. Myles parked in the garage and walked leisurely to the elevator. He arrived forty-five minutes earlier than his scheduled arrival. There was complete silence. He got up from his desk and walked into the kitchen for coffee.

"What!? There's no coffee!" exclaimed Myles in disbelief. "Why is there no coffee?" he continued.

He looked at the message on the wall in bold lettering: **The first one in the office must make the aromatic beverage.** Myles chuckled to himself as the message came with step-by-step instructions for making the coffee. He toyed with the idea of going back to his office and allowing a more experienced coffee maker to handle this task. He stood there a minute longer than he should have as he heard the ding of the elevator just as he was about to return to his office.

Just then he heard the familiar baritone of his boss behind him.

"Myles. What brings you in this early?"

"The commute was so horrible yesterday with road work, I decided to leave home earlier to avoid a repeat of yesterday."

"You're a smart man, Myles."

"Were you about to make the coffee?"

"Well, I just noticed signage stating that the first person in the office must make the coffee."

John Brimmer waited a beat before asking, "Do you know how to make coffee?"

"No," Myles said sheepishly.

His boss laughed in the way that only a baritone could. "That's okay. Just follow the step-by-step instructions I placed on the wall. Get your feet wet, young man. Get your feet wet." His boss turned and walked toward his office.

"When the coffee is ready, why don't you bring us both a cup? We can catch up while the office is still quiet," he called over his shoulder as he continued down the hall to his office.

Soon Myles entered the office with two steaming cups of black coffee. He placed the coffee, creamer, and sugar on a tray he found in the kitchen.

John Brimmer looked at Myles with pride. "Well, see what you can accomplish when you put your mind to it?" he said jokingly.

"John, this could not have been planned any better," Myles said cautiously.

"What do you mean?" asked his boss.

"Both of us arriving early," Myles explained.

Both men dressed their coffee and sipped in silence. Myles wasn't sure how much to reveal to his boss. He warred in his mind about confiding in him about yesterday's conversation with Agents McBride and Simmons. And then there was the breakup with Debbie and the directive from Agent McBride.

"Myles, spit it out," urged his boss. "What's on your mind, young man?"

Myles placed his coffee down and let out a sigh. "I had lunch with Agents McBride and Simmons yesterday."

"Okay. They seem nice enough."

"Well, I guess in order for you to understand the chain of events that unfolded yesterday, I will have to go back to Sunday," Myles suggested.

"Well, I'm ready. Take me back," he said as he slurped his coffee.

Myles took a sip of coffee and gently placed his mug on a coaster kept handy on his boss's desk. "Well, Myles," started. "Sunday was a crazy day. I broke up with Debbie."

"So far, so good," John Brimmer teased.

Myles cracked a smile before continuing, "Whenever I have something weighing heavy on my mind, I go see my grandmother. I planned this chance meeting by attending church services at Bethel AME."

"I know it well. That's where I met my wife."

"After church, we went to brunch and I ended up at her place where I confided in her about the investigation," Myles revealed.

John Brimmer stared at Myles for several minutes. Myles became uncomfortable and looked away while awaiting his boss's reaction. Soon he heard a low chuckle coming from his boss's direction. Soon both men were engulfed in laughter.

"Tell me, Myles. What made you reveal this to your grand-mother?" inquired his boss.

"Honestly, yesterday was crazier than Sunday. Agents McBride and Simmons accompanied me to lunch where they proceeded to inform me that they knew that I had broken it off with Debbie. They also revealed the bugging of her condo. Do you know how many times I have been to her place?"

John Brimmer held up his hands in protest. "I really don't want to know your private business."

"I guess that was a bit much," surmised Myles. "Anyway, these two agents tell me that they want me to get back in touch with Debbie and apologize. McBride was a little more forceful than Simmons as she told me to do whatever I need to do to get back in Debbie's good graces."

John Brimmer folded his arms over his stomach and leaned back in his chair in deep thought. He thought back to the day the Department of Justice contacted him about the mayor's office being under investigation and that two of their agents would need to use one of his offices. His thoughts floated to the day that Myles told him about the files Agents McBride and Simmons asked for. They stayed for hours after work pouring over the files looking for anything that might help him connect the dots. The only thing they learned was that the same firms that were consistently awarded city contracts were clients of his. Over the years, his firm profited from this business relationship but nothing more. John Brimmer was pulled away from his thoughts when he heard Myles say something about being under investigation.

"I'm sorry, Myles, did you say there is another investigation?"

Myles looked at John Brimmer for a beat before repeating, "I was informed that the reason they are here is to keep an eye on me. Because of my relationship with Debbie, I am also under investigation. Well, let me be clear on that. I was under investigation until they realized that I know absolutely nothing about the suspected pay-to-play scheme going on in the mayor's office."

His boss leaned forward and placed both elbows on his desk. "Isn't it horrible what the love of money will do to people? Take Debbie for example. She is beautiful, smart, and accomplished. She would not be on the DOJ's radar if she were not getting her palms greased. I always felt that something was a little shady about the mayor, but could not quite put my finger on it," he said. "Finish telling me about why they want you to get back in Debbie's good graces."

"They need to know how far up corruption goes in the mayor's office. If I can get her to talk about how she awards the contracts, why the same companies keep getting awarded city contracts, and especially how the mayor fits into this scenario, then the FBI can move in," explained Myles.

"Better you than me," said his boss. "Just be careful. Debbie did not get as far as she has by being careless. You don't want her to sniff out a setup," he cautioned.

"Got it. By the way, she called me last night. I wasn't in the mood to answer the phone, so she left a message on my answering machine. From her message, I think I might have an opportunity to get back into her good graces before the end of this week. I told McBride and Simmons to give me a couple of days to mull it over and I would report back on my decision."

John Brimmer looked up when he heard the ding of the elevator. He got up and closed the door to decrease the chance of anyone overhearing their conversation.

"Would you like to hear what I think?" Brimmer asked while returning to his chair.

"Sure."

"I would not wait too long before calling her back. I know men nowadays like to take their time before they call back. They don't want to appear desperate. However, if you want her to let you back in without a second thought, return with all humility. Tell her that you made a terrible mistake and that you started to call her on Monday but was embarrassed by how you treated her. Tell her that you are so sorry that you hurt her and that she did not deserve the treatment she received."

"Wow!"

"You are probably thinking that a real man would never be so open, right?" stated his boss.

"Uh, I was thinking something along those lines," admitted Myles.

"Well, young buck, news flash. A real man is always open and honest with not only the lady in his life, but with all things. It says a lot about the character of the man."

Myles considered the sage advice received from his boss. He felt honored to have a man in his life like John Brimmer. Growing up with a father that was incarcerated most of his life, Myles depended greatly on his grandparents for guidance. After the tragic loss of his grandfather, all he had was his grandmother. He smiled as he thought of their late-night conversations about his friends, sports, hobbies, and girlfriends. She never sugarcoated anything. She would tell him all the time that she was not going to be in his life forever and that he would soon navigate this life minus her. Secretly, he wished she would always be there for late-night conversations.

"Well, Myles, thanks for bringing me into your confidence. It is good to know that Agents McBride and Simmons have come to realize that the only thing you are guilty of is falling for a pretty face. You are not the only man guilty of that and you will not be the last."

"Thanks, John, for allowing me to unburden myself."

"Any time, Myles. My wife and I never got around to having children. I hope you don't mind if I think of you as the son I never had."

Myles looked at his boss with tears threatening to well up in his eyes. "I'm honored that you think of me that way."

"Well, now that we've gotten that out of the way, get to work," his boss said in an attempt to lighten the mood.

Myles arose from the chair and walked with a new sense of purpose back to his office. With the conversation he just had with John Brimmer fresh in his mind, he entered his office closing the door behind him. He sat down at his desk and reached for the phone.

"Hello, this is Debbie Adderly."

"Hello, Debbie Adderly. This is Myles Beyers."

"Hello, Mr. Beyers. What can I do for you?"

"Well, Ms. Adderly, would you do me the honor of meeting me after work? I thought about what you said, and you are right. I owe you an explanation for my poor manners on Sunday."

"I am not available this evening. However, there is an opening on my calendar for tomorrow say around six-thirty."

"Debbie, for what it's worth… I am so sorry I hurt you. You did not deserve the treatment you got from me. My behavior was shameful. If I could hold you in my arms right now and take it all back, I would. Thank you for agreeing to see me. I will be waiting for you in front of City Hall tomorrow. Talk to you later."

She sat holding the telephone in her hand as tears streamed down her face. If only he knew how much she loved him she mused. She wanted to spend the rest of her life with him. Now more than ever she needed to make this her last kickback. Soon the three of them would be living a life of luxury in Turks and Caicos. How could Myles refuse to leave New York once she talked to him about living a carefree life in the islands? Finally, all the things she desired had found their way into her life. She would have the man she dearly loved as well as enough money to live the life of luxury she always dreamed of. She hung up the phone, grabbed her makeup bag and walked down the hall to the restroom.

Myles got up from his desk and headed toward the office occupied by Agents McBride and Simmons. He knocked on the door and waited to be granted entrance.

Myles entered the office closing the door behind him. "Good morning! I thought I would let you know that I called Debbie this morning and set up a time to meet with her tomorrow evening."

Agent Simmons was the first to congratulate Myles. "That's great news!"

Agent McBride gave Myles a sly smile before offering, "Yeah, that's great news!"

Myles took a couple of steps backward before turning and exiting the office. He knew the objective of the assignment; however, he still could not get his brain wrapped around the fact that Debbie was caught up in such corruption. *Whatever happened to good, honest work*, he thought to himself. It might take you a little longer to reach the finish line, but it keeps you off the street and out of trouble is the advice his grandmother gave to him.

Myles returned to his office followed closely by Gloria. She sat down in one of the office chairs flanking his desk.

"So what's going on with the agents and you?"

"Can't talk to you about it right now. I have a lot to do. But you can make lunch reservations for the both of us. It doesn't matter where. It's your treat."

Gloria stared at him as if he had three heads.

"Okay, so that means I will be using the company credit card, right?"

Myles looked up from the paperwork on his desk and smiled. "I was kidding."

"You were kidding about which part? The 'lunch is on me' part, or the 'I don't care where' part?"

"Hmm…the 'I don't care where' part. Of course, I am paying for lunch."

"Will twelve-thirty work for you?"

Myles quickly checked his calendar. "Make the reservation for one o'clock. Pull the door closed when you leave."

Myles leaned back in his office chair and thought about the agents pulling him back in to assist with the investigation. It left him with a feeling of betrayal but did not know yet how to get around this. He had deep feelings for Debbie, but his hands were tied.

Gloria knocked on his door and informed him that she made reservations at a restaurant two blocks away from the office. They could leave at twelve forty-five and still make their one o'clock reservation.

Myles felt the walk would do him good as he had been sitting at his desk for hours. He needed to get away from the office, stretch his legs, get some fresh air.

"I have one other thing to do before we head out to lunch," he said. "It will not take me long."

"Okay, but don't forget our reservation is for one o'clock."

"Wait for me at the elevator," instructed Myles as he ran down the hall and disappeared into a colleague's office.

Gloria pushed the elevator button when she saw Myles sprinting down the hall toward her. Just as he reached the bank of elevators, the door opened.

They exited the building and Gloria looked at her watch. She was happy to see that they had ten minutes to walk the two blocks to the restaurant. She attempted to make small talk on the way to the restaurant.

"So how was your weekend?"

"It was the craziest weekend!" exclaimed Myles.

"What made it so crazy?"

"Why don't we talk about this over a nice meal?" suggested Myles.

They arrived at the restaurant with five minutes to spare. The hostess greeted them as they entered the restaurant.

"Hello, welcome to Sassy's," the hostess said with a smile.

"Hi. We have a one o'clock reservation," said Gloria.

"Can I have a name for the reservation?" asked the hostess.

"Gloria Reid," she replied.

"Follow me, please."

The hostess could not have placed them at a more private table. "Enjoy your lunch. Your waitress will be with you shortly," she added.

Myles slowly perused the menu while Gloria drummed her fingers on the table, stealing side glances at him. He smiled on the inside as Gloria's impatience grew. The waitress appeared with two glasses of water just as Gloria framed her mouth with her first question.

"Have you decided what you want, or do you need a little more time?" asked the petite waitress. She looked as if she could not be any older than twelve.

She looked at Gloria who answered, "Yes. I will have the watercress salad with a slice of lemon, please."

"And for you, sir?" the petite waitress asked.

"I will have the shrimp scampi with a small house salad."

"Will the house vinaigrette dressing be okay on your salad?" she asked.

"Perfect!" exclaimed Myles.

The petite waitress took their menus and stopped at the table across from them to take another diner's lunch order before mixing in with numerous wait staff.

"Okay," Myles started. "I know you want to know what's going on. I know this because you are having trouble sitting still in your seat."

Gloria chuckled slightly before replying, "You know me too well. So tell me what happened when you went out to lunch on Monday?"

Myles leaned across the table toward Gloria prompting her to do the same. Myles lowered his voice to just above a whisper, "I broke it off with Debbie on Sunday."

Gloria leaned back in her seat with a confused look on her face. "What does your breakup with Debbie have to do with you going out to lunch with the twin agents yesterday?"

Myles motioned for Gloria to lean back in toward him. "They strongly suggested that I apologize and somehow get back in her good graces."

"Why?" asked Gloria. "Honestly, I'm having trouble following this conversation," she continued.

Myles was having too much fun. He conceded and said, "Okay, I will give you the blow-by-blow. I just wanted to see you squirm a little bit."

"You are a horrible person, Myles Beyers? You are lucky I like working with you, otherwise I would get up and walk out of this restaurant. Also, my letter of resignation would be waiting on your desk when you returned."

"No, Gloria. You wouldn't do that," said Myles.

Gloria folded her arms across her chest feigning anger. It only lasted for a couple of minutes before they both broke out into laughter.

"In all seriousness, this is what is going on. I found out yesterday that the real reason the Department of Justice placed Agents McBride and Simmons next to me is to keep an eye on me. By that I mean that I was under investigation along with certain people in the mayor's office."

"Is this because of your relationship with Debbie?" she asked.

"Bingo!" he replied.

"Wait! So did you really break up with Debbie?" she asked.

"Yep. I broke up with her on Sunday. And before you ask, they already knew about it."

"How?"

"Her condo is bugged."

Gloria sat back in her seat trying to process what she had just heard.

"Is that the only place they bugged?" she asked.

Myles's eyes grew wide. "That's a good question. I wonder if my apartment is bugged."

"I guess there is no need to bug your office, right?" she questioned.

The waitress returned with their lunch orders. "Here you go, watercress salad with a slice of lemon for the lady and shrimp scampi with a small house salad for the gentleman. Can I get you anything else?" inquired their waitress.

"No," they answered in unison.

They ate their lunch in silence. The waitress returned with the check and Myles quickly provided her with his charge card. She took it and returned shortly with the credit card slip and his card.

On their way back to the office, Gloria was going over everything in her head.

"How did Debbie take the breakup?" she asked.

"Not very well."

"Why did they suggest you get back with her?"

"They suspect she is involved in the play-to-pay scheme in the mayor's office."

"Wow, this is better than watching those detective shows on television," exclaimed Gloria.

Myles held the lobby door for her as they returned to work. They walked across the lobby to the bank of elevators in silence. Gloria pushed the button to summon the elevator. When it arrived, they stepped onto the elevator and rode in brief silence to the executive level.

"Myles, did you suspect you were under investigation before they informed you?"

Myles looked at Gloria and motioned for her to follow him down the hall to the kitchen. "Yes, I did. One night I stayed late to catch up on some work. I was standing in the kitchen when I overhead them talking about the investigation. I guess they thought everyone had gone home for the evening. In any event, I heard Debbie's name mentioned as well as mine."

Gloria stood there in disbelief.

"They believe that I can get her to open up about her job within the mayor's office and, hopefully, get her to talk about this pay-to-play scheme."

"Don't you think she might be a little suspicious?" asked Gloria. "I know I would."

"Yeah, I thought about that too. However, she called me last night. I didn't answer the phone and allowed it to roll over to the answering machine."

Gloria stared at him for a beat before asking, "Was she crying?"

"No."

"So what did she say?"

"In so many words…I owe her an explanation."

Gloria chuckled. "I like her."

"Come on…let's go back to work before the day gets away from us," he said.

Myles noticed that McBride and Simmons were not in the office when he returned. He made a mental note to stop by their office before leaving for the day. He and Gloria glanced at each other before he entered his office and closed the door. She understood that what she learned today should not be shared with anyone outside of the four people who had been made aware of the investigation.

The rest of the day went by quickly. Gloria looked at the clock on the wall. It was five minutes before quitting time. She straightened up her desk, making a to-do list for the next day. She got up and knocked lightly on the office door belonging to Myles.

"Come in, Gloria," he said.

"I'm getting ready to leave for the evening. Do you need anything before I leave?"

"No. Have an enjoyable evening with your family. I'll see you tomorrow."

"Okay. By the way, Agents Simmons and McBride are in the office. They returned about an hour ago," informed Gloria.

"Thanks. Have a good evening."

Gloria passed Mr. Brimmer in the hall as she was leaving. "Goodbye, Mr. Brimmer. Have a good evening."

"Goodbye, Gloria. Is Myles still in his office?" he asked.

"Yes, he is."

"Thank you," he said as he hurried toward Myles's office.

John Brimmer could not wait to share the good news with Myles. As he turned the corner, he heard voices coming from Myles's office. He noticed that the door was slightly ajar, so he inclined his ear to better hear what was being said. Agents McBride and Simmons were speaking in hushed tones. It wasn't habit for him to eavesdrop; however, with the ongoing investigation of the mayor's office, he felt it was his duty to engage just this once.

After a couple of minutes, he elected to knock on the door. Since the door was ajar, he decided to open the door slightly and stick his head in.

"Oh, I'm sorry," he said apologetically. "I did not mean to interrupt."

Myles motioned for him to come further into the office. "You are not interrupting."

"Agent Simmons and I were just leaving," McBride said while getting up from her seat.

"Good evening, gentlemen," Agent Simmons said while following McBride out of the office.

"How long were you standing there?" he asked John Brimmer.

"About five minutes," he replied.

His boss snapped his fingers as he remembered why he was in a rush to talk to Myles. "I have good news to share," he sang.

Myles reclined in his chair and with a sly smile said, "Do tell."

"About a week ago, I was attending a fundraising event for Freeman Children's Hospital. I noticed a lady there who I could not take my eyes off. She moved with confidence and grace. To be perfectly honest, she reminded me of my late wife. She was soft-spoken as was my wife. All the time I was at this fundraiser, I watched as she moved through the crowd stopping to talk to people. Then it happened."

"What happened?" asked Myles.

"I was standing by the bar when I heard the sweetest voice behind me."

"The suspense is killing me," said Myles.

"I could not believe my good fortune."

"So what did this mystery woman say?"

She walked up behind me and said, "John Brimmer, I presume." I turned around with my fake looking mixed drink of ginger ale with a slice of lime and said, "You're good. How did you know who I was? That's when she informed me that it was her job to know the faces and names of those she invited to all fundraisers."

"No. Don't tell me that the mystery woman is Aubrey DeLoach!" exclaimed Myles.

"That's exactly what I am telling you," answered John Brimmer.

"Aubrey DeLoach is a philanthropist," continued Myles.

"I know," said John Brimmer excitedly.

Myles offered a verbal pat on the back, "Wow! I'm impressed John. So what does this mean for the firm?"

"Currently, it doesn't mean anything for the firm. That's what I came to tell you. She called me up and invited me to dinner. Of course, we both had to check our schedules but finally agreed on Sunday."

Myles reached across the desk and shook his boss's hand. "If anyone can hook her as a client, you can. The last time I checked, she was worth $42 billion and counting!"

Myles checked the time. "I wish I could stay here and strategize with you a little longer. However, I promised Debbie that I would meet her at six. It's a good thing City Hall is right across the street."

"That's fine. I think I will also pack up and head home," said John Brimmer. "Have a good evening."

"You too," said Myles.

As promised, Myles was standing outside City Hall as Debbie exited the building. He stood staring at her as she walked toward him. She is so beautiful he thought to himself. The soft pink dress she wore played nicely off her brown skin. As she walked toward him, he noticed that she was wearing her hair up with soft wisps of hair framing her face and the back of her neck. In all the time he was with her, he never saw her with her hair up, it was always down. He focused on her delicate neck and high cheekbones. Her eyes held his with a hold that was relentless. He told McBride and Simmons that he was committed to getting her to talk, but as he looked at Debbie, he wasn't so sure he could go through with it. How could he help put this vision of loveliness in prison?

"Debbie," he started. He just wanted to stand there soaking in her beauty for all eternity.

Debbie walked up and took his hand in hers. She looked up into his eyes and knew instantly that he felt remorse. But for what was yet to be determined.

"Hungry?" she asked softly. "I made reservations at Montrachet."

Myles was familiar with this restaurant. He did a quick calculation in his head as he was still more than a week out from payday. Debbie was not going to make this easy for him, he thought to himself. Next time, he would make dinner reservations at Myles's Kitchen and Bistro. He would be prepared to do all the cooking. But for tonight, he would allow her to have her fun.

They arrived at the restaurant and were seated at a table with a picture-perfect view of the New York skyline. Myles reached across the table and took Debbie's hands in his. He looked into her light brown almond-shaped eyes and apologized again for the way he tried to end their relationship.

"Myles, I'm not going to sit here and pretend that I understand what happened because I don't. One day we are the happy couple and the next day you are ending our relationship. I feel like there is something or someone else fueling your decisions."

"No there is no one else. Since we have been together, I have been faithful to you."

Debbie withdrew her hands from his and stared out at the sky-line. "Then, tell me. What caused the sudden shift in your feelings toward me? And before you answer, let me caution you. Do not lie to me. You owe me at least that much."

Myles reflected on the advice given by John Brimmer. He reached and took Debbie's hands in his. "Debbie with all sincerity, I apologize. I made a terrible mistake. When you left a message on my answering machine, I was so happy to hear your voice. I started to call you the following day but was embarrassed by how I treated you. I wish I could take back the hurt I caused. And you are right, you did not deserve any of that. When I think back to that day, I am so ashamed of myself. I don't know what got into me. You're right. I do owe you an explanation. When I saw you walking toward me today, I knew at that precise moment I had made the biggest mistake in life by pushing you away. Can you find it in your heart to forgive me?"

A single tear flowed down Debbie's cheek. Myles reached up and gently wiped it away. He inhaled her beauty as he brought her hands up to his lips and softly kissed them. He gazed deeply into her eyes and whispered, "I promise that I will handle your heart with care from this day forward."

They were so engulfed with the essence of one another they did not observe the wait staff standing there. Myles kept his eyes fixed on Debbie as the wait staff proceeded to place their dinner on the table.

"Enjoy your dinner," said the waiter as he turned and walked away.

As if Debbie could read his mind, she looked up and with a smile explained, "I called ahead and placed our orders. The Chef's Special on Tuesday night is to die for."

Debbie picked up the utensils scooping up a small portion of the special. As she raised the fork to her mouth, she heard Myles clear his throat. He was sitting there with his hands extended toward hers. She wasn't sure what to do.

"Give me your hands," instructed Myles.

Debbie did what he asked and observed as Myles bowed his head in prayer. She gazed around the restaurant uncomfortably to see if anyone was watching. After determining that no one was looking at them, only then did she conform. With eyes open, she bowed her head slightly and waited for him to finish. This was new to her as she and her mother never attended church or prayed over their meals.

Myles lifted his head and reached for the utensils. "This looks delicious! Debbie, you never cease to amaze me."

Debbie looked at him and smiled. She wondered in amazement at her good fortune. In her short time on this earth, no man had ever moved her the way Myles did. At that precise moment, she resolved in her heart to let the events of the past several days go. It did not matter to her that Myles attempted to walk away from their relationship. He had asked for forgiveness, and she was determined to do just that. Her heart would not allow her to do anything otherwise. The only thing that mattered to her was that he was back in her life.

They finished their dinner in silence; each caught up in their thoughts.

After dinner, Myles and Debbie stood outside of the restaurant awaiting the arrival of their cars.

"I wonder how far the valets had to go to retrieve our cars," pondered Debbie.

Myles laughed slightly as he had wondered the same thing. It was taking longer than usual to retrieve their cars. He silently watched as Debbie pretended to be upset.

"Debbie," called Myles.

"Yes, Myles."

"Can I kiss you?"

"What? Why are you asking me if you can kiss me? You have never asked before," protested Debbie.

Moving toward Debbie, Myles took her in his arms and kissed her deeply. He released her just as the valets arrived with their cars.

Debbie stepped back from him and took her car keys from the valet. "I will call you tomorrow," she called over her shoulder. Myles watched as the taillights of her car disappeared into the night.

Myles over tipped the valets and drove away.

Detective Stephenson emerged from the restaurant handing the valet his ticket. He determined there was no need to surveille them tonight as he had captured their entire conversation. Judging from what he observed, he wasn't sure what side Myles Beyers was on. He made a mental note to discuss his concerns with Agents McBride and Simmons. But as for tonight, he was headed home for some well-deserved shut-eye.

Myles arrived at the office early again the following morning. With thoughts of Debbie still fresh on his mind, he ran into Simmons and McBride as he exited the elevator.

"Good morning, Myles," said Simmons.

"Good morning to you as well, Agent Simmons…Agent McBride. You two are here early. What's the occasion?" he inquired.

"It's good that you are in the office early," said McBride. She scanned the corridor before motioning for Myles to follow them into their office.

"Please have a seat," McBride said while extending a hand toward a chair nearest her.

Agent Simmons sat on the edge of the desk. There was a small paperweight that he failed to notice before. It held his attention for several minutes before he became painfully aware of the tension in the air. He looked at Myles who was eyeing him with great uncertainty. "Myles, how are things going with Debbie Adderly?" he asked as he inspected the paperweight.

"Well, she and I had dinner together last night. But I'm sure you already knew that," responded Myles.

McBride sat quietly with her legs crossed. With interlaced fingers, she considered the intel Detective Stephenson provided late last night. She mused of all the ways Myles could be playing them. Stephenson wasn't sure what side of the fence felt more comfortable to Myles. The only way to find out was to put all their cards on the table. She had to know for sure where Myles stood.

"Myles," started McBride. "You have been dating Debbie Adderly for close to a year. You two have spent a great deal of time together, I'm sure. You appear to be quite smitten with her. Am I on the right track?"

"I'm not sure where you are going with this, but I assure…"

"Let me stop you right there, Myles," said McBride.

"Your assurance is definite. The reason it is definite is because of our conversation several days ago. We informed you that you were under investigation. We did not have to reveal that to you. However, after careful evaluation, surveillance and strategically placed listening devices, we concluded there was no way that you could be involved. What we need from you, Myles, is for you to keep your word. Do not…and I repeat…do not allow your deep feelings for her to cloud your judgment. Are we clear?"

"Crystal," Myles said with a little edge in his voice.

Myles was fuming inside. He could not believe these agents were talking to him like he was a child. He was a grown man and they were too involved in his personal life. The investigation, Debbie's involvement, and the possibility of losing Debbie to potential prison time was weighing heavily on him. If there was a way to save Debbie from all of this, he would.

"Are we done?" he asked while looking between both agents.

"Yes," replied McBride.

Myles got up from his seat and stormed into his office. He closed the door behind him but was wound too tight to sit down. He paced back and forth for several minutes before stopping to take in the panoramic view of the city. His thoughts turned to Debbie, but it was too soon to call her. He walked over to his desk and scribbled "set up a meet with Debbie" on his calendar.

He grabbed his coffee mug and headed toward the kitchen. He was walking back to his office when he noticed Gloria exiting the elevator.

"Good morning, Myles," she said. "How are you today?"

Myles gave her a frustrated look.

"That good, huh?" she said jokingly.

"If I kept a bottle in my desk, something else would be in this mug besides coffee," he reasoned.

"Well, it's a good thing there isn't," replied Gloria. "By the way, how did things go with Debbie last night?"

"You sound like them," said Myles disappearing into his office.

Gloria placed her things on her desk and followed him into his office. "So is that why you are on edge? I think I will go have a talk with them," she concluded.

"No, don't do that, Gloria," cautioned Myles. "Let me handle this."

Gloria looked at her boss and could not help but think that he was way in over his head. From her first day at this firm, he treated her with respect and kindness. She could not help but have a sisterly affection toward him. If she felt that anyone was taking advantage of him, she was quick to point it out. Yes, she could be a little out-spoken, but she also knew when to stand down. This was a time to stand down.

"Okay, well if you need anything, let me know," she said with a smile.

"Oh, before you leave, I think we might be getting another client."

"Really, who might this client be?" she asked.

"Are you familiar with Aubrey DeLoach?" Myles asked.

"The philanthropist!" she exclaimed. "Anyone who is not familiar with Aubrey DeLoach is living under a rock!"

Myles let out a hardy laugh at Gloria's assessment.

"Well, it's not engraved in stone but the 'big guy' was at a fundraiser for Freeman Children's Hospital a few days ago and ran into her. To be clear, she introduced herself to him. She called him yesterday to set up a meeting. And that meeting takes place this Sunday? How 'bout them apples?" Myles said enthusiastically.

"Can you imagine having her as a client?" asked Gloria.

"Well, keep this to yourself until it is official," admonished Myles.

"Will do," assured Gloria.

Gloria bounced out of Myles's office. She had always wanted to meet the great Aubrey DeLoach. If Mr. Brimmer were successful in bringing her on as a client, things would certainly change for the firm. Mr. Brimmer had done wonderfully over the years for the firm as well as his employees. With Aubrey DeLoach as a client, he would probably have to hire more people, she mused.

"Gloria, if you don't get your mind off of Aubrey DeLoach," she whispered to herself. "You've got work to do."

She sat at her desk with her chin placed squarely in her left palm staring at the agents as they moved around the office. If they only knew what Myles has gone through. How many young children witness their father killing their mother? His formative years with his mother and father were truncated by a senseless act brought on by jealousy. Because of Mr. Beyers' incarceration, he never got a chance to bond with his son, Gloria mused.

She was still reflecting on Myles's life when suddenly Valerie appeared at her desk. "Good morning, Gloria," she said with a broad smile.

"Good morning, Valerie," she sang. "To what do I owe the honor?"

"Do you have plans for lunch?"

"Not yet."

"Good. How about you and I go out to lunch?"

"Sure. What time?"

"I'm not free until one o'clock today. Mr. Brimmer has meetings up until twelve forty-five. I can go to lunch after that."

"I will let Myles know that I will be going to lunch a little later today. I don't think he will mind."

"Okay, see you then."

Valerie and Gloria left the office promptly at one o'clock. They had not been to lunch together in weeks and were excited to catch up. They walked around the corner to Jessie's Café and found a table in the center of the restaurant. From their vantage point, they could take note of all the activity in the restaurant.

Valerie and Gloria placed their purses on the empty chair separating them. "All right, give me the 411," pressed Valerie.

"Well, all I can tell you is that things are starting to heat up," stated Gloria.

"What do you mean by heat up?" inquired Valerie.

"Well, Myles tried to break it off with Debbie. The agents found out about it and told Myles to get back into her good graces. After a couple of days, Myles complied, and he went to dinner with Debbie yesterday. However, this morning Myles was a little put out with McBride and Simmons," Gloria revealed in a single breath.

"Why? What do you think happened?" asked Valerie.

"I'm not sure. Oh, did I forget to mention that they placed listening devices in Debbie's condo and the reason the agents are using an office at our firm is because Myles was under investigation too?"

Valerie gasped. "That's crazy!" she exclaimed.

Gloria sighed, "I know. Poor Myles. He is under so much stress."

"So do you think this investigation is going to wrap up soon?" asked Valerie.

"I sure hope so. I don't know how much more Myles can take," responded Gloria.

Soon a waitress appeared with menus and two glasses of water with a small plate of lemon slices and bread.

"Good afternoon, ladies," said the bubbly waitress. "My name is Samantha and I will be taking your orders when you are ready."

"Thank you," Gloria and Valerie said in unison. Both perused the menu and quickly made their selections.

The waitress returned to take their orders. "I will have the Caesar salad with chicken and my friend the broccoli cheddar soup with a small green salad."

"Thank you, ladies," the bubbly waitress said while taking their menus.

Debbie rushed back to her office after a long meeting with Glen and Mayor Stevens. Her phone rang just as she entered her office.

"Hello, this is Debbie Adderly," she said.

"Meet me at Jessie's Café," instructed the voice on the other end.

"I thought I told you never to call me at work. You have my pager number, use it!" reprimanded Debbie. "Can this wait until later, I'm really busy right now," continued Debbie.

"Ten minutes," said the voice on the other end. "Bring an envelope with you." The line went dead.

Debbie quickly scanned her calendar. She did not have another meeting until four o'clock. She picked up her purse and headed out of the office toward the bank. She entered the bank and withdrew five hundred dollars. This was less than what she typically gave him for information, but this would have to do until she heard what he had to say.

Debbie walked into Jessie's Café and scanned the restaurant looking for her contact. He was sitting with his back toward the wall at a table at the far end of the restaurant. His eyes were trained on the door and immediately saw Debbie as she entered the restaurant. He wasn't the only one that saw her.

"Don't look now but Debbie Adderly just walked in," Gloria whispered to her co-worker.

"How do you know it's her?" asked Valerie.

"I've seen her standing behind Mayor Stevens when he has given press conferences," explained Gloria. "She's walking toward us, so act natural."

When Debbie walked by their table Gloria and Valerie were engaged in conversation. "Without drawing attention to yourself, I want you to tell me who she is having lunch with," instructed Gloria.

"Okay...but I'm nervous. What if that guy she's having lunch with notices me? He looks a little worldly," suggested Valerie.

"You will be fine. Pick up your soup spoon and eat your soup. It is easier to steal glances when your head is bowed," said Gloria.

"I think you have been watching too many detective shows," said Valerie.

"Well, I would change seats with you but that would be too obvious," explained Gloria.

Debbie sat down at the table with her contact. "So were you successful in digging anything up on Michelle Jenkins?" she asked.

"Not yet. She appears to be squeaky clean but I'm sure there is something. I just haven't overturned the right rock yet."

"Well then, I'm confused. Why did you ask me to meet you here? Better yet, why did you ask me to bring an envelope with me?" Debbie asked.

"Before we get into all of that, slide the envelope my way."

"Valerie, what are they doing?" inquired Gloria.

"It looks like she is taking something out of her purse. It's an envelope. You know the kind you get from the bank when you make a withdrawal. She is sliding it across the table to him!" exclaimed Valerie.

Debbie's contact discretely takes the envelope and looks inside. "This is a little light," he said.

"That's all I could get on such short notice. There's more depending on information provided," assured Debbie.

Her contact took the envelope and placed it in his left jacket pocket while Debbie sat patiently waiting on the information she had just paid for.

He leaned in toward her and whispered, "I'm going to need you to watch your back. Word on the street is the mayor's office is under investigation," he said.

"Under investigation?" she said. "For what? Why do I need to watch my back?" questioned Debbie.

"According to my source, your name was mentioned."

A look of panic came across Debbie's face. Suddenly she felt like the walls were closing in on her. She needed fresh air and longed for the island breeze of Turks and Caicos. If what her contact said was true about the mayor's office being under investigation, she would need to put her plans in motion sooner rather than later. It was time for her to leave New York.

"There's more," offered her contact.

"More? Tell me," she begged.

"Meet me tonight at the regular spot around ten o'clock. Bring another envelope with you. I will do a little more digging to find out how much information they have. Look, I've known you since we were kids back in the neighborhood. I don't want to see anything bad happen to you, so I am going to need you to have your wits about you. I can feed you intel, but I can't be there with you."

"I understand." Debbie arose from her seat and exited the restaurant. As she walked back to work, she reflected on the information she just received. Had it not been for greed, she would have left New York years ago. However, the money kept coming and she was finally living the life she always dreamed of living. *How could the life I so carefully constructed begin to crumble?* she thought.

When she arrived back at her office, she immediately called her real estate agent and set up a time to meet. The time had arrived to place the condo on the market. She had to move quickly if she were going to escape New York. She had decided not to say anything to Glen or Mayor Stevens. The impending election, rumors of an investigation, dirty reelection campaigns and being told to award the same companies with contracts year after year was beginning to weigh heavy on her. This is not the life she envisioned for herself. How did she allow herself to be drawn into this cycle of deception and greed?

Gloria and Valerie watched as Debbie's lunch date left the restaurant. They paid for their meal and hurried back to the office.

"This is getting crazier by the moment," insisted Valerie.

"It sure is," agreed Gloria.

"Well, I am going to tell Myles what we witnessed. I think Agents McBride and Simmons should know as well."

"Okay. Keep me posted," said Valerie as she headed back to her office.

Myles was sitting at his desk eating his lunch when Gloria returned. She knocked on the door. "Come in." He stopped eating when Gloria entered. "How was your lunch with Valerie?" he inquired.

"Well, we went to Jessie's Café for lunch," she started. "While we were there, Debbie walked in."

"Oh yeah," Myles said half-heartedly. "She probably had a lunch date."

"Yeah, one can say that," suggested Gloria.

Myles looked at Gloria suspiciously. "I feel like there is something you want to say," he said cautiously. "So I would suggest you come right out with it."

"She was there with a guy. I was sitting with my back to them, so I asked Valerie to inform me of what they were doing."

"What did the guy look like?" he asked.

"Valerie described him as worldly," replied Gloria.

"Worldly? In other words, this isn't a guy you would find in the Boardroom," he surmised.

"Exactly!" agreed Gloria.

"What else did you and Valerie witness?" he asked.

"A bank envelope being pushed across the table. He took the envelope and placed it in his jacket pocket. Valerie said he leaned in toward her as if they were afraid of being overheard."

Myles took the napkin and wiped his mouth. "Well, she does work for a politician and the elections are coming up. You've seen the smear campaigns coming out of that office, haven't you? I'm not 100 percent sure about this, but I would imagine that she is paying for information. C'mon. Let's go see McBride and Simmons. I think this is something of which we need to make them aware?"

"I think Valerie should go with us," suggested Gloria. "After all, she was the one who witnessed the activity between Debbie and the 'worldly' guy. I did not want them to get spooked. If I had turned around, they would have gotten suspicious."

Myles eyed Gloria and asked, "Are you a detective in your spare time?"

"No. I just like watching detective shows," confessed Gloria.

166

"Okay. Call Valerie and have her join us."

Several minutes later, Valerie joined her coworkers.

Agent McBride looked at the three entering the office with slight amusement. "What's going on?" she asked.

"Well, these two ladies would like to inform you of something they witnessed while at lunch today," said Myles.

McBride and Simmons focused their attention on Valerie and Gloria. "What did you witness? Does it pertain to the investigation?"

"I believe it does," replied Valerie.

"Okay," said Simmons. "What do you have for us?"

"We saw Debbie Adderly at Jessie's Café earlier. She met with a guy there," offered Gloria.

"Go on," urged McBride.

"I saw her take an envelope out of her purse and push it across the table toward the guy she was meeting with," continued Valerie.

"Do you know what was in the envelope?" asked Agent Simmons.

"No, but it appeared as though he looked inside the envelope before putting it in his jacket pocket," added Valerie.

"Thank you, ladies," said McBride. "This is all very useful information."

"I wish we had been close enough to hear their conversation," said Gloria.

"Okay, well, let's allow Agents McBride and Simmons to get back to work," expressed Myles.

As they turned to leave the office, McBride called out to Myles, "Can I talk to you for a minute?"

Valerie and Gloria turned and looked at Myles with concerned interest.

"Sure."

"Close the door behind you, please."

"Have a seat, Myles," instructed Simmons.

Myles was getting anxious. He was nervous enough about being pulled back into the investigation. He silently prayed that they would not ask him how he planned to get her to talk about why the same companies won city contracts. He was not prepared to be interrogated by these agents today.

"Myles, my partner and I want all of you to know how appreciative we are of the willingness to assist with this investigation. We know it has been frustrating at times as well as stressful. You, more than anyone else, have experienced the brunt of the stress. If we could have gotten around involving you, we would have. But when we found out that you and Debbie Adderly were an item and that you worked across the street from City Hall…well, you see where I am going with this, right? It was the perfect opportunity to have someone with an inside track to someone on our radar assist us. Honestly, we were not sure we would be able to convince you to help us out, given your relationship with Ms. Adderly."

Myles quietly processed everything Agent McBride was saying. But what really got his attention is when Agent Simmons revealed something that caused some of the pieces to this puzzle to come together.

"Myles, we would not be doing our job if we did not know Ms. Adderly's every move. We listen to her phone calls. We follow her so that we know dates, times, and names of those she meets with. Also, we were aware of her lunch meeting at Jessie's Café."

Myles sat up a little straighter in his chair.

"So why do you need me?" asked Myles. "I mean, if you are having her followed, what can I bring to the investigation?"

"You, my friend, can get closer to her than we can," explained Simmons.

"Myles, the guy she met with today informed her that the mayor's office is under investigation and she is as well," offered McBride. "I would suspect that she is going to begin to dismantle her life here in New York and possibly flee to another country. We must move quickly. We also know that she is meeting this guy later tonight as he promised her more information on the investigation. Valerie was correct in her observation. From what we have gathered, Debbie has been paying this guy for some time. He is behind the information received and used in ad campaigns against the mayoral candidates. It's unfortunate that she has gotten herself entangled in all of this, but that's why your help is so important to us. We must put an end to the corruption in that office. We owe it to the people of this great city."

Myles was finding it hard to believe what he was hearing. He could not believe that Debbie was a part of all of this. It didn't seem possible.

"Myles, the intel she received earlier today spooked her. Believe me when I say she is preparing to run and it's our job to make sure she doesn't leave New York."

Myles sat quietly in his seat listening intently as both agents took turns describing the activities of the woman he believed he knew. His thoughts floated back to his last conversation with Debbie. He remembered taking her hands in his and saying, "*I promise to handle your heart with care from this day forward.*" Those were his exact words. How could he keep that promise if she were preparing to, as the agents believed, leave New York? He was beginning to feel conflicted about his feelings toward Debbie and his role in the investigation. He wasn't sure about revealing this to Agents McBride and Simmons. He would just have to trust himself to get the job done. He wondered how Debbie would feel toward him if she discovered that he was working with the Department of Justice to bring her and others within the mayor's office to justice for a pay-to-play scheme?

"Well, I guess I've heard enough for today," said Myles as he arose from his seat. "I will give her a call and invite myself over to her place. You mentioned that she was meeting a guy at ten o'clock tonight, right?"

"That's correct," answered Simmons.

"I have a suggestion," said McBride. "Give her a call and see if she is available to take tomorrow off. Take breakfast to her. Spend the day with her. See if you can get her to talk about the contracts awarded to certain companies. Get back with me so that I can clear this with your boss."

"I don't need you scripting anything for me," Myles said indignantly.

McBride held up both hands. "Hey, it's just a suggestion. As a woman, I think I know what women like."

Myles opened the door and walked out. He was growing weary of this situation and could not wait for it to be over. He walked over to his desk and placed a call to Debbie. He was determined to see her tonight. If he had anything to do with it, this would not drag on any longer than necessary.

Debbie answered on the fourth ring. "Hello, Myles."

"Hello, Debbie. I'm glad to see that we are dispensing of formalities today."

She chuckled slightly.

"Hey, are you able to take tomorrow off?" asked Myles.

"Maybe. What do you have in mind?"

"I was thinking that you and I could spend some time together. It has been a while since we have gotten out of the city for a long drive," rationalized Myles.

Debbie weighed his request against the information she learned from her contact earlier. She really needed to move on getting her condo listed and sold. Even with these issues looming, she decided to take Myles up on his offer. She needed time away to clear her head, so she jumped at the chance to spend time with him.

"That sounds heavenly! What time should I expect you?" asked Debbie.

"Early. The more time we have together, the better," replied Myles.

"How early is early?" pushed Debbie.

"I will be at your place by nine-thirty tomorrow morning," he said.

"Wonderful! See you then." Debbie hung up the phone and immediately informed the mayor that she would be taking the following day off. He wasn't too pleased about it, but he also understood the need for a mental health break. They had been going nonstop for months and with the upcoming election, all of them were working overtime to ensure he would get reelected.

"Debbie, do you have any information on Michelle Jenkins yet?" asked the mayor.

"I'm meeting with my contact tonight. I will let you know if it is anything that can be used against her."

Mayor Stevens looked at Debbie thoughtfully. "Take Friday off as well and make it a long weekend. We have all been working long hours preparing for this election. Even if we don't get anything useful to use against Michelle Jenkins, I believe we have the election in the bag."

Debbie was grateful for the extra time off from work. "Thank you," she said.

Mayor Stevens smiled and returned his attention to the papers on his desk. Debbie didn't put much thought into his sudden shift in demeanor, she had other things to contend with. She picked up the phone and called her mother. The next call was to her realtor.

Simmons was in the office alone when the phone rang. "Hello, Agent Simmons speaking."

"Agent Simmons, we just learned that Debbie Adderly is putting her condo on the market. She just set up a meeting with her realtor for Friday afternoon. She also made a call to her mother."

"I guess it is safe to assume that she is spooked and preparing to run. Why did she call her mother?" asked Agent Simmons.

McBride entered the office while he was still on the phone.

"It appeared to be a social call," responded the agent on the other end.

"Okay. I need to bring McBride up to speed. One of us will get back with you soon with instruction on how to proceed."

"Roger that," said the agent.

McBride reclined in her office chair and waited for Simmons to bring her up to speed. "You were right in thinking that Debbie Adderly would make a move soon. I just received a call from the surveillance team who informed me that Debbie Adderly made a call to her realtor for Friday afternoon. She is putting her condo on the market. She also called her mother. According to surveillance, the call appeared to be social, but you and I know that she will not leave her mother behind when she leaves New York. That would be heartless."

McBride sat with her eyes closed while she processed the information received from her partner of six years. After remaining in that position for several minutes she opened her eyes and got up from her chair, pacing back and forth in front of the window before turning to her partner.

"She is meeting with her contact at ten o'clock tonight. We need to know what she knows. Get in touch with Stephenson and inform him that we need his services tonight. He is more familiar with their meeting place. Other than that, we would need him to escort our surveillance team to the meeting spot. I don't want to take a chance on the van being spotted. We stand a better chance with Stephenson."

"I'm on it. Do you have any instructions for the surveillance team?" asked Agent Simmons.

"Have you heard back from Myles yet?" inquired Agent McBride.

"Not yet."

"I believe I saw him in his office. Go ahead and put in a call to Stephenson; I will stop by Myles's office and have a chat with him."

McBride heard Simmons on the phone as she exited the office closing the door behind her. She noticed that the door to Myles's office was closed.

"Gloria, is Myles in his office?"

"Yes, but he is on the phone. Please have a seat and I will let him know you are waiting."

McBride took a seat and waited patiently for Myles to complete his call. It wasn't long after when Gloria picked up the phone and informed Myles that she was waiting. He opened the office door and motioned for McBride to come in. Behind closed doors, Myles and McBride discussed new developments in the investigation. There were so many unanswered questions, Myles mused. He silently wondered how much Debbie's contact was prepared to reveal.

"I thought I would let you know that Ms. Adderly is preparing to leave New York," said McBride. Our surveillance team listened in on a call she made to her realtor and to her mother this afternoon."

"Is her mother aware of her activities?" asked Myles.

"I don't believe so. It's my guess that she doesn't want to leave her mother behind," explained McBride. "So have you given any thought to how you are going to get her to open up about the pay-to-play scheme?"

"We talked earlier. I asked if she could take tomorrow off from work. She was receptive to my idea of getting out of the city for a few hours," offered Myles.

"Sounds good. Do I need to talk to your boss, or have you already discussed this with him?" asked McBride.

"Not yet, but I will. As a matter of fact, I will discuss this with him when we are done," disclosed Myles.

"Well, don't let me hold you up," McBride said as she arose from her seat and exited his office.

"Debbie, what have you done?" whispered Myles. He got up from his seat and walked toward John Brimmer's office.

Valerie looked up when she heard footsteps nearing the office. "Hello, Myles," she said.

"Hello, Valerie. Is the big guy in his office?"

"Yes, he is." She picked up the phone to announce Myles. "You can go in."

John Brimmer got up from his desk and moved toward the conference table when Myles walked in. "What can I do you for, young man?" asked his boss.

"I don't know if Valerie told you, but she and Gloria saw Debbie at Jessie's Café during lunch. According to McBride and Simmons, she was meeting with her contact who has been feeding her information on the mayoral candidates. What's even more interesting, he informed her today that she is under investigation."

"Wow! The plot keeps getting thicker and thicker," exclaimed John Brimmer.

"Tell me about it. The reason I am here is to let you know that I will be taking tomorrow and Friday off. Normally, I would go through proper channels, but McBride and Simmons have just learned that Debbie is putting her condo on the market and meeting with her realtor on Friday. Now that she knows she is under investigation, she is spooked," explained Myles.

"So that is why you need the next two days off," surmised his boss.

Myles nodded a slow yes.

"No worries. The sooner they wrap up this investigation, the sooner we can all get back to our normal lives."

"I cannot agree with you more," Myles said.

"Be careful, Myles. None of us knows how high up this goes. Really, I'm surprised your lady friend is helping them with uncovering intel on the candidates. That doesn't appear to be in her wheelhouse."

"I must admit that I am cautiously concerned about my time with her tomorrow. McBride is hoping that I can get her to talk about how she determines the criteria for awarding city contracts. There are two companies that consistently win city contracts," Myles said.

"In order for that to happen, someone is getting paid off. It's been known to happen, however, when elected officials abuse their power, they must be held accountable and there will be consequences," concluded John Brimmer.

Myles was instantly saddened by what the "big guy" said. He, too, knew that everyone involved must be held accountable and that there would be consequences. If he could spare Debbie the pain and humiliation, he would.

"Thanks for your understanding John," Myles said.

"We'll catch up next week. Both of us should have much to discuss as Aubrey DeLoach and I are meeting for brunch on Sunday. I should know more after meeting with her. Hopefully, she is considering having this firm manage her billions."

Myles smiled as he arose from his seat. "I hope everything goes according to plan. See you next week."

"Yep...enjoy your time off."

Myles looked at the clock on the wall of his office and wondered where the day went. The workday would end in thirty minutes and it appeared as though most of his day was centered around the investigation. John Brimmer was correct. The sooner this investigation concluded, the sooner they could all get back to normal.

In the thirty minutes left to the workday, he called Gloria into his office and informed her that he would be taking the next couple of days off.

"Is this related to the investigation?" she half-whispered.

Myles did not want to reveal any more than necessary, so he lied.

"No. I just need some time off," responded Myles.

"Okay. Well we all need mental health days," agreed Gloria.

Myles smiled at her comment. "I hear you," said Myles. "We will discuss it more in depth when I return to the office. Deal?"

"Deal," said Gloria.

It was quitting time, and everyone was shutting their operations down and heading for as many avenues of departure available to them. Myles looked around his office to make sure everything was in order before hitting the light switch and locking his office. As he walked down the hall, he reflected on the past few days and what lay ahead of him. The whirlwind of activity these past few days left him spent. Myles was relieved when he unlocked the door to his apartment and shut the world out.

Debbie hopped in her car and exited the parking garage. She did not have to meet her contact until ten o'clock. She kicked her shoes off as soon as she entered the condo. Poured herself a glass of wine and relaxed on the balcony. She closed her eyes and listened to the hustle and bustle of city sounds and longed for the peace and quiet of island life. Soon this will all be behind me, she ruminated. Soon she drifted off to sleep. She awoke to the sound of a blaring car horn and loud voices. The hands on the face of her watch illuminated nine o'clock. She had been asleep for several hours. She quickly changed into a pair of jeans, T-shirt, and flats. She pulled the envelope of money out of her purse and counted it once more before stuffing the envelope back in her purse and heading out the door.

Detective Stephenson had arrived an hour earlier than Debbie's meet time. He wanted to make sure he positioned himself so that he was not spotted and able to capture their conversation. Just as he was getting in position, he saw car headlights coming toward him. He dropped down as low as he could to the ground careful not to make any sudden movements. When he felt the coast was clear, he stealthily made his way toward the parked car careful not to get too close but in range of capturing their conversation. Not long after the first car arrived, Debbie pulled up beside the parked car. She hopped out and slid into the passenger side of the all-black Dodge Charger.

When Debbie got in, her contact put his finger up to his lips indicating for her to remain silent. He reached into his left jacket pocket and pulled out a small device. Debbie watched as he turned the knob located on the top of this device and placed it on the dashboard.

"This is known as an audio jammer," her contact said. "This will protect any conversation from listening devices." He handed her a small package. "This one's for you."

Debbie looked in the package. "Thanks."

"So did you bring the money?"

"Before I hand the envelope over to you, what other information do you have for me?"

"My contact told me that they are close to bringing you in. The mayor's office is bugged so it's a safe assumption that yours is too. I'm quite sure they are tracking your every move. We have known each other since we were kids back in the old neighborhood. I don't want to see you take the fall for anybody. So whatever you have planned, I'm going to need you to do it quickly. Don't hang around any longer than necessary. Handle your business and get out of town."

Debbie handed him the money and eased out of his car into the driver's seat of her car. She glanced over at her childhood friend and they both looked at each other knowingly. As she drove back to her condo on the Upper East Side, she thought about all the times she awarded city contracts to those companies willing to pay to play. When she was approached by the mayor with the idea, she was a little hesitant. But then he explained the process, how much money they were entitled to, and that no one would be the wiser. Their perceived careful planning had come back to haunt them.

Detective Stephenson was the last to leave the abandoned building where he had staked out the perfect position to capture their conversation. What he did not count on was being outsmarted by a guy with an audio jamming device. He made a call to Special Agent McBride as soon as he found a pay phone.

"Hello," the sleepy voice on the other end said.

"Wake up, sleeping beauty," Stephenson teased. "I got some bad news for you. Ms. Adderly showed up at the meet, however, her contact had an audio jammer. So whatever they discussed, remains between the two of them."

"Dang it!" said a frustrated McBride.

"I guess I don't have to tell you that if you don't bring her in within the next day or so, she is going to be in the wind."

"Yeah, I know," responded McBride. "Thanks for the call."

"You bet."

McBride listened to the dial tone as she contemplated her next move.

Debbie parked her car and walked briskly out of the garage and across the lobby to the bank of elevators. She frantically pushed the button for the sixteenth floor. She went over the many conversations she had with her mother about leaving New York. It scared her that they were aware of her every move up until this point. She pushed the button again summoning the elevator.

Her eyes took in every inch of the lobby. Nothing appeared to be out of the ordinary. Maybe I am being paranoid, she thought to herself. Only when she heard the soft chime of the elevator and safely ducked inside, was she able to breathe. She began to second-guess her ability to get out of New York. If what she learned from her contact was true, time was not on her side. Any moves made in the coming days had to be so strategic that she would fly under their radar.

Debbie's mind raced as she entered her condo. She poured herself a glass of wine while contemplating her next move. With outstretched legs placed neatly on the coffee table, she settled back into the sofa and allowed her thoughts to take over. Myles was coming early the following morning. She was excited about spending time with him and the long drive outside of the city would allow her to think. Her realtor was scheduled to stop by on Friday. Those two things she was certain about. However, many uncertainties loomed ahead.

She grabbed her purse and removed the noise jammer so graciously given her by her childhood friend. She held it up and turned the knob to the on position. "Yes, you are going to be my new best friend," she said as she reached for the phone.

"I understand," said the voice on the other end.

Debbie finished her glass of wine and walked down the hall. She stood in front of the massive closet doors for a beat before opening them wide. She removed every suitcase and began packing.

A black van was parked across the street. "It's awfully quiet. What do you think she is doing?" asked the FBI agent.

His partner looked at his watch and shrugged his shoulders. "It's late. Maybe she is preparing for bed."

"Yeah. Maybe so."

"Let's not worry about tonight. How many agents are on for tomorrow?"

The rookie agent reached for the clipboard. "There are four agents assigned—two cars."

"Great…hopefully, tomorrow we have something concrete to use against her.

When Debbie finished packing, she pushed the suitcases toward the front door. Soon there was a knock at the door. Checking the peephole, she saw Matt and Jeremy standing in the hall. She opened the door allowing them free access to her condo.

"Thanks for agreeing to help out. Are you clear on what needs to be done?" asked Debbie.

"Yep. We will let you know once we complete the drop," said Matt.

Debbie reached for her purse as Matt opened the door and placed four suitcases in the hall.

"Wait!" exclaimed Debbie. "Here is something for your trouble."

"You don't have to give us anything," said Jeremy.

"He's right," echoed Matt. "You don't have to give us anything. We owe you." With that, Matt and Jeremy grabbed two suitcases each and headed for the garage.

Debbie stood in the hall until she heard the soft chime of the elevator. Only then did she reenter the condo, softly shutting and locking the door behind her. She stayed with her back against the door taking in the beautifully decorated condo, the New York skyline and modest collection of red and white wines. Slowly walking around the condo, she turned off the lights. Gently opening the sliding glass door, she stepped out onto the balcony and sat quietly listening to the sounds of the city. She turned the electric fireplace on and watched as the flames danced behind the glass. Soon, she thought, this will all be over. She awoke hours later to a rising sun and birds singing. She had slept on the balcony all night.

A normal person would have been stiff from sleeping on outdoor furniture all night. But she was far from normal in her estimation. She took great care in selecting every piece of furniture in her home to include the outdoor furniture. One could sleep on it and feel like they were sleeping in a bed made for a queen. It screamed luxury.

Debbie arose from her outdoor cabana and readied herself for Myles's arrival. While she showered, she wondered what Myles had planned for today. She dried off and threw on a pair of jeans paired with a white V-neck T-shirt. She looked in the mirror and decided to pull her hair back into a ponytail. She chose a casual flat shoe to complete the look. She surmised that today would begin a new chapter in her life. It was long overdue.

Myles called before leaving home to make sure Debbie would be ready when he arrived. He did not want to waste any time getting out of the city as his objective was to spend as much time with her as possible. She instructed him to enter the garage on the north side of the building and park in any available visitor's spot. He thought it strange but didn't question her request.

To his surprise, when he arrived at the door of her condo, she opened the door with jacket and purse in hand.

"Good morning," he said as he admired her choice of outfit and hairstyle.

"Good morning," she replied with a smile.

"So I was thinking we could take a drive up to Madison or New Canaan," Myles said.

"Well," Debbie started, "if we really want to get away from the city, why not drive to Cape May?"

Myles thought about Debbie's suggestion. Cape May was about a three-hour drive from the city and was doable.

"To be honest," Myles said. "I was hoping to keep our jaunt out of the city a little closer in. That would give us more time enjoying each other's company not to mention driving time back to the city this evening," he concluded.

"True. However, Cape May is so beautiful this time of year. I feel like I've been transported back in time whenever I visit. The Victorian architecture is amazing," she countered.

"You do realize that Cape May is three hours from Manhattan and after sightseeing, dining, and taking in the shops, I might not feel like making the three-hour drive back. I guess I could do it as today starts my long weekend," rambled Myles.

"You do know that I can drive, right?" Debbie said teasingly.

Myles stopped in front of a car that Debbie did not recognize. "Why are we stopping?" Debbie questioned.

"It's a rental," Myles said. "I thought it would be a nice surprise. You like it?"

"It's beautiful. Myles Beyers, you really know how to impress a lady," said Debbie as she climbed in on the passenger side. Myles climbed in on the driver's side and slowly navigated the car out of the garage, exiting on the north side of the building.

A dark sedan pulled away from the curb; careful not to follow too closely.

"Did you say earlier that you are starting a four-day weekend?" quizzed Debbie.

"Yeah, I have been putting in long hours at work. We picked up a couple new clients and getting everything in order has been a little stressful," offered Myles.

Debbie leaned her head against the headrest and took in the sights of the city as Myles pointed the car toward the Garden State Parkway. Twenty minutes into the trip, Debbie closed her eyes and wondered why she did not tell Myles she, too, was starting a long weekend. With everything she learned recently, she decided maybe it was better that he not know. All she wanted at this point, was a little peace and relaxation.

"Why so quiet?" asked Myles.

"Just enjoying my time away from the office, the drive, you, and a change in scenery," confided Debbie.

"I must admit that this is a nice drive. I can understand how one would want to remain quiet and just take in nature," offered Myles.

They drove in silence for another hour before Debbie drifted off to sleep. She awoke to the chimes indicating the opening of the car door. She sat up and noticed that Myles had exited the car. She opened the door and walked over to where he stood.

"Are you okay?" Debbie asked.

Myles put his arm around Debbie's shoulder drawing her closer to him. He had noticed a dark sedan following about four or five car lengths behind them from the time they got on the Garden State Parkway. He could not tell Debbie that he suspected they were being followed without revealing his knowledge of the investigation and that he was being used to trap her into talking about the pay-to-play scheme. When he pulled into the rest stop, the car passed by.

As the car continued by the rest stop, Myles sighed a sigh of relief. His focus and thoughts were on Debbie and did not notice another dark sedan pull into the rest stop. A middle-aged woman exited the car and walked toward the vending machines. She studied the overpriced snacks lining each row and decided to purchase two candy bars just as Debbie walked toward the restroom.

The FBI agent entered the restroom, stopping to wash her hands.

Debbie opened the door to the stall and walked toward the sink to wash her hands. The FBI agent used this time to engage her in conversation.

"Isn't it a beautiful day for a drive?" asked the FBI agent.

Debbie smiled as she responded to the image in the mirror. "Yes, it is a lovely day for a drive in the country."

"My husband and I are on our way to Cape May to celebrate our fortieth wedding anniversary," continued the FBI agent.

"Wow! Congratulations on your fortieth wedding anniversary," Debbie said.

"We decided that we would spend the weekend in Cape May. We love it there. I feel like I have stepped back in time when I see the Victorian homes and the quaint shops there. Oh, and the food…the food is delicious!" she said with closed eyes.

Debbie was amused by the middle-aged woman standing in front of her.

"My friend and I are also spending the day in Cape May," Debbie confided.

"Really?" said the FBI agent excitedly. "Maybe we will run into each other while there."

"Maybe. I will be sure to stop and say hello should that happen," Debbie said.

"Well, I better be going. My husband will wonder what happened to me."

"It was nice talking with you," Debbie said as the woman exited the restroom.

Myles was standing at the entrance to the building when the agent walked out. She smiled as she passed by. He was still watching her cross the parking lot when Debbie appeared by his side.

"Hey, you," she said. "I just met the nicest little old lady in the restroom."

"Is that right?" questioned Myles. "You were taking so long, I thought I would have to send in a search party."

Debbie laughed at Myles's attempt at humor.

"She told me that she and her husband are celebrating their fortieth wedding anniversary in none other than Cape May. Her excitement is contagious!"

Now it was Myles's turn to laugh. He had not seen Debbie this relaxed in months. Unquestionably, it was refreshing to hear her talk excitedly about the lady she met in the restroom. He opened the door for Debbie and walked around the car and climbed into the driver's seat. She was still chatting excitedly as he navigated the car back onto the Parkway.

"Myles," she started. "I do not have to work tomorrow. What would you say if I suggested that we not return to the city until tomorrow morning?"

He glanced her way briefly before asking, "Why didn't you mention that you had Friday off? We could have planned for it. Neither of us brought extra clothing."

"I don't know. It might have something to do with the lady in the restroom. The romance surrounding them celebrating their fortieth wedding anniversary. She said something that made me want to experience the magic of Cape May. Oh, c'mon! We can buy new outfits to wear. Let's be spontaneous this weekend."

Myles chuckled slightly. "I'm curious. What did she say about Cape May that excited you?"

"She said that spending time in Cape May is like stepping back in time. The Victorian homes and the quaint shops. She closed her eyes when she mentioned the food. The way she described being in Cape May would make anyone want to visit and never leave. explained Debbie. I agree. The first time I visited Cape May, I fell in love with the architecture," explained Debbie.

"Wow! You got all of that from your time with her in the restroom?"

"Yep! I want you to experience everything she mentioned," urged Debbie.

"Okay. I guess we will be staying over in Cape May," said Myles.

The FBI agents were careful to keep their distance as they continued to shadow Myles and Debbie.

"Candy bar," offered the FBI agent.

"Thanks," said her partner.

Myles, Debbie, and all the FBI agents arrived in Cape May within minutes of each other.

"I'm hungry. Do you want to get lunch before sightseeing?" asked Myles.

"Why don't we find a place to stay for the night first?" suggested Debbie.

"You're right," agreed Myles. "We definitely should find a place to stay. Maybe someone in one of these nice restaurants can suggest a place."

Myles took Debbie's hand in his and they walked the streets of downtown Cape May until they came to a stop in front of a restaurant. They were seated immediately and handed menus. After they finished their meals, the waitress returned with the check.

"I'll take that when you are ready," she said as she handed the check to Myles.

Myles took the check and asked, "Can you recommend a nice place to stay? This is our first time here."

"Sure. There is a nice Victorian bed-and-breakfast on Trenton Avenue. I haven't had the opportunity to stay there yet. However, people visiting our little slice of heaven have nothing but good things to say about the place," offered the waitress.

Debbie's eyes lit up when the waitress mentioned Victorian. None of which was lost on Myles.

He handed his credit card to the waitress. "Thank you very much for your suggestion."

"Not a problem. I'll be right back with this," said the waitress as she scurried off to process the card.

Myles and Debbie left the restaurant and set out to find the bread and breakfast mentioned by the waitress. When they drove up to the house, Debbie gasped with amazement. It was the most magnificent Victorian house with beautifully manicured lawns. The inside decorated with period furniture, Debbie allowed her mind to wonder about the many people over the years that had relaxed on the front porch perhaps sipping lemonade on a hot and humid day. The ladies or gentlemen of the day spending countless hours in the library thumbing through novels until they landed on the one with cool crisp pages, the one that instantly drew them into the story. Sitting with book in hand, they would not notice the hustle and bustle of the people around them as they were transported to another place in time.

Debbie returned to present day when she heard the innkeeper tell Myles there was one room left and if double beds would be okay.

"Yes, double beds are perfect," said Myles. The stars are aligning, Myles thought. With everything that is going on, he did not want to complicate things further. He realized now that he had not been as careful in the past with Debbie. He could hear his grandmother's voice quoting her most often quoted scripture as he grew into manhood, "Myles, watch and pray, that ye enter not into temptation: the spirit indeed is willing, but the flesh is weak." *Remember your assignment*, he told himself. Get her to talk about the contracts awarded.

The innkeeper escorted Myles and Debbie to their room. Upon opening the door, he handed Myles the key and left the two alone to admire the beauty of the room. Debbie walked around inspecting the intricacies of each piece of furniture. She could not believe she had allowed herself to get so caught up in the rigors of everyday life that she had missed out on countless opportunities to enjoy the simpler things in life. Being in Cape May, within minutes of the beach, shops and fine restaurants did not distract her from plans to leave New York for good.

"Myles," Debbie started, "do you see yourself living anywhere other than New York?" continued Debbie.

"I've not given it a thought. New York is all I know," answered Myles.

"What about you?" asked Myles.

"As a child," she began. "I always felt like I did not belong in New York. If ever there was an opportunity to leave city life behind for something more tranquil, I would jump at the chance."

Myles joined Debbie in one of the luxurious chairs by the window. "Sounds nice. Where would you go if given the chance?" he asked.

"I've always dreamed of leaving the United States and living on a tropical island," revealed Debbie.

Myles stared at Debbie for a beat. "Leaving the United States? You mean for good, right?" he asked.

Debbie stared down at her hands and quietly answered, "Yes."

Myles was taken aback by her answer. He never saw this coming. How could he? She never in all the times they have been together mentioned wanting to leave the United States to live on an island in the tropics. He needed a distraction from the bombshell Debbie dropped.

"Hey, come on," he said as he arose from his seat. "Let's go sightseeing before the day gets away from us."

"Here is Washington Street," Myles said. "From what I understand, these three blocks have many shops and restaurants. We should be able to find something to wear as well as toiletries. I picked up a brochure at the B&B. Cape May has an honest to goodness lighthouse. I've always wanted to visit a real lighthouse," concluded Myles.

"We can go check it out after we are done shopping," added Debbie.

They were going from shop to shop in search of the perfect outfit when they ran into the couple from the rest stop. The middle-aged FBI agent walked briskly toward Myles and Debbie waving and smiling along the way.

"Fancy meeting you here," she laughed.

Debbie returned the smile. "I guess you were right. You said we would probably run into each other while in Cape May."

The middle-aged FBI agent turned her attention to Myles. Extending her hand to him, "Hello, young man. I met your wife at the rest stop earlier today. We had the best conversation."

Myles graciously shook her hand and said, "Yes, she could not stop talking about your chance meeting in the restroom. I hear congratulations are in order. You are celebrating your fortieth wedding anniversary, right?" asked Myles.

"That's correct," responded the agent. "This guy beside me swept me off my feet forty years ago and we never looked back. It's been a rollercoaster ride, but I enjoyed every minute of it."

Myles could understand now why Debbie was so excited about her conversation with this woman. Her charismatic persona put everyone within arm's length at ease. She is someone that you could sit and listen to all day. Myles noticed that her husband stood patiently beside his wife. When there was a break in the conversation, Myles extended his hand toward the gentleman.

"Hello, my name is Myles."

"Hello, Myles, I'm Stanley."

"Oh, my goodness, where are my manners?" announced the FBI agent apologetically. "Here I am going on and on about who knows what and I forgot to introduce my husband."

Debbie extended her hand. "Stanley, it's a pleasure meeting you. My name is Debbie."

"The pleasure is all mine, Debbie."

"I have a great idea," exclaimed the FBI agent. "Why don't you two have dinner with us this evening? That is if you are going to be around."

"It's your wedding anniversary," chimed in Myles. "We don't want to intrude."

"No intrusion at all," said Stanley. "We would love for you and your wife to join us."

Debbie and Myles looked at each other in amusement.

"To be clear," started Myles. "We are not married."

"Oh dear," said the woman. "There I go again. I just assumed you two were married. I've been married so long I believe everyone is married," she waved her hands comically.

Stanley winked his eye at Debbie, "Marriage...s-marriage...you two are still invited. Come help us celebrate forty years of domestication. We insist."

"Don't pay him any attention. He has a warped sense of humor. By the way, my name is Shirley."

"Pleased to meet you, Shirley," Myles and Debbie said in unison.

"Stanley and I will make dinner reservations for five o'clock at Aleathea's. Hopefully, that's not too early for you. I just want you to enjoy the ocean views. Also, there is a beautiful wraparound porch with rocking chairs. You two are going to fall in love with this place."

"When you mentioned Victorian architecture while at the rest stop, I could not wait to get here," said Debbie. "We even found a lovely Victorian B&B not far from here."

"Really? I fell in love with one the last time we were here," said Shirley. Turning to Stanley, "Do you remember the name of that place?"

"Let me think about it for a minute. I remember that it was a huge place with well-manicured lawns. It reminded me of a castle," he said.

"It's on Trenton Avenue I believe," offered Shirley.

"The B&B where we are staying is on Trenton Avenue," said Myles. "Would the place you are trying to think of be Angel of the Sea?"

Stanley snapped his fingers. "Yes, that's it!"

"Sounds like a date," chimed in Debbie. "We will see you promptly at five o'clock."

Debbie and Myles continued shopping while the FBI agents disappeared into a nearby café to make a phone call.

"This is Special Agent Donohue," said the middle-aged FBI agent. "They are staying at the Angel of the Sea. I will need you to talk to the innkeeper and find out which room they are in. If the room next to theirs is occupied, inform the innkeeper that this is federal business and to do whatever to move the occupants out of that room. Should they need to put the current occupants up in another bread and breakfast or hotel, let the innkeeper know that we will reimburse for the inconvenience. Keep me posted on your progress."

"Well, fake husband, how about we take in some of the sights before dinner?"

"Sounds good, fake wife. There is a lighthouse on the peninsula. Let's go check it out."

Neither FBI agent had ever married. Their jobs were so stressful at times that both had decided years ago that the Bureau was their spouse. The number of hours spent at work or traveling would never sit right with a spouse. Remaining single eliminated any possibility of guilt.

Two FBI agents walked into the Angel of the Sea bread and breakfast. The innkeeper knew immediately that they were there on official business. They did not seem like the regulars that visited Cape May.

"Good afternoon, sir," said the taller FBI agent. "I am Special Agent Raymond, and this is Special Agent Johnston. Is there a place where we can talk in private?"

The innkeeper eyed them suspiciously. "Can I see your badges?"

Both FBI agents flashed their badges.

"Follow me to my office," said the innkeeper.

He invited the agents to sit down while he walked around his desk and sat in an oversized office chair. "So how can I help you gentleman?"

"What you hear today should be treated as confidential and not divulged to anyone. Two people checked into your establishment earlier today. They are part of an ongoing investigation," said one of the agents.

"Are they dangerous?" asked the innkeeper. "We have never had any trouble here."

"They are not dangerous. Do you recognize these two people?" the tall slender agent said as he pushed the photos toward the innkeeper.

"Yes, they checked in a little over an hour ago," revealed the innkeeper.

"We will need the room next to theirs to set up our surveillance equipment," said Johnston. "Is the room vacant?"

"No. We have a full house this weekend," said the innkeeper.

"Sir, I cannot express to you how serious this situation is. We will need that room. So the only thing we can suggest is that you move them to another establishment. The Bureau is prepared to reimburse you for the inconvenience," said Special Agent Raymond.

"What do I tell them? We have an exemplary reputation. I'm afraid this situation might put a blemish on our good reputation," responded the innkeeper.

"We have done this before," said Agent Johnston. "We promise that this will all work out according to plan and the reputation of your establishment will not suffer."

"Okay. I am putting my trust in both of you agents," said the innkeeper. "I will make some calls to see what I can do. Of course, I might have to put them up in a much nicer room than they have here."

Both agents exchanged knowing glances. "That's fine. How long do you think this will take?" asked Agent Raymond.

"Give me about fifteen or twenty minutes," said the innkeeper. "Why don't you two make yourselves at home on the wraparound porch. I will have the chef prepare our famous crab cake sandwiches for you."

The FBI agents left the innkeeper's office and took up residence on the wraparound porch.

As they were enjoying their crab cake sandwiches, they noticed two people struggling with their suitcases in frustration. They looked at each other knowingly.

The FBI agents ran to assist. "Here let us help you with that."

"Thank you. I have never heard of anything so bizarre in my life," the lady said as she threw smaller bags in the backseat of the car.

"Martha, he explained everything to us. And in his defense, I don't believe he really had a choice given the situation," remarked the stout man.

"Oh, I understand what he's saying. It's just that I had my heart set on staying at the Angel of the Sea!" she shrieked.

"If I'm not being too forward, what is going on?" asked Agent Raymond.

"Well, the innkeeper said there is a bug infestation. But what I fail to understand is how could a bug infestation only affect one room. Wouldn't it affect the entire property? Why are we the only people being placed at another facility?" questioned the stout man.

"Yeah I can see where that might raise questions," agreed the FBI agents. "Well, I hope that management at least put you in a place comparable to this one."

The man smiled. "They did us one better. We are staying in a suite at the Queen Victoria on Ocean. Don't say anything to the missus but I'm excited about staying in the King Edward suite at the House of Royals Building. I've always fantasized about being a royal. However, staying in that suite is about as close as I will ever come to being one," he said as he let out a hearty laugh.

The FBI agents watched as the man and his wife drove away from the Angel of the Sea before breaking out in laughter.

"A bug infestation?"

"Yep, in one room nonetheless!"

If they thought it proper, the FBI agents would have been rolling all over the well-manicured lawn of Angel of the Sea. Instead, they returned to the wraparound porch and what was left of their crab cake sandwiches. Soon the innkeeper joined them on the porch.

"Well, gentlemen, the room is all yours. Here is the key. If you will follow me, I will show you to your room," he said graciously.

The FBI agents had just moved the last piece of equipment into their room as Myles and Debbie returned to the B&B.

The door was slightly ajar allowing Debbie to see something that gave her pause. Maybe she had watched one too many detective shows, but it appeared as though she caught a glimpse of surveillance equipment. Had the person behind the door not shut it so abruptly, she might have known for sure. Am I being paranoid, she mused? She patted herself on the back for bringing the noise jammer with her. To be safe, she decided that she would turn it on whenever she and Myles were in their room.

"Debbie," called Myles as he stood in the doorway. "We need to get ready if we are going to meet Stanley and Shirley for dinner at five o'clock."

Debbie quickened her step into the room. "Now where did I put the bag with the dress and Pashima shawl I just bought?" Debbie half-whispered. "Aha! Here it is."

Temperatures at the beach dropped at night. The season was just entering late summer with warm days and cool nights. Soon it would be too cold for the beach, in her estimation. While she was in the shower, her thoughts turned again to the perpetual warm days and tropical ocean breezes of the tropics. Debbie finished her shower and dressed while in the bathroom. She looked at herself in the mirror and reflected on what she thought she saw in the room next to theirs. It unnerved her. She opened the door to the bathroom allowing the steam to proceed her. Myles picked up his outfit and entered the bathroom to shower and change.

While waiting on Myles to get ready, she brushed her hair and parted it in the middle but was not satisfied with the look. She quickly brushed it back and decided to wear it in a knot at the nape of neck. Debbie looked at her watch. They had an hour before they were to meet their new friends, Stanley, and Shirley.

It did not take Myles long to get ready. He walked out of the bathroom with an outfit suitable for dinner at a seaside restaurant. "You look stunning," he told Debbie.

"You clean up very nicely yourself, sir," she teased.

Debbie sat in a chair by the window. Myles joined her.

"What's on your mind, lady?" asked Myles. "You seem preoccupied. The whole idea of getting out of the city was to relax."

"I was just thinking about our time here at the beach. It is so beautiful and tranquil. Can you believe this place is just a three-hour drive from the city?" she asked.

"Amazing," agreed Myles.

"Sometimes…" Debbie's thoughts trailed off as she remembered that she had not turned on the noise jammer. Quickly changing direction, "sometimes I wish for simpler times."

"You too," asked Myles. "I think about that so much. As a kid, I didn't think about growing up or the responsibilities that come with being an adult. My only concern was hanging out with my friends. Leroy was my best friend. He and I would sell apples door-to-door every summer."

Debbie leaned her head back against the chair as Myles talked about his childhood memories but noticed a reticence when asked about his father or mother.

Myles checked the time. "It's only four-twenty, but I think we should leave now. It will take us about fifteen minutes to arrive and, I don't know about you, but I would prefer to get there before them. Especially since they were gracious enough to invite us to help them celebrate their fortieth wedding anniversary."

"You are a good man, Myles," said Debbie as she arose from her seat.

Myles and Debbie arrived at Aleathea's seaside restaurant with fifteen minutes to spare. They sat on the wraparound porch in one of the many rocking chairs lining the porch for guests. Debbie closed her eyes and listened to the sound of the waves crashing at the nearby beach. She could hear the sea gulls overhead and smell the salt air as it drifted over the peninsula. So relaxed was she that the mere thought of getting up from the rocking chair wasn't something she cared to entertain. Not even upon the arrival of Stanley and Shirley.

"Well, hello again," said Stanley. "Let's get this party started."

Shirley waved him off. "Don't pay him any attention. He's always like this."

"You two must have a lot of fun wherever you go," added Myles. "Stanley seems like a fun person to hang out with."

"Well, that's one way to describe him," laughed Shirley.

They entered the restaurant and were seated at a table with a view. From their vantage point, they watched as people biked along the boardwalk, couples strolled hand in hand as the sun began its descent and witnessed the sheer joy of children as they ran slightly ahead of their parents. All four seemed to be lost in thought as they savored the charmed ambience of Cape May.

"So is this your first visit to Cape May?" inquired Stanley.

"Yes, it is," said Myles as he adjusted himself in his seat. "What about you?"

"No. We try to come here at least twice a year. There is something about this place that makes you forget about your troubles. Maybe it's the ocean. I feel like I can caste all my cares into the water and they will float away," responded Stanley.

"That's wonderful," said Debbie as she joined the conversation. "My work is so demanding that I feel guilty taking any time off."

"Well, all I have to say to that is take time for yourself," encouraged Shirley. "One day you will look up and wonder what you did with your life besides work."

Myles nodded in agreement.

Stanley fixed his eyes on Debbie. "Might I ask what type of work you do?"

"I work at New York City Hall in the Office of the Mayor," responded Debbie.

"Oh, you work for Mayor Stevens," said Shirley. "I voted for him on more than one occasion."

"Thank you for your support," offered Debbie.

"What do you think his chances are for reelection," probed Shirley.

"I think he has a good chance of getting reelected," replied Debbie.

"Well, I think that's enough shop talk for now," said Stanley. "I'm starved."

"So am I," said Myles as he perused the menu.

The waitress appeared to take their orders. "Hi, my name is Tiffany and I will be your waitress for this evening. Are you ready to order?"

"Does everyone know what they want?" asked Stanley.

The all answered yes in unison.

"Okay, I will start with the ladies." Tiffany took the order for the table and repeated it so as not to leave anything out.

"So I have one stuffed flounder, one chicken marsala, one shrimp and crab cake, and one prime rib. I have two iced teas and two freshly squeezed lemonades. Would you like bread while you are waiting?"

"That would be lovely," replied Shirley.

"Please don't think I am being forward," started Shirley. "I am a hopeless romantic and I just love hearing stories of how couples became, you know, couples."

"How Debbie and I got together is complicated," said Myles.

"Oh, those are the best stories," urged Shirley.

Debbie grabbed Myles's hand and smiled at him in support. She was telling him with her eyes that it was okay to talk about his relationship with Cinnamon.

Myles let out a huge sigh before telling two complete strangers about his childhood friend, his best friend, Cinnamon. He told them about the night she was shot by her half-sister. Before the night was over, he told them about how Cinnamon's mother died at the hands of her half-sister's mother. He confided in them how hurt he was when Cinnamon pushed him away after she learned of her father's infidelity. He looked up into the shocked faces of Stanley and Shirley.

"Hollywood couldn't write anything this good," said Stanley.

"That's when I met Debbie. I work for an accounting firm in Manhattan. Actually, it is directly across the street from New York City Hall where Debbie works."

"How convenient," said Shirley while smiling at Debbie.

"Debbie," said Stanley. "What exactly do you do for the mayor?"

"I award city contracts," responded Debbie.

"That must be very stressful work," suggested Shirley. "I'm sure companies have to bid on the contracts. What sort of system does the city have for awarding contracts to companies?"

Debbie was not used to people asking her questions about her job. She was starting to feel a little claustrophobic.

"Will you excuse me, please? I need to get some air," said Debbie as she pushed back from the table.

"Oh my," exclaimed Shirley. "Did I say something wrong?"

"No. I'll go check on her," offered Myles.

Stanley and Shirley had sixty years with the Bureau between them. They knew without verbalizing their thoughts that they had struck a nerve with that last question.

"She's a smart one," whispered Shirley.

"Well, she's already on edge because of the investigation. Although, I must admit that you hit her with a punch to the gut with your question. Did you see the look on her face? She ran out of here like she just saw a ghost," acknowledged Stanley.

They both got a chuckle out of that.

The waitress had returned with their meals by the time Myles and Debbie rejoined Stanley and Shirley.

"Sweetie, I'm sorry if I upset you," said Shirley. "Sometimes I get a little carried away with all of my questions. It's just that I am fascinated with people and how they make their living."

"No worries," said Debbie. "I was feeling queasy and needed a little fresh air. I'm much better now."

"That's good to hear. Well, I guess we should eat. Everything looks so delicious," exclaimed Shirley as she admired everyone's selection.

Stanley rubbed his hands together in anticipation. "My stomach has waited long enough. It's time to feed the beast!"

The mood lightened as everyone joined him in laughter.

After dinner, the four walked the boardwalk laughing and talking. They stopped along the way to peer into the shops of windows and comment on the various displays. The more they walked and talked, the more Shirley felt that something wasn't quite right with the investigation involving Debbie. She had been an agent for many years and been in contact with many types of people. She considered herself a good judge of character, however, the only way she would know for sure about this nagging feeling was for Debbie to come clean about the consistent awarding of contracts to the same companies.

Debbie and Myles said their good nights to Stanley and Shirley and headed toward the parking garage. Myles put his arm around Debbie to keep her warm. As they drove back to the bed and breakfast, Myles seized the opportunity to find out what happened while at the restaurant.

"Hey, are you okay?" probed Myles.

"Sure. Why do you ask?" replied Debbie.

"Well, it appeared as though you were upset when Shirley asked about the procedure for awarding contracts," continued Myles.

"No, I wasn't upset. Like I explained earlier, I was feeling queasy and needed to get a little air," explained Debbie.

"But…" started Myles.

"Myles, please let it go," advised Debbie.

They drove the rest of the way in silence. Myles knew Debbie was hiding something. The mere fact that she got upset the moment Shirley asked about the awarding of contracts was indication enough that she wanted to keep that aspect of her job concealed. Myles would honor Debbie's wishes and would not push her to talk about something she was obviously uncomfortable discussing.

Myles parked the car and walked around to the passenger side to open the door for Debbie.

"Myles, I am sorry I snapped at you. It's just that the whole purpose of this trip was to relax, not talk shop which is what it turned out to be at the restaurant. I'm a little on edge with the upcoming election and other things. Sometimes I want to leave this life I've created for myself far behind and start anew somewhere else."

"Wow! Listen to you…start anew," uttered Myles attempting to lighten the mood. "Where would you go?"

"As mentioned earlier today, I have always wanted to live in the tropics. I've been to Turks and Caicos several times and that is the only island where I can see myself living," confided Debbie.

"So do you have a timeline for starting anew?" inquired Myles.

Debbie felt that she had revealed too much already. But it was Myles. What harm could it do to let him in on her plans to leave New York? If she had her way, he would come with her. She had squirreled several millions away in the British Caribbean Bank. Upon the sale of her condo, she would have another million or so to add to what was already there.

"Myles, what time are we leaving tomorrow?" asked Debbie.

"I see what you did there," replied Myles.

"What are you talking about?" asked Debbie.

"You ignored my question with a question," explained Myles. "That's okay. We will leave whenever you say we should leave."

"Thank you, sir," responded Debbie. "I would prefer to leave right after breakfast as I have a meeting tomorrow."

"Who schedules a meeting on their day off?" asked Myles.

"Someone who has business to attend to," replied Debbie.

"Oh, excuse me, Ms. Always Busy," teased Myles.

Debbie grabbed his arm as they ascended the stairs leading to the wraparound porch of the Angel of the Sea. They stepped back in time as they climbed the grand stairway to the bedroom which they occupied.

The FBI agents in the adjoining room patiently waited all day to capture something they could use against Debbie. They listened intently as they heard the door close and as Myles and Debbie made small talk.

"So do you think you might move forward with your plan?" asked Myles.

Debbie did not answer right away.

"Come on, Debbie. Give us something," said the FBI agent.

"It depends," replied Debbie.

"On what?" asked Myles.

"If you decide to come with me or not," suggested Debbie.

"Come with you where?" inquired Myles.

"Remember I told you…" started Debbie.

Suddenly Myles got up and moved toward the door. "Hold that thought," he said. "I'll be right back. I believe I left something in the car."

Before Debbie could finish her thought, Myles disappeared from the room. He was gone longer than she anticipated and was in bed by the time he returned. She turned on the bedside lamp and sat up in bed when she heard the door open and close.

"I'm sorry it took so long, but I drove back to the restaurant to get this," explained Myles as he sat the box on the small round table by the window.

Debbie eased out of bed and walked over to where Myles was sitting. She opened the box to discover a huge slice of carrot cake. To take the chill off the night, Myles started a fire where both reclined on the floor in front of the fireplace eating carrot cake and talking into the wee hours of the morning.

Finally, Myles looked at Debbie who was having trouble keeping her eyes open. "Maybe we should both get some sleep. We have a long drive ahead of us in a few hours."

Debbie agreed as she climbed into bed. "Get some sleep as you are driving back to the city," she teased.

"We will talk about this later," Myles said as he laid across his bed.

The FBI agent removed his headset and woke his partner so that he could get some sleep. He prepared his notes for reporting back to his colleagues, Stanley, and Shirley.

Several hours later, Debbie awoke to the sun gently streaming through the bedroom window. Myles was sleeping peacefully as she slipped out of bed to shower and dress before he awoke. As she showered, she reflected on time spent with Shirley and Stanley. She could not put her finger on it, but Shirley's line of questioning seemed oddly familiar to someone who was digging up information for a greater purpose. Debbie wondered silently if paranoia was setting after finding out about the investigation? Her contact warned her to be careful. She did not know how he came about this information, but she trusted him. He had never supplied her with anything that was not accurate. Although she only caught a glimpse of what appeared to be surveillance equipment, she could not afford to get comfortable.

She quickly dressed and brushed her hair. She was overdue for a visit to the salon, so she grabbed a hat from the weekender she purchased and placed it on the bed. Myles began to stir from sleep.

With eyes closed, "Good morning," he managed. He opened his eyes fully and noticed that Debbie was fully dressed.

"How long have you been awake?" he asked.

"Oh, I don't know. Maybe forty-five minutes to an hour," she shrugged.

Myles rolled over onto his back and stretched. He reminded Debbie of a cat stretching all four of its legs before curling up and falling back asleep.

"So do you have anything else you want to see before we head back to the city?" asked Myles.

"No. I think we have spent enough time in Cape May. I have to get back to the city as I have an appointment I simply cannot put off for another day," confided Debbie.

"Give me ten minutes, and I'll be ready to go," he said as he grabbed his clothes and headed for the bathroom. Forty minutes later, Myles emerged from the bathroom clean-shaven, showered, and dressed.

Debbie waited until Myles made eye contact before she pointed to her watch and smiled.

Myles smiled as he took inventory of all the things he liked about Debbie. Her whacky sense of humor was at the top of the list. He couldn't allow himself to go too deep. There were still some things he found hard to believe about her. One of which was the possibility of being involved in a pay-to-play scheme. How could she allow herself to get caught up in such corruption? Better still, why did she allow it? She was too intelligent for such debauchery. There was more to her story. He felt it in his gut.

In the room next door, the FBI agents had packed up their equipment and loaded everything in the car before Myles and Debbie checked out. They thanked the innkeeper for his assistance and reminded him to send the invoice for the suite at the Queen Victoria to the address provided.

The innkeeper smiled sheepishly and silently wondered how the agents knew about the suite at the Queen Victoria. "Yes. I will be sure to mail it to you," he stammered.

The agents drove several feet away from the Angel of the Sea. They parked and watched earnestly for the car driven by Myles. It did not take long before they recognized the car exiting the long driveway at the bed and breakfast to be that of Myles Beyers. Soon they were following Myles and Debbie back to the city.

Myles looked over at Debbie and said, "Thank you. I really enjoyed spending time with you. I have been under so much stress at work, I did not know until we left the city how badly I needed to get away."

"I understand and feel the same way. With the upcoming election, we have been working nonstop. If the mayor doesn't get reelected, we will all be looking for jobs come November," offered Debbie.

"You are an intelligent woman. You could probably go anywhere and find a job," reassured Myles.

"Maybe," she sighed.

"By the way, we were supposed to have a conversation about who would drive back to the city," teased Myles.

Debbie chuckled. "Sir, you are doing a lovely job of driving."

Myles could not help but laugh. Debbie always got her way. She was used to it and he had grown accustomed to letting her have her way. As he drove the Garden State Parkway, he mused of what he would do if she were in fact guilty and received some ungodly sentence for the part in this scheme. He quickly dismissed the thought. There had already been too much loss in his life. At that point, he decided to let everything go. Throw caution to the wind and enjoy the moment.

When Cinnamon was shot, he thought he would lose her. He didn't know what to expect when he arrived at the hospital. Now, there is Debbie. Again, he doesn't know what is ahead for her and he, sure as hell, doesn't know how this is going to end. His life played out like an opera full of trauma and tragedies.

Myles and Debbie arrived at her condo before the lunch rush hour. He parked in the garage and grabbed her weekender and escorted her to her door.

Debbie unlocked the door and turned facing Myles. "I had a lovely time. I'm sorry I can't invite you in, but I have an appointment I need to prepare for. I will call you later." She reached up and kissed him on his cheek.

"I understand. Have a good meeting and I'll talk to you later," said Myles as he headed toward the elevators.

Debbie looked at the clock on the wall. Her realtor would be there in an hour. She scanned the condo to make sure everything was nice and neat. She fluffed the pillows on the sofa and made sure the bathrooms and bedrooms were photo ready. If she were to leave New York, this was the first step.

She was in the kitchen drinking a glass of water when she heard a knock at the door. Who could that be, she wondered? She did not expect her realtor for another thirty minutes. She quietly tiptoed to the door and peered through the peephole. A young woman stood in the hall looking around nervously. Debbie put the chain on the door before opening it.

Eyeing the young woman suspiciously, Debbie asked, "Can I help you?"

Without saying a word, the young woman handed Debbie an envelope. As quickly as she had appeared at Debbie's door, she disappeared just as quickly.

Debbie closed and locked the door. She returned to the kitchen and opened the envelope. There were only two words scribbled on the note paper. Package delivered. Tears welled up in her eyes, spilling over and running down her cheeks. She tore the note in tiny pieces before throwing them in the trash. The next knock at the door was her realtor. Before opening the door, Debbie reached into her purse and turned on the noise jammer. If she were under investigation, she would not make it easy for them.

Sharon Michaels entered the condo and immediately began taking pictures. She assured Debbie that she could get top dollar for her condo because it was in a desirable neighborhood and not far from downtown Manhattan. The view, as Sharon Michaels pointed out, was worth a million dollars.

"Debbie, your condo is beautifully decorated. I give you my guarantee that it will sale within a week."

"Wow! A week. That soon?" exclaimed Debbie.

"Yes. Like I said. It's all about location. Listen, I have a client I would like to bring by soon to look at your condo. She wants to pay cash. I think a private sale is the way to go for you. She is traveling but I expect her back in New York within the next day or so. I would like this to be the first place I show her."

"That's fine, but I thought a private sale was without a realtor," said Debbie.

"Typically, it is. However, there are times when I do favors for people. My client asked for a favor and you need to sell your condo, right? I will walk you through the paperwork as if you were selling the house without a realtor and I will still get a commission. It's a win-win for everyone involved."

Debbie smiled as she thought about the noise jammer in her purse. If all goes well on Monday, she thought, she would be in Turks and Caicos by Tuesday.

"Please tell your client that the condo comes fully furnished."

"I will send these pictures to her tonight."

Debbie walked Sharon Michaels to the door.

"I'll be in touch," she said as she walked down the hall and disappeared around the corner.

Debbie stood in the door of her condo until she heard the soft chime of the elevator. She quietly closed the door. She opened the sliding glass door and stepped out onto the balcony listening to the sights and sounds of the city.

CHAPTER

LOIS ADDERLY ARRIVED AT THE AIRPORT on the island of Turks and Caicos fully expecting to see her daughter. The two men that arrived at her apartment assured her that Debbie would be waiting. They seemed nice enough. During the entire trip, they never left her side. Always asking her if she were comfortable enough or if they could get her something to eat or drink. They were hiding something. She was sure of it.

All three exited the airport and got into a cab. The guy who called himself Jeremy sat in the front with the cab driver and provided him with an address. The cab driver drove the winding roads of the island and came to a stop in front of the most beautiful villa.

"This is Grace Cay," said the cab driver as he got out and walked around to the back of the cab. He removed their suitcases and helped take them to the house.

"Whose house is this?" asked Lois in amazement.

"I'm going to take a wild guess and say it's your daughter's," said Jeremy.

Lois looked at him in unbelief as they both entered the house.

The cab driver held his hand out as Matt paid him for his services and tipped him generously.

Lois walked around the house peering into each room in amazement. After touring the house, she sat in silence around the Olympic-size pool, not knowing what to say. Clearly, she never expected to walk into something so luxurious. When Debbie mentioned a house in Turks and Caicos, she thought it would be a traditional island abode. But never in her wildest dreams would she have imagined such luxury.

As the hours ticked away, they were still sitting around the pool when suddenly Lois asked if they were hungry. "I don't know how long we have been sitting out here but I am hungry. I guess we should call a cab and go out to eat," said Lois.

"I'm with you," said Matt.

"Okay then. Let's get ready."

As Lois and Matt walked down the hall to prepare for dinner, Jeremy walked into the kitchen to inspect his handiwork. He walked into the pantry, opened the refrigerator and freezer to make sure his instructions were explicitly followed.

"Lois, Matt," he cried out. "You gotta see this."

Lois and Matt came running toward the kitchen. "What is it?" asked Lois.

He walked around the kitchen opening every cabinet door. Finally, he opened the refrigerator door to reveal a fully stocked refrigerator and freezer.

"How did this get here?" asked Lois.

"Well," started Jeremy. "At this point, I am happy to see that this kitchen is fully stocked. We don't have to go out. We can cook our own food."

They stopped talking when they heard the doorbell.

"Shush!" said Lois. "Who would be ringing the doorbell?" she said as she made her way to the front door.

There was an impressively dressed man standing there when she opened the door. He smiled and bowed his head slightly in acknowledgment of Lois.

"Are you Ms. Lois Adderly?" asked the impressively dressed man.

"Yes. I am she," responded Lois.

"May I come in?" he asked.

"May I ask the purpose of your visit," said Lois.

The impressively dressed gentleman smiled even wider. "I understand. You do not know me, and this is your first trip to Turks and Caicos. Your daughter, Debbie Adderly and I have been in constant communication over the past few years. She has made several trips to the island and on her last trip here, she engaged my services in the purchase of the land in which this elaborate house sits upon."

"Are you telling me that my daughter owns this house?" asked Lois.

"Not exactly. Can we discuss this inside? The sun is terribly unforgiving in the topics."

"Oh, my goodness. Where are my manners?" she said while opening the door wide for the man to enter the villa. "Please have a seat and I'll get you a cool glass of water."

Lois returned with a glass of water. They all watched as he turned the glass up and appreciated every drop of water.

"Well, I'm afraid I am at a disadvantage," said Lois.

"How is that?" asked the man.

"You know my name, my daughter, and my flight itinerary, but I don't know anything about you except that you have been in communication with my daughter for several years. I don't know your name and my daughter has never mentioned you," explained Lois.

"Well, I can't speak on that," he said while placing his briefcase on his lap. He opened it and took out a folder containing papers on the purchase of the land. He placed the deed to the property in Lois's hand.

"I will see myself out," he said. "It was a pleasure meeting you Ms. Lois Adderly. Enjoy your beautiful home. Your daughter must love you very much. I don't know too many children that would sacrifice their life's savings to honor their mother in such a way."

A gasp escaped Lois as her hand flew up to her mouth. Matt and Jeremy got up from their seats, flanking Lois on either side. The deed listed Lois as the owner of this beautiful villa with the Olympic size pool in Turks and Caicos. Tears streamed down her face.

"I need to call my daughter," sobbed Lois. "I need to tell her how much I love and appreciate her."

"She will be here soon," said Jeremy. "You can tell her then. Right now, we need to celebrate your good fortune. Who is cooking?"

Lois laughed as Matt and Jeremy engaged in horseplay as they made their way toward the kitchen. She looked at the deed once more before placing it back in the folder. There was so much she wanted to share with her daughter. She had a right to know who she was, and Lois purposed in her heart at that moment that she would know. If it were the last thing she did in life, Debbie would know her lineage.

She walked down the hall to her bedroom and placed the folder in the bottom drawer of the dresser. She could hear her house guests laughing in the kitchen as they cooked dinner. The smell of grilled steak filled the house.

There was a knock at her bedroom door.

"Ms. Lois, dinner is ready," said Matt. "I hope you like steak."

"I hope we are having more than steak," she teased.

"How does garlic butter grilled steak and shrimp with herb potatoes and salad sound?" replied Matt.

"It sounds heavenly," exclaimed Lois. "Honestly, where has my daughter been hiding you two?"

They ate dinner outside by the pool as the sky grew dark.

Lois ate the last piece of steak on her plate as she made a mental note to ask her house guests about their relationship with Debbie.

"Dinner was absolutely delicious," said Lois. "My compliments to the chef."

"Thank you," they sang in unison.

Lois moved to clear the table when she was stopped by Jeremy and Matt.

"Why don't you sit and relax by the pool. We will clean up the kitchen."

"Well, if you insist," said Lois.

"We insist," said the brothers. "It will not take that long to clean up the kitchen. We will rejoin you shortly. Can we get you anything while you are waiting on us?"

"No. I cannot eat another bite," replied Lois.

From her vantage point, Lois watched as the guys moved quickly around the kitchen. Her eyes roamed around taking in every inch of the property. She almost felt like she needed to pinch herself to make sure she wasn't dreaming. Thoughts of her childhood floated back while she relaxed around the pool. After her father had disowned her for getting pregnant out of wedlock, she never thought she would experience such luxury again. She never finished college and Debbie's father conveniently disappeared when he learned of the pregnancy. Abandoned by the one's she thought would be there for her, she went to work for New York's Housing Authority. She went into affordable housing and raised her daughter on the money she made, going without so that Debbie would have.

Her thoughts were interrupted when her two houseguests returned with a box of petite truffles.

"Look what we found while rummaging through the kitchen?" exclaimed Matt. "Yes, that's right! A box of petite truffles!"

"I would have preferred a slice of cake with a cold glass of milk myself," winked Jeremy. "However, these will do for now."

"Don't tell me you are a dessert snob," teased Lois.

"No, I'm not a dessert snob," replied Jeremy. "Be honest. Do I look like a petite truffles kind of guy?"

Lois chuckled at the thought of this big guy sitting around eating truffles. "I must admit. You do not fit the bill."

"So what's your story," inquired Lois. "How do you two know my daughter? Do you work together?"

"In a manner of speaking," said Jeremy. He reached for a truffle popping it into his mouth with all the elegance of an elephant. As he slowly chewed the truffle, he allowed himself to reflect on his first meeting with Debbie. In four short years, he and his brother had made more money than they could have ever imagined. Had it not been for Debbie, their small construction business would have shuttered its doors within a year. The first time they were awarded a city contract, they were elated. The second time his company was awarded a contract, they were able to expand and hire more people as the contracts kept coming.

He chuckled slightly as he noticed that Lois had not stopped smiling. "You have a special daughter," he exclaimed.

Lois turned her head slightly toward him, "I know. I've always known from the day she was born that she was special. Her eyes gave her away. Even when she was a little girl growing up in Baruch Housing, she never played with the other girls. I would watch her. There was a longing about her. I couldn't tell her…" she said as her thoughts trailed off.

"So, our story isn't extraordinary," Jeremy offered as he stretched his legs out and leaned back in the chair. "We are just two brothers from East Harlem."

"Fraternal twins to be exact," chimed in Matt.

Lois looked from one to the other. "I never would have known."

"My brother looks more like our mother; I am my father's son. However, I have more of my mother's personality. My brother is a combination of both. When we were in business together, sometimes making business decisions were hard. Sometimes I felt like four people were in the room instead of two."

They all laughed heartily at his comment.

"What sort of business were you in?" inquired Lois.

"Well, my brother and I spent our summers working with our uncle. He owned a small construction business. Some of the larger construction companies would bring him on as a subcontractor. Nothing big but enough to live outside of the city," explained Matt.

"Yeah. My mother made sure we spent our summers outside of the city working. She would always say a little hard work never hurt anybody," chimed in Jeremy.

"Was this your mother's brother?" inquired Lois.

"No. Our father's brother," they said in unison.

"Are they close?" asked Lois.

"Uh…their relationship was complicated. Our father and uncle refused to talk about it and we learned not to bring it up."

"So we worked with our uncle. This guy never slowed down and expected everyone on his construction site to be the best at whatever job assigned to them. He would say that his name was his reputation and everyone working for him was an extension of his name and reputation. Sometimes at lunch with the guys, we would mimic him."

"Do you think he knew?" asked Jeremy.

"If he did, he never let on," responded his brother.

"All those years of working with your uncle paid off," observed Lois. "I mean, you two went into business for yourselves, right? What sort of business was it?"

"Construction. When our uncle passed away, he willed his business to my brother and me. His house went to our parents."

"Your uncle never married?" asked Lois.

"No. He was married to his business. He told us one time that his biggest regret in life was never getting married. We were the closest he would ever get to having sons."

"We were in our early twenties when our uncle passed. Although we had worked every summer at various construction sites, we did not know anything about running a business, bidding for contracts or payroll. The list of things we did not know was exhaustive."

"We are sitting in my uncle's office one day going through the files and we noticed names of construction companies, architectural firms, etcetera. My brother and I are asking each other questions. Questions like…how can we get a bigger slice of the pie? Who can help us better understand the bidding process? I wrote everything down and kept reviewing the list of questions. In the meantime, contracts were being awarded consistently and for some reason we fell short every time."

"Then one day, my brother storms into the office and threw a stack of papers on the desk. Do you remember what you said to me?"

"I sure do. I said this ends today."

They both fell quiet, reflecting on the day they met Debbie. That's when everything started to turn in their favor.

"You have a very special daughter," reiterated Jeremy.

"Yeah, you said that earlier," responded Lois. "Care to elaborate."

"It is because of your daughter that our business did not fail. That day when I stormed into the office, I was livid. Contracts were being awarded all around the city and we were about to go under. We could not make payroll and we had lost all our guys to other construction companies. We felt that we had failed our uncle. So I called City Hall attempting to get in touch with someone that could give me answers. I left several messages until one day a lady returned my call. That lady was your daughter. I explained our situation to her. For the first time in a long time, I felt like someone was listening to me. She assured me that she would review the situation and get back with me. When she didn't keep her word, I paid her a visit at her office.

"After that, she made sure we were awarded contracts that we could handle. Soon we were competing for bids alongside more seasoned companies. She walked me through the bidding process and put me in contact with people that helped my brother and I understand how to run a business. We hired a person to run the day-to-day operations so that we could concentrate on bringing in more contracts. What we have, we owe it all to Debbie."

Lois sat silently as she processed what the twin brothers told her. Debbie never talked about her job in the mayor's office so, understandably, she did not know any of this. Nonetheless, she was happy to know that her daughter played a major part in the success of these two young men.

"Well, it has been a long day and I think I will retire for the evening," Lois said as she got up and walked toward the house. "I'll see you gentlemen in the morning."

"Good night, Lois," said the twins.

When they were certain Lois was out of earshot, they moved closer to one another and spoke in hushed tones.

"If things go sideways for Debbie, Lois will be crushed."

"Yeah, you might be right. Whichever way this situation plays out, we have to be there for both," said Jeremy.

His brother shook his head in agreement.

The brothers went inside and secured every window and door before retiring to their rooms for the night. Leaving Debbie behind in New York wasn't something they wanted to do nor did they feel comfortable in doing, but Debbie assured them she would be fine. She told them she had a few loose ends to tie up and she would follow within one week's time. If she did not make it within the specified time, they were to accompany Lois to First Caribbean International Bank. Debbie instructed them to have Lois speak only to the branch manager.

Confident in their assignment, they soon drifted off to sleep.

The following morning, all three slept longer than anticipated. In the fog of their sleep, they could hear knocking at the door. Lois arrived at the door first followed closely by the twins.

Slightly perturbed by the persistent knocking, Lois asked, "Can I help you?"

"I'm sorry to wake you, but I have been dispatched as your tour guide," said the slight man in Bermuda shorts and matching shirt.

"Tour guide?" all three said in unison.

This must have seemed funny to the tour guide as he roared with laughter. "That's okay. I can see that I have caught you off-guard." He checked his clipboard and pointed out Debbie's name on the paperwork. "Ms. Debbie Adderly called a few days ago and set up a half-day tour for Lois, Matt, and Jeremy. Are we going today?" the man asked with a smile.

"I guess so," said Lois. "However, we will need a little time to get ready."

The slight man looked at his watch. "Okay. I will wait for you on the bus."

Lois shut the front door and all three of them returned to their rooms to prepare for a tour of the island. None of them had ever showered and dressed in under fifteen minutes. The tour guide was just about to take a nap when he heard them getting on the bus. He could not believe they had gotten ready in such a short period of time.

"Is this your first time to the island?" asked the tour guide.

"Yes," replied Lois. "However, my daughter has been here before and assured me that I would love Turks and Caicos."

"Well, there is plenty to see on the island. I don't want you to think that I am bias, but, in my humble opinion, there is no other island quite like Turks and Caicos," said the tour guide.

"Aww...I bet you say that to all the girls," teased Lois.

"Okay. You found me out," laughed the tour guide. "I tell all the beautiful women that come to the island hoping that they will stay."

"Uh-oh, Lois," said Jeremy. "You better watch out. I think you have a not-so-secret admirer."

They continued to tease like that for the remainder of the tour. By the time they returned later that afternoon, Lois, the twins, and the tour guide had become good friends. Lois invited the tour guide and his family to a cookout the following weekend so they could get to know each other better and the kids could swim in the pool. By that time, Debbie would be there. He thanked her for her generosity and promised to return the following weekend with his family. He then got on the bus and waved goodbye as he maneuvered the tour bus back onto the winding road.

"Well, it's been a strange day," said Matt.

"Yes, it has," said Lois. "I cannot believe that my daughter is in New York running things in the Caribbean."

"We need a new name for her," said Jeremy.

"Well, while you are trying to think of a new name for Debbie, I think I will get something cool to drink and sit out by the pool and enjoy this tropical breeze," said Lois.

"We'll join you."

CHAPTER

CINNAMON AND HER FAMILY AWOKE EARLY
Saturday morning and drove to Bedford Correctional
Facility to visit with Shakira. They silently sat waiting for
the door to open allowing family members to visit with their loved
ones. John Harrelson thought about the last time he and Cinnamon
made this trip together. Shakira's reaction wasn't something he could
easily forget. He prayed that it would be different this time. He knew
she would have a lot of questions and he hoped that he would be able
to answer them to her satisfaction. He took inventory of his life and
knew that he had not done everything right. But what gave him hope
is that Cinnamon and Kyle had forgiven him. He could only hope
that Shakira would find it in her heart to do the same. He was tired
of living his life shrouded in lies and deceit. It had been that way for
years but now it was time for all of that to change. It was time to do
better.

Cinnamon heard the familiar click of the door as it opened. A
lone police officer stood by the door as people began to line up sin-
gle-file and enter the room. Cinnamon allowed her father to sit while
she and Kyle stood behind him waiting for Shakira to be escorted
in. Kyle looked around nervously as his eyes took in the room and
the people. How could people be so at ease, he silently wondered.

The constant sound of gates closing, buzzers every few seconds, and inmates only getting a short period of time to visit with family. However, he thought, the time spent with Shakira had to outweigh the long drive to Bedford.

Twenty minutes after they sat down, Shakira was escorted in. John Harrelson looked at his daughter and immediately broke down into tears. He could not contain himself. Tears streamed down Cinnamon's face and Kyle placed his hand on his father's shoulder to comfort him.

Shakira sat down and picked up the phone. She motioned for Cinnamon to do the same.

Cinnamon lifted the receiver to her ear. "Cinnamon," said Shakira. "Please put Dad on the phone. I need to talk to him."

"Dad," said Cinnamon. "Shakira wants to talk to you."

John Harrelson took the phone and for the first time heard his daughter's voice. "Dad, I need you to know that I love you and I forgive you. Please do not blame yourself any longer. What I did, I did out of jealousy. I have had plenty of time to think about why I am in this dreadful place and after spending countless hours with God, I have decided that I will no longer play the blame game. I take full responsibility for my actions. The hatred and jealousy I carried for years consumed me and caused me to do something uncharacteristic of who God created me to be. What I did that night can never be undone. Believe me it has haunted me night after night. But when Cinnamon came to visit me, she never stopped praying. She has so much love in her heart. She forgave me and asked if I was able to forgive myself. I must admit that it took a long time for me to get there, but it is because my sister never gave up on me. She never let me forget that God is a loving God. He forgives us of our trespasses. He doesn't remember our sins. He gave his only begotten son so that we can have everlasting life. Dad, I have so much love for you, Cinnamon and Kyle. Can you forgive me for almost destroying this family?"

John Harrelson looked at his daughter for the first time since her birth and placed his hand on the glass. Shakira's eyes followed his hand and placed her hand on the glass with his. "Shakira, I am so sorry. Right now, I feel like less than a man. What I allowed to happen was shameful, senseless, and selfish. Nothing I can say to you can wipe away the pain of growing up without a mother and a father. I thought acting like you didn't exist would wipe away the sin. I tried to cover it up but know now that was stupid. You are asking me for forgiveness. No, baby girl, I should be asking you for forgiveness. The time I wasted all these years is unimaginable. The lies and deceit I carried around for years weighed me down like a ton of bricks. When I finally came clean to my children, they let me have it. Cinnamon stopped talking to me. It hurt me to my heart that I had caused so much pain for so many people."

"Dad, the last time you came for a visit, I did not expect my emotions to be so raw. I thought I was ready to see you, but things got a little out of hand. I prayed to God that night that you would come back. All I wanted was another chance with you. I begged God to bring you back." Tears began to flow down her cheeks as she realized that God had answered her prayers. All she ever wanted was to not feel invisible.

"Shakira, please forgive me for not being there for you and for causing you so much pain," begged her father.

"I forgive you," she cried.

Kyle took the phone from his father and waited for Shakira to compose herself before telling her the good news.

"Shakira, I cannot believe you got me in here with all these crybabies," he teased.

"You're a crybaby too," retorted Shakira. "I saw you wiping your eyes, big brother."

"No. I had something in my eyes. It must be dust or something," he replied. They all laughed at Kyle's attempt to cover up the fact that he was just as emotional as the rest of them.

"So what's the good news?" urged Shakira.

"I found a lawyer who is willing to petition the court for your early release," revealed Kyle.

"Don't play with me Kyle," warned Shakira.

"Would I do something like that?" asked Kyle. Cinnamon and his father both looked at him before replying in unison, "Yes!"

Shakira could not contain her composure. She laughed so hard tears of joy ran down her face.

"Listen," continued Kyle. "She said she will have to review your case, but there is a good possibility that she might be able to get you an early release. I told her you were a model prisoner and we, as your family, are willing to vouch for you. You can live with Dad when you get out."

Shakira looked at her family and silently counted her blessings. For years, all she wanted was to be close to her father and siblings. To have them welcome her into the fold with open arms, no judgement or condemnation is more than she could ever ask for. At that very moment, she understood what it meant to be redeemed.

A police officer appeared behind Shakira. It was time to be escorted back to her cell. Before hanging up the phone, she told her family thank you and that she loved them with the love of God. John Harrelson, Cinnamon, and Kyle stayed in place until they could no longer see Shakira. The ride back to the city was silent as they each reflected on their visit with Shakira and the endless possibilities as they worked toward an early release for her. It was time to heal as a family.

Later that day, Debbie's real estate agent contacted her with good news. Her client arrived back in New York a day earlier than anticipated. She wanted to know if she could bring her by later that evening or first thing Sunday morning. Debbie had plans to see Myles, so she scheduled an appointment with her realtor for Sunday morning.

She hung up the phone and headed for her bedroom. Myles told her to not overdress as they would be outside most of the evening. The outfit she chose was comfy casual with equally as comfortable shoes. When she was satisfied with her selection, she showered and dressed. It was now seven o'clock and she expected Myles to arrive at any minute.

As she sat on the sofa, she wondered how her mother was doing. If only she could talk to her, she would feel much better about the situation. However, she trusted her friends to take good care of her. If anything were to happen, at least there was the letter in the safety

deposit box at First Caribbean International Bank to explain everything in detail. She silently hoped it would not come to that and that
she would be able to get out of New York without incident.

There was a knock at the door. She looked at the clock. "You're
early," she said as she opened the door. Her smile quickly dissipated.
She did not recognize the people standing at her door.

"Can I help you?" she asked.

"Debbie Adderly?" asked Special Agent McBride.

"How can I help you?" she asked again.

"Are you Debbie Adderly?" asked McBride.

"Yes," she replied.

"Ms. Adderly. I am Special Agent McBride, and this is Special
Agent Simmons. We will need you to come with us."

"Why?" she asked.

"We will explain everything to you downtown," offered Special
Agent Simmons.

Debbie reached for her purse on the table in the foyer and
removed the keys to lock the door. In the distance, Debbie heard the
soft chime of the elevator. Her eyes voluntarily looked toward the
sound and saw Myles walking slowly toward her and the FBI agents.
Myles could not let on that he knew McBride and Simmons, so he
remained resolute.

"What's going on? Debbie what's going on? Where are you taking her?" he asked.

"Sir, please step aside," said Agent McBride.

"Well, can you at least tell me where you are taking her?"

"Are you a relative?"

"No, but we are close. She's my…"

"She's your what, sir?" asked McBride.

"She's a special person that I care deeply for," revealed Myles.

"Ms. Adderly is being taken downtown for questioning. Here
is my card. You can reach me at that number day or night," said
McBride.

Myles did not know what else to do so he just stood there help-
lessly watching as the agents escorted Debbie from the building. In
his mind, he kept going over his time spent with her at Cape May. He

remembered that Debbie was careful not to talk about her work and he didn't pressure her. Even while at dinner with Stanley and Shirley she did not discuss her work. Myles thought back to the awkward moment when Shirley asked Debbie about the process for awarding contracts. He didn't think much of it at that time but now that the investigation had taken another turn, he thought maybe Stanley and Shirley were not who they pretended to be. None of this was making sense. Why now? What did they have on Debbie to bring her in for questioning?

Myles exited the building and stood on the sidewalk. The agents escorting Debbie out of the building play over and over in his mind. Why had he not noticed this before, he said to himself. There was a black van parked across the street. He watched as the agents pulled away from the curb. As soon as they pulled out, the van followed. Myles placed the card in his jacket pocket. Agent McBride would be hearing from him. Something else was going on and he would not rest until he got answers.

The concierge walked out and stood beside Myles. "Do you know what's going on?" he asked.

"Not yet, but I'm going to find out," replied Myles. "Let me ask you something," continued Myles. "There was a black van parked across the street. Do you know how long it's been there?"

"Sure. I noticed it a couple of months ago. It never moved. However, I would see different people getting in and out of the van," said the concierge.

"What do you mean by different people getting in and out of the van?" asked Myles.

"You know. Like a stakeout you would see on one of those detective shows," explained the concierge.

"Thanks," said Myles. "And I don't think the residents in this building have anything to worry about."

"Yeah, that's what I told them, but I wanted to make sure," said the concierge as he returned to the lobby.

Myles drove back to his apartment; however, he could not bring himself to get out of the car. Everything felt like it was crumbling down around him. He thought about going to Leroy's apartment, but he realized that would not be a good idea. Leroy would have too many questions. The only person he could talk to about what he witnessed is his grandmother.

Leona was sitting in the living room enjoying a cup of hot tea when Myles knocked at the door. She gingerly placed her teacup on the table and slowly walked toward the door.

"Who is it?" she sang.

"Hey, Granny, it's me," said Myles.

"I'm sorry I don't know anyone with the name me," replied his grandmother.

"Okay, I see we are going to play games today," teased Myles. "Granny, please open the door. It's your favorite grandson, Myles."

"Oh, Myles," cried his grandmother. She opened the door with a grand gesture reminiscent of old black and white movies from Hollywood. His grandmother made life fun. From the time he was a little boy, she made him feel special. The one constant in his life after his mother died, full of wisdom, or as the women around the neighborhood called, mother's wit. He and his grandmother would sit for hours talking about any and everything. She never held back. Most guys he knew would not talk to their parents about anything they were going through or go to them with questions. His relationship with his grandmother was different. She told him that he could come to her with anything. She would say, *"Myles, I don't care how bad you think it is, you can talk to me. I will tell you what I know. If I don't know the answer, I'm not going to lie to you. I'll tell you I don't know. But one thing's for sure, if I don't know, I will find someone who does. You can take that to the bank."*

"What brings you this way?" asked his grandmother.

"I need to talk to you. Granny, I just witnessed something that shook me up a little and I don't know what to do."

"Okay, well come on over here and sit down. Remember, there is nothing too bad that you can't tell your grandmother."

"Granny, it's about Debbie. She and I were supposed to spend the day together but…"

His grandmother held up her hand to stop Myles. "Sweetie, I thought you were going to break it off with her. What happened to that plan?"

"I did break it off with her, but the FBI agents had other plans for me," explained Myles.

"Humph! What plans did they have for my grandson?" asked his grandmother.

"Okay, please calm down, and I'll tell you everything. But you must promise me that you will listen to the story in its entirety before you express any comments. Deal?"

"Deal," said his grandmother reluctantly.

"Okay, as mentioned, I did break it off with Debbie. However, when I arrived at work the following day, the FBI agents called me into their office and disclosed that they knew that I had broken it off with Debbie. How did they know this information? They knew because her place is bugged. They even bugged my office and apartment. Not only that, I found out today that the FBI has for the past two months or longer, surveilled her residence. Who knows how many recordings they have compiled? The reason they wanted me to get back in good with Debbie is because she would not suspect me. They asked me to try and get her to talk about how the same companies were consistently awarded city contracts. She and I took a couple of days off from work and drove to Cape May. I have never seen Debbie so relaxed. I thought, finally I am going to get her to talk and all of this would be over."

Myles got up and walked to the French doors leading to the balcony overlooking the courtyard. He stood motionless for what appeared to be an eternity before continuing. "I felt like we were being followed so I pulled off the Parkway into a rest stop. The car I thought was following us kept going and I was so relieved. So while we were there, Debbie met a lady in the restroom. She found out that she and her husband were on their way to Cape May as well. To make a long story short, we ran into these two while sightseeing and they invited us to have dinner with them. According to them, they were celebrating their fortieth wedding anniversary. We met them at the restaurant and were having a nice time. Shirley and Stanley were making small talk with us. They asked about my job and I told them. I didn't see any harm in telling them. Then Shirley asked Debbie about her job. She informed Shirley that she worked in the mayor's office and that she awarded city contracts. Still I did not think anything of it until she asked Debbie about the criteria for awarding city contracts and how she went about determining who would get the contracts. The expression on Debbie's face was one that had seen a ghost," said Myles.

Leona reached for the teacup, bringing it to her lips, she quietly sipped the tea as Myles continued.

"I excused myself from the table and went after Debbie. She was standing outside of the restaurant. I asked if she were okay, but she told me she needed to get a little air as she felt nauseous."

"Was she?" asked his grandmother.

"Was she what?" inquired Myles.

"Nauseous," replied his grandmother.

"I took her at her word," said Myles. "Here's the kicker. I drove over to Debbie's residence to pick her up. When I got off the elevator, I saw two FBI agents escorting Debbie down the hall before coming here."

Myles heard the clanging of the teacup as his grandmother returned the cup to the saucer. He eyed his grandmother with trepidation. He was a grown man, but the reverence held for his grandmother goes without saying. He had never disappointed his grandmother and, hopefully, today he would not disappoint.

His grandmother sat quietly as she thought about everything Myles told her. The last time he came for a visit, he confided in her. He knew that information was confidential, but he trusted her enough to confide in her. When she advised him to cut ties with Debbie, it was for his own good. She was under investigation and they were looking at him as well. As she sat there trying to process everything she heard, she thought about the characteristics of her grandson. He is loyal, good-natured, hardworking, honest, and kind. When Myles considers you a friend, you are his friend for life. She has never met anyone as generous as Myles. But it saddened her to think that he had offered his heart up again to be broken. She didn't see any good coming from this.

"Myles, do you know why they took her today? From what you told me, it doesn't sound like they have anything on her," asked his grandmother.

"I tried to get information out of them as they were walking Debbie out of the building. One of the agents handed me her card. I will give her a call later today to see what I can find out."

"At this point, that's all you can do. For what it's worth, I really hate to hear this about Debbie."

"Yeah, me too," said Myles.

Leona stole glances at her grandson as he sat there silently flipping the agent's card between his fingers. He was all she had left in this life and she wanted him to be happy. It seemed like drama followed him around like a stray cat.

"Can I get you something to eat?" asked his grandmother. "I am having leftover tuna fish casserole for dinner. You are welcome to join me."

"Not right now…maybe later. I am still trying to get my head wrapped around what I saw. To bring her in for questioning, something happened. They definitely know something."

"You're right. But there is no reason for you to sit here worrying yourself sick about Debbie. I suspect she will be back at home tonight or no later than tomorrow morning," said his grandmother.

"You really think that the FBI is going to release her tonight?" asked Myles.

"Well, let's just say I am holding out hope that she will be back at home sleeping in her own bed tonight."

"I don't think so," said Myles. "When we were in Cape May, she kept talking about leaving New York. She even asked if I had thought about living somewhere other than New York. I remember asking her where she thought about going. She said she wanted to live on an island somewhere in the tropics."

"Do you think the FBI knows about her plans to leave New York?" asked his grandmother.

Myles thought back to a recent conversation with McBride. "Not sure. Maybe. Agent McBride mentioned a few days ago that Debbie might be making plans to leave New York and it was their job to stop her from doing so."

"My goodness," exclaimed his grandmother. "It appears as though Debbie has gotten herself into a heap of trouble. The elections are only a few months out. If the FBI investigation reveals corruption in the mayor's office, I'm afraid to think of what might happen with this election, to her, and anyone else caught up in this."

Myles beheld his grandmother and noticed that she looked tired. He watched as she slowly made her way to the kitchen. Typically, spry with a bounce in her step, she appeared to be less energetic. Her shoulders were no longer squared and her back straight. He noticed a slight roundness in the shoulders. When did all of this happen? He tried to remember how long it had been since he last saw his grandmother. He had been so caught up in the investigation that maybe he didn't notice it the last time he saw her. It saddened him to think that his grandmother, his one constant, was slowing down. He got up from the sofa and headed to the kitchen.

"Granny, that tuna fish casserole smells good. You haven't lost your touch," he teased.

"Sit down and I'll fix you a plate."

"I have a better idea. Why don't you sit down, and I'll fix both of our plates? It will be just like old times," said Myles as he pulled out a chair for his grandmother.

His grandmother watched as Myles moved about the kitchen. She wanted to hold onto this moment for as long as God would allow. She silently prayed a prayer of thanks for more time with her grandson.

Myles set a plate before his grandmother before taking a seat at the table. They bowed their heads as Myles said the grace. He looked up and smiled as this time spent with his grandmother reminded him of simpler times growing up in the old neighborhood. Sunday dinners after church and selling apples door-to-door with his best friend Leroy. Singing along to songs by Earth, Wind & Fire, or just hanging out with Cinnamon and Leroy.

During the meal, thoughts of Debbie crept into his thoughts threatening to steal time spent with his grandmother. For the sake of sanity, he pushed all thoughts of Debbie aside and gave his grandmother his full attention. Special Agent McBride had provided him with a number to call day or night. He would do just that. But right now, spending time with his grandmother gave him comfort. So much so, that what was on the other side of the door, he did not want to face. Myles wanted to make everything better for Debbie, but he was painfully aware it was not within his power. Nothing good is going to come from this, he thought.

Debbie sat in an interrogation room close to an hour before Special Agents McBride and Simmons joined her. They walked in carrying several files implicating the mayor, Debbie and the mayor's campaign manager, Glenn, in a pay-to-play scheme. The files contained the names of all companies awarded city contracts since the mayor took office. Names of shareholding banks, account numbers, dollar amounts, and property owned by all three littered pages throughout the files.

Agent McBride looked up from the open file on the table and asked, "Ms. Adderly, do you know why you are here?"

Debbie stared at Agent McBride as if she were not there.

"Ms. Adderly, I'm going to ask you again. Do you know why you are here?"

"All I know, is that you and…I'm sorry what's your name?"

"Agent McBride."

"Agent McBride, as I was saying, you and your partner knocked on my door and escorted me away from my residence without telling me why. So in answer to your question, no I do not know why I am here."

"Ms. Adderly," said Simmons. "In your line of work, have you ever heard the term pay-to-play? Before you answer, I want you to really think about how you are going to respond. You see, I would imagine that as the procurement officer in the mayor's office, one who is responsible for awarding city contracts to vendors, you are acutely aware of this and the consequences of participating in such a scheme."

McBride got up from her seat and walked to the other side of the table. She slid the open file in front of Debbie. "Ms. Adderly, the files we walked in with contain a year's worth of investigative work into this scheme. Please know that the Department of Justice and federal law enforcement will not tolerate public corruption at any level of government. I want you to take a good look at what is in this file. We have hours of recordings and surveillance tapes on you. I must admit, the noise jammer was a nice touch."

Debbie closed the file. "Are you charging me?"

"Look, Ms. Adderly," started Simmons. "We think you got in a little over your head. Why don't you tell us how it happened? Agent McBride and I will do all we can to help you."

Debbie knew this game. How many times had she seen actors on television playing good cop, bad cop. It did not matter that two federal agents sat across from her. She was not about to fall into their trap. She needed to lawyer up and it had to be done quickly.

"Agents McBride and Simmons, I appreciate that you are willing to help me. Or so you claim that you would like to help me. However, I think this is where I ask for my lawyer. I would like to make a phone call, please."

"Sure," said McBride. "You can call your lawyer. Come with me, please."

Agent Simmons gathered the files and followed them out of the interrogation room. Both agents waited outside the room as Debbie phoned her lawyer. When she hung up, she was escorted to the interrogation room where she sat silently contemplating her fate.

Sophia Crain, a prominent trial lawyer and managing partner at Percy & Crain, walked into the interrogation room and did what she did best, took charge. Retained by Debbie Adderly months ago for such a time as this, she was determined to earn every penny set aside for her client's defense. By the time she was through, Ms. Adderly would look like a choir girl.

She looked at Agents McBride and Simmons and said, "I'd like to have a minute with my client."

"You have five minutes," replied Simmons.

The lawyer smiled her appreciation before pushing out a firm, "Thank you."

Debbie looked up as her lawyer approached. "Sorry to interrupt your weekend. I'm quite sure you can think of more exciting places to be than here," said Debbie.

"Sure, I can. So what evidence did they present?"

"They claim to have a year's worth of surveillance tapes and recordings. Apparently, my office and condo as well as the mayor's office was bugged. From what I saw in the file, they have account numbers for offshore accounts, investments, and listings of property owned by the mayor, his campaign manager, and, of course, me. They asked questions about a proposed pay-to-play scheme in the mayor's office."

"What do you know about a pay-to-play scheme?" asked Sophia Crain.

"Nothing," Debbie whispered.

"Okay. Don't say anything else. Let me do all the talking," advised her lawyer.

Right on cue, Agents Simmons and McBride entered the room and sat down across from Debbie and her attorney.

"What crime are you charging my client with?"

"We have reason to believe that Mis. Adderly participated in a pay-to-play scheme. As the procurement officer responsible for awarding city contracts, naturally we had her under investigation along with the mayor and his campaign manager," explained McBride.

"What evidence do you have indicating that my client participated in this proposed pay-to-play scheme?"

McBride opened the file before her and handed the lawyer several pieces of paper. The papers contained the names of all companies awarded city contracts since the mayor took office. Names of shareholding banks, account numbers, dollar amounts, and property owned by all three littered pages throughout the files.

"Do you have any evidence linking my client directly to a pay-to-play scheme?"

"We have evidence that the same companies were consistently awarded city contracts."

"But you do not have any hard evidence that my client was involved," probed her attorney.

She looked between both agents.

"Based on your silence, I will take that as a no. If there is nothing more, I am walking out of here with my client. The evidence you have against my client is circumstantial at best. Until you have something concrete, you cannot detain her any longer."

"Wait," said McBride. "We know that something is going on and has been going on for years. Otherwise, we never would have received an anonymous tip and opened an investigation. We believe that your client knows more than she is letting on and we are going to prove it. She is the procurement officer in the mayor's office. All contracts are reviewed and awarded by her. You cannot get me to believe that she is not in some way involved in a pay-to-play scheme. She knows something and we are going to prove it."

"Have a good rest of your day." Sophia Crain and Debbie got up and walked out.

Agents Simmons and McBride watched as Debbie walked out with her lawyer. "We need to pay a visit to Davis Construction and Premier Architects. Maybe we can turn up the heat on Debbie Adderly by revealing to them that she was brought in for questioning," suggested Simmons.

"I concur," said McBride.

Debbie and her attorney emerged from the 1st Precinct and walked briskly toward a waiting car. They both entered the car from opposite sides with her attorney instructing the driver to drop them off at her office.

Debbie sat in silence staring out the window as the buildings zipped by and became one with the skyline. Every thought in her head competed with the other until there was no more room to accommodate another thought.

Her body language did not go unnoticed by her attorney. She knew she needed to act fast if she were to help her client. Pay-to-play schemes were not uncommon, and certainly did not come without consequence. But her gut told her there was more to Debbie's story. As her attorney, the more she uncovered, the better her chances of cutting a deal with the US Attorney's office.

The driver pulled up in front of a downtown high-rise office building. Debbie and her attorney got out and entered the building. Although it was Saturday afternoon, the foot traffic in the building was reminiscent of an average workday.

She and Debbie signed in at the front desk and waited for the elevator. When it arrived, her attorney pushed the button for the sixteenth floor.

"I brought you here so that we could talk more freely. The federal agents told me that you used a noise jammer a few times. That's why all the evidence they have on you thus far is circumstantial. However, do not think for one minute they are going to stop. They will make it their life's mission to find someone to implicate you. My guess, they are going after those who were awarded city contracts and anyone else to make a strong case against you. That's what I would do. Don't be surprised if they find someone to turn state's evidence against you. In any event, we need to be prepared for whatever they throw at us."

The elevator chimed when it reached the sixteenth floor. The law offices of Percy & Crain were conveniently located across from the elevator. The massive glass doors opened onto a beautifully decorated and spacious reception area. In the distance, Debbie could hear the ring of telephones and faint voices of lawyers hard at work for their clients.

On the way to her lawyer's office, they stopped by the kitchen. Her lawyer opened the refrigerator and retrieved a diet coke. "Can I get you something to drink? There's juice, soda, and water. Pick your poison. Scratch that. Poor choice of words."

Debbie moved closer to the refrigerator. She took note of the well-stocked refrigerator before reaching in and grabbing a ginger ale.

Her lawyer unlocked the office door and switched on the light as she made her way to her desk. "Make yourself comfortable and I'll be right with you."

Debbie sat down in a chair near the window and watched as an airplane disappeared behind the clouds. She wondered where it might be headed; silently wishing she had a window seat. A cabin in the woods would be more desirable than sitting in her lawyer's office. Her day had started out so promising. She and Myles had plans of spending the day together. The look on his face as the agents escorted her out of the building and the knock on her door earlier that morning was still fresh in her mind. The reality of two federal agents standing on the other side of the door was more than she could handle at this time. Her thoughts shifted to the warm tropical breeze of Turks and Caicos. She imagined the joy on her mother's face as she was handed the deed to the property. She thought about how much fun she and her mother would have watching as the ramshackle building inhabiting the property torn down and replaced with a stately dwelling. She thought about her good friends that accompanied her mother on her exodus from Baruch Houses. Debbie felt like she was struggling to awaken from a bad dream. She felt as if the walls were beginning to close in around her as her dream to leave New York faded into obscurity.

Her thoughts were interrupted by the movement of a chair being pulled back from the conference table.

"Debbie," her attorney said as she sat down. "If I am going to prepare a strong defense for you, I will need to know everything. Don't hold anything back. I don't care how insignificant you think it is, you let me be the judge of its significance. I have seen many defense attorney's cases unravel right before their eyes because their client withheld information. My gut tells me that you have a story to tell. So why don't you tell me your story starting at the beginning."

Debbie sat with both elbows on the conference room table; her mouth gently rested on clasped fingers. Finally, she sat back in the chair and began to narrate her story.

"I was young…just out of college when I secured a job at City Hall. I had returned to Baruch Houses after graduation. One day there was a knock at the door. A guy said he was running for City Council. He handed me a handful of pamphlets and moved on to the next apartment. Before he could knock on our neighbor's door,

I asked him if he needed any more volunteers. He asked if I were serious about volunteering for his campaign and to understand that this was strictly volunteering as there would be no pay associated with it. I was told what time to show up and that next day marked the beginning of many more opportunities for me."

"Impressive. Did he get elected?" asked her lawyer.

"Yes, and in return for working on his campaign, he helped me secure a position in the mayor's office."

"Have you been with the mayor since the beginning of his tenure?"

"No. There was someone in my position before my hire. I started working for the mayor six months into his first term."

"Would you happen to know what happened? Did your predecessor get fired or secure another position?"

"I'm not sure. No one would discuss it. So after a while I learned to keep my head down and nose to the grindstone," explained Debbie.

"Okay. Who introduced the pay-to-play scheme and how did you get involved?" asked her attorney.

Debbie reached for the can of ginger ale and took several sips before continuing with her story. "I was working late one evening when the mayor walked by and saw the light on in my office. He stuck his head in the door and inquired as to why I was working so late. I told him I was going through bids for city contracts and noticed something was a little off with how contracts were awarded. I pointed out where the same companies were awarded multimillion-dollar contracts consistently."

"What did he say when you pointed this out to him?" asked her attorney.

"It's not what he said, it's more about what he didn't say," replied Debbie.

"What do you mean?" inquired her attorney.

"He didn't ask what I was concerned about. He snickered a little and said that we could go over it another day."

"Did you?"

"Not exactly."

"What do you mean?"

"I was summoned to his office. When I arrived, he and his campaign manager were in deep conversation. They were speaking in a hushed tone and I could not make out what they were talking about."

"Did they discuss the pay-to-play scheme with you at that time?"

"No. Oddly enough, the mayor brought up my outstanding school loans."

"What about them?"

"You have to understand. I was fresh out of college with school loans to pay back. I really needed this job."

Debbie's lawyer considered her words carefully before continuing. "Debbie, I am not here to judge you, only to help you. You have hired me to do a job and I will do everything within the parameters of the law to help you through this. However, I cannot impress upon you enough how important it is to this case to reveal everything you know. If it smells like corruption, these federal agents will be all over it."

"I wanted to impress the mayor. I wanted him to know that I could hold my own and get things done. So when he offered to 'clear up' my outstanding school loans, I did not question it. It was one less thing I had to worry about."

"Were those his exact words?" asked her lawyer. "Did he tell you how he proposed to clear up your outstanding school loans."

"Those were his exact words. He never divulged how he proposed to clear up my student loans. All I know is that one day I received a letter from my loan provider that my loans were paid in full."

"How long from the time you received the letter from the loan provider did the mayor approach you about the pay-to-play scheme?"

"He did not bring me in on the pay-to-play scheme until it was time to send out more RFPs for city contracts."

"How did he approach you?" asked her attorney.

"He called me into his office. Again, Glen, his campaign manager was there. He invited me to sit down as they wanted to go over the process for awarding city contracts with me. I thought it was a little odd that the campaign manager would be in the meeting, but I kept my mouth shut and took note of what the mayor was saying."

"What did you learn from this meeting?" asked her attorney.

"I learned that the same companies were being awarded city contracts consistently. There were other companies that could easily have done the work, but I was told to find an excuse for not awarding them the contract. In other words, I had to make it seem that they were not qualified and did not meet the criteria. Some of the companies stopped bidding on city contracts, but there was one construction company that was a little more persistent."

"With the company that showed persistence, how did you handle them?"

"I continued to avoid them by not returning phone calls and discarding any mail received from them. When that strategy ceased to work, he showed up at my office. I guess you could say I was intrigued by his persistence, so I invited him into my office. I took the time to walk him through the bidding process and called in a favor with one of the bigger companies. They brought his small construction company in on a few of their contracts. I continued to call in favors to these companies so that he would not rock the boat, if you will. His company began to grow and eventually he was able to bid on contracts and win."

"So did this construction company participate in the pay-to-play scheme as well?" asked her lawyer.

"No. I found out later that Glen approached them about it, but they refused to participate. Not long after that, the mayor informed me that they were to be dropped from the list."

"Were you receiving money for participating in this scheme?"

"Yes."

"How much did you receive, and did you use any of it for personal gain?" inquired her attorney.

"Over the course of seven and a half years, several million has been deposited into an off-shore account," she replied. "I have not touched any of it."

"You live in a condo on the Upper East Side, correct?"

"Yes."

"Did you use any of the money to purchase the condo?" asked her attorney.

"No."

"How long have you lived on the Upper East Side?"

"Two years."

"Where did you live prior to purchasing the condo?"

"I shared a ratty two-bedroom apartment with a college roommate until I could save up enough money for a down payment. Because my credit report showed student loans paid in full, I was able to secure financing at an affordable rate."

"How much did you pay for your condo? Eight hundred and fifty thousand. How much did you save toward the down payment?"

Her attorney glanced up from her notes. "Debbie, need I remind you why I need you to be honest with me? Listen to me carefully. How much did you save, not borrow, toward the down payment?"

"I didn't."

"What are you telling me? You didn't save any money, or you didn't borrow money toward the down payment?"

"There was no need. The condo was a gift."

Sophia Crain was not afraid to ask the obvious. She removed her eyeglasses and placed them gently on the table. Leaning back in the chair, she stared out the window allowing her mind to run through the many ways this case could be argued. But if she were to fervently defend her client, she had to ask the hard questions. She must be prepared to attack at every opportunity. Her success at this firm did not come easily. There were many hard-won battles earning Percy & Crain the reputation of attorneys that never back down, never give in, and are always prepared for the fight.

"Who was the gift from?"

Debbie knew that one day she would have to reveal the arrangement but secretly hoped that day would never come. When Jeremy approached her about the condo on the Upper East Side, she was intrigued with his proposition. After all, she was living in a ratty two-bedroom apartment making a civil servant's wages. She desired more and felt she was deserving of it.

"J&M Construction."

Her attorney scribbled J&M Construction in her notes and placed an asterisk beside the company name. Sophia Crain had been in the game a long time and could smell when there was more to the story. And this story was as tangled as they come but she was up to the challenge of following every thread of evidence to get to the truth.

"Tell me about the companies that participated in this scheme?"

"Davis Construction and Premier Architects are the primary companies receiving city wide contracts," revealed Debbie. "The smaller companies were brought on as contractors. That was done to satisfy them and not bring attention to the pay-to-play scheme run by the mayor."

"Well, I'm going to point out the obvious here," started her lawyer. "The FBI opened an investigation. So I think someone was dissatisfied and called the FBI. That's the only way they would have known about it. Do you agree?"

"I'm not sure," replied Debbie.

Her lawyer scanned her notes. "You mentioned a company that the mayor approached but they refused to play along. Who was that?" she asked.

"J&M Construction."

"The same company that gifted you the condo?"

"Yes."

Sophia Crain reviewed her notes to see what she might have missed. Why would J&M Construction gift a condo to Debbie? Their vendor client relationship seemed a little skewed. Her notes revealed that Jeremy of J&M Construction was the primary contact and the one she helped through the bidding process.

"How did J&M Construction come upon the property eventually gifted to you?"

"Another side of J&M Construction is J&M Investment Properties. Before selling their company to Davis Construction, they invested in two condos on the Upper East Side. One to live in, the other as an investment property."

"They sound like shrewd businessmen. So now that I understand more about J&M Construction, tell me about your involvement with them."

"After a while, Matt, Jeremy, and I became good friends and looked out for each other. They confided in me about how Glen approached them about the pay-to-play scheme. I wasn't aware of Glen's visit until they told me about it. I cannot say I was surprised, however, the amount disclosed was more than the agreed upon amount. That's when I knew that I had allowed myself to be drawn into something all for the love of money. Every month, money was being transferred into my offshore account."

Sophia Crain removed her glasses and pushed back from the conference table. She walked to the wall of windows and stood staring down at taxicabs ushering people to various destinations. As forthcoming as her client had been thus far with information, she stumbled. She now knew that the missing link in this chain of events is the company acquired by Davis Construction.

"Debbie, do you trust me?"

"Yes."

"Then trust me when I tell you that I believe I know who alerted the FBI. I believe you know too. You might not be able to get your head wrapped around it at this moment, but you must. You are paying me to represent you. As your advocate in court, it is my responsibility to be prepared to fight any judgment brought against you. I would stake my reputation as an attorney that someone from J&M Construction alerted the FBI about the pay-to-play scheme."

"No. That can't be possible. We are friends. I believe they would have told me if they were planning to alert the FBI. Why would they need to tell the FBI? They made millions because of me. I looked out for them. They wouldn't do this to me," she said pleadingly.

"How can I get in touch with them?" Sophia asked softly.

For the second time today, Debbie felt like the walls were closing in around her. Everything she had carefully constructed felt like sand sifting through her fingers. Reluctantly, she reached for her purse and retrieved a small slip of paper containing the number where the twins, Matt, and Jeremy Bassey, could be reached in Turks and Caicos.

Sophia wrote the number down and handed the slip of paper back to Debbie. "I will give them a call tonight. We are through for now. I will give you a call after I speak with the Bassey brothers. My driver will take you home."

Neither woman said a word until they got on the elevator. "What do you think will happen?" asked Debbie.

"Well, this is definitely going to trial. So you and I must do our level best to be as prepared as possible. I will know a little more after I've had a chance to talk to your friends in Turks and Caicos. Don't worry," counseled her attorney.

"That's easier said than done," responded Debbie. "Looking back on it now, I wish I had not allowed myself to be pushed into this. All I could think about at that time is the mayor telling me that he owned me. I felt like I didn't have a choice."

"Wait. What did he mean by 'own you'?" inquired her attorney.

"He constantly reminded me that he paid off my student loans; therefore, he said he owned me," explained Debbie.

"Good to know. I can use that against him," responded her attorney confidently.

The elevator finally arrived on the lobby level. Debbie stopped by the guard's desk and signed out. The driver was waiting outside of the car for her when she arrived.

"Try to get some rest and I will be in touch on Monday. I will reach out to your friends in Turks and Caicos today to try and make some headway on the case. Depending on what I learn, they could be an asset or liability. Let's hope they prove to be an asset. Also, going forward, I will need you to not contact the Bassey's. I'm positive the FBI still has surveillance on you. They are waiting for you to slip up. Understood?" cautioned her lawyer.

"Understood," responded Debbie.

She walked Debbie to the car and instructed the driver to take Debbie home. "I'll be in contact soon."

Debbie climbed in the back seat of the car and closed her eyes as the driver navigated the car through the streets of Manhattan to her condo on the Upper East Side. She thought about Myles and how she would explain all of this to him. The expression on his face as she was being escorted out of the building was something she could not shake. How could she face him? The manipulative power the mayor wielded over her is something she could not comprehend, so how would she be able to explain this to Myles. She was spent. Right now, all she wanted to do was get home, soak in a hot tub of water, and climb into bed.

There was a message waiting on her answering machine when she arrived home. It was from Myles.

"Debbie, give me a call when you get home. I'm worried about you. I don't care about the time. We need to talk."

Debbie erased the message and walked down the hall toward her bedroom. She entered the bathroom and ran her bath. She eased down in the water and allowed the tears to flow. At this moment, she felt like the little girl growing up in Baruch Houses who longed to be anywhere but there. For the first time in life, she attempted to pray.

The sun streamed through the blinds in Debbie's bedroom the following morning. She lay across her bed not fully comfortable. Thoughts of her encounter with the FBI, the look on Myles's face, and exposing her vulnerability left her feeling not in control of her life. This was new to her as she had always been in control of her life.

She closed her eyes and tried to envision sitting on the beaches of Turks and Caicos. If she tried hard enough, maybe she could hear the sea gulls and feel the sun on her face and the warmth of the tropical breeze as she relaxed in a beach chair. The ringing of the telephone caused her to put a pillow over her head to drown out the shrill sound.

"Hello," she said sleepily.

"Hey," said Myles. "Are you okay?"

"About as good as can be under the circumstances," she replied.

"You want to talk about it?" he asked.

Debbie sighed deeply and rolled over onto her back. "Myles, I'm not ready to talk about this yet."

There was a long silence.

"Myles are you still there?" she inquired.

"Yeah," he replied.

"Give me a little time to process this situation. I give you my word that I will call you and explain everything," pleaded Debbie.

"I know," said Myles.

Debbie sat on the edge of the bed and said, "You know what?"

"Everything," revealed Myles.

Instinctively, Debbie's hand moved to her mouth. How could he know, she thought? The room felt like it was spinning. If the humiliation of being escorted out of her residence and placed in the back of a federal car and taken downtown for questioning wasn't enough, learning that the man she loved knew about her legal troubles executed a strategic blow. She had to find out how much he knew.

Debbie remained silent as she walked down the hall in search of her purse. When she entered the living room, she spotted it on the dining room table. She opened it and took out the noise jammer. She turned it on before she continued her conversation with Myles.

"Myles, I don't know what you think you know but I promise you it's not what you think," she said.

"I'm listening," he said.

"I don't want to talk about this over the phone. I have an appointment at two o'clock today. After that, my schedule is free," she said.

"Okay. What's a good time to stop by?" he asked.

"Six should be a good time," confirmed Debbie. "Bring your appetite. I will prepare dinner."

Myles chuckled. "You have not prepared dinner one day in your life. Be sure to order from a good restaurant."

The line went dead. Debbie sat holding the phone as she thought about how best to tell Myles that she wasn't the person he thought her to be.

Debbie glanced at the time. She had a couple of hours to herself before she met with her realtor. She looked around the condo and decided to straighten up a little. First impressions are often lasting she thought to herself. As she went from room to room, spot-checking everything, she remembered how meticulously she selected each item. Each piece of furniture and accessory had a story. When she was satisfied with the way things looked, she showered and dressed for the appointment with her realtor.

Promptly at two o'clock, there was a knock at the door. Debbie opened the door wide to welcome her realtor and prospective buyer. Debbie could not believe the prospective buyer of her condo was none other than the woman she met in Colorado. Flanking her on either side were two adorable twin girls. She could not have asked for a better scandal than to have the mother of Julius Carbozza's children standing in the foyer of her Upper East Side condo. Not only that but making plans to purchase her condo.

"Hello and welcome to my home," said Debbie as she extended a hand to Jolene Figueroa.

"Thank you. You have a beautiful home," complemented Jolene.

"Thank you. It was truly a labor of love. Can I get you something to drink or would you like to see the rest of the condo first?" asked Debbie.

"I would love to see more of this lovely condo," smiled Jolene.

"Let's start with the bedrooms and work our way back toward the front of the condo," suggested her realtor.

"This condo has three bedrooms. However, one is set up as an office. Next to it is the guest room, identical in size to the office. Across the hall is the master bedroom with an en suite. I would like to point out that all of the bedrooms have large walk-in closets," said the realtor.

"You have exquisite taste," offered Jolene. "From what I understand, the furniture conveys."

"That's correct," said Debbie. "Of course, that is if you want the furniture. I understand that it is my taste and women generally want to decorate a space to reflect their taste, but I thought it would be easier for all involved if the furniture conveyed with the sale of the condo," explained Debbie.

Jolene walked toward Debbie. When she was standing directly in front of her, she asked, "Can I give you a hug? That is the nicest thing anyone has ever done for me. Imagine purchasing a fully furnished condo on the Upper East Side. It doesn't get any better than this," she said as she wrapped her arms around Debbie.

"Well, I believe you just sold your condo," said the realtor. "Let's take a look at the rest of the condo and get started on the paperwork, shall we?"

The realtor walked Debbie and Jolene through the sale and provided them with names and addresses for filing the paperwork. Jolene provided Debbie with a check for $1.2 million dollars and the realtor a check for $150,000.

"Girls, we just bought a condo," exclaimed Jolene excitedly.

"All of this is ours?" asked the girls in unison.

"Yes, all of this is ours," said Jolene.

"Hey, girls, why don't we go check out the balcony," said the realtor. The twin girls followed the realtor out onto the balcony leaving Debbie and Jolene standing in the kitchen.

"Can I get you something to drink?" asked Debbie.

"Sure. A glass of water would be nice," she said.

"Imagine my shock when I opened the door and saw you standing there with my realtor," Debbie said as she handed the glass of water to Jolene.

"Yeah, I was just as shocked as you. Just so you know, I had no idea you were the seller," offered Jolene.

"This place is gorgeous. Can I ask why you are selling it?"

Debbie struggled with the answer to Jolene's question. How could she tell a stranger she had participated in a pay-to-play scheme along with the mayor and might be facing jail time? That's not something you want to tell the person who just bought your condo for $1.2 million dollars.

"Oh, I don't know. It's a combination of growing weary of city life and wanting something different," conjectured Debbie.

"I understand. City life isn't for everyone. Although I still live in New York, I travel to Colorado several times throughout the year just so I can breathe.

"What's stopping you from moving permanently to Colorado?" asked Debbie.

"Julius is running for mayor, correct?" asked Jolene.

"Yes," confirmed Debbie.

"It's been ten years. His father paid my family ten million dollars to keep quiet about the rape and subsequent birth of my daughters. I know that you work for the mayor and I have a good understanding of how politics work. Especially during an election year, smear campaigns can be vicious and relentless. If you go public with the information you have on Julius, what effect do you think that will have on my daughters?" asked Jolene. "They are impressionable young girls who might never get over the shame of being a product of a rape."

"So let me get this straight. You don't want me to go public with the information I have on Julius Carbozza?" asked Debbie. "Unbelievable! That information would cost him more than the mayoral race."

"I understand," said Jolene. "You already have the information. Get him to see that it is in his best interest, his wife, and extended family to drop out quietly. Let him know that you are aware of the rape and the ten million dollars in hush money his father paid to the Figueroa family. I believe he will do as you ask. I've been following him for years. I also know that he and his wife just celebrated their tenth-year wedding anniversary."

"Wow! You've really thought this through," said Debbie.

"I've had ten years to think this through. So what do you think about my plan to push him out of the running?" asked Jolene.

"I could not have thought of a better plan," said Debbie. "We are turning up the heat on Darren Jenkins and I believe he will drop out in the coming weeks, which leaves Michele Dobbs. I haven't been able to find anything on her."

"Hmm…who supplied you with information on Darren Jenkins and our friend Julius?" asked Jolene.

"I have a contact," said Debbie.

Debbie and Jolene exited the kitchen when they heard the sliding glass door open. The girls were chatting excitedly among themselves while Debbie confirmed that Jolene and the girls could take possession of the condo within one week's time.

"Girls, it's time to go. We've taken up enough of this nice lady's time," said Jolene.

Jolene and Debbie exchanged knowing glances as she walked them to the door.

Debbie shook her realtor's hand and said, "You're the best. This was the easiest transaction ever."

The girls took turns hugging Debbie before skipping off down the hall toward the elevator. Jolene reached in and hugged Debbie again before turning to follow her daughters. Selling the condo so quickly eased her fears slightly. She glanced at the clock only to realize that Myles would arrive within the hour. She picked up the phone and dialed the number to her favorite restaurant.

Myles arrived promptly at six o'clock to a candle-lit dinner of prosciutto-wrapped chicken with Romanesco florets. He was confused to see a set up like this considering what Debbie was facing.

"What's the occasion?" he asked when he walked in.

"Nothing special…I just wanted to do something nice for you. Why don't we sit down and eat?" suggested Debbie. "I know you came here to talk but why don't we take it slow. C'mon, let's eat before the food gets cold. We can talk later."

Myles removed his jacket and placed it across the arm of the sofa. "Everything looks and smells so good," he said.

Both Debbie and Myles ate in silence. Neither one knowing how best to broach the subject of the investigation, the chicken and Romanesco filled the emptiness otherwise occupied by great conversation and laughter.

Debbie looked over at Myles and said, "I ordered Tiramisu for dessert."

"Maybe later," said Myles.

"So I believe it is safe to assume that you enjoyed the meal. There's nothing left on your plate," said Debbie.

"Yeah. The meal was delicious," replied Myles.

He pushed back from the table and walked over to where Debbie sat. He took her hand and guided her toward the sofa.

"We *really* need to talk. And don't think that a meal ordered from your favorite restaurant is going to distract me from the issue at hand," he teased.

Debbie sat down next to Myles on the sofa and asked, "What did you mean when you said you knew everything?"

"I know about the investigation," revealed Myles.

"How long have you known?" asked Debbie.

Myles leaned forward and let out a sigh. "Debbie, the FBI approached my boss, John Brimmer, several months ago. They informed us at that time that they launched an investigation into possible corruption in the mayor's office. We were told that they chose our firm because we were located directly across from City Hall. They did not tell us much about the investigation. However, I got suspicious when they asked for certain files. I launched my own investigation by going through the files they had reviewed. The files were for Premier Architects and Davis Construction. Ring a bell?"

"Go on," urged Debbie.

Myles turned to face Debbie. "It did not make sense to me that two federal agents were sitting in an office next to me until one day I overheard Agents Simmons and McBride discussing the case. I was in the kitchen getting a cup of coffee; they were standing by the elevator. That's when I heard your name and mine. They knew before they approached John Brimmer, that you and I were a couple. Not long after that, I learned that surveillance equipment was everywhere. The day they showed up here to take you downtown, there was a van parked across the street. The concierge noticed the van also. He told me it had been parked there for weeks."

"Why didn't you tell me?" asked Debbie.

"I know this isn't going to make sense to you, but we were sworn to secrecy. I prayed that you were not involved in any of this."

"So what shocked you more yesterday? Seeing me escorted out of the building or Agents Simmons and McBride?"

"Both. You will never know how helpless I felt when I saw you with them. All I could think about is that I had failed to protect you."

"Don't beat yourself up Myles," said Debbie. "This is all my fault. I did not have to go along with the mayor and Glen. I did this to myself and I will have to suffer the consequence. I am no longer surprised by the extents people will go when money becomes their god. I am an example of that. Look around you. I acquired things.

Beautiful things. But these things cannot help me when I go before a judge and jury.

"I know this is going to sound strange, but I did not say anything to you because I was trying to protect you," said Myles.

Debbie looked Myles in the eye and asked, "Protect me how?" You were trying to protect me? You want to know what I think? I think you were trying to protect yourself. If you had given me a modicum of thought, you would have told me. Why did I have to hear about the investigation from someone who contributed information toward the mayor's smear campaigns? Why couldn't I hear this from the man I thought loved me?"

"That's not fair," countered Myles. "But if you really want to take it there, was it worth it? Was throwing your career away, everything you had worked so hard for, worth it? To be honest, the day I broke it off with you was the day after I overhead the conversation between Agents McBride and Simmons. I thought about my grandmother, my position at the firm and how hard John Brimmer worked to build something he believed in, and my reputation. I told myself that I needed to distance myself from you. Do you know how hard it was for me to walk away from the woman I love?"

"Why did you come back?" she asked forcefully.

Myles looked at Debbie standing there in front of him. She looked vulnerable, deflated, defeated. How could he tell Debbie that the FBI forced him back to her? The love he possessed for the beautiful, confident, businesswoman was strong as ever. In his mind, he believed he could protect her better with her than without her. He wanted desperately to tell her everything but wasn't sure if now was the right time.

"Debbie, please believe me when I tell you that my love for you transcends time. I only wish that things had turned out differently."

Debbie fought back tears of frustration as she listened to Myles. Her self-imposed plight landed her in an uncomfortable position.

"Myles, I can no longer hide behind all of the lies and deceit. I'm not innocent. Yesterday, I realized that the FBI was not going to stop until they got something concrete on me. So I called my lawyer who was able to walk me out of the 1st Precinct. We went to her office and I told her everything. I told her about the mayor paying off my school loans, the money that's sitting in a bank account untouched, and going along with the pay-to-play scheme out of fear. The reason I am sitting here with you right now is because the information the FBI has on me is circumstantial. You want to know why it's circumstantial?"

Debbie pulled the noise jammer from the pocket of her slacks. "I was informed about the investigation before we left for Cape May. The person who has provided me with information on two of the three mayoral candidates is the same person who provided me with this handy gadget. Every time you and I were together after that, I turned this on. I also used it while at Cape May. Especially after I caught a glimpse of the surveillance equipment in the room next to ours."

Myles sat dumbfounded.

"For the record, I did not know that you were under investigation. Nor did I know about the FBI agents parked in a van across the street or taking up residence at your firm. All my contact told me was that the mayor's office was under investigation and so was I. That's why the trip to Cape May was so special. I needed time away from the city to clear my head."

Myles reached for Debbie and pulled her closer to him. "If I could take all of this away from you, I would," he whispered.

"I know you would," responded Debbie. "You're a good man Myles Beyers."

"If I had told you earlier about the investigation, what would you have done?" asked Myles.

"I would have tried to get out of New York as quickly as possible. Even if I had attempted to leave, the FBI most likely would have stopped me at the airport. With my luck, the entire scenario would play out like a scene in a James Bond movie complete with intrigue, espionage, car chases and someone tackling me at the airport. I can see it all so clearly. A body comes flying through the air and tackles me right before I board an international flight."

The laughter did much to lighten the mood.

"Tiramisu?" asked Debbie.

"Tiramisu," echoed Myles.

As they sat eating Tiramisu on the balcony, Debbie realized that tonight might be the last time she and Myles would be together like this. She intentionally ate slowly; driving the fork into the dessert and pulling out just what she needed to satisfy her desire to spend as much time with him as possible. She took note of the sun beginning to set and the elongated shadows on the sides of buildings. The New York skyline had never looked more tantalizing.

Her thoughts were interrupted when Myles asked, "Does your mother know about the investigation?"

"Not yet," confided Debbie.

"To be perfectly honest, Myles, I hoped to be far away from New York before any of this came to light."

"Okay, Debbie. How…" started Myles.

"I know how crazy that sounds, but at least I was able to get my mom out of New York before any of this happened."

"Where's your mom?" inquired Myles.

"Turks and Caicos," replied Debbie reflectively.

CHAPTER

MONDAY BEGAN LIKE ANY OTHER MONDAY; quiet. However, Debbie felt this Monday was like the quiet before the storm. She walked around the office and quietly noticed that everyone was at their desks working but something seemed off-center. Then it happened. She noticed Glen rushing toward the mayor's office. Seconds later the door closed and competing voices went up and down the scales so quickly employees began to huddle together. They spoke in hushed tones wondering what could have the mayor up in arms. Debbie returned to her office and tried to appear busy.

Debbie grabbed her purse and stopped by the receptionist's desk. "I have an appointment outside of the office. It shouldn't take longer than an hour should anyone ask."

"Yes, Ms. Adderly," responded the receptionist.

Debbie pushed through the double doors just as the mayor exited his office in search of her. Before he could catch her, she climbed behind the wheel and sped toward the garage exit. Whatever was going on with the mayor, she was determined that it would not stop her appointment with Julius Carbozza. It was time for all of this to come to an end. If it were the last thing she did, it would be to make sure Julius Carbozza would not become mayor. She mashed on the gas like her life depended on it.

Julius Carbozza was on the phone when Debbie rushed into his office. His secretary trailed behind Debbie apologizing profusely to her boss.

"It's okay," he told his secretary. "Ms. Adderly, please have a seat."

"No, thank you. What I have to say won't take long."

"That's what I like," said Julius Carbozza. "A woman who knows how to get straight to the point."

"You are going to call a press conference and concede the mayoral race," said Debbie.

After a few seconds of disbelief, Julius Carbozza broke into laughter. "What makes you think that I would do something like that?"

"If you do not concede the race, I will have no other recourse than to go to the press about the ten mil your father paid the Figueroa family to cover up your rape of a sixteen-year-old girl. That same sixteen-year-old girl gave birth to twin girls. Your daughters. How do you think Sydney will take the news, Julius?"

"What are you talking about? My father never paid anyone ten million dollars. And I don't have any children. You're crazy. Who told you these lies?"

"Oh no, Julius, these are not lies. You see, I talked to the mother of your children. She told me that her mother worked for your family. She very vividly recounted the day you forced her into a back room off from the kitchen and raped her. Then you walked her to the pool and pushed her in. When she told her mother what happened, your father paid the family ten million dollars to not go public. So within the hour, Julius, you will call a press conference and concede the race. You simply do not have a choice. If you do not, then I will be forced to go public."

Debbie exited the office while Julius Carbozza sat frozen behind the massive desk.

Reluctantly, Debbie returned to the office. As she entered the building, people were abuzz with the latest development in the race for mayor.

"Ms. Adderly," the security guard called out. "Did you hear that Julius Carbozza just dropped out of the race? Man, they are dropping like flies."

"What do you mean dropping like flies?" she inquired.

"Darren Jenkins dropped out earlier this morning. It looks like Michele Dobbs is the last one standing," he said while rubbing his hands together.

"Wow! I'm sure the mayor is happy with this news," she said while walking briskly toward the mayor's office.

"Mr. Mayor," said Debbie.

"Debbie," responded the mayor. "Come in. Come in. Did you hear the good news?"

"Yes, I just heard. Everyone is so excited."

"Where did you disappear to earlier? Glen heard about the news before I did. I came out looking for you, but you were nowhere to be found. In any event, two of my biggest obstacles have been knocked out of the running. I understand Darren Jenkins, but I don't understand why Julius Carbozza dropped out so quickly. You wouldn't happen to know anything about that, would you?"

"Actually, I do. I paid a visit to Julius Carbozza and got him to see that it would be in his best interest to concede the race. I told him I was aware of the ten million dollars paid to the Figueroa family by his father to not bring charges against him for the rape and impregnation of a sixteen-year-old. Of course, he tried to deny it. I told him he had to concede within the hour, or I would have no other recourse than to go public with this information."

"Wow!" was all the mayor could muster.

"It looks like you will be going head-to-head with Michele Dobbs. Unfortunately, I do not have anything on her."

"Well, I don't think she has much of a chance or a fan base, so I'm not too worried about her," replied the mayor. "All in all, this has been a great start to the day."

Debbie walked back to her office feeling a sense of accomplishment. Politics can be a dirty business, but today she didn't mind getting a little dirty. Considering this guy should have gone to jail for a crime committed, she felt justified in bringing judgement against him. She could still hear the glass of his ivory tower falling to the ground.

She pulled the check for $1.5 million dollars from her purse. She made a mental note to stop by the bank and deposit it on her lunch hour. Once cleared, she would have the money wired to her bank in Turks and Caicos. She needed to make sure her mother would be comfortable with full access to her bank account.

Debbie pulled the files for Premier Architects and Davis Construction. She was on her third review of the files when her telephone rang.

"Hello, Debbie Adderly speaking."

"Hello, Debbie. Are you available to stop by my office say around four-thirty? There has been a new development in the case that I would like to discuss with you," informed her lawyer.

"Sure," responded Debbie.

"Great. See you then," replied her lawyer.

Debbie glanced at the clock on the wall of her office for the last time. She mentally ticked off the boxes. Darren Jenkins and Julius Carbozza conceded the mayoral race. She sold her condo. She successfully got her mother out of New York and settled in Turks and Caicos thanks to a little help from her friends. As she gathered her things and placed them in a box, she wondered if it would be prudent to inform the mayor and Glen of the investigation. When she turned around, the mayor was standing in the door of her office. He stared in disbelief.

"What are you doing?" he asked. He walked into her office closing the door behind him. "If I didn't know better, I would think that you were packing up your office."

"Mr. Mayor, I regret to inform you that today is my last day. You are in great shape now that Julius Carbozza and Darren Jenkins are no longer in the running. Earlier today, you said that you were not worried about Michele Dobbs."

"You're right. I'm not worried about Michele Dobbs. She doesn't pose a threat to me. But you do!"

The mayor walked around Debbie's office. He stopped to admire the photo taken of him when he first took office. He remembered the ambitious ideas he had for the city. The city he had lived in all his life. The pride he had for New York. All he ever wanted was to make New York the best place to live and work. He felt that he had accomplished what he set out to do. He did not want his legacy as mayor to be marred in scandal.

While the mayor stood admiring the photo, Debbie quietly reached into her purse and turned off the noise jammer. If the FBI were looking for something concrete to use, she was about to give them exactly what they were looking for.

The mayor turned around and looked at her with hatred in his eyes. In all the time she had worked for him, she had never seen this side of him. She sat quietly at her desk watching his every movement with cautious concern.

"Debbie, why didn't you tell me that this office, my office, was under investigation?"

"I'm sorry... I don't know what you are talking about," she said.

The mayor leaned in closer punctuating each word with a jab of his index finger, "You know exactly what I am talking about. It appears that the FBI brought you in for questioning Saturday morning. So don't you dare sit there and tell me that you are unaware of an FBI investigation into the awarding of city contracts. I thought you knew what you were doing. I put you in this position because you assured me that you could handle the responsibility of awarding city contracts in an unbiased manner."

Debbie's eyes grew wide with horror as he revealed how he could potentially lay all blame at her feet. She arose from her office chair and matched his game plan.

"You're right... I never should have feigned ignorance. However, the reason I did not say anything about it is because all the evidence they have is circumstantial. As long as everyone keeps their mouths shut, this will all blow over."

"C'mon, Debbie. You are smarter than that. How do you think I found out about you being brought in for questioning? The FBI paid Davis Construction and Premier Architects a visit earlier today. I can tell by the look on your face that you weren't aware of this little bit of information. My guess is their visit happened around the same time people were distracted by the concession speeches of Julius Carbozza and Darren Jenkins."

"No, I wasn't aware of this."

"Glen and I brought you in because we felt you could be trusted to do as told and not open your mouth about any of this. Your predecessor didn't want any part of it, so she decided to resign. But you... you were young, ambitious, and pliable."

"I assure you that I haven't mentioned anything about the pay-to-play scheme," said Debbie.

"How much money has been wired into your offshore account, Debbie?" asked the mayor. "Are you enjoying the benefits afforded to you. You live in a beautiful neighborhood in an expensive condo, right? How did you pay for all of that? Your annual salary in my office would not afford you the luxuries you managed to acquire. So remember this. If I go down, I'm taking you with me."

The mayor turned and walked slowly toward the door.

"Mr. Mayor, my only regret is not standing up to you years ago. You hired me because I was young and vulnerable. You knew that by paying off my student loans, I would feel obligated to you. So obligated that I would award city contracts to whomever you told me to."

"You satisfied that debt years ago. The only reason you stayed is because your love of money goes deeper than you care to acknowledge. I accept your resignation. There's no need to put it in writing."

The mayor walked out of Debbie's office, leaving the door wide open exposing her to prying eyes.

Debbie crossed the floor of her office and softly closed the door. She had an hour before meeting with her lawyer. When she completed packing, she picked up the box and walked out of her office.

She arrived at her attorney's office and relaxed in the reception area until she was ready to receive her.

"Debbie, what a day! Julius Carbozza and Darren Jenkins dropping out of the mayoral race within hours of each other. I don't know what all of this is about, but I'm sure we will know the truth soon. So allow me to bring you up to speed on a few things pertaining to the case. I learned earlier today that the FBI talked to the owners of Davis Construction and Premier Architects. From what I was able to find out, they are turning state's evidence. What does this mean for you? The FBI is going to come at you with everything they have. I am not trying to scare you. I need you to trust that I am going to do everything within my power to keep you out of jail."

"I understand."

"So what's going on? Did something happen today that I need to be aware of?"

"I resigned my position in the mayor's office today. Before I left the office, the mayor informed me that he received calls from Davis Construction and Premier Architects about the FBI paying them a visit. So you see, the mayor is very aware of the investigation. He even gave me a glimpse into his defense," Debbie chuckled slightly.

"How is that?" asked her lawyer.

"He tried to make it seem as though he wasn't aware of the pay-to-play scheme and that Glen approached him about it."

"None of which sounds plausible," offered her lawyer.

"The only saving grace is I got him to admit that he paid off my student loans and that he was aware of the pay-to-play scheme. That's why my predecessor vacated the position," explained Debbie.

"Wow! This is good stuff."

"Just so you know, the FBI bugged my office months ago. When the mayor came to my office to discuss the investigation, I discretely turned the noise jammer off. I am 99.9 percent sure that the FBI was listening to our conversation. Now they definitely have something concrete."

"Well, if they do, you can expect them to expedite warrants for the arrests of the mayor, Glen, and you. I will make some calls to see what I can find out. In the meantime, go home and stay close to the phone. As soon as I know something, I will give you a call. Okay."

Debbie got up and exited the office of her lawyer without looking back. Her lawyer told her to trust her and not worry. How could she not worry when her fate was in the hands of others? Debbie wished she could rewind time. If she could sit down and have a conversation with the younger Debbie, she would tell her to guard her heart with all diligence. There are many pitfalls in life. If not careful, you will succumb to the snares that so easily entangle you. But she couldn't go back and have such conversations with her younger self. She could only look in the mirror at the adult Debbie and hope for the best.

Debbie hopped in her car and carefully maneuvered it out of its parking space. She dreaded going home. It finally hit her that in a week she would have to vacate the premises and hand over the keys. As she drove around the city, she made a mental note to inform her lawyer about the sale of her condo and the check for $1.2 million dollars. After her conversation with the mayor today, I'm quite sure they have pulled bank statements. Maybe it's a good thing that she never made it to the bank to deposit the check. She pulled over and called Myles.

"Hello," said Myles.

"Hey, you. Are you busy?" asked Debbie.

"No. What do you have in mind?"

"I thought I would swing by for a visit. This has been a very strange day and I need someone to talk to."

"You can always talk to me. See you soon."

Debbie hung up the phone and headed across town. She thought about stopping to pick up something for dinner, but her body would not allow her to stop. If she did not keep going, she felt like she would never arrive. All she wanted was for Myles to hold her and hold her tight. She fully expected to be taken into custody before the end of the night. Myles was the last order of business before she headed home.

Myles was busy in the kitchen when he heard a knock at the door. He looked through the peephole and saw Debbie standing in the hall. When he opened the door, Debbie walked right into his arms. She was shaking so he held her tight. He continued to hold her tight until the shaking subsided. There are times when we must walk alone, his grandmother would say. This is one of those times when one can only go so far with the other. He brought his lips down and kissed her on the top of her head. He did not know what the future held for Debbie, but he prayed for God's favor upon her life.

"Are you hungry?" asked Myles.

"A little," responded Debbie. "It really smells good. I smelled it as soon as I entered the building," offered Debbie.

"I have to admit that I did not cook the chicken and dumplings. My grandmother sent it home with me the other day. It feels good to have a homecooked meal without having to do all the work. Chicken and dumplings have been my favorite meal since childhood. I cannot get enough of it. When I went to live with my grandparents, my grandmother would fix chicken and dumplings for my birthday every year. For dessert, she would bake an apple pie. She would tell me that I could invite a couple of my friends over for dinner and dessert. Every year I would invite Leroy and Cinnamon."

"But it's not your birthday. What's the occasion?"

"Thanks for pointing that out. I'm not sure but I'm also not complaining."

"Is there an apple pie tucked away in the kitchen as well?" asked Debbie.

"Yes, there is!" exclaimed Myles.

"Are you here to talk about the chain of events that unfolded this morning?" inquired Myles. "I called your office, but I was told you had a meeting outside of the office."

"Well, believe me when I tell you that this city will not be any better off with Julius Carbozza or Darren Jenkins at the helm."

"Why is that?

"Trust me. I believe Michele Dobbs is the best person for the job. So we did what we had to do to knock Jenkins and Carbozza out of the running. It's politics."

"I see," replied Myles thoughtfully.

Debbie glanced up at Myles and said, "I need a favor."

"You do. What's the favor?"

"Well, actually, I need several favors." Debbie reached for her purse and pulled out an envelope containing the check from the sale of her condo. The envelope was addressed to her mother in Turks and Caicos. I need you to get this to my mother as soon as possible. Also, here is the spare key to my condo. I will need you to go in and gather all my clothing and give it to charity. I will not need any of it where I am going."

"Debbie, what's going on?" asked Myles.

"I resigned today."

Myles sat in stunned silence as Debbie continued to tell him about her conversation with the mayor. Again, he felt helpless. He felt like he was in a bad horror flick set on repeat. The bad news kept coming.

"Debbie, have you talked to your attorney? What advice did she give you?"

"I met with her right before I called you. She told me to go home and stay close to the phone so she could reach me. Of course, that didn't happen because I am here with you."

"So you think they are going to make arrests tonight?"

"My attorney believes they will. Before I left her office, she was calling around. Maybe I should give her a call now."

Myles listened to the one-sided conversation between Debbie and her attorney. He silently prayed that God would strengthen Debbie for what faced her. He looked up when the call ended. "So what did she say?"

"The mayor was taken into custody at his home a few hours ago and Glen was just arrested. She arranged for me to turn myself in tomorrow afternoon. She will go with me. I guess it's time to face the music."

"Why? Why did this have to happen?" questioned Myles.

"Hey...don't worry about it. I could have stopped this, but I didn't. So now I take ownership of my bad decision. You know, the mayor said something earlier today that made me question myself. When I mentioned that he paid off my student loans because he knew that I would feel so obligated that I would award city contracts to whomever he told me to, his reply was that I satisfied the debt years ago. He accused me of staying because my love for money goes deeper than I care to acknowledge."

"Do you?" asked Myles.

"Do I what?"

"Do you have a love for money?"

"I never gave it a thought until he mentioned it."

"There's a story in the Bible about a rich man who could not part with all that he had when Jesus asked him to sell everything and follow him. He couldn't do it. However, I don't get that feeling from you. So I think the mayor is wrong on that one."

Debbie smiled. "You are a good man, Myles Beyers."

"I need one more favor," said Debbie. "I will leave the keys to my car with my attorney. Here is her card. Please call her so you can go get the car. I need you to hold on to it for me. There are too many uncertainties right now, so I appreciate it if you can take care of those three things mentioned."

"No problem. I will handle it."

"I don't know about you, but the chicken and dumplings are about to put me down," said Myles.

"Yeah, I understand. I think I will head home."

"Okay. I'll walk you out."

When they reached her car, Myles took Debbie in his arms and kissed her passionately. With tears streaming down her face, she pulled away and gazed deeply into his eyes. There was nothing more to say between them. Debbie climbed into the driver's seat and drove away. Myles stood watching as the taillights disappeared into the night.

"Please, God..." Myles walked slowly up the steps of his six-floor walkup. With everything that happened today, all he could think about was Debbie and what she was about to go through. It's unimaginable how she allowed herself to fall into this predicament. There were so many unanswered questions floating around in his head, he found it difficult to concentrate on one of them for long periods of time. Would she face jail time? Would she be able to post bond? How much money did she accept? Did she use any of the money? Why Turks and Caicos? Where is the money?

He picked up the envelope Debbie gave him and held it up to the light. "Debbie, what have you done," he whispered.

Debbie awoke earlier than usual. Halfway through preparing for work, she realized that she had resigned her position in the mayor's office. She reached for the remote and turned on the television and toggled between news reports on last night's arrests of the mayor and his campaign manager.

Slowly sipping her coffee, she continued to toggle between stations reporting:

BREAKING NEWS

Yesterday, in a strange turn of events, Darren Jenkins and Julius Carbozza suspended their campaigns. It is still unclear as to why they both decided to drop out of the race so close to the elections. Folks, I wish I could say that's where the drama ended, but I cannot. Later that evening, the mayor and his campaign manager were arrested. From what our sources tell us, the FBI opened an investigation into a reported pay-to-play scheme and has had the mayor's office under surveillance for a year. We have it on good authority that more arrests are sure to come. Stay with us as we continue to bring you up-to-the-minute coverage as this story unfolds.

Debbie turned the television off and walked out onto the balcony. She closed her eyes and enjoyed the warmth of the sun on her face. It was still early so she took the opportunity to enjoy the serenity. She watched as the birds flew from branch to branch. Her attention shifted to an airplane dancing across the sky; envying the freedom it represented. If only, she thought, things had been handled differently.

Debbie could hear the phone ringing. She knew that she should answer it, but her body would not cooperate. The call shifted to the answering machine and Debbie listened as her attorney left a brief message to get in touch immediately. She finished the last of her coffee and enjoyed several more minutes of solitude before calling her attorney.

"Good morning, thank you for calling the law offices of Percy & Crain. How may I direct your call?" answered the receptionist.

"Good morning. Debbie Adderly for Sophia Crain."

"Please hold while I connect you."

"This is Sophia Crain."

"Good morning, Sophia. This is Debbie returning your call."

"Good morning, Debbie. Thank you for returning my call. I wanted to touch base with you about this afternoon. As I mentioned last night, I arranged for you to turn yourself in this afternoon. I did not want a repeat of the FBI showing up at your door, so I will accompany you to the 1st Precinct and stay with you throughout the entire process. After law officials have done what they need to do, I will immediately ask that you be released on your own recognizance. If granted, you will have to sign a written promise to appear in court. If the judge refuses to honor the request, then bail set. The amount of bail is set by the judge. If the judge decides to go that route, will you have a problem making bail?"

"No."

"Wonderful. It is now ten o'clock. I will pick you up in about an hour and a half."

"I'll be waiting," said Debbie.

She hung up the phone and called Myles at his office.

"Good morning, Myles Beyers speaking."

"Good morning, Myles."

"Hey, Debbie, are you okay?"

"I'm a little nervous. I just got off the phone with my attorney. She did her best to walk me through the process of turning myself in. She will meet me here at my condo and stay with me throughout the entire process of being booked and, hopefully, being released on my own recognizance. If the judge decides not to grant her request, she's going to ask that I be released on bail."

"Debbie, I wish I had some encouraging words for you, but nothing seems adequate right now."

"It's okay. This is one of those times when ridiculousness goes beyond the boundaries of ridiculousness. I hope you haven't forgotten our discussion from last night."

"No worries. I'll take care of it."

Debbie disconnected the call and walked into the kitchen for a cup of hazelnut-flavored coffee. There was a knock at the door. She glanced at the clock. Her attorney wasn't expected for another thirty minutes. There was a second knock at the door. What's the rush, she thought as she approached the door. Debbie cautiously and quietly looked through the peephole and was relieved to see her attorney standing on the other side of the door.

She opened the door wide. "Hello, Sophia. I must admit that I was a little spooked when I heard a knock at the door. I wasn't expecting you for another thirty minutes or so."

"Well, I thought I would swing by early. Sometimes people experience anxiety when they are faced with uncertainty."

"I was just about to have a cup of hazelnut flavored coffee. Would you like a cup?"

"That would be wonderful," said Sophia.

"So how are you doing?"

"I am a bag of mixed emotions," confessed Debbie. "There are days when I feel in control of everything. Then there are days when I want to run and hide. On those days, my nerves are on edge and I'm weepy. When I am going through that phase, I want to reach out to my mother. I want her to wrap her arms around me and tell me everything is going to be all right."

"What's stopping you from reaching out to your mother?"

"I'm afraid," revealed Debbie. "My mother sacrificed her happiness so that I could have. My mother would go without when I was in college so that I would look nice on campus. She applied for loans and worked two jobs so that I could attend college. So that's why I haven't reached out to my mother."

"Debbie, how do you think your mother will feel once word gets out about your arrest? Don't you think you have kept her in the dark long enough?"

"I can't," she said between sobs. "I can't tell her that I willingly sabotaged my career. If you could have seen her face when she came for a visit. She told me how proud she was of my accomplishments. How can I tell her that I allowed myself to be part of the corruption permeating the mayor's office?"

"Write her a letter."

"What?"

"Write your mother a letter. If you feel that you cannot tell her over the phone, I suggest you write her a letter. Tell her that some things are going to come out about corruption in the mayor's office. Tell her that the FBI launched an investigation into a possible pay-to-play scheme and as the procurement officer responsible for awarding city contracts, you are part of the investigation. Also, mention that you have retained an attorney to advocate on your behalf."

Debbie looked at her watch.

"It's twelve o'clock noon," she said as she reached for the coffee mugs. "I will be ready to go as soon as I wash…"

Her attorney was startled by the sound of breaking glass. She got up and ran toward the kitchen. Debbie was standing in the middle of the kitchen floor with pieces of glass littered about. Sophia realized that Debbie had reached her breaking point. In her time as a lawyer, she had witnessed people handle stress in distinct ways. Some checked out completely, while others ignored the situation allowing stress to build up. Once the stress was too much to bear, they would explode.

"Debbie," Sophia called out as she approached her client cautiously. "Debbie," she called out again.

Sophia gently eased toward Debbie while her eyes searched the kitchen for sharp objects. She did not want Debbie to hurt her or herself. She quietly moved toward Debbie until she was within arm's length of her.

"Debbie," she said while reaching out to her. "C'mon. Let's go sit down. Whatever it is, we can talk about it, okay?" Sophia took Debbie's hand and led her out of the kitchen.

Sophia sat down beside Debbie on the sofa and continued to hold her hand. They remained silent until Debbie was ready to talk about what she experienced in the kitchen.

"You must think I'm crazy," said Debbie.

"No. I don't think that at all. Believe me when I say I've seen worse."

"I am just so frustrated with myself. All the hard work I put in trying to make something of myself only to watch it go down the drain. How crazy is that?"

At the risk of sounding judgmental, Sophia decided it was best to allow Debbie to vent. After what she witnessed in the kitchen moments earlier, the only thing on her mind was the safety of her client. So she listened.

A half hour later, Debbie had calmed down and was ready to leave. She looked at her attorney and said, "Let's get this over with."

"Not before we've gotten the glass up off the kitchen floor," exclaimed her attorney. "You stay right there, and I'll clean it up."

On their way to the 1st Precinct, Debbie looked over at her attorney and said, "Thank you for being so patient with me."

"Not a problem. Like I said before, I will advocate on your behalf and do everything within my power to ensure the best outcome for you. By the way, you have a beautiful condo. If all goes well, you will be sleeping in your own bed tonight."

"It would be nice, but it really doesn't matter."

"Why do you say that?"

"I sold my condo a few days ago. My realtor contacted me about a client who was in the market for a condo. She arranged a private sale. I sold the condo and everything in it for $1.2 million dollars. The new owner will take possession within the week."

"Let's hope she is able to take possession that soon."

"Why wouldn't she be able to?" asked Debbie.

"I know that you said the condo was gifted to you. However, the kink in your defense is your relationship with J&M Construction and your accepting a gift from a company you helped via city contracts. I know you told me that you didn't use any of the money and that it is sitting in an offshore account. The FBI can hold the new owner from moving into that condo until they determine that the property is not connected to any of the monies received. This process can take months or even years. It's known as forfeiture or seizure of property."

Debbie closed her eyes and leaned her head back against the headrest.

"She paid $1.2 million dollars for the condo. All furniture conveys," offered Debbie. "I promise you that I did not use any of the money from this pay-to-play scheme for personal gain."

"I believe you. Now, all we have to do is get the jury to believe you."

Debbie and her attorney exited the car and walked into the police station. Agents Simmons and McBride were in conversation with the police chief and two other officers when they entered the lobby of the precinct.

"Ms. Crain, Ms. Adderly," said Agent McBride. "I was getting a little worried that you weren't going to show up."

"Why would you think that?" asked Sophia.

"Well, you arrived fifteen minutes later than when you said you would be here," said McBride.

"Is that all? Just fifteen minutes? Usually, traffic has one snarled longer than fifteen minutes."

Agent Simmons turned toward the chief of police and said, "Can you have your officers read Ms. Adderly her rights and then take her to Booking, please?"

The chief of police motioned to his officers who proceeded to read her the Miranda Rights and escort her to Booking. Within minutes of being booked, all news networks reported on the alleged pay-to-play scheme in the mayor's office and the latest arrest of Debbie Adderly.

Those throughout City Hall and the mayor's office were stunned by the news. They found it hard to believe that the person elected to

STACY JOHNSON

oversee the great city of New York, was using his office and power in such a corrupt way.

Myles, Gloria, and Veronica watched the latest news from John Brimmer's office. They all sat in stunned silence as one station after the other reported on the chain of events over the past two days.

"When justice comes, it comes swiftly," muttered John Brimmer. He stole a glance at Myles who sat motionless with downcast eyes. He thought back on the day the federal agents walked into his office and revealed that there was possible corruption in the mayor's office. So much has transpired from that day until now. But he could not help but wonder about Myles's mental state. He and Debbie had a close relationship. If he weren't mistaken, he believed Myles might have strong feelings for her.

"Gloria, Valerie, can you give me and Myles a minute?"

"Sure," they said in unison. They exited the office quietly closing the door behind them.

"Myles, how are you doing?"

"I knew this day was coming. However, I didn't expect it to hurt so much. I cannot tell you how many times I prayed that Debbie wasn't caught up in anything illegal. I wanted so desperately for the FBI to be wrong about her."

"Yeah, one can only imagine the pain you must be feeling right now. Do you love her?" asked his boss.

"I don't know. Sometimes I think I do and other times I feel like it's more of a deep friendship, if that makes sense."

"Trust me. When you are truly in love, you will know it. Maybe what you experienced with Ms. Adderly was nothing more than a close friendship or infatuation. Or maybe she represented comfort and security. I point all of this out because there is a strong possibility that she might be sentenced. If so, what are you prepared to do?"

"Right now, I can't think that far ahead."

"I understand. But there will come a time when you will have to address that question. My wife and I never had any children and I've come to think of you as the son I never had. I need you to promise me that when the time presents itself, you will address the question with integrity."

"I appreciate your concern. Thank you."

"Your lady friend has a long road ahead of her as well as the mayor and his campaign manager. The people of New York deserved better than they gave us."

"Given what has transpired since yesterday, Michele Dobbs might be a shoo-in for mayor."

"Well, I'm not convinced that Michele Dobbs is the right person for the job," revealed his boss.

"We are sixty days out from election. I don't think there will be anyone contesting her," surmised Myles.

"Yeah, you might be right. But I see that as a problem. There has to be someone in this great city to challenge her."

"Well, unless someone steps up soon, Michele Dobbs will be the next mayor of New York. By the way, I promised Debbie I would handle a few things for her. Can you spare me for a couple of days?"

"You are taking more time off. Weren't you just in Cape May?"

"Yes, I was. However, I need to make a special delivery to her mother in Turks and Caicos."

"Turks and Caicos? Aww, man, this just keeps getting better and better. Considering what you have just been through, take the rest of the week off."

"Thank you."

Myles walked back to his office and asked Gloria to look for flights going to Turks and Caicos. The look she gave him was priceless.

"Don't tell me you are taking another vacation," she said.

"It's not a vacation…it's business."

"We don't have any clients in Turks and Caicos," she responded. "Since you are flying to Turks and Caicos, I think I will take some time off as well."

"I agree. You definitely need some time off."

"Great. So why are you going to Turks and Caicos?"

"Has anyone told you that you are nosy?"

"I prefer inquisitive."

"Same difference. Can you go research flights for me? Now, please."

Two hours later, Gloria walked back into Myles's office and said, "It took a lot of calling around, but I was able to get you on a direct flight into Providenciales International Airport. Your flight leaves at noon tomorrow afternoon, arriving on the island at 3:25 p.m. Your return flight leaves at one o'clock Saturday afternoon arriving at JFK at 4:25 p.m. You can pick up your boarding pass and ticket at the airport. Be safe and I'll see you when you return to the office on Monday."

"Wait a minute! What about hotel accommodations? I can't sleep on the beach."

"You can, but that's not a good look."

"And you can be replaced. You know this, right?"

"I'll secure hotel accommodations for you before close of business."

An hour later, Gloria walked back into his office with a revised itinerary. "You're all set. Anything else?"

"Thank you. Since you have been such a big help to me, you can leave early."

"You're a good man, Myles Beyers."

"That's funny."

"What is?"

"Debbie told me the same thing."

"That's because you are. Enjoy yourself in Turks and Caicos."

Myles finished his work and made sure everything was in order before leaving for the day. He stopped by his boss's office to let him know his schedule and that Gloria would also be out of the office.

"Safe travels and we'll catch up when you return," said John Brimmer.

"Sure thing."

Myles headed for the garage and decided to stop by for a visit with his grandmother before heading home. He was sure she would have many questions after what's being reported on the news. The arrest of Debbie Adderly would be at the top of her list for discussion.

He arrived at Chesterfield Assisted Living and parked his car so that his grandmother could see him from where she sat on her balcony. She waved at him as he made his way to the front entrance of Chesterfield.

When he arrived at his grandmother's apartment, she was already waiting for him at the door. "Isn't this a nice surprise," she said as she wrapped her arms around him. "Come on in and sit down. We have a lot to talk about. What are your thoughts on Julius Carbozza and Darren Jenkins dropping out of the race? When I heard that on the news yesterday, I almost spit out my false teeth. Oh, my goodness! Then that whole ordeal with the mayor and his campaign manager getting arrested. I was so outdone. And to think I voted for Mayor Stevens."

"Yeah, like everyone else, I was surprised by the turn of events. And it happened so suddenly. So Debbie was taken into custody earlier today. She called and we got a chance to talk briefly before her attorney arrived. Her attorney was with her when she turned herself in."

"I feel just awful for her. There was another guy who got caught doing the same thing several years ago. What is his name? Well, anyway, his name will come to me tomorrow," she snickered.

"Former County Executive Joseph Pinkerton. However, if memory serves me correctly, he resigned from office when faced with federal indictment."

"So now we have to wait and see what is going to happen with the mayor and the others," said his grandmother.

"Well, Granny, let's hope for the best."

"Tell me, what brings you out this way on a workday?" asked his grandmother.

"I'm traveling to Turks and Caicos tomorrow afternoon. I promised Debbie that I would handle something for her."

"Why do you have to travel to the tropics to do it?" inquired his grandmother.

"Well, at first I was going to mail it. But after Debby's arrest earlier today, I decided it would be a good idea for me to hand-deliver the envelope to her mother. Also, I'm not sure how much she knows about what's going on here in New York and I just feel that someone needs to be there for her when she finds out."

"Sweetie, listen to me. You can't be there for everyone."

"I understand what you are saying, but I have to do this. You always told me that a man always keeps his word. I promised Debbie that I would handle a few things for her so I'm going to keep my word. Now, how I decide to handle it is up to me."

"Okay," she said as she put her hands up in surrender. "Are you hungry?"

"To tell the truth, I am. What's for dinner?"

"Actually, I did not cook so it's whatever you find in the refrigerator."

"How do you feel about going out to eat?"

"I'll get my jacket," said his grandmother.

Myles arrived home later that evening and decided to pack his suitcase before getting into bed. He made a mental note to thank Gloria for booking him on an afternoon flight instead of an early morning flight. He slept in a little longer than anticipated the following morning but was still able to make it to JFK in plenty of time.

He glanced at the departure schedule; Flight 458 for Turks and Caicos was departing on time. He had a little time on his hands, so he stopped by the newsstand across from the gate of departure. Beautiful faces graced every magazine. He stopped and read the inside flap of several books in search of something interesting to read. He was still looking for an interesting book to read when he overhead a conversation between the clerk and the person delivering the afternoon edition of the newspaper. From his vantage point, he could see the headline on the front page of the New York Times which read: Mayor Stevens resigns in face of federal indictment. He could not believe what he was reading. Where does that leave Debbie, he thought. He stood there staring at the photo of the mayor walking out of the precinct with his lawyer. How could this be happening? It appeared to Myles that Debbie was being set up to take the fall. How were they able to get an indictment so quickly? He wasn't a lawyer, but something did not seem right.

Myles picked up a copy of the *New York Times*, placed a dollar on the counter, and walked out. He walked back to his gate and began reading the story. The more he read, the more questions he had about this entire ordeal. The question of how this would affect Debbie still loomed before him. With Debbie still in custody, he could only hope that her attorney had a rock-solid defense. He folded the paper and placed it on the seat next to him. His focus shifted to Debbie's mother. With the envelope from Debbie safely tucked in the breast pocket of his jacket, he got up and waited in line to board the plane. Once seated, he stared out the window and wondered silently how all of this would turn out.

Three and a half hours later, Flight 458 from JFK International Airport touched down in Turks and Caicos. He and others waited patiently with passports in hand to speak with the immigration officer. Once granted permission to enter Turks and Caicos, he headed straight for Baggage Claim where he retrieved his luggage. Drivers were lined up outside of the airport, each competing earnestly for their next fare. A guy ran up to Myles and grabbed his suitcase.

"Where are you going, sir?" he asked.

"In hot pursuit of the man and his suitcase, Myles provided the driver with the address listed on the envelope. He was surprised that the address was only twenty minutes from the airport. The driver got out and removed the luggage from the trunk of the car and placed it at the door to the house. Myles paid the driver handsomely and turned his attention back toward the beautiful house before him. He knocked on the door and waited for someone to answer. When no one answered, he knocked again. Still there was no answer. He heard voices coming from the back of the house, so he picked up his suitcase and walked around the side of the house. The closer he got to the back of the house, the clearer the voices became. People carried plates of food in and out of the house; others lounged around the pool. He observed several children in the pool and wondered if he were at the right house. Suddenly, he was noticed by a woman he perceived to be Debbie's mother. There was an unmistakable resemblance that became more apparent as she came closer.

"Hello, young man, can I help you?" she asked as Matt and Jeremy saddled up beside her.

Myles was at a loss as to how to respond. How do you tell someone you have never met that their daughter has been arrested for participating in a pay-to-play scheme? He looked between Debbie's mother and the two men casting a shadow on him and found his voice.

"Ms. Adderly, can I speak to you in private?"

"How do you know my name? Did my daughter send you? I swear, there have been so many strange people showing up saying that my daughter has dispatched them to this house," she exclaimed.

"I know your daughter and she did not send me. I took it upon myself to travel to Turks and Caicos. Please, I really need to speak with you in private."

Lois Adderly felt something was wrong. For what reason would this young man travel all this way? As she escorted Myles to her home office. "Is my daughter okay?" she finally asked.

"Please, make yourself comfortable," said Lois Adderly.

Myles retrieved the envelope from his jacket pocket and handed it to Lois Adderly.

She sat down and opened the envelope. A small slip of paper dropped to the floor when she removed the check. Lois did not notice the slip of paper on the floor. Myles bent down and picked up the slip of paper and read Debbie's scribbled note, "Sold condo. Please deposit check. I'll explain later."

Myles glanced at Lois who was still staring at the check. "Young man, please tell me why you are here? I don't understand what this check is for. The check is made out to my daughter. Why are you handing it to me?"

He handed her the note.

"Ms. Adderly, I wish I were coming to you with good news, but I'm not. So I'm just going to come right out and tell you that the FBI launched an investigation into an alleged pay-to-play scheme in the mayor's office. A couple of days ago, the mayor, his campaign manager, and Debbie were arrested."

"Oh my God," she cried. Tears flowed from her eyes as she thought about her daughter being arrested. "How could this be? There must be some mistake. Debbie has never done anything wrong in her life."

Myles moved his chair a little closer to Lois Adderly. "Please know that Debbie is in good spirits. She called me before she turned herself in. We also talked at great length the night before. She understands completely what's facing her and has retained an attorney."

"I cannot get my head wrapped around this," said Lois Adderly. "None of this is making sense."

"I'm right there with you."

There was a knock at the office door. "Come in," said Lois.

The door opened and Matt and Jeremy walked in carrying Myles's luggage. "You left your luggage outside."

"Yeah, I guess I got sidetracked given the circumstance," said Myles.

"Lois, you want to tell us what's going on? It looks like you've been crying."

"Debbie has been arrested," said Lois.

"We were afraid of this?" said Jeremy.

"What are you talking about?" asked Lois. "You two knew about Debbie's legal troubles and didn't tell me?"

Jeremy and Matt sat down across from Lois and Myles. "Debbie wanted us to wait until after the arrest before we said anything. I know that sounds crazy, but that's how she wanted it to play out," said Jeremy.

Jeremy and Matt took turns filling Lois and Myles in on how an unlikely friendship forged between Debbie and them.

"In order for you to understand how we came to be friends with Debbie, we have to take you back to two brothers in New York who worked their way up in construction and headed one of the most successful construction companies in the city. We owe our success to your daughter, Debbie Adderly. But before we get into all of that, I think you might want to go check on your guests. We can talk about this later."

"Oh, my goodness. I forgot all about my guests. By the way, young man. What is your name? Where are you staying?"

"My name is Myles Beyers and my secretary made hotel accommodations at a hotel. I came here from the airport, so I haven't checked in yet."

"Please call and cancel your reservation. You can stay here with us. There's plenty of room," said Lois. "Also, I need you to tell me more about the FBI investigation. So between now and Saturday, everyone in this room will fill me in. Right now, there are too many missing pieces."

The three men looked at each other and without saying a word understood that things were about to get uncomfortable for all involved.

Matt and Jeremy showed Myles to the guest room. "There is a telephone in the living room that you can use to call the hotel. Also, I hope you brought your swim trunks. Swimming is the only relief from the sun when outside," said Jeremy.

"Indeed, I did," replied Myles. "There is absolutely no way I would travel all the way to Turks and Caicos and not bring several pairs of swim trunks."

As the sun began to set on the horizon, Lois's guests gathered their children and said their goodbyes. How she managed to entertain her guests after learning her daughter had been arrested, was something she learned from her mother. Lois remembered her mother always said, "Never let them see you sweat." Her personal favorite, "It's your wagon, you can push it, or you can pull it." She never fully comprehended these colloquialisms; however, they brought her comfort at this moment in time.

Lois walked into the living room and plopped down on the sofa. "Whew! It has certainly been a day. I must admit that learning of my daughter's arrest wasn't something I was prepared for. Myles, when I saw you, I thought you had lost your way or something. You were just standing there staring."

Myles smiled and confessed, "I was staring because you and your daughter look so much alike. Now I know where Debbie gets her beauty."

Lois blushed. "You are too kind."

Jeremy and Matt confirmed what Myles confessed.

"So, Myles, how did Debbie get caught up in a pay-to-play scheme?"

"According to her, she was pulled into it by the mayor and his campaign manager."

"Pulled in how?"

"Student loans. From what I understand, he paid off her student loans and held it over her head for years so that she didn't have a choice but to do whatever he asked of her? As of Monday, she resigned her position in the mayor's office when he found out about the FBI investigation and Debbie being brought in for questioning. They had some words and she told him that her only regret was not standing up to him sooner. She told him that he knew that in paying off her student debt, she would be willing to do what was asked of her out of appreciation."

"My Lord!" exclaimed Lois. "So the mayor and his campaign manager orchestrated this pay-to-play scheme and pulled Debbie into it," confirmed Lois.

"That's what it sounded like to me," replied Myles. "Then he engaged in a little belt lining."

"In what way?" asked Lois.

"He told Debbie that her debt was paid years ago, and her love of money is what kept her there. In other words, her greed and love of money is what kept her there. Because she accepted the money only made his words more real."

"I don't care what he said. Clearly, he doesn't know my daughter and he doesn't know me," said Lois angrily. "Right now, I am so angry."

"There's more that you need to know," said Myles.

"Not tonight, Myles. I'm tired and I've heard enough for one day. Let's all get a good night's sleep and resume this conversation tomorrow morning," suggested Lois.

Having said that, Lois got up and walked down the hall toward her bedroom. She walked in and sat on the side of the bed. With tears streaming down her face, she felt helpless in her own power. "Why, Lord?" she whispered. "Why is this happening?" Lois slid off the bed onto her knees and sought the Lord's guidance through prayer. Somehow, she knew that He would be her guiding force, her strong tower. Lois felt better after talking to God. Wiping the tears from her face, she climbed into bed and allowed sweet sleep to comfort her throughout the night.

Lois awoke the following morning to the chatter of male voices and the occasional splash in the pool. The clock on her nightstand registered 11:00 a.m. She had never allowed herself to sleep that long and immediately hopped out of bed. After a quick shower, she joined the others outside by the pool.

"Gentlemen, I'm sorry I slept in so late. Have you had breakfast?" asked Lois.

"You were sleeping so peacefully, we didn't want to wake you," offered Myles. "I can only imagine how you felt when I told you about Debbie's arrest."

"None of us have had anything to eat," said Jeremy. "We decided to wait on you. Why don't you sit down and visit with Myles? Matt and I have this all under control." Jeremy and Matt headed toward the kitchen leaving Myles and Lois sitting by the pool.

"You said last night that there was more that I needed to know. I'm ready to hear what you have to say," said Lois.

"While you were still asleep, Jeremy and Matt filled me in on other missing pieces. I will say this. Your daughter is not only smart, but extremely strategic. Having said that, I would suggest we wait until we can all sit down together so that nothing gets lost in the translation."

"Okay. You will be here for a few days. I guess there is no need to rush into anything. However, I wish my daughter had trusted me enough to tell me herself. I've always told her that there was nothing so terrible that she could not talk to me about."

"My grandmother raised me after my mother died and my father incarcerated for her murder. She would tell me the same thing. She would say, "Myles, there is nothing too bad that you cannot come to me with. You can talk to me.""

"Your grandmother is a very smart lady. Is she still alive?"

"Yes. She moved to Chesterfield Assisted Living about a year or so after I got my own place."

"What about your grandfather?"

"I'm sorry to say that he is no longer with us. He succumbed to injuries received from a tragic accident on the job."

"Oh, Myles. I'm sorry to hear about your loss."

"Thank you. I really miss him. He was a good dude. We spent so much time together. But I think that is why I am so close to my grandmother. We are all we have. My grandmother is getting up in age and I know that one day she will no longer be here, but I'm not prepared to lose her."

Lois reached for Myles's hand and held it tight. She, too, knew all too well what it was like to not have someone you cared deeply for to no longer be in your life. There were many nights she cried herself to sleep grieving for those she longed for. Now, there is the situation with Debbie. No longer would she give up and allow decisions made by others to dictate how she lived, and she was not going to allow it to happen to her daughter. Lois said a silent prayer.

Jeremy and Matt exited the house with a bountiful feast and set it before Myles and Lois. They all joined hands and bowed their heads and gave thanks for food on their table and new friendships. Once they had finished eating and clearing the table, they all came back together for a heart-to-heart conversation. What was revealed left all of them pondering the fate of Debbie.

"Lois," started Jeremy. "My brother and I need you to know that you raised a special young woman. She has a heart bigger than most. Believe us when we say that we owe her a lot because if it were not for her, we would not be in Turks and Caicos."

Lois listened intently. So intently, in fact, it almost looked as if she were holding her breath.

"So our story of success is due, in part, to the sacrifice of your daughter. There might be some twists and turns to our story. You might have to buckle up because the ride gets a little bumpy."

"I understand. Please, proceed."

"Several years ago, our uncle passed and left us his business," started Matt. "It was a small construction company. He mainly did rehabs. There were times when he got hired on as a contractor on larger construction jobs throughout the city. My brother and I worked with him every summer. He never married or had children so, as mentioned earlier, he left us his business. We knew absolutely nothing about how to process payroll or how to bid on contracts, but we were willing to learn. As time went on, business got slower and slower and we lost all our staff to other construction companies. Still, we were not willing to give up. We would bid on contracts and was never awarded one contract. Then we noticed a pattern. It appeared that the same companies were being awarded major contracts. These were multimillion-dollar contracts. Then one day my brother stormed into the office and said he had enough. He began calling the mayor's office daily demanding to speak to the person in charge of awarding contracts. When that didn't work, he decided to walk into the mayor's office and not leave until he had been seen by the person awarding city contracts. Matt looked at Jeremy and said, "Would you like to tell them what happened next?"

"Well, that was the day things began to turn in our favor. Debbie invited me into her office for a brief meeting. I explained to her about our uncle leaving us a small construction company that my brother and I did not want to lose. I also mentioned that I noticed that the same construction companies were consistently being awarded city contracts. There was an unmistakable look in her eyes that told me I was on to something. She told me that there was a contract coming up and that an RFP would go out soon to vendors. That day, she took the time to go through the bidding process with me. Step by step, line by line until I understood what to do. Soon we were brought on as subcontractors with larger companies. Money began flowing into our bank account and we were able to hire people. But she didn't stop there. She put us in touch with people that were more knowledgeable about payroll, payroll taxes, benefits, and the day-to-day operations. Debbie grew our small fledgling construction company to a first-class operation able to compete with other companies city-wide."

Lois beamed with pride. Matt and Jeremy painted a picture of Debbie that far surpassed anything she could have imagined.

Jeremy picked back up with the story. "We were doing a brisk business around the city. You can go into any borough and see our handiwork. So one day the mayor's campaign manager, Glen, paid us a visit. I remember both my brother and I looking at each other in utter confusion. He came in and introduced himself. Ten minutes into his visit, we understood why he was there. I believe he said, 'You have a first-class operation. The city must be treating you well. I'm not going to beat around the bush. I've looked at Ms. Adderly's files and noticed that your company has been awarded several contracts and made a substantial amount of money. Since the city has been so good to you, it's only fair that you give back.' So my brother asked him to come right out with it. He was sitting on the edge of the desk when he got up and moved toward Glen. He got right in Glen's face and wanted to know exactly what he meant by giving back. I have to give it to Glen, though. He did not flinch. He looked my brother right in the eye and said, 'Are you familiar with a pay-to-play scheme? If not, then this is how things are going to work going forward. From every contract awarded to your company, you will give back 30 percent. If not, work will dry up for your construction company.'" Then he got up and left the office.

Lois and Myles exchanged glances of unbelief.

Jeremy continued. "My brother and I could not believe what had just happened. By this time, we were about two maybe two and half years into the business and had grown exponentially. My brother and I went home that night and discussed Glen's terms for doing business with the city. Of course, it did not sit well with us. That's when we began to formulate a plan of our own. We called Debbie and invited her over for dinner. As luck would have it, she was free that night and eagerly accepted our invitation."

All eyes were on Myles as he chuckled at the thought of Debbie accepting their invitation to dinner.

"What's so funny?" asked Lois.

"You know your daughter can't cook, right?" Myles could no longer hold back the laughter. "If it doesn't come in a bag or from a restaurant, she's not eating."

They all broke out into laughter as they knew this to be sure of Debbie.

"Cooking has never been of interest to her," admitted Lois. "Thank you for helping to lighten the mood."

"I'm sorry," said Myles. "I didn't mean to interrupt like that, but I had this vision in my head of Debbie running to your house for dinner."

"No problem. I think we all needed a good laugh, and it was well timed," said Matt.

"Debbie arrived, and we informed her of Glen's visit to our office," continued Matt. "It did not go unnoticed by either of us that Debbie did not seem surprised by his visit. However, when we mentioned the 30 percent, that's when we noticed she was slightly uncomfortable. So my brother being the type of person he is, sat down beside Debbie. She never moved nor did she make eye contact with him. He just sat there and stared at her. In fact, he stared at her so long, I was uncomfortable for her. Then he asked, "How could you allow yourself to get caught up in this?" Debbie's head hung just a little lower after he put forth the ask. That night, Debbie confessed to everything. We discovered that Glen and the mayor had been running a pay-to-play scheme since he had taken office. Just like Myles mentioned earlier, she told us that she had a lot of student debt that would take her years to pay off. One day she arrived at the office only to find out that the mayor had paid off her entire debt. But it came with a price. From that day forward, he told her to whom to award city contracts."

"Also," chimed Jeremy, "that's the night the three of us strategized on how to beat the mayor at his own game. You see, it's not by accident that we are here in Turks and Caicos. Lois, when we showed up at your apartment, took a cab to the airport, and got on a plane to Turks and Caicos, that was a well-thought-out plan to get you out of New York before Debbie's arrest. She knew that once news broke about corruption in the mayor's office, it would only be a matter of time before she would be arrested.

"We made millions of dollars from city contracts, so my brother and I would not allow ourselves to be strong-armed into kicking back money to the mayor and his campaign manager just to ensure city contracts. So we stopped bidding on contracts and sold our company to Davis Construction. We made several millions from that sale. When things started to heat up for Debbie, she contacted us and handed over four suitcases. When we saw the suitcases, we knew instantly to get you out of the city. Everything was planned right down to the minute," explained Jeremy. "Now, how the house came about is another story."

"I'm very interested in hearing about the house," said Myles. "You mentioned that you and your brother were in construction, but you sold your business. What I noticed when I first arrived, is that this house does not look like a typical house you would find in the Caribbean. Is it safe to assume that you and your brother built this house?"

"C'mon, man, you are jumping chapters ahead," teased Jeremy.

"Well, if you two did all of this, I am about to get up and shake your hand. Because this looks great."

"Thank you. Just know the house has a story as well. Right after we sold the business to Davis Construction, my brother and I were hanging out with Debbie when she mentioned leaving New York. She told us that she wanted a change of scenery and had always dreamed of living in the Caribbean. We asked her if she knew what part of the Caribbean she wanted to live in, and she immediately said Turks and Caicos. A couple of weeks after that, we surprised her with a trip to this fabulous island. While here, we explored the island, talked to residents, and got a feel for the island. We ran across a plot of land with an extremely sad looking house sitting on it. My brother and I looked at each other, the wheels started turning, and our imaginations took off. Debbie walked toward the sad looking house and said, and I quote, 'My mother would love living here on this property. While here, I'm going to see how much this plot of land costs. It will take a while, but I think if I sell my condo, I will have enough money to build a beautiful house on this plot.' We stayed and walked the property until the sun began to set. I must admit, it was as if an artist had taken a paintbrush and used the sky as the canvas. That's how nice it was."

"Debbie did just that," offered Matt. "Before we left the island, she had purchased this plot of land and vowed to come back and build a house for her mother. She told us that her mother sacrificed everything so that she would have. All she wanted was to give back to you, Lois."

"So, what my brother and I decided to do was build the house for you, Lois. Debbie had no idea what we were planning. We felt it was the least we could do since she helped us become who we are today. Had it not been for her taking the time to walk us through the bidding process, we probably would have given up and shuttered our doors long ago. Although we no longer own a construction business in New York, we started another business here on the island. Admittedly, it is our goal to expand our business to other islands throughout the Caribbean," explained Jeremy.

"Oh, my goodness. I'm overwhelmed with joy. This is a lot to take in at one time. Thank you so much for being such a good friend to my daughter. She never talked much about her work in the mayor's office, nor did she invite me into her life and talk about her friends. Now that I think about it, I always thought Debbie didn't have any friends."

"My impression of Debbie is that she chooses her friends wisely. She needs to be able to trust those around her, so she keeps her circle of friends small," offered Myles.

"That sounds plausible," said Lois. "I know that you have a story to tell as well. However, you only have two days left before you head back to New York. Why don't we take in a little sightseeing today? Tomorrow, you can tell me what you know. Deal?"

"Deal. By the way, Lois, I believe we should stop by the bank while we are out."

"Oh!" exclaimed Lois. "Thanks for the reminder. I had forgotten all about depositing the check for Debbie. Yes, we will definitely stop by the bank."

It was midafternoon by the time they left to explore the island.

"Myles," started Lois. "Have you ever ridden a horse?"

"That's a negative."

"Well, why don't we head over to Long Bay. If we are lucky, maybe we can go horseback riding along the beach. From what I hear, the fish fry at Bight Park is enjoyable. There's live music and plenty of island food to sample. We can do that on Friday?" suggested Lois."

Myles thought it felt strange that they were enjoying Turks and Caicos while Debbie was sitting in a New York jail cell. Then he thought back to what Jeremy and Matt had said about Debbie knowing she would be arrested. Whether he wanted to believe it or not, they were all part of a well-thought-out plan. He couldn't help but wonder if he were part of that plan too. When he listened to Jeremy and Matt talk about the methodical plans constructed, it left him a little uneasy.

"Myles," said Lois. "What do you think about the fish fry at Bight Park tomorrow?"

"Let's do it."

"All right. Long Bay here we come. If for some reason, however, we cannot engage in horseback riding today, we need a backup plan," said Lois.

"Honestly, I don't think we will be able to go horseback riding today. Look at the time," said Jeremy. "I suggest we either go to Cockburn Town or take a tram tour of Grand Turk. Since Myles is leaving Saturday afternoon, I vote for the tram tour. He will get to see more of the island that way."

"You're right. The next time you come for a visit, we will go horseback riding and take in all the other amenities offered on this beautiful island as well as connecting islands. Now, let's get out of here."

Myles had such a relaxing time with Lois, Jeremy, and Matt frolicking in the sun that he almost forgot that he had a life in New York. A life he had worked hard to establish. His granny was there. Two of his best friends lived there. And with realizing all of that, he still hated that his time in Turks and Caicos was about to come to an end. Saturday afternoon he would board a plan heading back to the hustle and bustle of city life. More importantly, he needed to get back to New York and check on Debbie. It worried him that no one had heard from her or her lawyer. Maybe I should approach Jeremy and Matt to determine if contact has been made, he thought to himself.

They had a full day exploring all the island had to offer. When they arrived back at Lois's home, they were tired. One by one, they plopped down in chairs, on the sofa, and even on the floor. They all howled with laughter as Myles lay prostrate on the floor.

"You can laugh all you want, but I have never been this tired in my life. Honestly, I don't think I have enough energy to get up off the floor and walk. If you see me crawling down the hall to my assigned bedroom, please don't judge me."

They laughed even harder.

"Well, I don't know about the rest of you," started Lois. "But I am going to bed. Good night to all and to all a good night."

"Why does that sound like a line from some Christmas story?" asked Jeremy.

"That's because it is!" exclaimed Matt.

They were deliriously tired. Matt and Jeremy helped Myles up and all three trudged down the hall to their respective bedrooms.

Myles heard a telephone ringing in the distance. In the fog of sleep, he thought he heard Lois's soft voice answer the call. He struggled to emerge from the sleep that held him captive, but it was useless. Sleep held him hostage for several hours before he opened his eyes and briefly wondered where he was. He stretched and grunted allowing his body to fully awaken. He lay for several minutes before swinging his long legs over the side of the bed and bringing his six-foot, two-inch frame vertical.

He lingered in the shower longer than usual as he thought about what the day beheld and how Lois would react to what he had to tell her. Jeremy and Matt filled in one-third of the puzzle the previous day; however, it was now his turn to reveal all he knew. It wouldn't be easy to tell her how the FBI pulled him in to assist them in securing intel on Debbie. The only thing she needs to know is that the FBI had surveillance equipment in her office and her condo, he rationalized. There was no need for him to do anything. No matter how he tried to spin this, Lois would want to know why he did not tell her from the beginning that she was under investigation. What did John Brimmer tell him before he left? He asked, "What will I be prepared to do when the time presents itself?" Myles heard John Brimmer's voice, "Promise me that you will address the question with integrity." He remembered the conversation being centered around whether he loved Debbie. But Debbie is an extension of her mother. He concluded that whatever question or questions posed by Lois would be addressed with integrity. Transparency was the order for today. She deserved to know the truth.

Myles exited his bedroom and noticed the bedroom doors for Matt and Jeremy were pulled closed. He walked into the kitchen and noticed Lois sitting on the patio deep in thought. He opened the refrigerator and removed the orange juice. He began opening cabinet doors in search of juice glasses. On the third attempt, he removed two juice glasses and filled them with orange juice. Quietly moving around the kitchen, he found a serving tray where he proceeded to place breakfast breads, fruit, and two glasses of orange juice. From the look of things, today did not appear to be a day for cooking. He picked up the tray and walked it out to Lois. Before he could reach the table, Lois turned toward him. He could see she had been crying.

"Good morning, Myles," she muttered.

"Is it?" he replied.

Lois looked down at her hands as she folded and unfolded a tissue. "I guess that depends on if you see the glass half empty or half full."

"You care to talk about it?" he asked.

"Yes. I need to unburden. Myles, I am trying to remain strong for my daughter but, honestly, the news of Debbie's arrest hit me like a ton of bricks. I thought I was doing okay until Debbie called this morning."

"I heard the phone ringing this morning, but I thought I was dreaming," offered Myles.

"When I heard her voice, all I wanted was to wrap my arms around her. I'm less than a four-hour plane ride from her but it feels like it's longer than that."

"Sometimes, Lois, in times like these we feel helpless. But what gives me comfort is knowing that the God I serve is strong enough to fight my battles for me. I've never been faced with legal troubles, but

I am convinced that if that unfortunate situation were to ever arise, he would be there standing by my side."

"My daughter sure knows how to pick them," she said quietly. "Myles, I did not raise Debbie in the church, but I wish I had known about God much sooner. I came to the Lord late in life. It was after Debbie had finished college and moved out on her own. One of my coworkers asked me one day if I was a believer. When I told my coworker that I didn't know what she meant, she asked me if I believed in God. I must admit I felt a little awkward admitting that I wasn't sure. But I was curious. I began asking her questions and she was so patient with me. Then one day while browsing through a neighborhood bookstore, I picked up the Bible and thumbed through it. I cannot explain what happened, all I know is that I was drawn into this book. So I purchased it and would read scriptures every day. The rest, as they say, is history."

"Lois, thank you for sharing your testimony. My grandmother raised me in the church. She always said that it doesn't matter when you come to Him. All that matters is that you do. You know, there are things that happen in this life that we cannot explain. There are times when we feel that we just can't bare our burdens another day. That's when God steps in and does all the heavy lifting. Honestly, there were times when I would look at Debbie and wonder how she was able to function given what she knew."

Lois eyed the juice and breakfast breads. "What do you mean?"

"When the FBI approached my boss about the investigation into possible corruption in the mayor's office, I was called into the office as well as my secretary and his executive assistant. We were told about the investigation and they requested to use the vacant office next to mine to better keep an eye on City Hall. Just so you know, the building I work in is directly across the street from there. Out of all the offices in the building, why did they choose our office. I was instructed to work closely with the FBI agents and provided them with any files they requested."

Lois listened intently as she cut a small piece of breakfast bread and placed it on a small plate with several pieces of fruit.

"Please go on. I'm listening."

"So one day they asked for files on Premier Architects and Davis Construction. I did what I was told and provided them with the files."

"Wait a minute! Davis Construction? Isn't that the firm Jeremy and Myles sold their company to?"

"The one and only," confirmed Myles.

"More pieces to the puzzle are dropping into place," said Lois.

"So curiosity got the better of me and I stayed late one night going through the files for Davis Construction and Premier Architects. I had gotten up from my desk and walked into the kitchen for a cup of coffee when I overheard Agents Simmons and McBride discussing the investigation. That's when I learned that Debbie was under investigation and so was I."

"I can understand why Debbie was under investigation, but why were they investigating you?"

"Based on my relationship with Debbie, they thought that I might know something about what was going on in the mayor's office. What they did not know is that Debbie is about as tight-lipped about her job as they come. I remember asking her about her job when we first met, and she basically told me only what she was comfortable in telling me. I learned not to ask her anything about her job."

"So did you tell Debbie about the investigation?"

"No, I did not."

"If you and Debbie were as close as you claim you were, why did you not tell her what you learned?"

There it is. The elephant just stormed into the room, thought Myles. He leaned back in the chair and looked off into the distance before responding to Lois.

"I did not tell her immediately because I had been sworn to secrecy. So I started my own investigation. I revealed what I overheard to my boss and both of us went through the files looking for clues. Then I did what anyone in my position would do. I broke up with her. You might not believe me, but it hurt me to walk away, but I felt that was the only way to protect her."

"Why did you feel that breaking up with her was the only way to protect her? In my opinion, you left her exposed."

"I hear what you are saying but try to see this from my vantage point. The FBI not only bugged her condo and apartment but my apartment. They had hours of recordings of me and Debbie. Our conversations and intimate time together. Debbie wasn't the only one exposed in this situation."

"Obviously, you two could not stay away from each other. Otherwise, you would not be here, right?"

"That very next day, the FBI called me into the office and told me they were aware of my breakup with Debbie. That's when I found out about the recordings. I was informed, no I was told, that I needed to get back into Debbie's good graces. They did not care how I did it, but they needed me to help them get something concrete on her."

"I cannot believe what I am hearing," shouted Lois.

"Please, calm down," said Myles.

Just then Jeremy and Matt exited the house. "Lois, what's going on?"

"I just learned that Myles was being used by the FBI to help gather intel against my daughter," shouted Lois.

"It's not what you think, Lois," explained Myles.

"It isn't? Then please explain to me why you agreed to help the FBI?"

"I went along with the FBI because I felt that I could protect Debbie better if I were with her than apart from her," explained Myles. "However, I wasn't sure how to get back into Debbie's good graces after the way I treated her. But she made it easy for me when she called demanding to know why I walked out on her. That's when I decided that if the FBI wanted Debbie, I wasn't going to make it easy for them."

Reluctantly, Jeremy and Matt sat down and listened to what Myles had to say.

"Let's talk about something else Debbie was doing for the mayor. You all are familiar with Michele Dobbs, Darren Jenkins, and Julius Carbozza, right?" asked Myles.

"Yeah, they are all running for mayor," said Lois.

"Well, as of a few days ago, Michele Dobbs is the only one running for mayor. Julius Carbozza and Darren Jenkins dropped out of the race. The reason they dropped out of the race is because Debbie was gathering information for the mayor's campaign manager to use against them in smear campaigns."

"Yeah, I saw some of those ads. They were vicious," said Lois. "How is that Debbie's responsibility?"

"Good question. However, Debbie is the only one that can answer that," said Myles.

"So who provided her with the information?" asked Jeremy.

"From what I was able to find out, she knows a guy who knows a lot of unsavory people. They have their way of getting information on people. This guy doesn't come cheap."

"How did you find out about him?" asked Lois.

"Well, I have a secretary who is extremely nosey. She likes to say inquisitive. Not long ago she and my boss's executive secretary were at lunch at a downtown restaurant and noticed Debbie having lunch with a guy. I didn't think much of it until she described the guy. There's a guy from the old neighborhood that fancies himself a street investigator."

"I'm not sure what is meant by a street investigator," said Lois.

"Let me put it this way. There are people who work but not in the traditional sense. They get in good with others and find out information on people. This information is traded for money. That's who Debbie was working with. How she hooked up with this guy, only she can answer that. So I went back to the old neighborhood and asked one of my friends about him. He told me where to find this guy. It took a few weeks before I was able to catch up with him, but when I did, I told him about the FBI investigation. I handed him two noise jammers, one for him and one for Debbie. That's how I helped Debbie without the FBI finding out."

"I take back everything I was thinking about you," said Lois.

"I appreciate that," replied Myles. "You mentioned that Debbie called. How is she doing? Is she in good spirits?"

"Yeah. She was released on her own recognizance and told me that her attorney is working hard on her behalf. Also, there is a list of witnesses that her attorney has compiled for the defense. I mentioned that you were here. I got the impression she was relieved," said Lois.

"Hopefully, I will get a chance to see her when I return to New York."

"There's something else that is bothering me," started Lois. "How did the FBI know to launch an investigation? Do you think it was one of the companies that was overlooked during the bidding process?" asked Lois.

"It's hard to say," replied Myles.

Jeremy and Matt sat quietly taking in the conversation between Lois and Myles. Jeremy warred within himself about the investigation, the agents, and what he knew about the investigation. He wasn't sure if now was the time to open that can of worms. But if not now, then when would be the right time, he thought. If confession is good for the soul, then he had to step in with all fours.

"The plan," started Jeremy. "It was all part of the plan."

Myles and Lois stared at him in amazement. "What plan?" asked Myles.

"I had to find a way to get Debbie out. She and I discussed everything that transpired in the mayor's office. I explained to her that there were rumblings throughout the industry about being overlooked for major contracts. People were tired of seeing the same companies be awarded city contracts year after year. She understood but did not know how to untangle herself. There were offshore accounts with large sums of money. These accounts were set up by the mayor and his campaign manager in Debbie's name. All accounts are in her name and point to her. When she found out about it, she confronted the mayor. That's when he told her that he owned her. Can you imagine someone telling you that they own you? I realized that if she wasn't going to make the call, then it was up to me. I couldn't act like I didn't know about it. I had to make the call."

"Oh my goodness. I don't know what to make of all of this," said Lois.

"Please believe me when I tell you that the call was necessary. That was the only way to stop the mayor from getting back in office and getting Debbie out of the pay-to-play scheme," explained Jeremy.

"I know I took a huge gamble, but it was one I was willing to take to save a good friend."

Myles nodded his head in agreement. "It took guts to do what you did. I respect you for it."

Lois sat in disbelief. She felt like the world was spinning out of control and she needed it to stop. "Before this story gets any more bizarre, is there anything else I need to know?"

"There is one more thing, but it's a good thing," said Jeremy. "Debbie's attorney called a couple of days ago to go over a few things with me. I was informed that I would be called as a witness for the Defense. We can only pray that Debbie comes out of this unscathed."

Lois considered Jeremy's last statement. She prayed with all her heart that Debbie would come out unscathed. She wouldn't be totally sure of her attorney's abilities until she had an opportunity to speak with her. That conversation would present itself sooner rather than later. Without looking into the faces of the three men sitting around her, she knew they too pondered the uncertainties before them. In the coming days, her steps would be just as strategic, if not more than, Debbie's. The success of her daughter's defense depended on it.

Later that evening at the fish fry, they made their way through the crowd. Musicians graced the stage while people gathered and swayed to island music. From the time they spent among the laughter and friendly faces of the people, their thoughts came under the spell of the music. They did not allow themselves to think about the corrupt nature of the mayor or the impending trial. Just for that night, they allowed themselves to be totally free. The rest would take care of itself. Music, laughter, and the aroma of island delicacies filled the night sky until the wee hours of the morning. Lois and the others stayed, enjoying the festivities, as if they would miss out on something magical if they left too early. After hours of dancing and sampling conch fritters, conch chowder, and conch salad from the best chefs in the Caribbean, they were ready to return home for a couple hours of sleep before accompanying Myles to the airport.

Myles lay on his back staring up at the ceiling while the others slept. In the quietness surrounding him, he thought back over the events of the past week and felt he now understood why Debbie fell in love with Turks and Caicos. In the short time spent on the island, he experienced another side of life that many people yearned for but not many had an opportunity to encounter. Unable to shut his mind down and embrace sleep, he lay tossing and turning until sunrise. He quietly got out of bed, showered, and packed his suitcase for the return home.

He slowly walked down the hall of this beautiful house, allowing his eyes to roam, taking in every corner. Entering the kitchen, he noticed the massive island, the backsplash, the appliances, the elongated cabinets which gave the kitchen depth. He opened the French doors leading out to the elegantly designed swimming pool and the landscape showcasing plants indigenous to the Caribbean. Myles returned to the kitchen and walked into a well-stocked pantry. Exiting the pantry, his eyes fell on the living space and the furniture defining each space. He was aware that someone had taken great care in designing and furnishing this house. Someone who not only wanted to show gratitude, but their undying love. He wondered if Debbie knew.

Myles heard a door open. Jeremy emerged slowly into the living space, wiping sleep from his eyes. "Hey, did you get any sleep?" he asked as he made his way to the kitchen. He poured a glass of juice and joined Myles in the living room. "I really enjoyed myself last night, but my body is telling me that I am not twenty anymore."

"I hear you," agreed Myles. "There is something about island music and food which cannot be explained."

"Say no more. It's like being transported to another place in time."

"Okay. I'm quite sure that's a lyric from an Earth, Wind & Fire song," added Myles.

"Yeah, well that's the best I can do on such short notice," laughed Jeremy. "That's what island music and food will do to you."

They continued talking until they were joined later that morning by Matt and Lois. They looked as if they needed another twenty-four hours of sleep. Lois plopped down and curled up in the far corner of the sofa. Matt commandeered the other plush chair in the living room.

"What time is your flight?" asked Lois.

"One o'clock," answered Myles.

"What time is it now?"

"Island time," chuckled Matt as his face caught a pillow thrown by his brother.

"Please excuse my brother, sometimes he forgets how old he is."

"Clearly," said Lois sleepily.

"It is nine o'clock. Myles, you have four hours before your flight leaves. Why don't you dress for the weather and come with me? I have something I want you to see."

Myles walked back to the guest room and put on a pair of shorts and short-sleeved shirt. He decided on a pair of tennis shoes instead of sandals as he wasn't sure where they were headed. Jeremy was waiting for him when he returned to the living room.

"It sure gets hot early in the Caribbean," said Myles.

"Yeah, but you get used to it after awhile. However, that's why I positioned the house so that Lois and Debbie would feel the breeze coming in off the ocean."

"So you designed the house?" asked Myles.

"Yeah. My degree is in architectural design. My brother; construction engineering. You might remember that we worked every summer at our uncle's construction company. He told us that he was going to leave the business to us. However, we needed to go to college. I remember the day he asked us what we were interested in. I have always been interested in architecture. My brother and I would walk around the neighborhood and explore abandoned buildings wondering who used to live there or what the houses used to look like. I can honestly say, it was in the blood because my uncle was the same way."

"My grandfather worked in construction as well," said Myles.

"Really? There is a possibility that my uncle knew your grandfather."

"I only wish he were still alive so that I could ask," said Myles. "There was a crane accident on the construction site where he worked, and he didn't make it."

"I'm sorry to hear that."

"After that, it was just me and my grandmother."

"Here we are," said Jeremy as he put the car in park. "Once a contractor, always a contractor."

Myles stood in front of a three-story office building with a gorgeous view of the ocean. J&M Builders was in stenciled lettering on the glass door.

"I just wanted you to know that things aren't always what they appear to be. The mayor and his campaign manager thought we were out for the count. My uncle taught us to fight smart. By all appearances, it looked like my brother and I were giving up. But that was far from the truth. We decided to shut down our operation, make a little money in the process, and set up shop here in Turks and Caicos. The same way we helped the City of New York, we can do the same throughout the Caribbean."

Myles was speechless. The resilience of the twin brothers from the inner city let him know that they refused to be defeated.

"C'mon. I'll give you a tour of the place." Jeremy unlocked the glass doors and walked Myles through the office floor by floor.

As they walked around the unfurnished office building of J&M Builders, Myles couldn't help but notice there was a glimpse of the ocean from every part of the building. At that moment in time, he was glad that he had traveled to Turks and Caicos. He wasn't sure what he would find when he arrived, but he was glad he made the trip.

"So when will the office be ready for business? Is there a place to buy office furniture on the island?"

"I am working with a local shop owner on the island to help furnish the office. Understandably, there are some items that will need to be shipped to the island."

"The furniture in Lois's house. Did that come from the island as well?"

"No. I handpicked every piece of furniture and accessory and had it shipped by boat from New York."

"Wow! You really went all out," said Myles.

"Debbie means a lot to me. She helped my brother and I when we were at our lowest. I would do anything for her."

At that moment, Myles knew that Jeremy's feelings for Debbie went deep. He had always heard that when a man goes deep in his pocket for a woman, he is in love. The other elephant in the room had shown up. He now knew that Jeremy was prepared to go the distance for the woman he loved. Myles thought about what John Brimmer said before he left for Turks and Caicos. "What are you prepared to do, Myles, when the situation presents itself? Promise me you will handle it with integrity."

Myles looked at his watch. "I guess we should head back to the house. Congratulations on your new business. I wish you and your brother great success."

"Thanks."

Jeremy and Myles climbed back in the car and drove back to the house in silence. When they arrived, Lois was just putting the finishing touches on breakfast.

"You two got back just in time. Sit down and let's eat. I don't want you getting on the plane without something on your stomach, Myles."

"Wow! Everything smells so good. I cannot wait to dig in," said Myles.

For the remainder of the time spent with Lois and the twin brothers, Myles enjoyed good conversation and new friendships. He was happy he made the trip.

Myles arrived at the airport an hour before takeoff. He said his goodbyes to Lois and the twin brothers promising to return for a visit. As he walked through the airport, memories of all he learned while in Turks and Caicos flooded back keeping him company on the return flight home. Had he known what was facing him when he returned, he never would have left New York.

CHAPTER

MYLES OPENED THE DOOR TO HIS apartment and pushed his suitcase inside. The blinking light on the answering machine alerted him of five missed calls. He pushed the button and heard the familiar voice of the administrator of Chesterfield Assisted Living. "Mr. Beyers, this is Charlotte Adams at Chesterfield Assisted Living. Please give me a call at your earliest convenience." Myles scrolled through the remaining messages. They were all from the administrator of Chesterfield. Each message more urgent than the other. The fifth and final message from Charlotte Adams, "Mr. Beyers, I've tried several times to reach you. As your grandmother's point of contact and power of attorney for making medical decisions, it is vitally important that you contact me."

Myles frantically dialed Chesterfield and asked to be connected to Charlotte Adams.

"This is Charlotte Adams," said the voice on the other end.

"Ms. Adams, this is Myles Beyers returning your call. I'm sorry to just be getting back with you, but I was out of town on business."

"Yes, Mr. Beyers. Thank you for returning my call. I'm sorry but I have some distressing news. Your grandmother suffered a stroke a few days ago and was taken to Mercy General. I spoke with the doctor earlier today and was told that she has fallen into a coma.

She listed you as having power of attorney and able to make medical decisions for her."

Myles found it hard to speak. He felt his world turning upside down. His grandmother, the one who had always been there for him, the one who he could depend on was in a coma. They talked and joked the day before he left for Turks and Caicos. She didn't look sick to him…not really.

"Mr. Beyers, are you still there?"

"Yes, I'm still here. She's at Mercy General, correct?"

"Correct."

"What's the doctor's name?"

"Dr. Philips. Again, Mr. Beyers, I am sorry to be the bearer of such news. My prayers are with you and Leona. The family of Chesterfield is very fond of her."

"Thank you." Myles disconnected the call and ran out of the apartment. He could not get to the hospital quick enough. He mentally scolded himself for making the trip to Turks and Caicos. Had he mailed the check instead of hand-delivering it, he would have been here for his grandmother. It hurt to think that his grandmother went through this all alone.

He arrived at Mercy General and pulled into the first empty parking space. He jumped out of the car and rushed into the hospital lobby.

He ran up to the Information desk, "Hi. My grandmother, Leona Crutchfield, is a patient here. Can you tell me what floor she is on, please?"

The young lady at the desk searched for her name. "Yes. She is on the fourth floor. The elevators are down the hall to your left. When you get to the fourth floor, turn right, and go through the double doors."

Myles followed the young lady's instruction. When he pushed through the double doors, the gold letters on the wall informed him he had entered the intensive care section of Mercy General. A nurse with kind eyes and compassionate smile looked up as he approached the nurse's station. He stopped at the desk and asked where he might find his grandmother, Leona Crutchfield. She told him she was in 403B.

He gingerly walked the corridors of Intensive Care in search of his grandmother. As he walked, he took note of people as they lay quietly in their beds; their bodies fighting to live. Machines tracking blood pressure, oxygen levels, and heartbeats kept watch. He walked into 403B and drew back the curtain. Tears welled up and spilled over onto his cheeks as he saw a once vibrant woman hooked up to a ventilator. The bedside monitors played the same song as the others along the corridors of ICU.

"Granny, please forgive me for not being here for you," said Myles. He sat by his grandmother's bedside allowing the tears to flow. "You're all I have left is this world. Please. You have to get better."

He looked up when the nurse entered the room.

"Hello," she said. "Are you a family member of Mrs. Crutchfield?"

"Yes. I'm her grandson, Myles Beyers."

"It's good to meet you. The administrator of Chesterfield called and said you would be stopping by. Do you have any questions for me or Dr. Philips?"

"All Ms. Adams told me is that my grandmother had a stroke and slipped into a coma. I do have questions for Dr. Philips. However, in the meantime, can you tell me if my grandmother is in any pain?"

"She's not responding to any stimuli, which lets us know that she's not in any pain. Since she is in a coma, it's too early to know if her speech or limbs are impaired. Dr. Philips is conducting his rounds and should be in to check on your grandmother shortly. Do you have any further questions?"

"No. You've been helpful."

The nurse massaged Leona Crutchfield's left hand as she checked the monitors. "God has the final say," she whispered.

Myles saw her lips moving but could not hear what the nurse was saying. She picked up the clipboard hanging from a hook at the foot of the bed and made a few notations before turning to walk out of the room. She stopped at the door and looked over her shoulder at Myles. "Mr. Beyers, I heard you praying as I walked into the room. Remember, God has the final say."

Myles was comforted by her encouraging words. Not long after the nurse left, Dr. Philips walked in and introduced himself to Myles.

"Hello, I'm Dr. Philips," he said while extending his hand to Myles.

Myles shook the doctor's hand and said, "Hello. I'm her grandson, Myles Beyers."

"Good to meet you. I'm looking after your grandmother while she is with us. You certainly must have questions for me, and I'll do my best to answer them. So what have you been told about your grandmother's condition?"

"I was told that she had a stroke and then lapsed into a coma. What I don't know is what caused her to stroke. Also, is it normal to lapse into a coma after stroking?"

"These are all valid questions so let's start with what we do know. There are two types of hemorrhagic strokes. One being intracerebral and the other subarachnoid. The most common, and the one that caused your grandmother's stroke, is intracerebral. Essentially what happens is the artery bursts and blood flows in around the tissue, which can be caused by a history of high blood pressure, drinking, or, unfortunately, old age."

"We can rule out drinking and high blood pressure," said Myles.

"Yes, we can. Her primary physician confirmed that she was neither a drinker nor suffered with high blood pressure. The administrator at Chesterfield told me she was outside when this happened. This might have worked in her favor. I say this because this could have had a different outcome had she stroked while alone in her apartment. Others saw her fall and immediately called 911. Now, the reason she is in a coma, can be contributed to the hit to the head when she fell causing swelling in the brain. Because of the swelling, there was no blood flow to a major part of the brainstem resulting in a comatose state. Please rest assured that we will take good care of her at Mercy General. I am hopeful that she will begin to show signs of improvement in the days and weeks to come. But right now, all we can do is remain hopeful and keep a close eye on her for signs of improvement. Do you have any more questions?"

"Will there be paralysis or problems with her memory or speech?" asked Myles.

"There is always a possibility for a stroke victim to experience some or all of these conditions. But let's not worry about that yet, okay? Talk to her. Let her hear your voice. She might not be able to talk to you, but she can hear you. Some other things you can do is play music. If she has a favorite artist or favorite song, let that play. Remember, she can hear even if she can't open her eyes or speak. Read to her as well. Data proves that all these things aid in the recovery process. I'm going to give you my office number. If you don't hear from me, feel free to call me."

"I will. Dr. Philips, thank you."

Myles bent down and kissed his grandmother on the top of her head; a kiss only reserved for her. He put his lips close to her ear and prayed, "*Father, in the name of Jesus, touch and heal her body. I pray that when it is time to walk out of this hospital, she will walk out in true form. Amen.*"

He stayed by her bedside until visiting hours were over. He kissed his granny and told her he would return the following day. Myles slowly walked out of the hospital uncertain what the days ahead would offer. He could only pray that there would be better days ahead.

The following morning Myles lay in bed staring at the ceiling. He made a mental note of everything he needed to do before going to the hospital. He looked at the clock and forced himself out of bed to shower and dress for church. He needed to let her pastor know that she was in the hospital and stop by her place to pick up some music.

Just as he was preparing to leave, the telephone rang.

"Hello."

"Hey, Myles, welcome back."

"Hey, Debbie. I was going to call you when I got a chance."

"When did you get back?"

Myles knew where this was going, and he wasn't in the mood to play twenty questions.

"I got back yesterday afternoon, but I really need to go. I will give you a call later, okay?"

"Myles, wait a minute. After all that I have gone through and what's facing me, it seems like you could make time to talk to me. While you were having fun vacationing in Turks and Caicos, I was sitting in jail, remember? Then, you tell me that you arrived back in New York yesterday afternoon and didn't bother to call me. Don't I mean anything to you?"

"Debbie, I cannot do this with you right now. When I got home, there were five messages waiting for me. All five messages were notifying me that my grandmother had a stroke while I was in Turks and Caicos. I wasn't vacationing, Debbie. I was handling business for you. Remember the check for $1.2 mil? I hand-delivered that check to your mother. So excuse me while I attend to my grandmother. I'll call you when I get a chance."

He abruptly hung up the phone, slamming the door as he exited the apartment.

After church, he drove to Mercy General and sat with his grandmother. He read several pages from a book he grabbed off her nightstand. He would look up from the book periodically to watch for any signs of life only to return to the book. Soon he would reach the end and made a mental note to stop by the local bookstore. He now believed he had a strong grasp of his grandmother's taste in literature. Visiting hours were over so Myles moved the chair back to its original position and placed the book in the cubby with her other personal items. He leaned over and kissed his grandmother on the top of her head and wished her sweet dreams. "We'll finish the book tomorrow, Granny. I love you."

Myles returned home later that evening and stretched out across his bed; not bothering to change out of his clothes. He was awakened the following morning by the sound of a ringing telephone.

"Hello?"

Gloria was talking every excitedly, "Myles, are you coming in to work today? Mr. Brimmer stopped by your office and I didn't know what to tell him as I had not heard from you."

Myles looked at the clock; it was ten o'clock. He could not believe he had forgotten to set the alarm before going to sleep.

"What would you like me to tell Mr. Brimmer?"

"Tell him I overslept but I will arrive within the hour?"

"Are you okay? You don't sound like yourself. Plus, you have never overslept or been late in all the years I have worked for you."

"Thanks for your concern. Please let Mr. Brimmer know that I am on my way."

"Okay. See you soon."

Myles took a quick shower and threw on a pair of slacks with a button-down shirt and argyle sweater. Not his typical dress but considering he was late for work he did not have time for a suit and tie today. He arrived at the office around noon and stopped by John Brimmer's office to apologize for his tardiness.

"Myles, welcome back. Come in and have a seat."

He entered the office closing the door behind him. "John, I apologize for being late. After leaving the hospital last night, I was so tired I lay across my bed without setting the alarm."

"Back up. You were in the hospital?"

"No. My grandmother. She suffered a stroke while I was out of town and is in a coma."

"I am so sorry to hear this," said his boss. "Of course, if you need additional time off, we can work something out."

"I appreciate your concern, but I think the best thing for me right now is to remain busy. I have the doctor's number and, in the brief time that we discussed my grandmother's condition, I have complete confidence in him."

"Okay, but if you change your mind, let me know. This might not be the appropriate time to ask this, but how did everything go in Turks and Caicos?"

"Things went better than I expected. However, it would take me three days to tell you everything that happened while there."

"Wow! It's like that?"

"Yes. I can tell you this though. Everything is not as it seems. Debbie's mother was in the dark about everything. And I was in the dark about Jeremy and Matt."

"Who are Jeremy and Matt?" inquired his boss.

"Get this. They used to own a construction firm here in New York. They did well for themselves, too. When the mayor's campaign manager approached them about participating in the pay-to-play scheme, they decided to shut their operation down. As a matter of fact, they sold their company. Who do you think they sold their company to? I'll give you one guess."

John Brimmer leaned back in his oversized executive chair and thought for a minute. There was a twinkle in his eyes when he answered, "Davis Construction."

"Exactly!"

"So Debbie is friends with Jeremy and Matt?"

"From what I was told, Debbie helped them through the bidding process. Eventually, their firm got hired as contractors on some of the larger jobs around the city. They made a reputation for themselves and their company grew large enough to hire staff. Apparently, Debbie put them in touch with the right people. Jeremy and Matt told me that they successfully bid on contracts and were awarded multimillion-dollar contracts."

"Would the name of their construction company by any chance be J&M Construction?"

"One and the same. You know them?"

"Do I know them? Yeah, I know them. They used to be one of my biggest clients," explained John Brimmer.

Myles sat back in the chair and allowed himself a few minutes to process what he'd just heard. He thought back to the files Agents Simmons and McBride requested. They were attempting to connect the dots by following the money. Now this was all beginning to make sense.

"I wonder why they took their business away from you?" pondered Myles out loud. "They are still in business, you know. Before I left, Jeremy took me by their new office in Turks and Caicos."

"Well, one could speculate all day," started John Brimmer. "Maybe they were trying to cut all ties with New York. Especially if they refused to go along with the mayor's pay-to-play scheme. They were smart enough to know that they would not be awarded any contracts without paying. So they got out of the business while they could. Selling, in my opinion, was a smart move. I hated to lose their business as J&M Construction was a multimillion-dollar account. If memory serves me correctly, we lost them as a client right before you were hired."

"Well, it's safe to say that between the upcoming trial and election, things are going to get pretty interesting," surmised Myles.

"I agree." Myles looked at his watch. "Well, I've taken up enough of your time. I should get to work."

"Yes, you should," said his boss jokingly.

Myles was in better spirits after sitting and talking with John Brimmer. His boss always said that he thought of him like the son he never had. What he failed to tell his boss is that he felt that he stepped in to fill the void that his biological father wasn't there to fill. He had a decent relationship with his biological father now that he was no longer incarcerated. They saw each other from time to time, and it was always good to catch up. Now that his father had secured full-time employment, he moved out of the halfway house into his own apartment. It was because of forgiveness that he was able to forge a relationship with his father. Myles knew that forgiving a person that has committed a crime as heinous as taking another's life could be considered unforgiveable by most. However, when his father asked for his forgiveness, he felt that was the only way to move forward. He had to forgive. Myles thought back on the many heated conversations he had with his father. Forgiveness did not come overnight. Raw conversations followed by hot tears running down both their faces was the scene on many nights spent with his father. He remembered the look on his father's face when he told him that he had stolen the one thing that made life bearable. Crushed was the only word that could describe the pain. He remembered his father getting up from the chair he sat in and slowly walking toward him with outstretched arms repeatedly saying I'm sorry...please forgive me.

Myles leaned back in his office chair and thought about the events of the past few weeks and wondered where all of this would end. There was a soft knock at his office door. He looked up and his secretary was peering around the door.

"Myles. I'm sorry to disturb you but you have a visitor." She opened the door a little wider and his childhood friend, Cinnamon entered.

He got up from his chair and walked around the desk to welcome her. "You are a sight for sore eyes," he said as he hugged her. "What brings you downtown?"

"I heard about your grandmother and I decided to stop by to check on my friend. I needed that face-to-face with you, not a phone call."

"Wow, Cinnamon, you do not know how much this means to me."

"What can I do to help?" she asked.

"I don't know. I mean, I've been going by the hospital and sitting with her. Her doctor told me that playing music and reading to her is a good thing to do. So I took some of her favorite music and I play it while I'm there. Honestly, listening to the music helps me as well."

Cinnamon smiled when he mentioned playing music for his grandmother.

"Myles, do you remember how you, Leroy, and I would sit on your grandmother's porch and play Earth, Wind & Fire's song 'Keep Your Head to the Sky' repeatedly. We really thought we could sing."

"I sure do. Leroy's voice would crack every time he tried to hit the high notes. Remember the time my grandmother was standing at the front door with a wooden spoon in her hand. She looked at him and said, 'Leroy, if you don't stop all that noise, you will be banned from my sidewalk for all eternity.'"

"Yeah, and Leroy looked at her and said, 'I didn't know people could own the sidewalk.' Your grandmother opened the door and before she could get out of the door good, he jumped off the porch and ran home. He was afraid to come back to your house for weeks after that."

"As he should have. My grandmother would always ask about my smart-mouth friend. She really got a good laugh that day."

"Every birthday, you would invite Leroy and me to dinner for chicken and dumplings with apple pie for dessert. Man, I thought your grandmother was the best cook in the neighborhood."

"She hasn't lost her touch either. I try to swing by Chesterfield at least once a week for a visit and dinner with her. Sometimes she cooks and then, there were times when we go out to eat. Cinnamon, when I found out about my grandmother, all I could think about was that I'm not ready for her to leave. I still need her here with me."

"Try not to think that way, Myles. Your grandmother is a fighter. Remember, God has the final say."

"The nurse said the same thing the first night I was at the hospital."

"She's right. Everything happens in God's timing, not ours."

"You always come with words of encouragement. Thank you."

"Anytime. But as your friend from the neighborhood, I would like to help you out. How about I go sit with your grandmother today. I have some free time. It's the least I can do. Oh, before I forget, we secured early release for Shakira."

"Did you say we? I'm assuming you are talking about your dad, Kyle and, of course, you."

"Exactly. She moved in with our father and they are bonding quite nicely."

"When did all of this happen?" asked Myles.

"About a month ago," confirmed Cinnamon.

"Wow…this is great news! I'm happy for you and your family."

"Hey, I'm going to get out of here and head over to the hospital to sit with your grandmother for a few hours."

"Cinnamon, thank you so much. There's a book there as well as her favorite gospel tunes. And, Cinnamon, if I haven't told you lately, I appreciate you."

She smiled. "I appreciate you, too."

After Cinnamon left his office, he considered himself lucky to have friends as caring and true blue as Cinnamon and Leroy. They grew up and took separate paths that continuously brought them back together. No matter what they went through, one or all would show up when needed. From the first time he went to live with his grandparents, Cinnamon and Leroy were present. They befriended him, and they all remained friends throughout their academic and professional careers. His granny called them the three musketeers. You never saw one without the other.

Myles looked at the time and determined that he should at least attempt to get some work done in the office.

His secretary walked into his office and offered to get him something for lunch. "I'm going to step out for a salad. Would you like me to bring you a sandwich?"

"I had no idea it was this late. If you don't mind, I would appreciate it. Here, take this. It should be enough there for a salad and sandwich."

"Thank you. I'll be back shortly."

Myles turned his attention back to the files on his desk hoping to keep his mind off the FBI investigation, the upcoming trial, and now, his grandmother's hospitalization. He scribbled a note on his desk calendar to talk to his boss about Aubrey DeLoach. If he was looking to replace the revenue lost when J&M Construction closed their account, Aubrey DeLoach and all her billions might be worth pursuing.

Myles was deep in thought about Aubrey DeLoach when Gloria returned with lunch. He invited her to stay and have lunch with him. He thought it strange that she did not quiz him on his time in Turks and Caicos, nor did she ask him any questions about Debbie or the trial.

"How was your time away from the office?" asked Myles. "Did you do anything interesting?"

"Truly, we did. We dropped the kids off with my mother-in-law and hubby and I flew to New Orleans. We had a great time. Thank you so much for suggesting that I take time away from the office."

"Actually, I didn't suggest that you take time off. You told me what you were going to do, and I went along with it."

"Well, if that's how you are remembering it."

"Gloria has anyone ever told you that…never mind."

She looked at Myles and answered, "Yes."

For the second time that day, Myles laughed. He felt that God was smiling down on him and sending people his way to keep his spirits up. He briefly thought about Debbie and that he might have been a little abrupt with her. He made a mental note to call and apologize.

"Gloria, after lunch I would like you to help me research a potential client."

"Sure. Who is the client?"

"Aubrey DeLoach. A few weeks ago, John mentioned that he was having dinner with Ms. DeLoach. Anything you can find out about her philanthropic efforts will help make my case with him."

"I must admit, it will be a nice boost for the company to have her as a client. Between us, do you think there might be something brewing between the two of them?"

Myles chuckled slightly. "I'm not sure but I don't think it will be a bad thing if there was. John confided that he poured himself into his work after his wife died. Let's wait and see if their business relationship evolves into something more permanent."

"I'm right there with you. Thanks, again, for lunch and I'll let you know what I turn up on Aubrey DeLoach."

Myles reached for the phone to call Debbie but stopped short of dialing the number. There was no way he could divide his time between his grandmother and Debbie. Not now. No matter how much he wanted to be there for her, his heart was with his grandmother. He rationalized that Debbie had a strong support group with Matt, Jeremy, and her mother. If he explained why he could not be with her right now, he felt she would understand. He reached for the phone and dialed her number.

"Hello."

"Hey, Debbie. Look I just wanted to call and see how you are doing."

"I'm doing okay. Today has been a day of meetings with my attorney. She thinks we have a solid case showing that I was black-mailed into participating with the pay-to-play scheme. Remember when I told you that the mayor paid off my student debt without my prior knowledge? The FBI has a recording of him admitting to it which worked in my favor. However, all three of us are facing indictment but I have confidence in the attorney as she has never lost a case."

"That's great. I pray all works out for you, Debbie."

"The trial starts in a couple of weeks. It would mean a lot to me if you could be there throughout the trial."

"Debbie, that's not something I can do. I cannot afford to take any more time off from work. I took time off when we drove to Cape May, and my boss was very understanding when I traveled to Turks and Caicos on short notice. This is the firm's busy time and unless I am compelled to testify, I don't think it's fair to my boss to take any more time off work unnecessarily."

Debbie was so silent Myles thought she might have disconnected the call.

"Debbie?"

"I'm still here. I'm just trying to process what I'm hearing right now. The one person I thought I could count on was you. So, forgive me if I don't share your sentiment about work."

"Debbie, I think you are being unreasonable."

"Unreasonable? I don't think so. If it were you facing trial and being scrutinized, I would be in court showing my support."

"What about my grandmother?" asked Myles. "Am I to forget about her as well?"

"I'm sorry about your grandmother, Myles, but didn't you say she's in a coma. She doesn't even know you are in the room."

"That's where you are wrong. Why didn't I see this before?"

"See what?"

"I never saw the selfish Debbie. All I saw was the fun loving, beautiful, businesswoman. But now you have shown me another side of you. The side that wants everything to go her way. You might not understand what it's like to lose someone you love. It's a void that cannot be filled. My grandmother tried to fill that void to the best of her ability, and I will not abandon her when she needs me the most. You have your mother, Jeremy, and Matt. My grandmother only has me and I her. End of story."

"I see. So you are not going to be in court for moral support?" asked Debbie.

"I really shouldn't have to choose. But if you cannot understand my position, then I would have to say I will not be there. Frankly, I think this is definitely the end of us."

"Well. I guess that settles that. Do me one last favor."

"Sure."

"Mail the key I gave you to Baldwin Realty. Address the envelope to Sharon Michaels. I will call her in the morning so that she will know to look out for it. Myles, I'm going to miss what we had together, but I guess it is time to move on. Take care."

"You too."

Myles hung up and leaned back in his chair. He assured himself that this was for the best. His grandfather always told him that when setting priorities, a man should figure out what's most important to him and go from there. At this moment in time, his grandmother was his priority. He, too, would miss Debbie but the uncertainty of his grandmother's condition demanded his attention. He was deep in thought when Gloria walked into his office.

"Myles. I'm sorry to disturb you but I thought I would get back with you on Aubrey DeLoach."

"Great. Let's see what you were able to find."

"Well, the DeLoach Foundation's philanthropic efforts have been substantial and impressive. For example, four clinics were built in western Africa. From what I was able to find out, these clinics are in areas that previously did not have any doctors let alone clinics. When someone got sick, they had to travel miles to the nearest town and stand in line for hours for someone to examine them. The clinics are fully staffed state of the art facilities with large waiting rooms so that people do not have to stand out in the hot sun. The best part is that these clinics are free."

"Free?"

"Yes. She partnered with the government. They agreed to provide free medical care to all residents of these villages after establishing the clinics."

"This woman is a saint!"

"As close to one as anyone of us will ever get," offered Gloria. "There's more."

"More than building four clinics?" asked Myles.

"Yes. Recently, the DeLoach Foundation donated twenty million dollars to community colleges and universities to assist disenfranchised children wanting to attend higher learning institutions. She personally worked with each institution to establish an articulation agreement between community colleges and universities to ensure credits earned are transferrable."

"There are so many children that have given up on progressing beyond high school because of finances," said Myles. "To have someone like Aubrey DeLoach donate twenty million of her own money so that children from low-income families can compete on a level typically reserved for those with means is commendable. We need more Aubrey DeLoach's in this world."

"I agree. From what I have read, the scholarship fund is replenished each year. As long as there is money in the fund, children will have a chance."

"I'm impressed by this woman," said Myles. "How is the fund replenished?"

"Fundraising," replied Gloria. "Actually, there is a fundraiser planned next week." Gloria quickly scanned her notes. "Yes, here it is. There is a fundraiser scheduled next Friday at the Four Seasons."

Myles smiled broadly as he gave Gloria a congratulatory clap. "Good job. That's why you should get paid the big bucks."

"I will remember you said that when it is time for my performance review."

Myles looked at the clock. It was officially the end of the workday and decided he would swing by the hospital and sit with his grandmother for about an hour before heading home. He and Gloria rode down on the elevator together.

"I'm sorry to hear about your grandmother," said Gloria. "Normally, Mr. Brimmer doesn't share this type of information, but since I work so closely with you, he thought it was best that I knew."

"Thank you."

"If I can do anything for you, please let me know."

"I will. Thank you."

They rode the rest of the way in silence. The soft chime of the elevator awakened both from solemn thoughts. Gloria looked at Myles and smiled before exiting the elevator. Myles returned the gesture and leaned back against the wall of the elevator as it ushered him to the garage level. As he walked toward his car, he noticed a man walking briskly in his direction. He kept his eye on the person headed in his direction as he quickened his step.

His hand was on the door handle when he heard someone call his name. "Myles Beyers?" Myles turned toward the person. "Are you Myles Beyers?"

"Yes. I'm Myles Beyers."

He followed the motion of the hand placing a folded piece of paper in his hand. "You have been served." As quickly as the person appeared, he was gone.

Myles unfolded the paper and realized he had received a summons of process to appear in court. He read it twice before it dawned on him that Debbie had gotten her way. If he would not appear in court from his own volition, he would be forced to appear as a witness for the Defense. He crumpled the summons and threw it in the backseat of his car out of frustration.

On the drive to the hospital, Myles tried not to let his mind linger too long on the summons received. The only thing that mattered to him was that his grandmother recovered. In the past few days spent at the hospital, Myles got to know the familiar faces of the nurses. They would give him updates on his grandmother as he passed by. When he arrived at his grandmother's room, he was surprised to see Cinnamon.

"Hey, I'm surprised you are still here," he said.

"I wanted to wait for you so that I could give you the good news," responded Cinnamon.

"Don't keep me in suspense. I can use some good news right about now."

"When I arrived, I popped in a cassette. I leaned in close to her ear and told her that I was here and would be visiting with her for a couple of hours. At first I thought my mind was playing tricks on me because I saw movement."

"What type of movement? Did she move a finger or movement of the eyes? Does her doctor know?"

"Slow down. All these questions are making me dizzy.

Myles ran his hands over his hair and stared at his grandmother with great expectation. If only she would move while I'm here, he thought to himself.

"Has there been any additional movement?" he asked.

"No. She only moved once. However, I mentioned it to her doctor, and he said that sometimes coma patients experience non-purposeful movements. He checked her feet for stimuli, but there was no response."

While talking to Cinnamon, Myles absent-mindedly leaned on the foot of the bed with one hand. He thought he noticed eye movement, so he moved a little closer to his grandmother. Although her eyes were not open, he noticed slight eye movement.

"Did you see that?" he asked Cinnamon.

"See what?"

"Her eyes moved," he exclaimed excitedly. "Come on, Granny. Let me see you move your eyes again. Come on."

Both he and Cinnamon waited patiently for any signs of movement. They alternated between holding her hand to rubbing her feet for any signs of life. Cinnamon took her hand in hers and began to pray. Myles did the same and joined her in prayer. Dr. Philips quietly entered the room and stood respectfully until they finished praying.

When Myles opened his eyes, he was surprised to see Dr. Philips standing there. He walked toward the doctor and shook his hand.

"Dr. Philips, this is a good friend of the family, Cynthia Harrelson."

"Yes, we met earlier." He stepped a little further into the room. His attitude was one of deep reflection.

Dr. Philip cleared his throat and with great earnestness said, "I entered the room as you and Ms. Harrelson were praying. It was such an impassioned prayer, that I believe all the angels in heaven stood at attention. You work great as a team, and your grandmother is lucky to have the both of you fighting on her behalf. Keep praying," he said as he put his hand on Myles's shoulder.

Myles took the opportunity to question Dr. Philips about the eye movement he noticed.

"Dr. Philips, before you arrived, I noticed eye movement. Is this a sign that she might be coming out of the coma?"

"It's not uncommon for coma patients to experience spontaneous eye movement. You might see them open and close their eyes periodically, but until they are able to open their eyes and keep them opened for extended periods of time, she is still in a comatose state. When coma patients begin to respond to the calling of their name or react to pain, they are getting closer to coming out of a coma. Some other things to look for is how easily is the patient awakened from sleep. Awaking easily from a gentle shaking of the shoulder or sounds such as calling her name or footsteps walking into the room are all signs of someone coming out of a coma."

"I understand. Thank you for taking the time to explain this to us."

"She is making progress. Her vitals are good, and she doesn't appear to be in any pain. Earlier today, I started her on an anti-blood clotting medication. This is standard procedure for stroke patients. Before I leave, do you have any other questions?"

"No, not at this time."

"Do you still have my number? If not, I can give you another card."

"I still have it."

Dr. Philips put his hand on Myles's shoulder in comfort. "Don't worry. I will take good care of your grandmother."

"I have no doubt," replied Myles.

Dr. Philips left the two alone. As he exited the room, he considered the statistics of stroke being the leading cause of long-term disability. In his twenty-five years as a doctor, he had treated many stroke victims. Most of them had a recurring stroke within five years of the first one. But there was something about the prayer he heard moments earlier that led him to believe that Myles's grandmother would defy the odds. He recalled an incident that happened early in his medical career. Fresh out of medical school, he decided to pursue residency for additional training. He smiled at the thought of how cocky he was at that time. He remembered a young lady being rushed into the ER with massive hemorrhaging on the brain. He was called in as the attending physician. Surgeons spent hours rushing against the clock to save this young lady's life. The stroke suffered caused too much damage and she died during surgery. He remembered it like it was yesterday. She was only seventeen years old. When the primary surgeon went out to talk to the family, he remembered the mother of this young girl cursing God. He vividly remembers the mother yelling that she would never forgive God for taking her daughter away from her. She would ask repeatedly, how could a loving God let her daughter die from a stroke at seventeen? In his twenty-five years as a doctor, he had seen people of all ages die for whatever reasons. There were those who would lose their faith, and then there were others who held fast to their faith when tragedy struck. This is what he witnessed from Myles and Ms. Harrelson. Yep, in his twenty-five years of practice, he had witnessed more than he cared to remember. He walked into his office, hung his white coat on the back of the door, and headed home to have dinner with his wife; something he had not the luxury of in some time.

Myles kissed his grandmother on the top of her head and whispered, "Pleasant dreams. I'll be back tomorrow."

He and Cinnamon walked slowly down the corridor, past the nurse's station, and pushed through the double doors exiting the ICU. Myles pushed the button summoning the elevator. Cinnamon moved closer to him and placed her head on his shoulder.

"Myles, your grandmother is lucky to have you," she said.

"No. I'm lucky to have her. I don't think I am able to articulate how much she means to me. When I lost my mother, she wrapped me in love. A day never went by that she did not remind me how much she cared about me. It's because of her that I am who I have become. I owe everything to her."

"Are you going to give yourself a little credit?" teased Cinnamon. "I remember how driven you were in school. I could see it in your eyes. You were determined not to become a product of our environment. You and I know many people that allowed street life to suck them in."

"Yeah. My grandparents were engaged in every aspect of my life. My grandfather took up time with me. When he took me fishing, he was giving me life lessons. He imparted wisdom in me at a young age. I know everyone did not have the home life that I experienced and my heart aches for them."

"I feel the same way. I have heard so many people say that the young people of today are a lost generation. I feel like they just need a little guidance. Someone to take an interest in them and put them on the pathway to success."

"I think you might be onto something, Ms. Cynthia 'Cinnamon' Harrelson."

"Wow...did you have to use my whole name plus the nickname?"

"Yep!"

"It's good to see that you haven't lost your sense of humor," teased Cinnamon.

"In times like this, it helps to have one."

The elevator arrived and Myles and Cinnamon had it all to themselves.

"So when was Shakira released?"

"About a month ago. Kyle contacted a lawyer who petitioned the court for an early release. Check this out. She was a model prisoner."

"No joke."

"No joke. Talk about a complete turnaround. I believe in the power of prayer. In the beginning, I was the only one she would agree to see."

"Cinnamon, I am intrigued by the transformation. I remember the night when you were shot. It was a nightmare because we all thought we were going to lose you that night."

"Yeah, it was a long journey back, but I made it."

"I'm glad you did."

The doors of the elevator opened onto the lobby level. "Where did you park? I'll walk you to your car."

"My car is in the shop, so I caught the bus."

"Okay. Now I get to hear the rest of the story. You want to go grab a cup of coffee? There's a diner right across the street."

"Sure."

They grabbed a booth near the back of the diner and ordered something to eat. Hours passed as they talked.

"What are your thoughts about Shakira and your dad forging a relationship?"

"I'm all for it. It did not come right away, though. In the beginning, Dad would drive to Bedford every Saturday hoping to see Shakira. He would wait for hours only to be turned away. This happened every weekend for a little more than a year. I was the only one she would agree to see."

"So I'm interested in knowing how those visits went. Was there a lot of anger, tears, or silence?"

"For real, all of the above. Then one day I walked in and started praying. Every Saturday after that I would pray for and with her. Suddenly, during one of our visits, she broke down, and a floodgate of tears emerged. Eventually I told her about Dad driving to see her every Saturday only to be turned away. I asked her to put him on the visitor's list."

"Was she amendable to that?"

"Yes. By that time, she and I had spent a lot of time together talking and allowing the act of forgiveness to come forth. Then she started attending church services and reading the Bible. The transformation was phenomenal. Then, and only then, was she ready to allow Dad to visit. At least she thought she was ready."

"Why do you say that?"

"The first visit did not go well. She freaked out. Screaming and crying and banging on the glass. We didn't know what to think."

"We returned the following Saturday and she and Dad talked and asked each other for forgiveness. That's the day Kyle revealed that he had been talking to a lawyer about an early release for Shakira. We all thought it was a good idea and that she and Dad should live together. Kyle and I had him all our lives. Now, it's Shakira's time to bond with our father. And in case you did not know, Leroy and Shakira are seeing each other again."

"Well, it seems like everything is falling into place."

"Yes, it is. Dad and Shakira are like two young children. She dotes on him as much as he dotes on her. It's fun to watch."

"That's great!"

"So what about you? How are you and your lady friend doing?"

"We aren't."

"Don't tell me you two broke up."

"Actually, it happened earlier today, but maybe it's for the better."

"Did the breakup have anything to do with her involvement in the pay-to-play scheme in the mayor's office?"

"Not really. Although some of my frustration with her might be indirectly related to what's going on with the impending trial and her involvement. But the biggest reason for our breakup is that she didn't understand why I couldn't be in the courtroom every day of the trial. I told her that my priority is to my grandmother. She's laying in a hospital bed in a coma and I pray to God that she makes it. So I told her that if she couldn't understand my position about work and my grandmother, then maybe we should go our separate ways."

"How did she take it?"

"Surprisingly calm."

"Well, there is a possibility that with the upcoming trial and her fate lying in the balance, she is stressed as well."

"Whose side are you on?"

"I'm not on anyone's side. But I do know that if it were me in her position, I would be freaking out."

"Well, I'm freaking out because I have to tell my boss that I was served with a summons to appear in court. So you see, even though I told her that I could not be in court, she found a way to get me there. I don't have to be there every day, but I still have to be there."

"Wow."

"My sentiments exactly."

Myles checked his watch. "It's getting late and I have an early day tomorrow."

Like clockwork, the waitress appeared with the check. Myles left the money on the table and they walked out of the diner back toward the hospital where he left his car parked. He opened the door for Cinnamon and waited as she climbed into the passenger side. Once behind the wheel, he started the car and navigated it out of the parking lot onto the main street. The ride to Cinnamon's apartment was pleasant and they continued to talk and laugh about old times. Traffic was remarkably light for this time of day, but Myles did not complain. An oldie but goodie played on the radio. Myles reached over and turned the volume up slightly. Just enough volume to lean back and enjoy the ride. It had been a long time since they had enjoyed each other's company in this way. Simpler times, Myles thought. Simpler times.

He parked his car in front of Cinnamon's apartment. He turned off the engine and got out of the car so that he could open the door and escort her to her apartment. Before unlocking the door to her apartment, Cinnamon turned and gave Myles a hug.

"Good night, Myles. Remember to call me should you need me to go sit with your grandmother. I can probably squeeze in a couple of hours this Saturday or after church on Sunday. Just let me know."

"Cinnamon, I really appreciate it. I never know what's going to happen from day to day so, I appreciate the offer.

"Well, look at it this way. Soon the trial will be over, and you will not have to worry with it any longer."

"I guess that's the only way to look at it. I'll be in touch."

Myles exited the building, hopped in his car, and headed home. It had been a long day and he needed to rest. He silently prayed for God to watch over his grandmother as she slept.

"Tomorrow, young man, is another day," he said to himself.

The next day, Myles arrived at work earlier than usual. The office was quiet which gave him time to review his notes from the previous day's impromptu meeting with his secretary. Impressed with the Aubrey DeLoach Foundation's philanthropic efforts, he thought it would be wonderful to establish a program in the city for low-income children wanting to attend college. A pathway directing recent high school graduates through the application process, educating them on the college experience, and removing the worry of affordability so that their minds would be on success, not failure. It sounded good to him. Now he had to get John Brimmer on board so that they could pitch the idea to Aubrey DeLoach. He saw this program as one that would set these children up for high-paying jobs so that they could amass wealth a lot sooner. He thought about the people in his old neighborhood that had never been to college so were not able to help their children. These kids needed a bridge to get them to the other side. That bridge, he believed, was Aubrey DeLoach.

He heard the soft chime of the elevator. One chime after the other alerted him that soon the office would be teeming with people. Myles continued to work on his idea, formulating his thoughts and organizing it on paper. Before the end of the day, he felt he would have something to go to his boss with.

Gloria popped her head into his office.

"Good morning, Myles. You are here early."

"Good morning, Gloria. I thought I would come in early and get a jump on work. Yesterday was such a weird day."

"Weird how?"

"After work I was served with a summons to appear in court."

"Geez! Just when you thought it was safe to go back in the water, the FBI comes for you."

"The FBI didn't do this. I am a witness for the Defense."

"Oh, I see. Does Mr. Brimmer know?"

"Not yet. I'll tell him later. Let him enjoy his coffee."

"I hope everything works out."

"Yeah. So do I."

He returned his attention to his notes and tweaked the idea about a pathway to success. The more he reviewed his notes, the better this program sounded. This had the potential of helping many people rise above their circumstance Myles thought. He couldn't sit on this idea. It must be shared with his boss and sooner rather than later. Since John Brimmer had a working relationship with Aubrey DeLoach, they could both sit down and pitch the idea to her. If established correctly, this would be a wonderful venture for her Foundation.

While envisioning this idea, his office phone rang.

"Hello, this is Myles Beyers."

"Myles, this is Debbie."

"Hey, Debbie." Myles noticed she was calling from a different number. "Did you change your number?"

"No. It's my mother's number?"

"Your mother's number. I don't understand. Is she in New York?"

"No. I'm staying at my mother's old apartment in Baruch Housing since the new owner has taken occupancy of the condo."

"Oh, okay. So how can I help you?"

"I understand from my attorney that you were served a summons to appear in court. I just wanted you to know that I feel so much better having you there to support me."

"Debbie, let's not do this. I told you why I could not be in court. Why didn't you let your attorney know my situation?"

"I didn't mention it because it means more to me to have you by my side in court."

"This conversation is over." Myles gently disconnected the call.

How could someone be so heartless? he thought. Recently, all Debbie thought about was herself. She never asked about his grandmother. She never once told him that she understood his situation. Where was the empathy and compassion? This situation revealed a different side of her, one that he could not deal with. He told himself many times that he was prepared to go the distance with her; settle down and have a couple of children. Yes, he would be there and answer every question presented by the prosecution and the defense. But that is all he would be prepared to do. Maybe his grandmother had seen something all along that did not bode well with her. She wanted more for her grandson. Now he knew.

Myles finished the workday without having discussed his idea with John Brimmer or informing him of the summons. Tomorrow is another day. He straightened the files on this desk, turned off the light and headed to the hospital to sit with his grandmother. After the day he had, he felt like reading a good book.

WHAT'S NEXT FOR STACY JOHNSON?

Shades of Freedom

A sequel to Apples and Cinnamon

FOLLOW THE CHARACTERS OF APPLES AND Cinnamon as they continue to unveil their stories. What will happen to Debbie? Will she make if out of New York? What about Myles, Cinnamon, and the rest of the characters? Stay tuned as their stories promise to take you on a literary journey filled with many twists and turns.

CHAPTER 1

THE VOICE OF THE FLIGHT ATTENDANT came over the speaker clear and crisp instructing passengers to fasten their seatbelts and prepare for landing. Debbie's mother stared out the window at her beloved city. The city where she lived for so long. The city where she raised Debbie. She wondered if the city had turned on her child or if her child had turned on the city. Nevertheless, she would not allow this city to destroy her daughter. She would not stop fighting for her daughter.

The plane touched down and taxied the runway for several minutes before arriving at the gate. She waited as others lined up to exit the plane. Once the last person in line passed her seat, she grabbed her purse and exited the aircraft. By the time she arrived at Carousel 10, her lone suitcase was waiting. She picked up her baggage and exited the terminal and climbed into the back of a New York City taxicab. She provided the driver with the address. It was rush hour and Lois knew it would be a long commute. She leaned her head against the back of the seat and closed her eyes. An hour later, she arrived at her destination. She paid the cab driver the fare with a generous tip and climbed out of the cab. The cab driver removed her suitcase from the trunk of the cab and placed it on the sidewalk. It had been years since she walked out of these gates.

She picked up her suitcase and pressed the button. A soft voice floated through the intercom.

"Mother. It's Lois."

There was a long silence before she heard the buzz unlocking the gate. The gates swung wide. Lois continued up the long driveway leading to the front of the house. She took her time, looking at every tree, flower, and shrub. It was just as she remembered. Nothing had changed. She climbed the steps to the front door and rang the doorbell.

The door opened.

"Hello, Daddy."

ABOUT THE AUTHOR

STACY JOHNSON IS AN OFFICE ADMINISTRATOR whose first job immediately upon graduating high school was for a United States senator. She received a bachelor's from University of Maryland Global College (formerly University of Maryland University College) in communications studies and a master's from American InterContinental University in business administration with a specialization in project management.

She entered the literary world after the birth of her first grandchild, prompting her to write several books for children in honor of her granddaughter. Hailing from a long line of ardent readers, she loves watching characters come alive as the story progresses. Stacy has mentioned on more than one occasion that her characters will not leave her alone until she has told their story. She jokingly says that her characters move into her home and pull up a chair and refuse to leave.

Her earlier years as a child were spent in the local library where she would check out Nancy Drew mysteries three at a time. Stacy believes that the best stories are the ones yet to be told. Stacy is the proud mother of three and grandmother of two.